Also by Bernard Knight

The Elixir of Death
Figure of Hate
The Witch Hunter
Fear in the Forest
The Grim Reaper
The Tinner's Corpse
The Awful Secret
The Poisoned Chalice
C[illegible]'s Quest

Professor Bernard Knight, CBE, became a H
pathologist in 1965 and was appointed Pr
Forensic Pathology, University of Wales C
Medicine, in 1980. During his forty-year career
Home Office, he performed over 25,000 autops
was involved in many high profile cases.

Bernard Knight is the author of twenty-one novel
biography and numerous popular and academic no
fiction books. *The Noble Outlaw* is the eleventh novel i
the Crowner John [illegible] *The Elixir of Death*
Figure of Hate, T[illegible]
Grim Reaper, The Ti[illegible]
Poisoned Chalice, Cro[illegible]

The Noble Outlaw

Bernard Knight

SIMON & SCHUSTER

LONDON • NEW YORK • SYDNEY • TORONTO

First published in Great Britain by Simon & Schuster UK Ltd, 2007
A CBS COMPANY

1 3 5 7 9 10 8 6 4 2

Simon & Schuster UK Ltd
Africa House
64–78 Kingsway
London WC2B 6AH

www.simonsays.co.uk

Simon & Schuster Australia
Sydney

A CIP catalogue record for this book is available from the British Library

ISBN-13: 978-0-7432-9498-0
ISBN-10: 0-7432-9498-X

Typeset by Palimpsest Book Production Ltd,
Grangemouth, Stirlingshire

Printed and bound in Great Britain by
CPI Bath

Acknowledgements

My sincere thanks go to my publisher, Kate Lyall Grant, and to my editor, Gillian Holmes, for their unfailing help and encouragement.

AUTHOR'S NOTE

When William of Normandy conquered England in 1066, he dispossessed or killed most of the Saxon earls and thegns. He declared himself to be the sole owner of the whole land, but parcelled out a great deal of it to his Norman supporters, as 'tenants-in-chief'. He ensured that these 'honours' that each received were composed of manors scattered about the country, to avoid any baron having a block large enough for him to raise an army, and possibly a rebellion, against the king. However, for several centuries, it was not uncommon for barons and manor lords to seize land belonging to neighbours, if they could get away with it. The court records of those early times are filled with disputes over land – and this story is partly concerned with one such event, albeit fictitious.

The manor of Hempston Arundell, near Totnes, is now known as Littlehempston. The 'noble outlaw' of this book was a great-grandson of Roger de Arundell, the founder of the dynasty, who is thought to have come over with the Conqueror and who has many West Country entries in the Domesday Book of 1086 – and who incidentally, is the grandfather, twenty-seven times removed, of the author!

All the names of people and places are authentic, the former being either real historical characters or taken from the Exeter Crown Pleas roll of 1238. Unfortunately, history does not record the names of Devon coroners until the thirteenth century, so Sir John de Wolfe is a product of the author's imagination.

One of the problems of writing a long series, of which this is the eleventh, is that regular readers will have become familiar with the background to the stories and may become impatient with repeated explanations in every book. However, new readers need to be 'brought up to speed' to appreciate some of the historical aspects, so a Glossary is offered with an explanation of some medieval terms, especially those relating to the functions of the coroner, one of the oldest legal offices in England.

What were to become universities began in England in the twelfth century, starting in a small way as 'schools', usually for young clerics. They were private establishments, unlike the schools attached to cathedrals and religious houses, and they were run by individual masters or groups of teachers, themselves clerics and often canons, teaching a set curriculum. Oxford and later Cambridge became predominant, but other towns including Lincoln, Exeter and Northampton were competitors; by the early thirteenth century, however, these had faded away, even though Exeter had the famous Joseph Iscanus as a poet and teacher.

Attempting to use 'olde worlde' dialogue in a historical novel of this period is futile and unrealistic, as in Devon during the late twelfth century most of the people would have spoken Early Middle English, which would be incomprehensible to us today. Some would still have spoken a Celtic tongue, similar to Welsh, Breton and Cornish, the latter surviving in the West Country for many more centuries. The ruling classes would have spoken Norman-French and the clergy used Latin, in which virtually all documents were written.

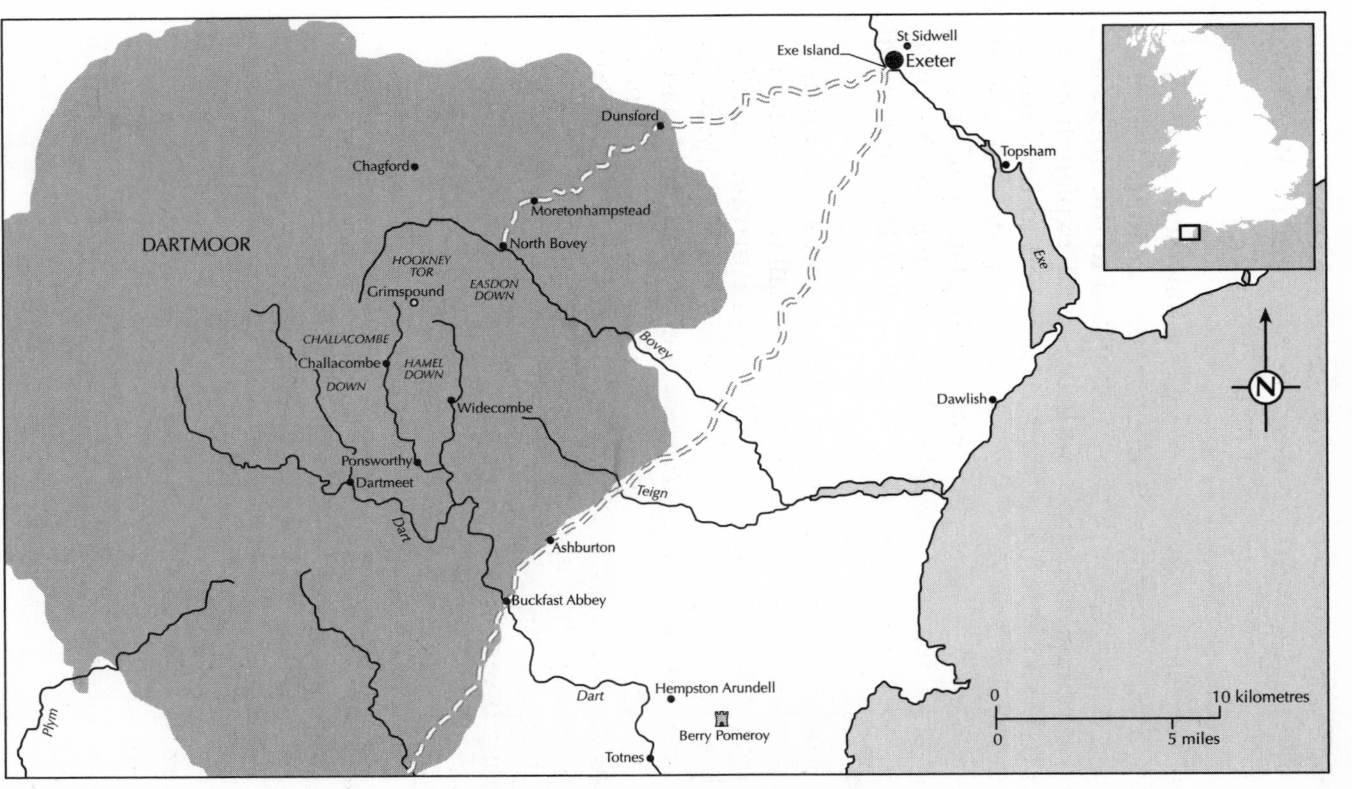
St Sidwell
Exe Island
Exeter
Dunsford
Topsham
Chagford
Moretonhampstead
DARTMOOR
North Bovey
HOOKNEY TOR
Grimspound
EASDON DOWN
Exe
CHALLACOMBE
Challacombe
HAMEL DOWN
DOWN
Bovey
Widecombe
Dawlish
Ponsworthy
Dartmeet
Teign
Dart
Ashburton
Buckfast Abbey
Dart
Hempston Arundell
Berry Pomeroy
Totnes
Plym
0
10 kilometres
0
5 miles
N

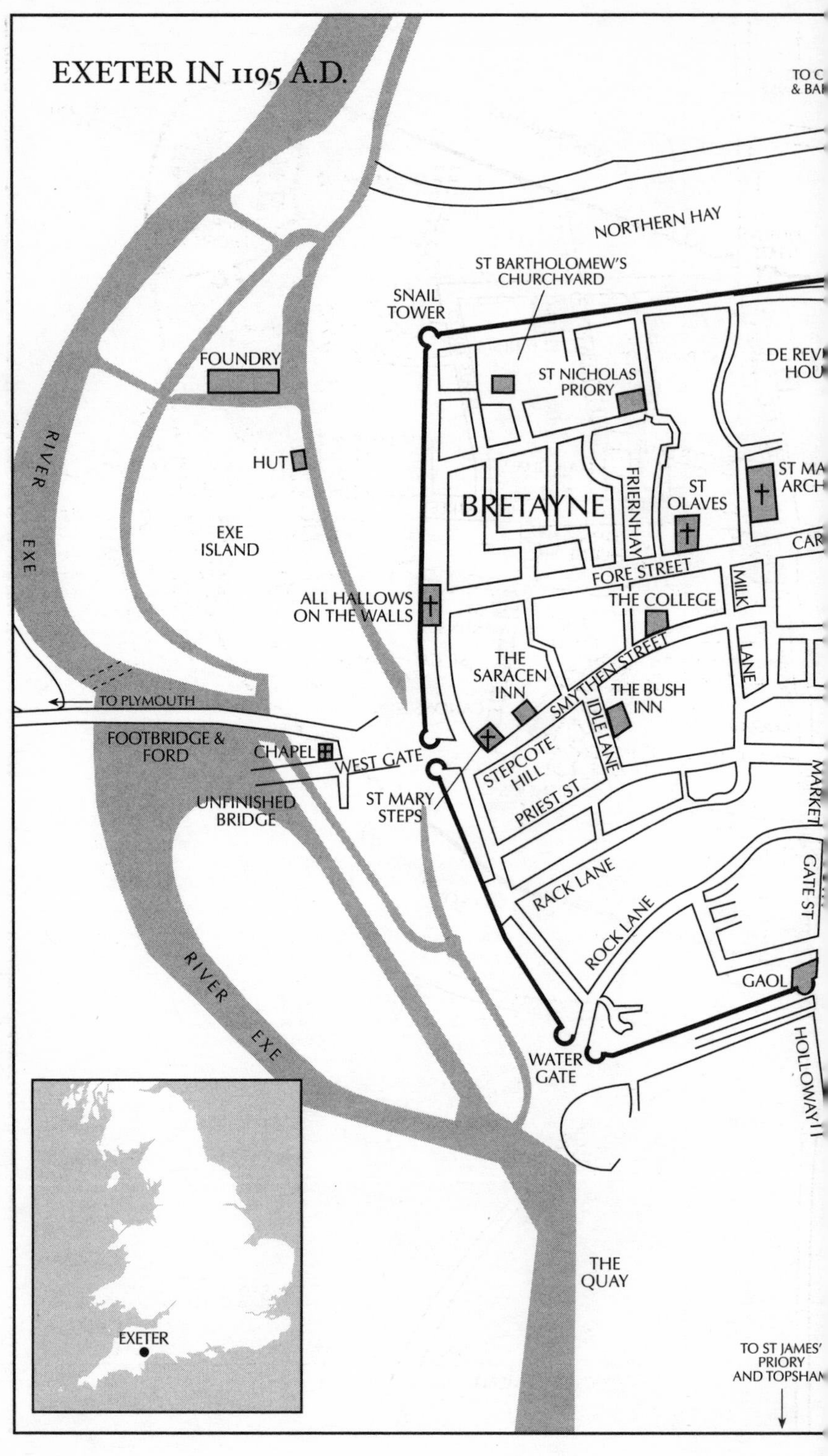
EXETER IN 1195 A.D.
NORTHERN HAY
ST BARTHOLOMEW'S CHURCHYARD
SNAIL TOWER
FOUNDRY
ST NICHOLAS PRIORY
HUT
RIVER EXE
BRETAYNE
FRIERNHAY
ST OLAVES
EXE ISLAND
FORE STREET
ALL HALLOWS ON THE WALLS
THE COLLEGE
MILK LANE
THE SARACEN INN
SMYTHEN STREET
THE BUSH INN
IDLE LANE
TO PLYMOUTH
FOOTBRIDGE & FORD
CHAPEL
WEST GATE
STEPCOTE HILL
PRIEST ST
ST MARY STEPS
UNFINISHED BRIDGE
GATE ST
RACK LANE
ROCK LANE
GAOL
RIVER EXE
WATER GATE
THE QUAY
EXETER
PRIORY

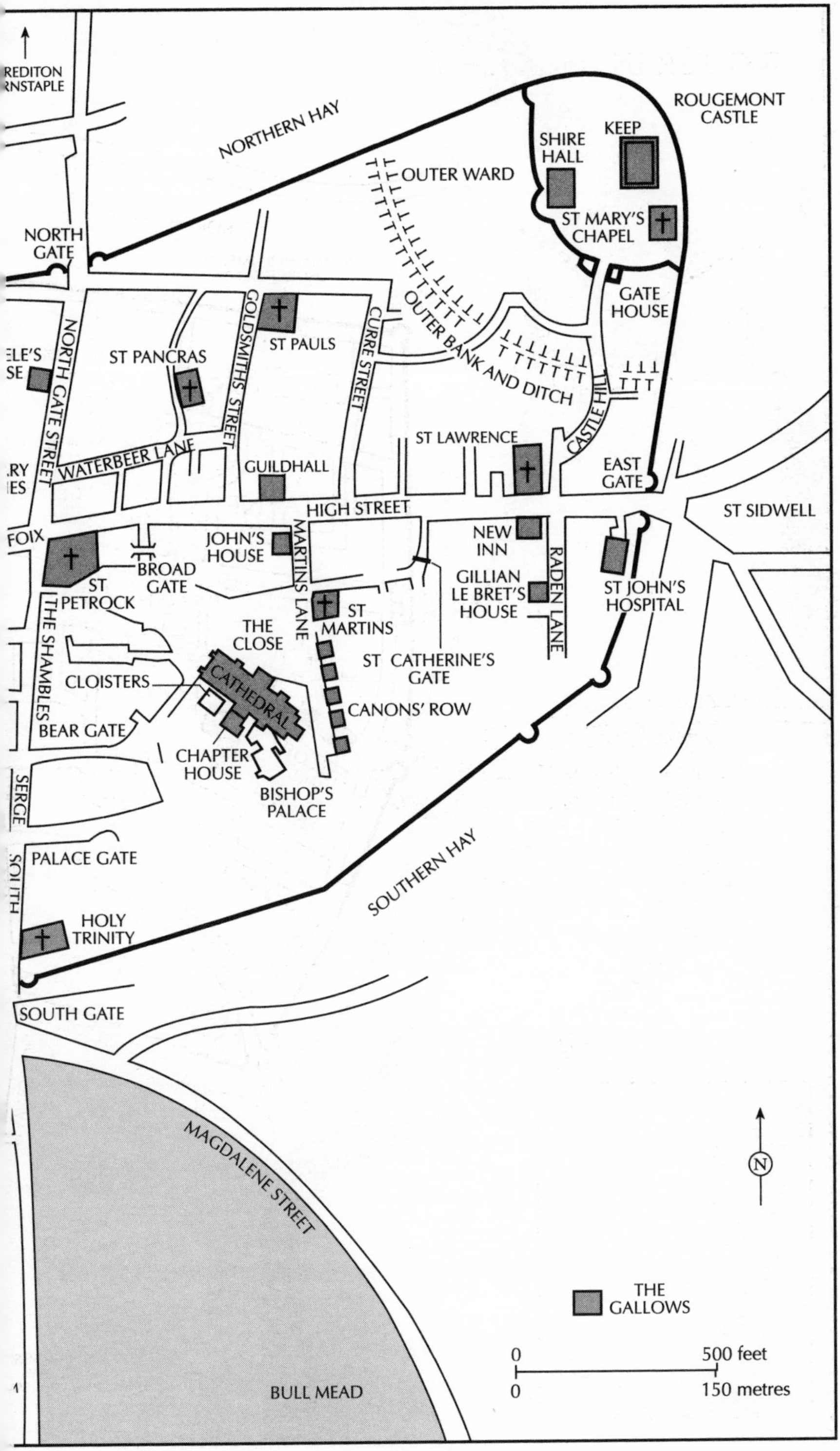
REDITON
RNSTAPLE
NORTHERN HAY
ROUGEMONT CASTLE
KEEP
SHIRE HALL
OUTER WARD
ST MARY'S CHAPEL
NORTH GATE
GATE HOUSE
OUTER BANK AND DITCH
NORTH GATE STREET
ST PANCRAS
GOLDSMITHS STREET
ST PAULS
CURRE STREET
ELE'S
SE
CASTLE HILL
ST LAWRENCE
WATERBEER LANE
GUILDHALL
EAST GATE
RY
ES
HIGH STREET
ST SIDWELL
FOIX
JOHN'S HOUSE
NEW INN
BROAD GATE
ST PETROCK
MARTINS LANE
GILLIAN LE BRET'S HOUSE
RADEN LANE
ST JOHN'S HOSPITAL
ST MARTINS
THE CLOSE
ST CATHERINE'S GATE
THE SHAMBLES
CLOISTERS
CATHEDRAL
CANONS' ROW
BEAR GATE
CHAPTER HOUSE
BISHOP'S PALACE
SERGE
PALACE GATE
SOUTH
SOUTHERN HAY
HOLY TRINITY
SOUTH GATE
MAGDALENE STREET
N
THE GALLOWS
0
500 feet
0
150 metres
BULL MEAD

GLOSSARY

ABJURING THE REALM

A sanctuary seeker, if he confessed his crime to the coroner, could abjure the realm of England, never to return. He had to dress in sackcloth and carry a crude wooden cross, then walk to a port nominated by the coroner and take the first ship abroad. If none was available, he had to wade out up to his knees in every tide to show his willingness to leave. Many abjurers absconded *en route* and became outlaws; others were killed by the angry families of their victims.

ALE

A weak drink brewed before the advent of hops. The name derived from an 'ale', a village celebration where much drinking took place. The words 'wassail' and 'bridal' are derived from this.

AMERCEMENTS

Arbitrary fines imposed on a person or community by a law officer for some breach of the complex regulations of the law. Where a fine was imposed by a coroner, he would record the amercement, but the collection of the money would normally be ordered by the royal justices when they visited at the **Eyre** (q.v.).

APPROVER

A criminal who attempted to save himself by implicating his accomplices. His confession had to be recorded by the coroner.

ATTACHMENT
An order made by a law officer, including a coroner, to ensure that a person appeared at a court hearing. It resembled a bail bond or surety, distraining upon a person's money or goods, which would be forfeit if he failed to appear.

BAILEY
Originally the defended area around a castle keep, as in 'motte and bailey', but later also applied to the yard of a dwelling.

BAILIFF
An overseer of a manor or estate, directing the farming and other work. He would have manor reeves under him and be responsible either directly to his lord or to the steward.

BONDSMAN
An unfree person in the feudal system. Several categories, including villein, serf, cottar, etc.

BURGAGE
A plot of land, usually comprising a house and garden, in a town or city. Long and narrow at right angles to the street, it was often the property of a burgess.

BURGESS
A freeman of substance in a town or borough, usually a merchant or craftsman. A group of burgesses ran the town administration; and in 1195 they elected two portreeves (later a mayor) to lead them in Exeter.

CANON
A senior priest in a cathedral, deriving his living from the grant of a parish or land providing an income (a prebend). Exeter Cathedral, a secular not a monastic establishment, had twenty-four canons.

CHAPTER
The administrative body of a cathedral, composed of the canons (prebendaries). They met daily to conduct business in the chapter house, so-called because a chapter of the Gospels or of the Rule of St Benedict was read before each session.

COB
A plaster made of straw, clay, dung and horsehair which was applied to panels of willow or hazel withies, which filled the spaces between the frames of a house. Small cottages might be constructed entirely of cob.

COIF
A close-fitting cap or helmet, usually of linen or felt, covering the ears and tied under the chin: worn by men and women.

CONSTABLE
A senior commander, usually the custodian of a castle, which in Exeter belonged to the king. The word was also used of a watchman who patrolled the streets to keep order.

CORONER
Though there are a couple of mentions of a coroner in late Saxon times, the officer of coroner really began in September 1194, when the royal justices at their session in Rochester, Kent, proclaimed in a single sentence the launch of the system that has lasted for over 800 years. They said, 'In every county of the King's realm shall be elected three knights and one clerk, to keep the pleas of the Crown.'

The reasons for the establishment of coroners were mainly financial: the aim was to sweep as much money as possible into the royal treasury. Richard the Lionheart was a spendthrift, using huge sums to finance his expedition to the Third Crusade and for his wars against the French. Kidnapped on his way home from the Holy Land, he was held for well over a year in prisons in Austria and Germany, and a huge ransom was needed to free him. To raise this money, his Chief Justiciar, Hubert Walter, who was also Archbishop of Canterbury, introduced all sorts of measures to extort money from the population of England.

Hubert revived the office of coroner, which was intended to collect money by a variety of means relating to the administration of the law. One of these was by investigating and holding inquests into all deaths that were not obviously natural, as well as into serious assaults, rapes, house fires, discoveries of buried treasure, wrecks of the sea and catches of the royal fish (whale and sturgeon). Coroners also took confessions from criminals and fugitives seeking sanctuary in churches, organised **abjurations of the realm** (q.v.), recorded the statements of **approvers** (q.v.) who wished to turn King's Evidence, attended executions to seize the goods of felons, and organised the ritual of **ordeals** (q.v.) and trial by battle.

As the Normans had inherited a multiple system of county and manorial courts from the Saxons, the coroner also worked to sweep more lucrative business into the new Royal Courts. This gave him the title of Keeper of the Pleas of the Crown, from the original Latin of which (*custos placitorum coronas*) the word 'coroner' is derived.

Although the coroner was not allowed to try cases (this was later again specifically forbidden by Magna Carta), he had to create a record of all legal events to present to the royal justices when they came on their infrequent visits to the **Eyre** (q.v.). The actual recording on the 'coroner's rolls' was done by his clerk, as the coroners, like the vast majority of people, were illiterate. Reading and writing were almost wholly confined to those in holy orders, of whom there were many grades besides the actual priests.

It was difficult to find knights to take on the job of coroner, as it was unpaid and the appointee had to have a large private income: at least £20 a year. This was supposed to make him immune from corruption, which was common among the sheriffs. Indeed, one reason for the introduction of coroners was to keep a check on sheriffs, who were the king's representatives in each county.

COVER-CHIEF
More correctly 'couvre-chef', a linen head cover flowing down the back and shoulders, worn by women and held in place by a band around the forehead. Called a head-rail in Saxon times.

CURFEW
The prohibition of open fires in towns after dark, for fear of starting conflagrations. The word is derived from 'couvre-feu', describing the extinguishing or banking down of fires at night. During the curfew, the city gates were closed from dusk to dawn. A thirteenth-century mayor of Exeter was hanged for failing to ensure this.

DESTRIER
A sturdy warhorse able to carry the weight of an armoured knight. Destriers were not the huge beasts often portrayed in historical art; they were rather short-legged, the rider's feet being not that far from the ground.

ESCHEAT
If a baron or manor lord died without an heir of full age, his estate reverted to the king, either permanently or until the heir came of age. Felony or treason could also lead to the escheating of property.

EYRE
A sitting of the King's Justices, introduced by Henry II in 1166, which moved around the country in circuits. There were two types, the 'Eyre of Assize', which was the forerunner of the later Assize Court, which was supposed to visit each county town regularly to try serious cases. The other was the General Eyre, which came at long intervals to scrutinise the administration of each county.

FARM
The taxes from a county, collected in coin on behalf of the sheriff and taken by him personally every six months to the royal treasury at London or Winchester. The sum was fixed annually by the king or his ministers: if the sheriff could extract more from the county, he could retain the excess, which made the office of sheriff much sought after.

FRANKPLEDGE
A system of law enforcement introduced by the Normans, where groups (tithings) of ten households were formed to enforce mutual good behaviour amongst each group.

FREEMAN
A person other than a bondsman of the feudal system. The villeins, serfs and slaves were not free, though the distinction did not necessarily mean a different level of affluence.

FLETCHING
The feathered flights on the end of an arrow made by a fletcher. On crossbow bolts, the fletching was usually of leather.

GAOL DELIVERY
As the circulation of the King's Justices at the Eyre of Assize was so slow, with years between each visit, the

counties were visited more often by lower judges, called Commissioners of Gaol Delivery, in order to clear the overcrowded prisons of those held on remand.

GUILDS
Trade or merchant associations set up for mutual protection. Merchant guilds mainly functioned to ward off foreign competition and to set prices. Trade guilds were organisations for the many crafts and manufactures, controlling conditions of work, the quality of goods and the welfare of workers and their families.

HAUBERK
A long chain-mail tunic with long sleeves to protect the wearer from neck to calf, usually slit to enable riding a horse.

HUNDRED
An administrative division of the county, originally named for a hundred hides of land or a hundred families.

JOHN LACKLAND
A sarcastic nickname for Prince John, Count of Mortain. The name came from the refusal of his father King Henry II to endow him with significant territory. When his brother Richard came to the throne in 1189, he gave much land to John, including Devon and Cornwall.

JUSTICES
The king's judges, originally members of his royal court, but later chosen from barons, senior priests and administrators. They sat in the various law courts, such as the Eyre of Assize or as Commissioners of Gaol Delivery. From 1195 onwards, Keepers of the Peace, later to become Justices of the Peace, were recruited from knights and local worthies to deal with lesser offences.

KIRTLE
A ladies' floor-length gown. Many variations of style and fit, especially of the sleeves, existed in the fashion-conscious medieval period.

LEAT OR LEET
An artificial water channel usually constructed to drain a marsh or to conduct water into an ore-washing system during tin extraction.

MAGISTER
A learned teacher in a school or early university.

MANOR-REEVE
A villien in a manor elected by his unfree fellows to represent them. He organised their daily labours and was in turn responsible to the lord's bailiff or steward.

MANTLE
A cloak, either circular with a hole for the head, or open-fronted with the top being closed either by a large brooch on the shoulder or by a top corner being pulled through a ring sewn to the opposite shoulder.

MATINS
The first of nine offices of the religious day, originally observed at midnight or in the early hours.

ORDEAL
A test of guilt or innocence, such as walking over nine red-hot ploughshares with bare feet or picking a stone from a barrel of boiling water. If burns appeared within a certain time, the person was judged guilty and hanged. There was also the Ordeal of Battle where a legal dispute was settled by combat. For women, submersion in water was the ordeal: the guilty floated. Ordeals were forbidden by the Lateran Council in 1215.

OUTLAW
A man who did not submit to legal processes. Usually an escaped felon or suspect, a runaway sanctuary seeker or abjurer, he was declared 'outlaw' – by a writ of exigent – if he did not answer to a summons on four consecutive sessions of the county court. An outlaw was legally dead, with no rights whatsoever, and could be legally slain on the spot by anyone. If caught by a law officer, he was hanged. A female could not be outlawed, but was declared 'waif', which was very similar.

OUTREMER
Literally 'over the sea', the term was used to refer to the countries in the Levant, especially the Holy Land.

PELISSE
An outer garment worn by both men and women with a fur lining for winter wear. The fur could be sable, rabbit, marten, cat, et cetera.

POSSE
The *posse comitatus*, introduced by Henry II, was the title given to a band of men raised by a sheriff to hunt felons or enemies of the realm across the county.

PREBENDARY
The canon of a cathedral, deriving an income from his prebend, a tract of land granted to him (see **canon**).

PRESENTMENT
At coroner's inquests, a corpse was presumed to be that of a Norman, unless the locals could prove 'Englishry' by presenting such evidence from the family. If they could not, a 'murdrum' fine was imposed on the community by the coroner, on the assumption that Normans were murdered by the Saxons they had conquered in 1066. Murdrum fines became a cynical device to extort

money, persisting for several hundred years after the Conquest, by which time it was virtually impossible to differentiate the two races.

QUIRE
The area within a church between the nave and the presbytery and altar, which gave rise to the name 'choir'. The quire was usually separated from the nave by a carved rood screen at the chancel arch, bearing a large crucifix above it.

SACKBUT
A medieval wind instrument similar to a trombone.

SANCTUARY
An ancient act of mercy: a fugitive from justice could claim forty days' respite if he gained the safety of a church or even its environs. After that time, unless he confessed to the coroner, he was shut in and starved to death. If he confessed, he could **abjure the realm** (q.v.).

SERGEANT
The term was used in several ways, denoting *inter alia* an administrative/legal officer in a county hundred, or a military rank of a senior man-at-arms.

SECONDARIES
Young men aspiring to become priests and under twenty-four years of age. They assisted canons and vicars in their duties in the cathedral.

SHERIFF
The 'shire reeve', the king's representative in each county, responsible for law and order and the collection of taxes. The office was eagerly sought after as it was lucrative; both barons and senior churchmen bought the office from the king at high premiums, some holding several shrievalties at the same time. Sheriffs were notorious for

dishonesty and embezzlement – in 1170, the Lionheart's father, Henry II, sacked all his sheriffs and heavily fined many for malpractice. The sheriff in the earlier Crowner John books, Richard de Revelle, though fictional, was named after the actual Sheriff of Devon in 1194–95. He was appointed early in 1194, then lost office for reasons unknown; he returned to office later in the year, but was dismissed again the following year.

SOLAR
A room built on to the main hall of a castle or house for the use of the lord or owner, usually for the use of the lady during the daytime and often as a bedroom at night.

UMBLE PIE
The umbles were the less desirable parts of venison, such as the offal. Especially at Christmas, they were given by a lord to the poorer people to make 'umble pie', from which the expression 'to eat humble pie' arose as an indicator of subservient status.

VICAR
A priest employed by a more senior cleric, such as a canon, to carry out some of his religious duties, and especially to attend the many daily services in the cathedral. Such a priest was often called a 'vicar-choral' because of his participation in chanted services.

WIMPLE
A linen or silk cloth worn by women to cover the neck and upper chest, the upper ends being pinned to their hair to frame the face.

WOLF'S HEAD
An outlaw was said to be 'as the wolf's head', for like a wolf, he could be beheaded with impunity and a bounty of five shillings could be claimed from the sheriff.

Chapter One

Exeter, December 1195: in which Crowner John goes back to school

Even Thomas de Peyne, still squeamish after serving for more than a year as coroner's clerk, found little to upset him in the appearance of this particular corpse.

What little flesh that could be seen reminded him more of the cheap dried cod that hung from the fishmongers' stalls than of a human being. The leathery face and shrivelled hands protruding from the mouldering clothes looked unreal, like some amateur woodcarving.

'Been here some time, Crowner!' boomed the broad Cornish accent of Gwyn of Polruan, the coroner's officer and right-hand man. 'Dried up like an old boot, not a trace of corruption about him.'

They stood with their master in the back yard of a house in Exeter's Smythen Street, a lane that ran down to Stepcote Hill and the city wall in the southern part of the city. It got its name from the number of smiths' forges and metal-working shops that lay along its length, though a few of the burgages, like the one they were in now, had recently been turned into places of education.

Behind the main building, which fronted on to the street itself, was a yard with a large outhouse which had been the forge. A square box, it was built of cob plastered on to woven withies held between oak frames. It had a large chamber at ground level, where until recently the furnace and anvils stood. The old forge was roofed with stone tiles, as thatch was too hazardous to use so near the flames and sparks of a smithy. Under this roof lay a loft formerly used for storing iron rods and strips, reached by a crude ladder in the corner. It was there that the corpse had been discovered an hour earlier, before being dragged down to the yard – causing the short-tempered coroner to be incensed even before he had started his investigation.

'For God's sake, does no one ever obey the law?' snapped Sir John de Wolfe, glaring at the discomfited James Anglicus, the magister of this establishment, one of the new schools in Smythen Street. 'When a dead body is found, it must be left exactly where it was until a coroner can view it in its original surroundings!' He scowled around at the gaping onlookers. 'Who was the First Finder?' he rasped irritably.

Magister Anglicus, a mournful, middle-aged man in a long cassock of clerical appearance, pointed at a stringy artisan of about the same age, his fustian tunic tucked up between his bare legs and held in place by a leather belt. 'Roger Short here discovered the cadaver. He's the builder that is turning the old forge into another lecture room for me.'

Roger touched his grubby woollen cap in deference to the coroner. 'Proper shock it was, sir,' he gabbled, displaying a mouthful of rotten black stumps. 'I went to pull up those old boards that floor the loft, to give more headroom. There was a heap of old wood in the angle between the roof rafters and the floor. When I pulled it out, I found him lurking behind.' He jabbed a thumb towards the body lying on the ground. 'My labourer and me hauled him down the ladder straight away, sir. We didn't know we wasn't supposed to, but no one could have got at him up there, tucked tight under the eaves.'

James Anglicus hurried back into the dialogue,

anxious to head off any further criticism. 'Straightway I sent my servant Henry up to the castle to inform either you or the sheriff, Crowner. I could see no point in raising the hue and cry, when obviously this poor creature has been dead for months!'

The hue and cry was supposed to be implemented whenever a crime was discovered, the four nearest households being knocked up to pursue any miscreant found red-handed at the scene. John de Wolfe recognised that in this case, Anglicus was entirely right; it would have been a waste of effort. He gave one of his all-purpose throat clearings in response and bent over the sad remains of the man that lay on the dusty ground. Gwyn, the red-haired giant who had been his servant and trusted companion for two decades, came to crouch on the other side of the corpse, prodding the hardened skin of the face with a finger the size of a pork sausage.

'Who the hell is he, I wonder?' he growled.

'Could he be a Musselman, with that dark complexion?' ventured Thomas timidly, keeping his distance but fascinated by the strange appearance of the cadaver.

'He's not dark, he's just dried up,' snorted de Wolfe. He motioned to his officer, and Gwyn began trying to remove the clothing from the pathetic bundle. The dead man was curved almost into a ball, with his legs drawn up and his head bent down into his arms.

'Rigid as a plank, Crowner!' he complained. 'Not ordinary death stiffness, he's just dried into a bundle of sticks. I'm afraid of breaking him in half if I try too hard.'

John de Wolfe dropped to a crouch himself and started to help Gwyn lever off the brown woollen tunic which was peppered with moth holes and nibbled by mice. It ripped easily, which at least helped them to clear it from the body, revealing blue serge breeches underneath.

'Is it seemly to render the poor fellow naked out in the open?' asked James Anglicus rather pompously.

'We'll not expose his nether regions here, but I need to know if he has injuries that would make this a felony,' snapped the coroner.

'I assume he crawled into the loft and had a stroke or seizure, poor fellow,' persisted the magister, anxious to distance his school from any criminal activity.

The coroner and his henchman ignored him and began looking at the dead man's head, back and chest. Gwyn lifted him over on to his other side, picking him up as if he were a feather. 'Weighs no more than a spring lamb!' he observed. 'All the substance has dried out of him.'

The corpse's face had shrunk down to a mask of skin, tightly stretched across his jaw and cheekbones. The eyes had collapsed into almost empty sockets and the brittle lips had drawn back into a grinning rictus, revealing large, crooked teeth.

'Plenty of hair left, though,' observed Gwyn, ruffling a brown thatch which sat above a neck shaved up to a horizontal line level with the top of the ears, a style introduced by the Normans many years earlier.

'More than you can say for some of the skin,' grunted de Wolfe. 'Look at the back here.'

From the neck down to the waist, more on the left side, the surface of the body had fared much worse than the face and hands. Decomposition had destroyed much of the skin, exposing ribs and spinal bones. The wet rot had dried up eventually and there was no unpleasant foulness left, but the sight made the sensitive Thomas hurriedly avert his gaze.

'No sign of injury, Crowner. No stabs, slashes or a smashed head,' said Gwyn in a somewhat disappointed tone. 'Maybe he did suffer from some sort of seizure.'

De Wolfe climbed to his feet again, uncoiling his long body which, as usual, was dressed all in black and grey.

James Anglicus, who had never met him before, regarded this powerful man warily, as he was second only to the sheriff in the hierarchy of the county law officers. He saw a tall man with a predatory, slightly menacing stoop as he hovered over those around him. His jet black hair, still untouched by grey at the age of forty-one, was swept back unfashionably low to his collar and was matched in colour by the dark stubble on his cheeks; he was days away from his weekly shave. A long face and big, hooked nose were relieved by full, sensual lips and deep-set eyes beneath heavy brows.

'What happens next, sir?' asked the teacher anxiously. He wanted this thing off his premises as soon as possible, concerned that he would be blamed by his patron for bringing the college into disrepute.

The coroner rasped his fingers over the bristles on his chin, a mannerism that seemed to stimulate his thought processes. 'Cadavers are usually taken up to the castle to await burial, but as we have no idea who this fellow is, I'll hold an inquest here. That old forge is as good a place as any to keep him out of the rain or snow.'

James Anglicus was aghast. 'That's not possible, my students will be back from their devotions at the cathedral in an hour,' he blubbered. 'Their instruction cannot be disturbed for some ancient corpse.'

De Wolfe glowered. 'Administering the king's peace is more important than gabbling Latin at a bunch of youths,' he snapped. 'If necessary, I will order the whole house to be cleared while we search it.'

The pedagogue stepped back a pace, conscious of the angry glint in the coroner's dark eyes, but managed to stammer a last feeble protest. 'My patron will be most disturbed to hear of this. The school is in its formative days and most vulnerable to adverse gossip.'

It was clear from de Wolfe's expression that this plea made little impression on him, but grudgingly he followed it up. 'What exactly is this place? And who is this sensitive patron of yours?' He knew that in recent years, seats of learning had been set up in a number of towns to offer a higher level of education than those provided by the cathedral schools, which were mainly concerned with teaching youngsters to read and write and with training older boys for the priesthood.

'I was appointed to lead this establishment three months ago, Crowner,' began James importantly. 'It is the most recent of the four schools in this road, chosen for its proximity to Priest Street, where so many of the cathedral clerics lodge. Most of our pupils are clerks in holy orders at various levels, the majority of them quite young men.'

De Wolfe nodded impatiently. 'And who is this patron of whom you speak? Does he own the school and run it like any other business?'

The magister was indignant. 'Profit is of little importance, sir. Naturally, each student pays fees, but the prime motive is the education of young minds. Our patron has expended much money and effort in setting up this temple of learning. Any breath of scandal might harm his ambition to attract more students.'

'But who is this paragon of virtue?' demanded John, weary of the teacher's long-windedness.

James Anglicus stared at him in some surprise. 'I would have thought you would be well aware of that, sir. It is your own brother-in-law.'

De Wolfe never gaped, but at this news, his jaw came close to sagging. 'Richard de Revelle!' he exclaimed incredulously. 'You're jesting with me, surely.'

'Indeed I am not,' exclaimed James indignantly. 'Sir Richard is a man of high academic ambition – he most earnestly seeks to establish Exeter as a seat of learning.'

And as a seat of profit for himself, thought de Wolfe cynically, though grudgingly he had to acknowledge that his brother-in-law was well-educated. In fact, Richard never failed to rub it in to John that while the latter was illiterate, Richard himself had attended the cathedral school in Wells, his parents having originally wished him to enter the Church. John shrugged and turned back to the body on the ground.

'It makes no difference to whom the place belongs, magister. There was still a corpse found on the premises and I have to deal with it in the usual way.'

A few flurries of snow were twisting in the cold breeze: both living and dead needed to find some shelter. John gestured to Gwyn and with little effort, the Cornishman picked up the flimsy bundle and carried it back through the wide doorway of the forge, kicking aside some tools and boxes to make space for it on the cluttered floor. John and the builder followed him inside, and Thomas and James Anglicus tagged along more reluctantly, together with a fussy, pompous fellow who the magister had earlier introduced as Henry Wotri, his servant and general factotum in the school.

'We can shut this door and leave the deceased here until my inquest,' announced de Wolfe, indicating the rickety collection of planks that hung on rusted hinges. 'Then you can carry on with your lessons in the house undisturbed for the time being.'

'When will that be?' quavered the master, his morose features looking even more depressed.

'Certainly not today; we first need to make some effort to discover who he was,' snapped the coroner. 'My officer and clerk will make some enquiries around the city and then I will probably call a jury together either tomorrow or Wednesday.'

He stared down at the twisted figure on the ground. 'At least we should do our best to put a name to him and avoid burying him in an unmarked grave, though I doubt we'll ever know how he died.'

For once, Sir John was soon to be proved wrong.

The coroner and his two assistants were in John's

chamber in the gatehouse of Rougemont, Exeter's castle built in the northern angle of the ancient town walls. It was a bleak room high in the narrow tower, a draughty cell with two unglazed window slits looking down over the city, as Rougemont itself was at the highest point of the tilted plateau that rose from the River Exe.

De Wolfe sat at a rough trestle table, which together with a bench and a couple of milking stools, was all the furniture in the room. Thomas de Peyne sat on one of these stools at the end of the table, copying out documents on to rolls of parchment, while Gwyn perched in his habitual place on one of the stone windowsills.

There was a metallic clatter from the table, as de Wolfe played with something on the boards in front of him. Thomas stared at the rusted object, a crudely shaped nail about the length of his little finger. One end was sharply pointed, the other fashioned into an irregular head.

After laying the corpse down in the old forge, the coroner and his officer had decided to make a closer examination in the hope of finding something to explain the death. Though they stripped the shrivelled body to examine every inch of its surface, they found no wounds at all until Gwyn looked at the back of the neck. Here skin and muscle had been lost so that some of the bones of the spine were exposed. Stained yellowish-brown by dust and dirt, they seemed unremarkable until Gwyn's sharp eyes noticed a darker brown nodule nestling between two vertebrae. Unable to remove it with his fingers, watched by the others he used the point of his dagger to lever at this alien lump, before drawing out a full three inches of metal that had been jammed between the bones. Now, as it rested on the table, John poked at it pensively with his forefinger.

'When men fall from a warhorse or a hayrick and break their backs, even when they survive, they often lose all feeling and motion in the legs – sometimes even arms as well,' he ruminated. 'So whatever is contained in the spine must be mightily important – and having this nail stuck through it must be a devilishly dangerous matter.'

Gwyn stroked his red moustaches, which hung down to his collarbones. 'When I worked as a slaughterman in the Shambles years ago, the poleaxe sometimes missed the back of the head and hit the beast high on the neck – but they seemed to drop dead just as effectively.' The sensitive Thomas winced and Gwyn, who could never resist baiting his little friend, turned the screw. 'Inside the neck was a thick white cord, joined to the brain. Very tasty it was, dropped in a stew with some turnips and onions.'

As the clerk blanched at the thought, de Wolfe picked up the nail and turned it in his fingers. 'This hammered through that white cord would kill, I have no doubt. If not immediately, then within a short time, as those who break their backs never survive for long.'

'Could it be an accident, Sir John?' asked Thomas, his mild nature hoping as always for an innocent outcome.

Gwyn laughed raucously. 'Accident? How the hell could he get an iron nail three inches deep into the back of his neck by accident? You'll be saying next it was suicide.'

'He could have fallen backwards, on to a plank that had a projecting nail,' hazarded the clerk stubbornly.

'So where's the plank? It's not still nailed to the back of his neck, is it?' jeered the Cornishman.

De Wolfe sighed and held up a hand to halt their bickering. 'He ended up hidden in that loft, so someone must have put him there. No, this is murder, but until we discover who the fellow might be, I don't see how I am even going to start finding his killer.'

Their clerk still worried away at the problem. 'Why

should a man stay still while another hammers a nail into his neck?' he demanded.

'Maybe he was asleep – or dead drunk,' suggested Gwyn.

'Or he could have been drugged,' added de Wolfe. 'Syrup of poppy or some other stupefying herb. He might even have been given a buffet on the head, hard enough to make him lose his wits for a while. We would find no trace of that, given the state of him now.'

The coroner hauled himself up from his bench and made for the doorway, an arch in the rough stone wall. It had been draped with ragged hessian in an attempt to reduce the draughts that whistled up the narrow spiral stairs from the guardroom two floors below.

'I'm going over to see the sheriff, for this death is odd enough to tell him about. Gwyn, you get out into the town and see if you can pick up news about anyone gone missing in the last few months or so. And Thomas, you do the same over in the cathedral Close. Your priestly friends are the biggest gossips in the city.'

De Wolfe clattered down the stairs and came out into another bare chamber, where two soldiers were playing at dice on an upturned barrel. A third man-at-arms shivered on guard duty outside, just within the archway that led out to the drawbridge over a deep dry ditch that separated the outer ward of the castle from the inner bailey. Inside the latter, walls of red sandstone enclosed an area containing three buildings, the tiny garrison chapel of St Mary, the plain stone box of the Shire Hall, and, straight ahead across the inner ward, the two-storeyed keep where the sheriff had his quarters.

The snow had petered out before it settled and under John's feet was hardened mud, churned by the horses, oxen, cartwheels and innumerable boots that had crossed the bailey to reach not only the keep, but the many sheds and wooden buildings that lined the walls. Some were barracks for the men-at-arms, others storehouses and stables, a few huts even housed wives and families of the soldiers, though most of these lived in the larger outer bailey, which was almost a village in itself. John climbed the wooden steps to the entrance of the keep, the main hall being ten feet above ground for purposes of defence. Beneath it was the undercroft, a semi-basement which housed the castle gaol.

Inside the large hall, the chill December day was tempered by a blazing fire in a hearth-pit and the body heat of scores of men, some sitting at trestles, others standing in groups, the rest milling about as they tried to get their varied business done. Merchants, clerks, stewards, a few knights and men-at-arms were talking, shouting, eating and drinking in what was probably the busiest place in Exeter.

John pushed his way through them and made for a side door on the left, where a soldier in a leather jerkin and round iron helmet stood guard outside the sheriff's chamber. At the sight of the king's coroner, the man jerked upright and smacked the butt of his spear on to the flagged floor in salute. All the men-at-arms knew and respected Sir John de Wolfe as a seasoned warrior, a former Crusader and veteran of a dozen campaigns in Ireland and France. From the colour of his hair and stubbled cheeks, as well as his preference for dark clothing, he had become known as Black John among the troops, a name that had often been matched by his moods – though fair and just, he was not a man to be trifled with.

De Wolfe gave the man a nod and opened the heavy oaken door. Inside, the Sheriff of Devon, Henry de Furnellis, was suffering the persistent attentions of his chief clerk, who loaded more parchments on to Henry's already cluttered table. Like John, Henry could neither read nor write, and his clerks had to read every document to him and take down replies as dictation.

De Furnellis looked on the coroner's arrival as

welcome relief and waved the clerk Elphin away, reaching for a wineskin and a couple of pottery cups. De Wolfe sat down in a leather-backed chair opposite Henry and gratefully accepted a cup of good Loire red.

The sheriff was an elderly man, almost sixty, and had a heavy face like that of a mournful bloodhound. An old soldier like John, he had been given the shrievalty of Devon as a reward for his faithful service to the king. In fact, he had been given it twice, as almost two years ago the previous sheriff, Richard de Revelle, had been ejected from office almost as soon as he was appointed, suspected of sympathy for the rebellion of Prince John, Count of Mortain, against his brother Richard Coeur de Lion, whilst the latter was imprisoned in Germany.

De Furnellis had temporarily taken over the post, but a few months later de Revelle was reinstated as a result of the political influence of Exeter's Bishop Marshal, himself a Prince John sympathiser. However, a year later, he was again ejected from office, mainly because of de Wolfe's exposure of his corrupt behaviour, and once again de Furnellis had been recruited to fill the gap.

After a few pleasantries and mutual complaints about the icy weather, John told the sheriff about the discovery of the body in Smythen Street.

'I've no idea who the man might be, Henry,' he finished. 'He wore garments of a decent quality, so is unlikely to be some beggar who crawled in there for shelter.'

'And who would want to slay a beggar with a nail in the back of the neck?' agreed de Furnellis. He was a shrewd man, experienced in the ways of the world, though the fire had gone out of his belly as the years passed by. He had accepted the post of sheriff reluctantly, out of duty to his king, but hoped that he was only looked on as a stopgap and could go back to retirement as soon as possible.

'Have you any recollection of someone having gone

missing in the city this past year?' asked John, hopefully. The sheriff had a manor a few miles out in the country, but lived most of the time in a town house on Curre Street, so might have heard some local gossip.

He scratched his bristly jowls thoughtfully. 'Folk are always vanishing, John, usually for reasons of their own. This is no village, where all men belong to a frankpledge and their neighbours know every time they cough or fart. In towns, men conveniently slip away because of debt or to escape from a shrewish wife – or run off with a pretty mistress.'

De Wolfe knew that the bluff older man was not making personal remarks, though either of the last two reasons could have applied to himself. 'But no particular disappearance comes to your mind?' persisted the coroner.

Henry shook his head dolefully. 'Sorry, John, no one of sufficient importance to be reported to me, anyway. Unless they are arrested or appealed for some crime, our citizens try to give me a wide berth. If they are dead, they come to your notice!'

After a few more minutes, the chief clerk began to get impatient and glare accusingly at his master for neglecting yet another armful of documents, so de Wolfe finished his wine and took his leave.

'You do what you think fit, John. You have more experience in tracking down corpses than me,' was Henry's parting shot as the coroner went to the door. Typically, the sheriff was content to leave any investigating to de Wolfe, though as the king's representative in the county, enforcing law and order was his responsibility.

Outside the keep, snowflakes were being whirled about by a keen east wind. John pulled his mottled wolfskin cloak tighter about him as he loped across the inner bailey and made for the gatehouse. Instead of going up to his dismal chamber, he carried on through the arch, through the outer ward and down Castle Hill to the high street. It was not far off midday, according to the cathedral bell ringing for Nones, so dinner was next on the agenda. He made his way back to his house in Martin's Lane, a short alley which joined High Street to the cathedral Close.

Pushing open the door of the narrow timber building, he wondered which would prove to be more frosty, the weather or his wife's welcome.

Chapter Two

In which a knight of the realm crosses Dartmoor

At that moment, about sixteen miles west of the city, a group of men were huddled under a turf roof in what was virtually a hole in the ground. Like the king's coroner, they were waiting for their midday meal, though theirs was to come from a blackened iron pot that sat on three stones set over a small fire.

'What have you got in there for us, Robert?' demanded a burly young man whose nose and cheeks were reddened by the cold. He had a shock of bright ginger hair poking from under the pointed hood of his leather jerkin.

'A rabbit and a cock pheasant. And lucky to get those in this weather,' grunted their cook for the day, a gaunt fellow of part-Saxon blood. He stirred the small cauldron with a length of twig pulled from the roof, swilling round the onions and chopped turnips that simmered in the salted water.

'And bloody awful weather it is, especially for the likes of us,' grumbled a third man, clutching his soiled but expensive worsted cloak more tightly around his shoulders. Philip Girard had taken it last month from a fat monk he had waylaid on the Plymouth road, reckoning that it would be of greater benefit to him on Dartmoor than to the owner sitting in the warming room of Buckfast Abbey.

'Thank God we've got a better place than this to go home to,' grunted Peter Cuffe, the ginger-haired youth. 'Though some living rough on the moor have not even a burrow as good as this one, poor sods.'

He looked around their shelter, which was formed by a couple of drystone walls built at right angles to an overhanging rocky bank. The walls narrowed to an opening, outside which was another barrier of moorstones to stop the wind, rain and snow from beating directly into the den. The whole was roofed over with untrimmed branches supporting grassy turfs. From a distance of a few score yards, the whole place was virtually invisible, blending in with the uneven terrain of the moor, especially now that everything was covered with a powdering of snow. Long ago, it had been a shelter for the tinners who used to work a nearby stream, but it had been abandoned as the lode was exhausted. Last year, their gang had repaired the crumbling walls and put a new roof across them, providing another hideout to add to the others they had concealed across the central part of Dartmoor.

'Isn't that damned broth ready yet?' demanded the fourth member of the group, who had been squatting on a log at the back of the cavelike shelter. He had an air of authority which marked him out as the leader and though his clothing was plain, it was of a better quality than the jumble of garments that the others wore.

'It'll do, sir. At least it'll be something hot to pour down our gullets,' replied Robert Hereward. There was a general shuffling around as each of them groped in his small pack and drew out a wooden bowl and horn spoon. The cook had a stale loaf which he broke into quarters and handed round; then he dipped the bowls into the pot and speared some meat and bones into each with his knife.

He passed the first bowl to their leader, then they crouched again around the fire, as the shelter was too low for anyone to stand up.

'This is all we'll get until we reach Challacombe,' warned Hereward. 'God willing, Gunilda will have something better for us when we get back.'

There was silence for a time, broken only by the slurping of hot soup and the noise of small bones being spat on the ground. When the last drops had been scraped from the bowls and the crusts finished, Peter Cuffe produced a small wineskin with a silver neck and stopper, another prize obtained by highway robbery. He passed it first to the man on the log, who drank deeply before wiping his mouth with the back of his hand and passing the bag on to Philip Girard.

'That was good stuff, these Exeter merchants do themselves well,' exclaimed Sir Nicholas de Arundell. The dispossessed lord of Hempston Arundell was a powerfully built man of average height, with a strong, handsome face. His close-cropped fair hair was a legacy from his Saxon mother Henneburga, but the rest of him was pure Norman, the first Arundell having arrived with William the Bastard. He was thirty-three, but the hardships of the last decade showed in his face, making him look older than his years.

As the men stuffed the bowls back into their shoulder packs, Girard questioned their chief. 'Are we going back in this weather?' he growled. A former huntsman, he was tall, with a weathered face pitted with cowpox scars.

De Arundell rose to his feet, stooping under the damp brushwood of the ceiling. 'Let's get out before the weather gets worse,' he answered in his deep voice. 'If it snows more heavily, we'll never cross the moor. I'm not going to starve for days in this rat hole.'

While the others gathered their few belongings and as Robert stamped out the embers of the fire, Nicholas thought longingly of the house at Hempston, his manor near Totnes in the south of the county. Though he had not been able to live in it for almost five years, he wistfully recalled sitting out snowy weather there in the comfort of his own hearth and with his wife Joan to keep him company. Now here he was slinking from hole to hole across a desolate landscape, like a fox seeking its den. True, this place was merely a convenient refuge on the moor, but even their more permanent quarters at Challacombe were hardly an attractive domicile. If any determined sweep were to be made by the law officers, they would even have to flee from that and seek one of their other hideouts, which were little better than this crude shanty.

Hauling his heavy woollen cloak around him and pulling up the hood, he slung his satchel over his shoulder and grabbed a heavy staff, the top weighted with iron bands to make it a formidable weapon. Leading the way past the outer wall, he emerged into the open and stretched upright, scanning the leaden sky. The snow had stopped for the moment, but a keen east wind was whipping up wraiths of white from the uneven moorland and the pinkish-grey horizon threatened a blizzard to come.

'We've less than five hours of daylight, so let's get going,' he commanded and set off towards the south, guided by landmarks that had become all too familiar these past three years. The grotesque outlines of the tors, irregular columns of granite standing against the skyline, together with upright stones set up by men long ago, marked the tracks that only sheep and moor men could recognise. In single file, the four men trudged steadily onward, thankful that the snow was only up to the insteps of their leather boots, which had been greased with hog fat to make them at least partly waterproof.

They marched in silence to conserve their breath. Though they had ponies back at Challacombe, they seldom used them for relatively short expeditions: on foot they could drop to the ground and lie invisible when either setting an ambush for unwary travellers or hiding from more powerful forces. With almost ten miles to go from where they had come up on to the high moor from South Tawton, they loped along steadily, occasionally stumbling on rocks hidden under the snow and plodding laboriously when they had to climb out of the sudden steep valleys that small tributaries of the Dart and Teign rivers had hacked deep into the moor.

As the shortest day of the year was only a week away, daylight faded early, especially with such a heavily overcast sky. By the time they came into the final mile of their journey it was getting dark, and though for a while their silhouettes against the whiteness of the snow helped them to follow in Nicholas's footsteps, soon only their familiarity with the turns and twists of the sheep tracks kept them on the right path. Eventually they descended into a valley where a tiny glimmer of yellow light guided them the last few furlongs. Their approach was soon heralded by the deep barking of a pair of dogs.

'Gunilda's set that old lantern outside for us, God bless her,' said Robert Hereward. Following a stony stream downwards, they passed through some bare trees to reach an opening in a low boundary wall and came into a tiny settlement of half a dozen stone huts, most of them derelict. The light had been placed on a boulder outside one which still had its roof of reed thatch. Daylight would have shown that this was tattered and rotting, but still held down against the gales by ropes slung over the top with heavy stones hanging on their ends. A door of rough planks was thrust open as they approached, and two wolf-like hounds rushed out, then cringed along the ground towards them, tails wagging. Behind them, outlined against a dim glow from a fire inside, was the figure of a tall woman, a sack around her shoulders to act as a shawl.

'I wondered if you would get here or stay the night at the Cosdon shelter,' she said in greeting, her voice deep and harsh. Gunilda Hemforde was a formidable widow of about fifty, of extremely ugly appearance. Her deeply lined face was like leather, her greying hair was sparse and patchy, and the few teeth she had left were blackened stumps. Gunilda was a widow because she had killed her husband with an axe when she found him on their bed with her younger sister. Rather than face inevitable hanging, she had taken to the moor two years ago, later being declared by the shire court to be a 'waif', this being the female equivalent of an outlaw. Now she kept house for the dozen men of the Arundell gang at their main hideout in the deserted village of Challacombe.

The woman stood aside to let the four weary travellers enter. Each greeted her warmly, for she made life more bearable for them by her simple ministrations.

'Rest yourselves and I'll bring your meat directly,' she promised, going to the other end of the single, square room where she had a table for preparing food. The men slumped gratefully onto piles of dried ferns set back from the circle of stones that enclosed the firepit in the centre of the hut. Three other men were already there and the conversation centred around the day's activities.

'We had very little luck,' observed Philip Girard. 'Two days lurking about the Okehampton road and almost nothing to show for it.'

'An Exeter burgess who carried no more than thirty pence in his purse and a flask of wine on his saddlebow!' added Peter Cuffe, in disgust. 'And we had to chase off a hulking great servant waving a sword to get even those.'

Nicholas de Arundell pulled off his boots and held his feet towards the fire, steam soon coming off his damp hose. 'Any news of Martin and the others?' he asked. The remaining five men had gone south three days before to try their luck along the high road that ran between Plymouth and Exeter. There was some head-shaking and grunting, then Gunilda replied from where she was hacking a large loaf into chunks as if it was her late husband's head.

'By the sky today, I reckon the snow was worse down that way, so perhaps they've holed up in the cave near Dunscombe.'

The outlaw band lived partly by armed robbery, especially during the winter months when there were few other sources of income. However, crime was not their only means of survival. Sometimes, they got casual work with the tinners, as the headmen of the teams often wanted extra labour when regular workers fell ill or were injured. At haymaking or harvest time, some village reeves would turn a blind eye to the employment of a stranger, and payment in kind, a goose or a small sack of corn, would be added to Gunilda's store of provisions.

Tonight, their supper came from poaching, a deer that Philip Girard had shot with a crossbow the previous week in the park of a manor near Widecombe. Thanks to the icy weather, it had hung outside the hut in good condition, providing venison for many days, and now Gunilda had used the last of it in another stew, eked out with winter cabbage and stored carrots and turnips.

They ate their food from a motley collection of tin, pewter and wooden bowls at a long table with benches on each side, luxurious surroundings compared with their refuge holes dotted over the moor. A couple of tallow dips, cord wicks floating in a dish of animal fat, provided the only light apart from that of the fire, but it was sufficient to dispel the gloom as they washed down the food with pottery mugs of ale and cider brewed by their grim housekeeper.

As they drank, they talked, the topics ranging from the best wood for making quarterstaffs to the usual nostalgia for homes and families from whom they were for ever banned, at least in theory. This last theme was pursued by their leader, to the concern of some of the others.

'I've made my mind up, I'm going into the city this week,' announced Nicholas.

This obviously worried Robert Hereward, who in their former life had been de Arundell's steward. 'Sir, I well know how badly you wish to see your good lady, but is it wise to put your head into the lion's mouth?'

His master shook his head, Hereward recognising the obstinate look that appeared on his weathered face. 'Not only do I wish to see my wife, but I need to talk to her about our situation,' he grated. His voice shook with anger. 'I'm damned if I'm to stay an outlaw for the rest of my life, especially when those bastards de Revelle and Pomeroy are at the root of it all!'

There was a growl of agreement from the others.

'But can you get into Exeter and stay there unrecognised?' persisted Peter Cuffe doubtfully.

'Getting in is no problem, I'll wait outside the West Gate at dawn and push in with the press of people entering for the market. With a wide pilgrim's hat and a few badges sewn on an old cloak, the porters'll not look twice at me.'

'And when you're in, what then?' persisted Robert Hereward, anxious for the safety of his hot-headed leader, as the penalty for discovery would be a summary hanging or beheading.

'Lady Joan is lodging there with a cousin, using a different name. No one knows of the connection between her and a noble outlaw, so she's quite safe. She's supposed to be on a pilgrimage to pray for her sister's health at the shrine of Saint Radegund in the cathedral.'

'And you'll be sheltered by them?' asked Peter dubiously.

'Yes, almost no one knows me in Exeter,' said Nicholas confidently. 'We're Cornish people, even though I inherited a Devon estate.'

He waved his mug at Gunilda for a refill and she plodded over with an earthenware pitcher of cider. 'I just hope you don't stay too long, that's all,' she growled fiercely. 'Every day makes the risk greater for you.' He shook his head as she poured the murky liquid.

'A day or two at the most. Then I'll be back here with some sort of notion of what to do next. My wife has sharp wits and talking to her will settle my mind.'

The old woman went round the circle of men, topping up their pots. 'Then may God and his Blessed Mother protect you, for if you were caught, this gang of numbskulls would perish without your guidance.'

That evening a biting east wind was whistling down the narrow tunnel of Martin's Lane as Sir John de Wolfe loped towards his house, the second of two dwellings in the short alley. Opposite was the side wall of an inn on the corner of High Street, next to a livery stables, where the coroner stabled his old warhorse Odin. The house was tall and narrow, being timber-built with a roof of wooden shingles. It had an almost blank front, with a single unglazed window at ground level, covered with heavy shutters. The only other opening was the front door of blackened oak with studded metal hinges. This led into a small vestibule, with a passage around to the backyard at one end. At the other, a door led into the hall, a high gloomy chamber which occupied all the interior of the building, though a solar had been added on upstairs at the back.

John entered the vestibule, thankful to be out of the wind, though it was still freezing inside. He took off his wolfskin cloak and sank on to a bench, wearily pulling off his boots in favour of house shoes. Going into the hall, he passed between the wooden screens that attempted to block the worst of the draughts, then advanced on the hearth, which was his pride and joy. Most houses still had a central firepit, the smoke having to rise to the roof and find its way out under the eaves, leaving a great deal behind to smart the eyes and irritate the throat. Several years before, copying from a house he had seen in Normandy, he had had a stone wall built at the back of the hall to support a conical chimney that passed through the roof and took the smoke from the hearth beneath. Together with the stone-flagged floor, which his wife had insisted upon as being a cut above the usual rush-strewn beaten earth, it made his house one of the most up-to-date in the city, about which Matilda could boast to her snobbish cronies at St Olave's Church.

She was sitting by the fire now, waiting for their serving woman Mary to bring in supper, another innovation, as most people were content with a single large dinner at noon.

'My brother is calling upon me tomorrow, John,' she snapped, without a word of greeting. 'I trust that you can manage to be civil to him for once.'

Considering that he had saved the man's life less than a month ago, de Wolfe thought this less than gracious, but Matilda was woefully short of grace. He rapidly scanned a mental list of possible excuses not to be at home for Richard de Revelle and hoped for a murder or a rape in the morning to keep him away.

Sitting in a wooden monk's chair, which had side panels and a hooded top to deflect draughts, John looked across at his wife on the opposite side of the hearth. Matilda's stocky body was enveloped in a thick kirtle of heavy green wool, with a long velvet mantle around her shoulders for warmth. Her head was encased in a tight-fitting helmet of white linen, tied with laces under her double chin, framing a square, pugnacious face with heavy-lidded eyes. A big fire of crackling logs kept their faces scorched, but behind them the bleak hall, towering up into the darkness of the rafters, was icy.

'Well?' snapped Matilda. 'Are you going to be here or not?'

Bereft of any excuse on the spur of the moment, he nodded reluctantly. 'What brings him here tomorrow? I thought he would be at Revelstoke or up at Tiverton.'

Richard had several manors in Devon and another in Somerset, and compared to John, he was a rich man. His wealth came both from lands inherited by his haughty wife Lady Eleanor and from his own incessant pursuit of money, some of which had come from his embezzling activities when sheriff.

'You surely must know that he has recently bought a house in North Gate Street as a *pied-à-terre*!' said Matilda sharply. 'Is it so unnatural for him to want to see his only sister when he is in our city?'

John glowered at her, wondering again how he had survived seventeen years of marriage to this woman. Neither of them had wanted to be wedded to the other, but they were forced into it by their families, one lot anxious to see their plain daughter married off to a knight, the other keen to marry the youngest son into a richer family.

'Richard is rarely happy to set eyes on me,' he replied dourly. 'So why do you want to inflict me upon him tomorrow?'

His wife glared at him. 'Because he has asked to speak to you, that's why. Something about that fellow who was found dead in the school in Smythen Street.'

De Wolfe groaned. 'I might have guessed that was it. He's afraid the gossip will harm his bloody purse, by putting off rich students from signing up to his poxy college. We don't yet know who the dead man was.'

Matilda began a scandalised tirade against his denigration of her brother's educational initiatives, but was diverted by Mary bustling in with a tray bearing their supper. Ever eager for food and drink, Matilda heaved herself up and went to her stool at one end of the long table, ready to attack the spit-grilled trout that lay on a thick trencher of bread.

Slitting it expertly along the backbone with a small knife, she picked up the succulent flesh in her fingers. Afterwards she washed them in a bowl of rosewater and wiped them on a napkin, all produced by the tireless Mary from her journeys back and forth from the kitchen hut in the backyard, where she cooked, ate and slept.

John poured his wife a cup of wine, then went to sit at the opposite end of the table to have his own meal, the distance between them exemplifying the emotional gulf between them. He was grateful for the silence that the serious business of eating required, a silence which went on through the second course of slices of cold pork with onions, followed by fresh bread and hard yellow cheese.

Eventually, they finished and Matilda rose, as he knew she would, seeking Lucille, her browbeaten French hand-maid, to prepare her for bed.

'I'll expect you home for dinner tomorrow, John,' she said in a tone that invited no contradiction. 'Richard needs to hear from you about this corpse and I'll not have him disappointed.'

With that, she sailed out of the hall to go around to the yard, where there were outside stairs to her solar. This was a room built high up on to the back of the hall, supported on stout timbers, under which Lucille lived in a small boxlike chamber.

Left to himself, John sank with a sigh into his chair by the hearth and waited for Mary to come to clear the debris of the meal. As she entered, his old hound Brutus slunk in and laid at his feet to enjoy the warmth of the fire, knowing full well that his master would soon be taking him out for a stroll – a nightly excuse to visit the Bush Inn and its attractive Welsh landlady.

As an unfrocked priest only recently restored to grace,

Thomas de Peyne was not overly fond of visiting taverns, but the Bush was an exception. Just around the corner from his modest lodging in Priest Street, the building in Idle Lane was the nearest thing to home for him, as the kindly Nesta insisted on mothering the little cleric. Even though he had a few more pennies to spend since his rescue from abject poverty, the landlady fed him gratis whenever he appeared, convinced that his weedy frame, with the slight hunchback and lame leg, needed more sustenance than he bothered to give it.

Tonight, he was just finishing a bowl of mutton stew, sitting at a table near the hearth with Gwyn, who had just demolished his favourite pork knuckle with a pile of beans and onions. The big Cornishman seemed always hungry and thirsty and justified his appetite by the soldier's adage that one should sleep, eat, drink and make love whenever the opportunity arose, as one never knew when the next chance would come along. On the other side of the trestle sat John de Wolfe, with a quart of Nesta's best ale in front of him, just topped up by old Edwin, the one-eyed potman. Brutus lay under the table, waiting expectantly for Gwyn to drop the stripped bone down to the rush-covered floor. This peaceful tableau was completed a moment later by the appearance of the shapely landlady herself, who slipped down on to the bench alongside the coroner and pushed her arm through his.

'Tell me all the day's gossip, John,' she demanded.

The lean, dark face of her lover broke into a rare smile as he looked down at the pretty redhead. 'Not a great deal today, my girl. Just a mouldy old corpse found around the corner from here, hardly a hundred paces away.' He told her briefly about the finding of the body in the nearby forge.

'Have you any idea who it might be, given that you are almost neighbours?' he demanded, with mock severity. The question was not completely facetious, as

Nesta was a fount of gossip, her inn being one of the most popular in Exeter, especially amongst travellers passing through the city. Like his maid Mary, Nesta had often been the purveyor of titbits of information that were of use to the coroner.

'No one has gone missing from this part of the town,' she replied seriously. 'How long had the poor man been there?'

De Wolfe shrugged. 'Hard to say, given that it was dried out like a smoked herring, up above that forge. Some months, I would guess.'

'When did the metalworkers leave there, I wonder?' asked Gwyn, brushing bits of food from the luxuriant ginger moustaches that hung down each side of his chin.

The landlady had the answer to this. 'Michaelmas, that was. I heard that their lease ran out then and it was bought for this college, whatever that place might be.'

Thomas could never resist airing his knowledge of anything remotely academic. 'It's one of these new schools that are springing up in some cities – Oxford was the first, but a few other places are now aping Paris and Bologna.'

'I thought schools were where young boys and girls learned to read and write,' offered the more philistine Gwyn, picking shreds of pork from his teeth. 'Like the one in Winchester where you got into trouble, Thomas,' he added slyly.

The clerk's pinched face coloured immediately. 'I was totally innocent, as you well know – you great Cornish clown,' he retorted, with a sharpness that was unusual for him. Now that he had been vindicated of the allegations that had got him ejected in disgrace from the priesthood, he was even more sensitive than before about having the matter brought up.

'Who's this man Anglicus they call Magister?' asked Nesta.

'He's the fellow who runs the establishment, the prime teacher there, though I understand there are two others under him,' explained de Wolfe. 'But what amazed me was to find that my dear brother-in-law actually owns the place – and no doubt puts the profits into his purse.'

Thomas nodded eagerly, his annoyance with Gwyn forgotten. 'He may be on to a good thing, such schools are becoming popular now. Some have sprung up in Northampton and Norwich, but the best-known outside Oxford is here in Exeter, where the poet Joseph Iscanus is magister.'

'So what do they teach, if it's not reading and writing?' asked Nesta.

'How to smoke corpses, by the looks of it!' scoffed Gwyn, getting another scourging glare from Thomas.

'Here it would be the *trivium*,' the clerk expounded, his own enthusiasm as a teacher spurring him on. 'The three great subjects, Grammar, Rhetoric and Logic. If the school succeeds, then later they may go on to the *quadrivium*, Arithmetic, Geometry, Astronomy and Music – and even Physic.'

Impatient with this academic lecture, the coroner turned to his officer and demanded to know if he had any news about the dead man.

'There's no gossip at the four taverns I visited earlier to suggest anyone's missing,' said Gwyn dolefully. 'The trouble with a big city like Exeter is that folks come and go every day, and no one takes any notice.' He paused to take a huge draught of ale, before continuing. 'In a manor, the tithings keep a strict watch on each member and every villager knows every other freeman and villein – but here, you can walk in and out of the five gates and unless you're driving a pig or pushing a barrow, no one says a word to you.'

The coroner turned to Thomas de Peyne. 'What about you? Any whispers amongst you holy men?' As well as being his clerk, the little man had part-time employment in the cathedral, teaching some of the choristers to read, working on the archives in the scriptorium and saying early masses for the wealthy deceased who had left annuities for perpetual prayers. It gave him a good opportunity to keep his ear to the ecclesiastical ground, as he was probably the most inquisitive man in Devon. However, today he had drawn a blank in respect of the murdered corpse from the forge.

'Nothing at all, Crowner,' he admitted sadly. 'From the appearance of his clothing, I think he was a tradesman or merchant, rather than anything to do with the cathedral Close, though of course there are plenty of lay people associated with the running of the diocese.'

With an admonition to them both to keep trying on the following day, John lazily stood and, with a wink at Nesta, said he was going out into the backyard of the inn to unburden himself of some of his ale against the fence. Gwyn and Thomas knew from experience that this was their cue to leave and reluctantly tore themselves away from the firepit to go out into the cold night air of Idle Lane, where Thomas set off for the room which he shared with a vicar-choral from the cathedral and the Cornishman made for yet another alehouse, with the excellent excuse that he was spying for his master.

Chapter Three

In which Crowner John suffers his brother-in-law

Next morning, the coroner was obliged to attend the Tuesday hangings, to record the event and officially to seize the property of the four felons, which was forfeit to the Crown. The executions were held outside the city at Heavitree, where the gallows stood along Magdalene Street, one of the main roads going eastwards.

Thomas was there to scribe the details on his parchment sheets, and as usual Gwyn followed in the shadow of his master, partly as bodyguard, but mainly as assistant and companion, as he had done for twenty years in Irish rain, French mists and Levantine sunshine.

After the wretched victims had dropped from the crossbar of the high scaffold with ropes around their necks, the coroner's team made their way back to the South Gate and de Wolfe strode reluctantly towards his house, aggrieved that no legal emergency had cropped up to use as an excuse to avoid dinner with his brother-in-law. He heard Richard de Revelle's braying voice as soon as he entered the vestibule and groaned as he lifted the latch of the hall and went inside.

Richard was sitting in John's chair near the hearth, drinking their best wine from one of the glass goblets that were brought out only on special occasions. Matilda, in her best brocade kirtle, sat opposite and scowled at her husband as he entered.

'You're late, John. I've had to tell Mary to wait before serving the food.'

'Well, I'm here now. Some of us have duties to attend to,' he retorted, with a meaningful nod at her brother.

He went to a side table and poured himself some wine, pointedly using a pottery cup instead of one of the heavy glasses he had bought at considerable cost in France some years earlier. 'Matilda tells me you had something to discuss with me, Richard,' he grunted.

'Let that rest until we have eaten,' commanded his wife, as Mary came in with a wooden tray bearing a boiled duck. They came to the table and began eating, today using pewter plates instead of the usual bread trenchers. Bowls of cabbage, onions and beans were brought in from the kitchen shed, together with a large jug of a different wine. The courteous Richard cut slices from the plump bird with his knife and placed them on his sister's platter before serving himself, leaving John to fend for himself.

As de Wolfe had recently ruined de Revelle's political ambitions and come within a whisker of having him arrested and possibly hanged, it was hardly surprising that the atmosphere was strained. However, the former sheriff was beholden to John several times over, and he could not afford to be too openly antagonistic to the coroner, especially as de Wolfe still had enough evidence to have him indicted for treason over Richard's support for the rebellious Prince John.

They began eating in a state of muted truce, the dapper Richard making some small talk, largely with his sister, leaving John to chew undisturbed and to regard their visitor from under his black eyebrows. He saw a slight man of average height, with wavy brown hair and a small pointed beard which made his face look triangular. Like his sister, Richard had rather small brown eyes, which darted restlessly around, giving him a shifty appearance that matched what John knew of his nature. But what most drew the attention was the splendour of his dress, for though he was not as showy as John's trading partner, Hugh de Relaga, de Revelle had expensive tastes in costume. He wore a calf-length tunic of the best green linen, heavily embroidered around the neck and hem with gold thread, and, clinching his waist, a wide belt of elaborately tooled leather. Over these he wore an open surcoat of fine yellow wool, while on a hook behind the screens hung a further defence against the chill of winter, a heavy, fur-lined mantle of blue cloth. As they ate, Richard regaled his sister with details of the house he had just bought in the city.

'In an excellent district, of course,' he brayed. 'Just inside the North Gate, with a hall, a solar and two extra rooms.'

'Starting another school, are you?' observed John with heavy sarcasm. Impervious to the jibe, de Revelle explained that he needed somewhere to stay in the city when he was attending to his various business interests in Exeter, his manors at Tiverton and Revelstoke being far away at opposite ends of Devon. The fact that he no longer had quarters in Rougemont because he had been ejected in disgrace, was carefully avoided.

When they had eaten a dessert of stewed figs imported from Provence and sampled Mary's bread and cheese, they returned to the wine and the problem that Richard had brought.

'It's this damned corpse found in my new school in the lower town,' he began in his rather effeminate, high-pitched voice. 'I gather that you are dealing with the matter, John?'

'I'm the only coroner in Exeter, so I have little choice,' growled de Wolfe.

'Then I trust that you will settle the case with the

utmost speed and discretion. Such unwelcome publicity can do nothing but harm to my venture there.'

'I'll do what I have to do, Richard. No more nor no less than my duty.'

Brother and sister exchanged looks loaded with exasperation at this unhelpful attitude, but John was damned if he was going to do any special favours for this rogue who was only interested in his own profit.

'I swear this corpse was put there deliberately to embarrass me and spoil my efforts to bring some more culture to this city,' whined Richard. 'Both potential students and prominent families who are considering enrolling their sons can only be discouraged by such goings-on.'

'Are you accusing the masters of your rival schools as the culprits?' asked John mischievously. 'Maybe this famous poet Joseph Iscanus slew the fellow and dragged him up into your loft?'

'Don't be so ridiculous, husband. Listen to what my brother is telling you,' snapped Matilda. 'This death is an embarrassment to Richard and can only do a disservice to both him and the progress of education in this city,' she added pompously.

'Iscanus is a good teacher,' said Richard condescendingly. 'I only hope that our new establishment can match his excellence, given time. If we can all urge more students to enrol, then Exeter could come to rival Oxford.'

Remembering the main reason for his visit, he changed the subject. 'Have you made no progress at all in clearing up the death of this damned intruder into my school?' he demanded.

De Wolfe grunted into his wine cup, his usual response to being nagged. 'We don't even know who the fellow was, yet. Have you any idea how he came to be in your property?'

'He must have been hidden there to cause us trouble,' claimed de Revelle.

'But I'm told you acquired the place only at Michaelmas,' countered John.

Richard shook his head stubbornly. 'I'll wager he wasn't there when we took over. Depend on it, he was dumped there deliberately.'

The coroner shrugged. 'And who would want to have done a thing like that, for God's sake?'

'I know one, for a start,' replied Richard, darkly. 'The man who has been plaguing me for many months, damn him.'

John waited for an explanation. His brother-in-law had a legion of enemies and he wondered which one would be chosen this time.

'That thrice-cursed outlaw from Cornwall, I'll wager he's behind this,' snarled Richard. 'That bloody Arundell fellow.'

John pricked up his ears. 'Arundell? Which one is that? There were several of that name out in Palestine when I was there.'

'They're scattered all over the West Country like a swarm of flies,' grumbled de Revelle. 'William of Normandy should never have given them so much land after Hastings, they became a plague on the country.'

'Which one, I said?' snapped John impatiently. If a fellow Crusader was involved, he wanted to know about it.

'Nicholas, who used to hold Hempston Arundell years ago, though he should have stayed with the rest of the barbarians in Cornwall.'

De Wolfe shook his head. 'I don't know of a Nicholas from my time in the Holy Land. But Hempston is near Totnes, isn't it?'

De Revelle nodded his elegant head. 'A dismal little manor next to Henry Pomeroy's lands.' He seemed to John to become suddenly evasive.

'So why should he want to harm you? What have you done to him?' he demanded.

Richard waved a be-ringed hand dismissively. 'It's a long story, John. Suffice it to say that he has threatened me a number of times and tried to bring an action against me in the courts. But of course, an outlaw has no legal existence, so he has no chance of that, unless he wants to lose his head.'

He refused to enlarge upon the issue and John guessed that he had swindled this Arundell out of something. He was not sufficiently interested to press his brother-in-law further, so Richard repeated his earlier request.

'I trust you, and that senile sheriff we have now, will clear up this mystery with the utmost speed. I can expect little from de Furnellis, but I hope that you will do all you can to settle the matter before it becomes the talk of Devon.'

John stood up, his bench grating on the flagstones. 'I'll do what I can, as always. But you have no idea at all who this dead man might be?' When Richard shook his head, de Wolfe persisted. 'You are always parading about the county between your manors, have you heard of anyone going missing this past half-year?'

'John, I have better things to occupy me than listening to gossip, other than that concerning the gentry of this county.' De Revelle was an even bigger snob than his sister.

'This man was no beggar or serf, he wore good clothing, so he need not have been beneath your notice,' said John, sarcastically.

His brother-in-law had the grace to look a little abashed. 'I still have no notion of who he might have been. Perhaps you can stir your sheriff into enquiring amongst the tithings and the serjeants of the Hundreds, to see if anyone has gone missing?'

De Wolfe began backing towards the door. 'That is being done, but somehow I suspect he is a townsman rather than a villager.'

Matilda glared at his retreating figure. 'Are you leaving

so early, husband? Can you not stay to entertain our guest longer?'

Reaching the screens, he raised his hand in a perfunctory farewell. 'I have urgent business at the castle. This morning's business at the gallows has put me behind, I must go.'

Before more protests could be made, he marched out of the door, grabbed his boots and cloak from the vestibule, and made a hurried getaway into the street.

The chapter house of Exeter cathedral was a timber structure built just outside the massive south tower. It was an old building, now indisputably inadequate for housing both the chamber on the ground floor where the canons daily debated their business, as well as the scriptorium and archives on the upper level. The bishop had promised to donate part of the nearby palace garden for a new building in stone, but so far it was still no more than a drawing on a sheet of parchment.

It was to the scriptorium that Thomas made his way that afternoon, climbing the wooden stairs in the corner of the bare chapter house with joy in his heart. A born academic, he loved both the Church and its historical accoutrements, so to him the steps up to this dusty library were like the first flight of a stairway to heaven. After two years in the wilderness following his unfrocking, to be legitimately returned to the fold and also to have the run of the books and manuscripts in the archives was paradise on earth. When recently he had been restored in Winchester to the priesthood, one of the conditions was that he should be found some ecclesiastical employment, so his uncle John de Alencon, Archdeacon of Exeter, had arranged some part-time jobs for him. As well as teaching young choristers to read and write, Thomas was to begin cataloguing the cathedral archives, which over the years had declined into a disorganised jumble of manuscripts. This was a delight to Thomas, for he could spend as much time as he liked reading them, as well as the several score valuable books which were chained around the walls.

Today, however, he had an added motive in spending a few hours in the chapter house, as he wanted to discover if anyone there had any idea of the identity of their most recent corpse. There were usually a few people in the scriptorium, either laboriously copying old papers or researching some obscure point of canon law. Exeter was one of the nine secular cathedrals in England, staffed by canons and their minions, so there were no monks there, only various grades of cleric like Thomas himself. These were at least as prone to gossip as the butcher or baker, and Thomas had no difficulty in getting them talking, albeit in low tones so as not to disturb the couple of old prebendaries who were dozing at their desks.

Adept at worming out information without giving rise to suspicion, the little clerk spent the whole afternoon interrogating a pair of vicars, three parish priests and an old canon who spent most of his time in the scriptorium because of the pleasant warmth given off by the stone chimney that came up from the hearth in the chamber beneath. Thomas had hoped that one of them might have had parishioners who had vanished or perhaps had known of a missing member of the congregation from one of the twenty-seven churches in the city. In addition, though the confessional was sacrosanct, priests were known when amongst themselves to let drop anonymous information, but perhaps this was too much to expect. In the event, his afternoon was wasted, as absolutely nothing turned up that might shed any light on the identity of the unknown corpse. John could only hope that Gwyn would have better fortune than Thomas de Peyne.

In fact, his officer's attempts at gaining information were not only more successful, but much more exciting than the clerk's placid hours in the cathedral scriptorium. The big Cornishman had spent the afternoon and early part of the evening making a tour of Exeter's taverns. Having at least one large jar of ale in each, by twilight a lesser man would have sunk unconscious into the gutter, but Gwyn's iron head and large bladder could deal with prodigious quantities of drink without much effect upon him. But a couple of hours after nightfall, he had still learned nothing of any use and he decided to make his way in the icy moonlight back down to the Bush to report his failure to his master. On his way down Smythen Street, where their problem had begun, he resolved to make one last call and carried on down towards Stepcote Hill, a lane leading down towards the West Gate and so steep that it was terraced to offer safe footing. At its top was the most disreputable alehouse in the city, the Saracen. A haunt of thieves, whores and assorted villains, the tavern was run by Willem the Fleming, an obese giant almost as big as Gwyn, who ruled his disorderly house by sheer physical force. Gwyn rarely went there except when there was an affray or a murder, not only because he represented unwelcome law and order, but also because the ale was so foul compared with Nesta's brew.

Tonight he ducked under the low lintel of the front door, above which was painted a crude representation of a Moorish head, complete with turban. Inside, the taproom was foul with smoke from the central firepit, its odour mixed with the stench of unwashed bodies, spilt ale and the miasma rising from month-old rushes rotting on the floor. A pair of stray dogs competed with rats in searching for old food scraps dropped beneath the rickety tables, at which drunken patrons sat with a few raucous whores. The rest of the room was filled with rough-looking men who stood drinking, shouting and arguing, when they were not pinching the bottoms and bosoms of the three slatterns who pushed through the crowd bearing large jugs to refill empty pots.

Gwyn got himself a mug of cider, which was slightly more palatable than the ale, ignoring the hostile looks of some men who recognised him as the coroner's officer. Picking on an older man sitting alone against the wall, he began a conversation about the weather and then the iniquities of rising prices until he felt able to bring the talk around to missing persons in the city. He soon discovered he was wasting his time with the taciturn fellow and moved on to try the same ploy with others. His efforts fell on equally barren soil and he was about to give up in disgust and go to the Bush, when he felt a hand grip him roughly by the shoulder.

'Why the hell are you asking all these questions, man?' snarled a voice. Turning, Gwyn saw a big black-bearded fellow, whose scarred face seemed vaguely familiar, though he could not put a name to him.

'What's it to you? Unless you've got some answers for me!' responded Gwyn, not a man to take kindly to being spoken to in that tone.

'Bloody spy, that's what you are,' spat Blackbeard. 'I know who you are – the crowner's nark, nosing your way in here like this.' He raised his fist in a threatening gesture and shook it under Gwyn's large nose.

Gwyn, who was always partial to a fight to liven up the evening, pushed the fellow in the chest. Large as he was, Blackbeard staggered back under the thrust of a hand the size of a horse's hoof. Though fights were almost an hourly event in the Saracen, this one promised to be better than the usual run of squabbles, as it involved a red-haired Goliath and their own pugnacious tavern-champion.

The patrons rapidly scattered to form a ring around the combatants and began yelling encouragement at Blackbeard, advising him to tear off the law officer's head. Though Gwyn was unusually large, the other man was also heavily built and a decade younger, as well as evidently being the possessor of an evil temper. He rushed back at the Cornishman, fists flailing, and landed one heavy blow on his upper belly and a sideswipe at Gwyn's lantern jaw. For all the effect it had, Blackbeard might as well have punched the stone wall opposite. Almost lazily, the coroner's officer reached out and repaid him with an open-handed slap across the side of the head, which sent him reeling.

'I don't want to hurt you, son,' growled Gwyn. 'So for God's sake, stop irritating me!'

Now livid with rage and humiliation, Blackbeard began mouthing invective at the ginger giant as he regained his feet and crouched in preparation for another assault. He was encouraged by renewed yells of support from the tipsy spectators, and especially the frenzied screams of the strumpets, who seemed near-orgasmic at the prospect of blood. One of them wore the red wig and striped gown of a Southwark prostitute, being for some reason far from her home territory. This time, the resident fighter managed to land a heavy blow on Gwyn's face, making blood spurt from his nose, and this so annoyed the coroner's officer that he grabbed Blackbeard by the throat and shook him like a dog shakes a rat.

'Will you stop your bloody nonsense, man?' exploded Gwyn, exasperated now at this uncalled-for provocation. 'All I was asking was whether anyone here knew of someone gone missing in the city these past few months.'

His adversary was incapable of speech with Gwyn's massive hand clamped around his throat, though as his face went blue, he continued to thrash his arms and legs in a futile attempt to land some blows. Seeing their champion getting the worst of the contest, the crowd began to quieten, but one moderately sober man, wearing a blood-stained butcher's apron, challenged Gwyn.

'Why d'you want to know that, ginger? What business is it of yours?' he called aggressively.

Gwyn flung Blackbeard back, so that he again staggered

into the arms of the spectators behind him. Turning to the butcher, Gwyn bellowed an answer. 'Because we want to know the name of the corpse found in the forge just up the street. After all, he was a neighbour of yours, albeit as dead as mutton!'

Instead of replying, the butcher suddenly pointed behind Gwyn. Swinging round, he saw that Blackbeard was running at him again, this time waving a wicked-looking knife that he must have snatched from his belt.

'Oh Christ, not again,' muttered Gwyn, just having time to kick the man in the crotch as he came within reach. He grabbed his knife arm and wrenched it up and back, extracting a scream of pain as the shoulder dislocated, pain that merged into the agony of having his genitals hammered by a large boot. This time Blackbeard went down and stayed down, curled into a ball and moaning as he tried to clutch simultaneously his nether regions and his injured shoulder.

The crowd now seemed divided between those who resented their man being defeated by an outsider and those who felt that drawing a knife on an unarmed opponent was unsporting. Gwyn felt it diplomatic to leave, especially as the uncouth landlord, Willem the Fleming, was pushing his way through the throng, intent on restoring order with a large club that he kept near the ale casks.

Gwyn shoved his way through to the street door, went out into the cold night air and crossed the narrow street to where Idle Lane went off at right angles. On the corner, he stopped to wipe the blood from his nose with the back of his hand, hawking and spitting out some that had trickled down into his throat. He chuckled at the memory of the brief fight, as he had felt that recently life had been getting too staid, with little to get the pulses racing.

As he gave a final sniff, he suddenly heard a footstep behind him. He whirled around in case someone from the Saracen had decided to pursue him with retribution in mind. With fist half-raised, Gwyn peered in the wan light of the gibbous moon and saw a small man of indeterminate age, swaddled in a dark cloak, a woollen cap on his head, the tasselled point hanging over one ear.

'Who the hell are you? Are you following me?' he growled. The fellow looked on closer inspection to be well past middle age and seemed an unlikely assailant.

'I heard what you said in the alehouse just now. I know you for the squire of Sir John de Wolfe and I might have some information for him.' Gwyn peered more closely and saw a pair of sharp eyes glinting in a lined face free of any beard or moustache.

'What sort of information? Who are you anyway?'

'I am Walter Pole, a harness maker from St Mary Arches. You were asking about persons who have gone missing from the city and I may be able to help you.'

Gwyn gripped Walter by the shoulder. 'We can't talk out here, it's as cold as a witch's womb! If you'll walk a few hundred paces with me to the Bush tavern, you'll be able to tell your story to Sir John himself.'

Gwyn displayed the harness maker to the coroner with a proprietary air, as if he had manufactured the fellow himself for de Wolfe's edification.

'This is Walter Pole, Crowner. He says he has something useful to tell us about our corpse,' he announced, as they stood before John's table in the taproom of the Bush.

De Wolfe's long face glowered up at the new arrival, but he waved him down to a bench opposite and beckoned to Edwin to bring Walter a jar of ale. Glad to be near the fire and out of the biting cold outside, the craftsman lowered himself gratefully on to the seat and pulled off his pointed cap, revealing a shock of wiry grey hair.

'So what's this you've got to say to me about the dead man in Smythen Street?' demanded John. He had already decided that Pole had an honest face and might be worth listening to.

'I think I might know who he is, Crowner,' began the harness maker, taking a swallow of the ale that the potman had placed before him. 'Or at least, I can tell you about someone who's gone missing from the city.'

De Wolfe's black eyebrows climbed up his forehead. 'Indeed? Who is he – and why has no one noticed his absence before this?'

'I'm talking about Matthew Morcok, a former master saddler, sir. He had given up his trade due to bad health, almost a twelve-month ago.'

'So why has no one raised a hue and cry about his disappearance?' asked John. 'Had he no wife or family to question his whereabouts?'

Walter Pole shook his head firmly. 'That's the point, Crowner. He had been a widower these many years and had no children except a married daughter living away in Oxford. Morcok lived a solitary life in a small house in Priest Street and kept very much to himself.'

'Didn't his neighbours miss him?' said Gwyn, hovering over the table.

Walter sighed into his ale. 'To tell the truth, Matthew was not a very sociable person and Priest Street is not very neighbourly, with so many different clerks and suchlike coming and going all the time. I suspect he had snubbed those few who tried to befriend him, so they kept well clear.'

'So how is it that you happen to know all this?' snapped de Wolfe.

'I worked for him for ten years, first as a journeyman, then as a partner. We had a workshop in Rock Street, making leather accoutrements for horses and oxen. When he gave up due to ill health, I bought his share in the business.'

'What sort of ill health did he suffer?'

Walter shrugged and turned his hands palms up. 'God alone knows its nature, sir. But he began shuffling as he walked and had a spasmodic twitch of the head. His fingers were always working, as if he was rolling pills between them.'

Gwyn broke in again. 'I remember seeing such a man about the streets a year or so back. Did he lean forwards as he walked as if he was going to fall on his face at every step?'

Walter nodded in agreement. 'That he did! But his mind was clear, even if his speech wasn't. He could get about well enough, but his disability made him shun the company of others, which is why he hasn't been missed.'

De Wolfe gave one of his grunts, which could signify almost anything. 'So how is that you know he vanished? And when was this?'

'As I worked with him for so long, I tried to keep in touch, though even with me he was distant in his manner. I think he was so conscious of his ailments that he wanted to be left alone. But as he had been so active in the Guild of Leatherworkers, I usually went down to see him after a guild meeting to keep him abreast of what was being discussed – not that he seemed that interested.'

'And the last time?' asked John, striving to conceal his impatience at the longwindedness of Walter Pole.

'Soon after Midsummer's Day, it must have been. I called upon him and tried to be sociable, but he was in his usual sour mood. Then I went again after the guild meeting at Michaelmas, but I got no answer at his house. I went back a few days later, but again I had no reply, the place was all shut up.'

'Was that the last time you tried?' said the coroner.

'No, I went down to Priest Street again a few weeks ago, but still no sign of him. I asked a couple of neighbours, but they said they hadn't laid eyes on him for months. Mind you, several of them had only been there that long themselves, there are so many lodging houses in that street with folks coming and going all the time.'

'Couldn't he have gone away, maybe to live with his daughter?' suggested Gwyn.

Walter Pole's lined face took on a dubious expression. 'They were never that close, sir. Morcok made no secret of the fact that he disliked the fellow she married, especially when he took her to live halfway across England. She hadn't visited him for a good three years that I know of, so I can't see him going to Oxford. In any case, what about his house? It was a decent freehold burgage, worth a few pounds of anyone's money, but it's never been put up for sale. So where is he?'

John saw Nesta weaving her way through her patrons to come to sit with him and decided that her company was preferable to that of the harness maker, as he seemed to have exhausted his tale about the missing saddler. Standing up, he gravely thanked Walter Pole for his help.

'You asked where is this Matthew Morcok?' he finished. 'Possibly still in the old forge, just up the street. I want you to come there an hour after dawn tomorrow and see if you can identify him for me. He's in bad shape, but you might still be able to recognise him.'

Taking the hint, Gwyn ushered Walter to a stool on the other side of the firepit, where a glowing pile of logs threw out a comforting heat. Motioning to one of the serving wenches to fetch the leatherworker another quart, Gwyn went back to his master's table and sat where Walter had been, opposite de Wolfe and the fair Nesta, who had her arm through that of her lover.

'What d'you think of that tale, then?' he demanded of them.

John had just told Nesta the gist of Pole's story, while Edwin eavesdropped shamelessly. The old one-eyed servant, standing at the end of the table with a brace of empty jugs in his hands, took it upon himself to answer.

'I remember that old man from Priest Street, the one with the shaking palsy. He used to shuffle up this way now and then, I always was afeared that he would pitch forwards on to his nose, poor fellow. But I've not clapped my eye on him for many a month.' As if to illustrate this, he rolled the sunken, white orb of his horrible dead eye in its deformed socket, the legacy of a spear thrust during the Battle of Wexford.

'Well, we should know in the morning, if this man Pole can make anything of the features of the corpse,' observed John, gently massaging Nesta's shapely thigh under the table. 'Richard de Revelle has got some crazy notion that he was planted there by a Dartmoor outlaw just to discredit his bloody school.'

'What outlaw would that be, John?' asked Nesta, sliding her fingers over his.

'Another landless knight, I suppose. There are so many about these days. Since the Crusade ended, many warriors, mostly second sons without an inheritance, find themselves without either a war to fight or a manor to farm, so they take to armed robbery.' He paused to lift his pot with his free hand and take a long swallow, before continuing. 'This fellow is from some Cornish family. Maybe you know of them Gwyn, coming from those parts. He's Nicholas de Arundell, according to my dear brother-in-law. I vaguely recall the name, but our paths never crossed in Palestine.'

'It's a well-known family in Cornwall,' replied his officer. 'Been there since the Conquest, for William the Bastard handed out many parcels of land to the Arundells, all over the West Country.'

The potman, a champion nosy-parker well able to rival the inquisitive Thomas de Peyne, still hovered with his empty mugs, reluctant to leave without adding to the discussion.

'I know something of this outlaw fellow Nicholas,' he said. 'Some call him Nick o' the Moor and many have a lot of sympathy with him.'

John was willing to listen to Edwin, as the old man often had useful snippets of information. Endlessly passing amongst the patrons of the Bush, distributing ale and collecting pots, he heard all kinds of conversations from men who travelled to Exeter from all over England and beyond.

Resting his pottery mugs on the end of the trestle, Edwin leaned forward and in a lowered voice, as if what he had to say was confidential, he told them what he knew about Nick o' the Moor.

'Gwyn's right about him being from this big Cornish family, but he inherited a small manor in Devon from his father. Somewhere near Totnes it is, I forget the actual name, but it's nigh to Berry Pomeroy.'

The coroner nodded, as this was what Richard de Revelle had told him. 'Hempston Arundell, that's the manor,' he grunted as Edwin went on with his story.

'Seems he had not long taken over the place after his father's death, when he was persuaded to take the Cross, back in 'eighty-nine. Doesn't get back for a few years and then finds that he has been declared dead and his manor confiscated by the Count of Mortain, who puts Pomeroy and de Revelle in his place.'

De Wolfe groaned. 'It's no surprise to hear those treacherous bastards would be involved in some underhand scheme like that. But how came this Nicholas to be outlawed?'

Here the potman had run out of gossip. 'I'm not sure of that, Crowner, I only overheard part of the talking and that was a year or two past. I seem to recall that this Nicholas is a hothead and he assaulted and killed somebody in his rage over the loss of his estate. He was arrested but escaped and ended up on the moor with a band of other men, most of them his own retainers.'

De Wolfe prodded Edwin a little more, but the old man had nothing further to offer. 'Now that I know the bones of it, I must discover the whole story,' John said ruminatively. 'De Revelle must have been up to his tricks before I got back from Austria.' That return was a sore memory for de Wolfe, for he had been one of the king's bodyguard when the Lionheart had been seized in Vienna and held to ransom in Austria and Germany for eighteen months. John still felt guilty of letting his monarch down, even though in fact he had been away foraging for fresh horses when the mayor of Vienna burst into the tavern and arrested Richard.

Pushing the recollection away, he decided to probe further into this affair of Nicholas de Arundell, though he thought it was preposterous to suggest it had anything at all to do with the death of the man in the forge. Slipping an arm around Nesta's shoulders, he looked meaningfully at the ceiling planks, which were also the floorboards of her little chamber up in the loft.

'Tomorrow, I'll get the full story from our sheriff,' he said, standing up as a signal to Gwyn and Edwin that he had other, more immediate plans in mind. 'Henry de Furnellis is of old Devon stock, he'll know all the scandal about the gentry. This might be another useful stick with which to beat my brother-in-law.'

Chapter Four

In which Crowner John gossips with the sheriff

Soon after first light the next morning, the coroner's trio was back at the school in Smythen Street, where they found Walter Pole already waiting for them outside the yard of the old forge. When Gwyn banged on the weathered boards of the gate that stood at the side of the plot, they were eventually pulled aside by Henry Wotri, the servant they had met when the body was found. As they trooped into the yard, the sounds of chanting could be heard from the main building, which used to be not only the residence of the forge master and his family, but also a shop on the ground floor where he sold his wrought-iron products. Now Magister Anglicus lived on the upper floor along with two other teachers, the lectures being given in the big chamber down below, which had been formed by knocking the old shop and the metal store into one large space.

'What are they doing?' demanded de Wolfe, as they walked across the empty yard. 'Singing their lessons or what?'

Henry gave a lopsided grin. 'No, sir, that's their morning prayers. The master starts the day with a service, them being all clerics of one sort or another.'

Henry led them towards the old forge, where work had ceased on pulling the floor down until such time as the cadaver would be removed. 'Magister James has been in a proper state, having the builders sent away because of this body,' the servant said with ill-concealed delight. 'He's got eight more students arriving next week and nowhere to put them until this place is finished.'

It looked as if de Revelle's venture into education might pay off after all, thought John. More scholars meant more fees, which would be music to his mercenary brother-in-law's soul.

'The deceased is just where you said he was to be left, Crowner,' said Henry. 'I'll not come in with you, if you don't mind. He's not a pretty sight.'

This was hardly encouraging to Walter Pole, who already looked anxious, but at that early hour de Wolfe was in no mood to pander to sensibilities.

'Come on, this will take but a moment. Just one look at him – and especially at his clothing.'

He stamped on ahead into the forge and Gwyn urged the harness maker to follow him. A moment later, Gwyn pulled off the old canvas that had been thrown over the body.

Walter peered at it, nervously at first, then curiosity got the better of his revulsion and he bent to get a closer look. 'Looks more like the cheapest leather I have to deal with, rather than a man,' he observed.

'But do you recognise him?' growled the coroner.

Walter scratched his head and thought for a moment. 'He's about the right height for Matthew and a thin fellow with it, which tallies. But that face – more like a dried monkey, I can't swear to it being him.'

'What about the clothing?' prompted Gwyn.

The leatherworker stared again, then bent down and tugged at the edge of the tunic. 'It's very much like what he used to wear. But so many other folk favour the same sort of garments. I couldn't be sure.'

John ground his teeth in frustration. 'Is there nothing else you might recognise?'

Walter looked abashed at being unable to please this

intimidating man. He rubbed his forehead in a desperate attempt to think of something useful. 'What about his arm?' he ventured.

De Wolfe glared at him. 'Well, what about his damned arm? He's got two of them, hasn't he?'

'He broke one a few years ago, falling off his pony. It never healed properly, there was always a lump under the skin.'

Gwyn seized upon this at once, as he had used a similar ploy once before. 'Which arm was it, left or right?' he demanded, already bending down to the corpse.

Walter Pole thought for a moment, muttering under his breath and looking at his own arms as he twisted them at the wrists to help him remember.

'The left . . . yes, it was the left, as he said it wouldn't stop him having full use of his right when he was pushing his needle through the leather.'

John stooped to look as Gwyn pushed up the left sleeve of the tunic almost to the shoulder. 'Where was the damage, Walter?' he boomed.

'Just below the elbow. He would rub it sometimes, as he said it ached.'

Gwyn lifted up the hand, the brown, wrinkled skin of the arm looking like old parchment against the almost black claws of the fingernails. He felt all along the forearm from wrist to elbow and then gave a loud exclamation.

'Ha! There's a hard lump here. Would this be it?'

Hesitantly, the harness maker stretched out his own hand and tentatively felt the area that Gwyn indicated. He nodded vigorously. 'That's it. This must be poor Matthew. No one else would have a lump like that in that very spot.' He looked sadly at the withered corpse. 'His staggering sickness must have got the better of him in the end.'

John de Wolfe shook his head. 'Not so, Walter. He was murdered!'

* * *

An hour later, the coroner strode across Rougemont's inner ward to the keep and shared a pot of ale with the sheriff. Henry de Furnellis was fond of men's company and, unlike his haughty predecessor, the old soldier was happy to forsake the sheriff's chamber for the noisy, bustling hall outside.

They sat at a table near the firepit and ignoring the attempts of clerks, merchants and others to seek an audience with him, Henry listened to the latest news about the mummified corpse.

'God's teeth, how did a master craftsman like that get himself slain in such a bizarre fashion?' he asked, his grizzled old face displaying his surprise.

'There's some meaning to it, I'm sure,' replied John grimly. 'But what it signifies is beyond me at present. As far as we can make out, the fellow had been an ordinary tradesman with nothing to mark him out as a victim.'

The sheriff nodded over his mug. 'A saddler seems an unlikely target for an assassination. Too old to have ravished the wife of some ill-tempered husband. And if he owed money, this was no way to set about repayment.'

De Wolfe stared for a moment into the fire, watching the flames flicker around the pile of oak logs. 'This body was found on de Revelle's property and he has some fanciful tale about it being dumped there to discredit him.'

Henry groaned and rolled up his eyes. 'Bloody de Revelle! I might have guessed that he would turn up again before long. I thought his experiences last month might have encouraged him to lay low for a while.'

'He claims that this corpse was planted in his school by some outlaw bent on revenge,' said de Wolfe. 'What do you know of this Nicholas de Arundell, the one they call "Nick o' the Moor"? All I've learned about him was from the one-eyed potman at the Bush.'

De Furnellis cradled his chin in a hand as he dug into

his memory. 'Nicholas de Arundell? There was a scandal concerning him about three years back, before I was made sheriff for the first time. The county was in the hands of that bastard John Lackland then, so although theoretically he was sheriff, the prince left all the work to the serjeants and bailiffs of the hundreds.'

This obscure complaint told de Wolfe nothing and he waited for further explanation.

'De Arundell went off to the Crusade as soon as our king called for recruits, and I seem to recall that on the way he stayed to fight for the Lionheart in the Sicilian war. Anyway, when more than two years had gone by without word from him, it was claimed that he was dead and the Count of Mortain, who had been given Devon and Cornwall by the king at his coronation, declared his estates to be escheated.'

'And who put that claim about?' growled de Wolfe.

'The de la Pomeroys of Berry Castle, which stands next to Hempston, said that a monk returning from Palestine had told them this, as he was passing through. Of course, no one could ever produce this monk to confirm it, but as you know only too well, Henry de la Pomeroy was one of Prince bloody John's most ardent supporters in these parts.'

'And then this Nicholas causes a big problem when he turns up very much alive?' suggested the coroner.

'Indeed he did! It seems he arrived with a couple of his men and finds his wife gone back to Cornwall and a strange bailiff running his manor. Unfortunately, in his anger, he went about righting the situation in the wrong way.'

'So what happened to get him outlawed?' asked John.

'This Nicholas is a man of very short temper and he and his retainers, together with some villagers who were loyal to him, tried to throw out the bailiff and Pomeroy's men. There was a fight and in the mêlée, one of the local men got a crack on the head which killed him.

Someone got a warning to Berry Castle and a large force rushed over to arrest Nicholas, but he and his men escaped.'

By now, a few people had gathered behind the sheriff and were listening to his tale with interest. Any tales of conflict and violence were a welcome diversion in these peaceful times in Devon. One of the older men was Gabriel, the sergeant of the garrison's men-at-arms and a close friend of Gwyn. He broke in with his own memories of the affair.

'I don't know the details, but I heard that somehow he and some of his men vanished into the moor, where they've been ever since. He knew it was no use seeking justice from the sheriff, for there wasn't one worth speaking of, as it was the Count of Mortain who nominally held the shrievalty.'

'But why could he not get justice from someone?' demanded John. There were some derisory noises from the men gathered around. It was clear where their sympathies lay, and one man, a clerk to Ralph Morin, the castle constable, put them into words.

'Who could he appeal to, Crowner? He was declared outlaw in the county court a few weeks later, so he ceased to exist as far as the law was concerned. He couldn't bring any legal action for restitution of his estate – he couldn't even show his face anywhere for fear of being beheaded or hanged on sight.'

De Wolfe nodded his understanding at the fearful significance of being declared an outlaw, and the sheriff's next words confirmed de Arundell's plight.

'He was a relatively insignificant knight with no powerful friends, even though he had been on Crusade. Then he made matters worse by starting a vendetta against de Revelle and the Pomeroys, father and son. He and his men hid themselves on Dartmoor and struck at various farms belonging to their adversaries.'

Henry grinned at the memory of de Revelle's anger

at the time. 'They burned a few barns, stole sheep and cattle and poached deer from their lands. They even kidnapped a few of de Revelle's servants and tried to hold them to ransom, but he wouldn't pay so much as a bent penny, so they had to let them free.'

Eventually, the sheriff had to succumb to the pleas of his chief clerk and reluctantly go back to his chamber to give audience to the many people who were waiting impatiently to see him. John strode back to the gatehouse and sat behind his table, watching Thomas carefully scribing away at his manuscripts. The little clerk's tongue protruded from the corner of his mouth as he hunched over his quill pen, concentrating on forming the excellent script that would be put before the royal justices when they next came to hold the Eyre of Assize. One of the main functions of the coroner system was to record all legal events in each county for presentation either to the judges on their infrequent visits or to the Commissioners of Gaol Delivery, lesser officials who came more often to clear the endless backlog of cases, whose alleged perpetrators languished in the prisons. Though juries of men from every hundred had to present their local cases to the courts, anything in which the coroner was involved had to be documented on his rolls for examination by the justices. It was Thomas's pride that ensured that his yards of parchment were the neatest and most legible of all the documents presented.

De Wolfe had been trying to learn to read and write, taught both by a vicar from the cathedral and by Thomas, but his lack of patience made him a poor student and he had hardly progressed beyond being able to read a few simple sentences and sign his name. Now he looked with wonder, rather than envy, at his clerk's dextrous fingers forming the regular lines of Latin script on the creamy parchment before him.

After a few minutes, boredom began to overtake him. He missed Gwyn's boisterous company, as the officer was still down in Smythen Street organising the inquest which John would hold just before noon. At this time of morning, the three of them would usually have a second breakfast, but with Gwyn away, there was no bread and cheese and the large jug of cider on the floor was empty.

De Wolfe drummed his fingers on the table and shivered as a cold blast of air whistled through the slit-shaped windows. The snow had held off, but it was frosty and the wind was rising from the east.

Thomas looked up, his pointed nose bright red with cold, the beginnings of a dewdrop forming at its tip. He sensed that his impatient master wanted some diversion.

'How will you pursue this killing, sir?' he asked.

'Start by discovering more about this saddler,' replied John. 'Search his dwelling for a start, then question those who knew him in life, I suppose.'

'He seems to have been a stalwart guild member,' offered Thomas. 'I heard Walter Pole mention that this Matthew had once been the treasurer of the Cordwainers, which includes all kinds of leatherworkers.'

The coroner had learned over the sixteen months since he had taken office that his clerk was both intelligent and perceptive, so that anything he suggested was usually worth considering.

'The guilds! We must follow that aspect. I'll speak to Hugh de Relaga about it, he has his finger in every scheme the merchants devise in Exeter.'

De Relaga was the garishly dressed portreeve, one of the two leaders of the city council, as well as being John's business associate in their wool-exporting business. When de Wolfe returned home from Palestine, he had invested his booty wisely and had become a sleeping partner in this enterprise with Hugh. They bought fleeces from all over the Southwest and shipped them across to Normandy, Flanders and even as far as Cologne. Recently, they had invested in three ships so that henceforth, instead of the partners paying freight, their own crews would sail the Channel when the new season began in the Spring and come back with finished cloth as well as wine and fruit, to make a steady profit on the transaction.

'The present warden of that guild might be worth questioning, Crowner,' suggested Thomas. 'I took the liberty this morning of finding out who it was. He's Archibald Wasteper, a master cordwainer. He sells his footwear from a shop in North Gate Street.'

John nodded. 'I know of the place, my wife has bought shoes there – and damned expensive they were,' he added, with feeling.

The clerk sensed that the coroner still wanted some distraction until Gwyn returned, so he kept the dialogue going.

'Sir, do you think that there is anything in this claim of Sir Richard, that this outlaw has some part in the death?'

John scratched his head; a flea was irritating him. 'I don't rule out anything, but it's a pretty unlikely story.'

Thomas nodded his agreement. 'And there is the problem of a Dartmoor outlaw getting into the city.'

Here de Wolfe declined to agree with his clerk. 'Not as difficult as you might think, Thomas. With the many hundreds of folk in and out of the gates each day, it's impossible to check everyone, even if those idle porters on the gates made an effort to do so – which they don't.' He gave a lop-sided grin. 'Outlaws not uncommonly squirm their way back into society. I've heard of several who rose to become respected pillars of society again, under new names and in a different city.'

The sounds of heavy feet on the stairway heralded Gwyn's return and a moment later his large figure pushed its way through the doorway curtain. He was clutching a gallon jar of cider and three hot mutton pasties, bought from a stall outside the castle gate.

As they ate and drank, Gwyn reported that the inquest was set up and a jury had been impounded from all the neighbours in Smythen Street, as well as the occupants of the school.

'Properly put out, was that magister fellow,' he chortled. 'Said it would disturb his lecture on Homer, whatever the hell that is!'

Thomas pursed his lips in academic disapproval. 'You ignorant Cornish savage. Homer was probably the most famous writer in history.'

Gwyn leered at the little priest. 'Well, he wasn't too well-known down in Polruan, I can tell you!'

John raised a hand imperiously. 'That's enough, you two. After dinner, we'll talk to some people about this Morcok fellow. Surely someone should know what he did to get himself killed.'

The inquest was a low-key event, with few people present apart from the jury whose members had been reluctantly dragged in from the surrounding area. Though in the countryside, all males over twelve from the four nearest villages were supposed to attend an inquest in case anyone had any information about the death, this was impossible in the more populous towns and cities. Here, it was only practicable to round up a score or so of those from the immediate neighbourhood to act as jurors. Their duty was not only to consider a verdict, but also to act as witnesses, as local people were most likely to have knowledge of what went on in their street.

Gwyn had been around all the nearby houses and workshops to order their attendance, on pain of fines if they failed to turn up, and now a couple of dozen men and older boys had shuffled into the yard of the smithy. They stood in a ragged half-circle outside the open doors of the outbuilding, looking sheepish and uncertain of their role in this legal ritual. The coroner's system was little more than a year old and few people understood it – though anything connected with the law was always to be avoided wherever possible, as fines and even imprisonment were an inevitable result of failing to abide by the tortuous rules.

At the end of the line of men stood Magister James Anglicus and his pompous acolyte Henry Wotri. Behind them lurked a dozen students, ranging from fresh-faced boys of fifteen to some serious young men of twenty, all dressed in black clerical habits similar to that of Thomas de Peyne, who was seated on a box just inside the doors. He had an empty cask in front of him to support his parchments and ink bottle, which he always carried in a leather pouch slung over his shoulder.

A few curious spectators clustered inside the gate, mostly old men with nothing else to occupy their time, plus a sprinkling of goodwives and some cheeky urchins. John spotted old Edwin from the Bush, who obviously could not resist nosing into anything that took place within a few hundred paces of the tavern.

Gwyn bellowed out the official summoning of the inquest, exhorting 'all who have anything to do before the king's coroner for the county of Devon' to 'come forth and give their attendance'. Then he walked to stand behind John, who glowered around at the jurors, looking like a big crow in his wolfskin cloak of mottled grey over a long black tunic. The cold breeze swirled his swept-back hair over his collar as he harshly instructed the men as to their functions.

'This is an inquest held to investigate a breach of the peace of our sovereign lord, King Richard,' he began. 'You must consider who, where, when and by what means the man who lies here came to his death.'

He glared around the ring of jurors, as if defying them to contradict him. 'First, let me hear from the First Finder, who discovered the corpse.'

Reluctantly, the builder stepped forward and stood before John de Wolfe. In response to some impatient prompting, he said that he was Roger Short, a carpenter, who was adapting the building for use as an additional lecture room. Describing how he had unearthed the cadaver from the angle between the upper floor and the rafters, he went on to emphasise that he had rushed to report it to the magister. Roger wanted to avoid any amercement for delay and promptly passed the buck to James Anglicus.

After determining that the carpenter had no idea who the body was nor how it had got there, de Wolfe asked him a last question. 'How long would you say it had been up in that loft?'

The scruffy little builder hitched up his sagging breeches and shrugged. 'Hard to tell, sir. There was a thick layer of dust all over the rubbish that covered him, so that hadn't been moved in a long time. Months, I'd say.'

Roger had nothing else to contribute and thankfully stepped back, allowing Walter Pole to take his place. De Wolfe got him to repeat the reasons why he thought the corpse was that of Matthew Morcok.

'This deformity of the arm bone will be shown to you all in a moment,' the coroner promised the jury. 'Meanwhile, I will presume that you agree that the body is that of the cordwainer.'

Then he moved on to the contentious matter of Presentment of Englishry, which he had to explain to them, well aware that they resented the financial implications.

'After King William first took possession of this country, many Saxons took it upon themselves to slay what they considered to be Norman invaders,' he began, not shirking his words even though there were men of obvious Saxon blood in his audience.

'To discourage this, a heavy murdrum fine is levied on any community amongst whom a man is found murdered, unless his family can prove he is English –

or Welsh or Scottish.' Again he scowled around the ring of jurors, well aware that over a century after the Battle of Hastings, intermarriage had blurred the distinction between Saxon and Norman. The murdrum fine was now just a cynical means of extracting more taxes from the population, but to the loyal John, the king's law was absolute and he had no option but to carry it out.

'Is there any man here related to Matthew Morcok who can present him as English?'

There was a silence, as de Wolfe had known there would be, as the only kin was a daughter many miles away – and women were not allowed to make presentment, which was normally carried out by two male relatives.

'Then this will be recorded by my clerk in his rolls and it will be up to the justices, when they arrive, to decide upon the amount of the fine.'

There were no other witnesses to call, so Gwyn rounded up the jurors and drove them nearer the doors of the forge. Going inside, he dragged out an old door on which lay the pathetic remains of Matthew Morcok, covered with a dirty piece of canvas from the loft.

'You will all look upon the cadaver before you advise me of your verdict,' said the coroner. 'But first, I will show you this.'

He held up the rusty nail and passed it to Walter Pole, who was the spokesman for the jury. They all passed it from hand to hand and examined it with obvious curiosity.

'This was found driven into the bones of his neck. You will see the hole it made when you view the remains.'

They filed past as Gwyn lifted off the canvas and their reactions varied from the stolid to the revolted. The sight of the twisted, leathery mummy caused some to gasp, but most of the older men, especially those used to the carnage of battle and the cruelties of farming and slaughtering, merely nodded or grunted. When the viewing of the body was complete, de Wolfe again faced the assembled citizens.

'It is clear that this man, who surely must be Matthew Morcok, a master saddler of Priest Street, was foully done to death by a spike being hammered into his spine. When this happened, we cannot tell, but I will assume that it was during the past year, the sixth in the reign of our sovereign lord King Richard.'

He paused and his piercing gaze swept along the row of faces before him.

'Who killed Matthew, we do not know, but it is my duty and that of the sheriff to discover that. Until then, the only verdict of this inquest can surely be that he was murdered by some unknown person or persons.'

The men shuffled their icy feet on the frozen mud of the yard and looked at each other uncertainly.

'To allow this poor fellow a decent burial at last, I must complete these proceedings – though the inquest can be resumed at any time when further information comes to light. So now confer amongst yourselves and let me know your decision.'

This was said with a final glare that betokened dire consequences for anyone who challenged his decision – and within a moment, Walter Pole had muttered to the men next to him and come back with total agreement.

'We say the man is Matthew Morcok, sir – and he was foully killed against the king's peace.'

That was good enough for de Wolfe, and with a nod at Thomas to get everything down on his parchment, he waved away the crowd, who began drifting towards the street. He beckoned to Walter Pole, the harness maker.

'What about burying this poor fellow?' he asked. 'Are you going to send for his daughter?'

'Our guild will see that everything is done right, Crowner. But I don't think we can wait for the daughter, even if we knew exactly where she lived. It would take two or three weeks to get a message to Oxford, and then for her to get back here.'

John knew that part of the function of the various guilds was to ensure that the widows and families of dead members were looked after and this extended to seeing that deceased guildsmen had a decent funeral if there was no one else to provide for them. But his own duty to the corpse was now fulfilled, apart from finding the murderer, so with a yearning look across the road towards the Bush, he made his way back home for dinner.

John found Matilda to be in a less frosty mood than he had expected and she even listened to his account of the inquest with less than her usual indifference. He always studiously avoided any topics that could trigger her scorn and anger, which severely limited the range of acceptable subjects for conversation. Naturally mention of the Bush alehouse was forbidden, and even talk about the shipping venture with Hugh de Relaga was banned, for the simple reason that their three vessels were owned in partnership with Hilda of Dawlish, one of his former lovers before Nesta came on the scene.

But today, his wife seemed moderately civil, if not actually affable. Sensitive to her moods after years of suffering, John wondered what was making her so mellow. It was only after finishing their meal that he found out. When Mary's boiled bacon and a pease pudding had been consumed, followed by dried apricots stewed in honeyed cider, Matilda took her cup of small ale to the fireside and divulged not one, but two reasons for her relatively benign mood.

'We are invited to a feast, John,' she announced. 'A messenger from the Guildhall came this morning, requesting our attendance there tomorrow evening. The Guild of Mercers are holding a banquet to celebrate something or other. It will be a chance for me to wear my new blue velvet, the one I bought at the October Fair.' She preened herself at the thought of outshining some of the merchants' wives who were her cronies from the congregation of St Olave's Church in Fore Street.

Her husband grunted as he settled down on the opposite side of the hearth. Not much given to social occasions, he was indifferent to such gatherings, but then the thought of a free meal and fine wine made him accept the prospect with moderately good grace. It also occurred to him that it gave him an opportunity to ask amongst the many guildsmen present, to see if they could throw any light on the death of one of their former treasurers.

Matilda's second reason for being in a good mood was even less exciting, as she was enthusing about a new friend she had acquired amongst the small congregation at St Olave's, a church obscurely named after the first Christian king of Norway. Along with the nearby cathedral, this was her favourite place of worship, where as the wife of a knight she could flaunt her rank amongst the wives of merchants and craftsmen, even though many of them were far richer than her husband.

'There is a new lady recently arrived in Exeter,' she announced. 'Joan de Whiteford, the young widow of a manor lord from Somerset, though I suspect she has fallen on hard times since his death, as she is living off her relatives, poor thing. Still it is pleasant to have someone of equal status to converse with, a person of breeding instead of the clodhopping goodwives that usually attend the services.'

John was sleepily staring into the fire, about as interested in his wife's social life as he was in the number of stars in the sky, but she continued to drone on about Lady Joan.

'She is lodging with her cousin Gillian le Bret, who I've known as a devout churchgoer for some years. I had no idea that Gillian had noble relatives, for her late husband was only a merchant – though a very rich one,' she added, as if his affluence was partly her doing.

When John responded with a snore, Matilda gave a *tut* of irritation and flounced out to find her maid to settle her in the solar for her afternoon nap.

Chapter Five

In which a noble outlaw comes to town

As the first pale glimmer of dawn appeared in the eastern sky next morning, people began converging on the city gates like iron filings to a lodestone. There were four main entrances to the city, a legacy of the symmetrical Roman plan that still governed the layout of Exeter. Recently a fifth opening, the Water Gate, had been knocked through the south-western corner of the old walls to give direct access to the quayside, necessary now that trade was burgeoning in the city.

Although Exeter was too far upriver to be prey to the sea raiders and pirates that sometimes ravished the towns on the coast, the city gates were still closed from dusk to dawn, and at the West Gate that morning, a hundred or so people waited patiently to be admitted. As well as farmers driving beasts to be slaughtered in the Shambles, there were many traders and peasants with goods to sell, as Thursday was a market day.

Though in winter the range of foodstuffs was limited, ox-carts hauled cabbages and root vegetables, and men pushed wheelbarrows piled with other produce, including live chickens trussed by their legs. Fishermen who had boated up on the flood tide from Topsham had wicker creels of fresh fish, and old women stumbled up with baskets of eggs or a goose or duck tucked under their arms.

Nearby, the new stone bridge across the River Exe was still far from complete, as the builder had once again run out of money, so the figure merging amongst the latecomers had to pass over the rickety footbridge that was the only dry route. In times past, Sir Nicholas de Arundell would have ridden his horse across the ford next to the bridge, but today he trudged with the peasantry, wearing a floppy, wide-brimmed hat, a tall staff in his hand. The grey woollen cloak that enveloped him was thin and stained, and from his shoulder hung a shapeless hessian bag. In the cold wind and the dim morning light, no one gave him a second glance; all were too intent on both their own business and their shivering bodies to concern themselves with another pilgrim, probably on his way to the shrines in the cathedral – or even making for distant Canterbury. With a few days' growth of stubble on his cheeks and a cloth wound round his chin as a scarf, Nicholas was next to unrecognisable, even if there had been anyone in Exeter who might have known this man from a small manor way out in the countryside.

He crossed with the others on to the marshy ground of Exe Island, and followed the well-beaten track from the bridge to the gate. Here he hunched himself into his cloak and stamped his feet with the other freezing travellers until dawn was unmistakably streaking the sky and the porters took pity on the perishing folk huddled outside. There was a rumble as the bars were slid from their sockets; then, to squeals from the rusty hinges, the huge pair of oaken doors slowly swung open.

As the press of humanity surged through ahead of the livestock and the carts, the two gate guards made no attempt to check anyone's identity. This was a routine that had been going on for centuries and, except in times of war or rebellion, security was lax. Those who would have to pay market dues for trading would be seized upon by the tally clerks as soon as they set up stalls or crouched at the roadside to sell their eggs or onions, but that was no concern of the gate men. The man in the pilgrim's hat had banked on this and walked boldly into Exeter alongside a man leading a goat on a length of cord.

Though Nicholas was not very familiar with Exeter, he walked steadily up Fore Street, which climbed from the river up to Carfoix, the junction where the roads from the four original gates met in the centre of the city. This was bustling with activity, as booths and stalls were being set up along the sides of the streets, making the narrow lanes even more congested as early-morning shoppers came out to get the freshest produce. He carried on up High Street past the new Guildhall, looking neither to right or to left in his effort to remain inconspicuous. However, he had to dodge many passers-by, especially those porters who jogged along with great bales of wool hanging from a pole across their shoulders, and milkmaids with a pair of wooden buckets swinging from their shoulders. When he got within sight of the East Gate at the other end of the town, he searched his memory for his only previous visit with his wife to her cousin, which was now fully five years ago. A landmark he remembered was the New Inn, Exeter's largest hostelry, where the judges and commissioners stayed when they came to hold court. Turning right just past it, he thought he recognised a quiet street where the burgage plots were large and the houses amongst the best in the city.

'Is this Raden Lane?' he asked a ragged urchin who was standing on the corner with a smaller child on his hip, begging from passers-by. The boy, barefoot and blue with cold, nodded jerkily, his teeth chattering. He gave a beatific smile as Nicholas slipped him a quarter-penny, which had come from a fat purse taken from a waylaid horse dealer a week before.

Raden Lane was almost empty of people and he felt

more exposed as he walked along, looking for the house where his wife was staying. Some dwellings were right on the lane, their doors opening straight off the street. Others were further back on their plots, with a fence and gate at the front. Most were built of wood or were half-timbered with cob plastered between the frames, but a few of the newer houses were made of stone. Some were tall and narrow, others low and wide, half of them with two storeys. The city wall was visible at the end of the lane and he knew that the cousin, now a widow of comfortable means, lived about halfway along on the right. He spotted the house, distinguished by its arched gate leading into a garden plot, and not wanting to draw attention to himself by hesitating, he strode up to the gate and pushed at the stout boards. It was locked and there was no handle. Cursing under his breath short-temperedly, he rapped on it with the end of his staff until he heard slow footsteps on the other side. The gate creaked open and a man in late middle age peered out, an iron-tipped wooden spade in his hand – whether intended as a weapon or an implement was not clear. He was unusually tall and thin, with a large purple birthmark of coarse, thickened skin disfiguring the whole of one side of his face. The apparition gaped toothlessly at the visitor, but said nothing.

'Is this the dwelling of Mistress le Bret?' demanded Nicholas. He had a deep voice, and a brusque manner even when he was in a benign mood, which was not often these days.

The servant nodded, but still seemed suspicious of early-morning callers. 'Who wants her?' he croaked.

'I am Philip de Whiteford, returning from Canterbury,' he lied. 'I am husband to Mistress Joan, who is staying here.'

These were aliases he and his wife had decided on long before; she had kept to her real Christian name as she feared she could never avoid answering to it.

The servant's strange features relaxed and he pulled the door open. 'Welcome, Sir Nicholas! Your good lady will be glad to see you.'

Obviously, the true state of affairs was no secret within the house, and Nicholas fervently hoped that the servants kept their mouths firmly shut when they left it. He was led through a well-kept garden to an old timber-framed building with a steeply pitched roof of stone tiles. Inside, a hall occupied most of the ground floor, with a solar and a bedroom built on at the side. It was a substantial dwelling, as Joan's cousin, Gillian le Bret, was the widow of a wealthy tinmaster and on his death, five years earlier, he had left her comfortably off, for they had no children to share the inheritance.

As Nicholas entered, a small, fair woman rushed out of an inner door and threw herself at him, sobbing and laughing in turns. As they hugged each other and kissed, an older, handsome woman appeared from the solar.

Gillian le Bret watched indulgently as the pair made an emotional reunion, then went across to the old servant Maurice, who had stood uncertainly in the doorway, and whispered something to him, drawing a warning finger across her lips. He wandered off in the direction of the kitchen shed in the back yard, with orders for the cook-maid to prepare food and drink for the visitor.

Gradually, the de Arundells settled down, and Nicholas greeted Gillian with a kiss and profound thanks for sheltering Joan for the past month since she had come up from her exile in Cornwall. The widow was considerably older than her cousin, with greying hair peeping from under the white linen wimple that framed her pleasant face. When the knight and his lady had prised themselves apart again from a second embrace, Gillian managed to set them down on a long settle facing the burning logs in the firepit.

'Are you sure you went unrecognised in the city?' asked

Joan. Though her pretty face was now flushed with tears of joy, she lived with the constant worry that her husband would be arrested, which inevitably would mean he would be hanged or beheaded. At twenty-six, she was seven years his junior, and sometimes she looked even younger. Pretty rather than beautiful, she had a determined set to her face, partly born of the troubles they had suffered these past few years.

Nicholas slid a brawny arm around her slender shoulders, which were becomingly draped in a green pelisse over a pale yellow kirtle.

'Don't fret, my love. No one was interested in a scruffy pilgrim like me. I'll have to leave in a day or two, but until then, I'll not show my face outside the gate. As long as everyone in this household keeps a tight hold on their tongue, there'll be no problem.'

A few minutes later, their chatter was interrupted by the arrival of cold meats, bread, cheese and ale. After eating, de Arundell spent the rest of the morning until dinnertime talking to Joan about his existence on Dartmoor. He told of life in the abandoned village and tales of his men, many of whom had been retainers in Hempston and were well remembered by his wife. After a hearty dinner at noon, Cousin Gillian diplomatically went off to her solar to give the pair some privacy.

'I just had to see you, Joan, apart from talking about a plan of campaign,' he began, hugging her on the settle in front of the glowing logs. 'D'you realise that I've only been with you for a few days since I went off to Outremer?'

When he returned so unexpectedly from the Holy Land, his wife had already returned to Cornwall, dispossessed by Pomeroy and de Revelle and convinced that Nicholas was long dead. After the news of his resurrection percolated down to her relative's manor in Cornwall, she had had great difficulty in getting a message to him on Dartmoor, and it was due to Gillian le Bret and her servant Maurice that contact had been made again. Since then, they had only managed two fleeting meetings such as this, both in Totnes, where the risk of his being recognised was becoming too great for him to venture there again.

'So what is to be done, my love?' asked Joan, a very practical woman despite her winsome prettiness. 'If you were not so shamefully outlawed, you could bring an action in the courts and certainly should win.'

They had been over this ground many times before, and Nicholas shook his head impatiently. 'Impossible. I have no legal rights and if I dared show myself publicly to try to retrieve them, I would be dead within the day. There are too many supporters of the Count of Mortain around to risk it – to say nothing of that bastard de Revelle!'

Once again, they talked the problem through, up hill and down dale, without coming to any conclusion.

'Some new approach is the only hope,' he said with anger, for this emotion was never far below the surface with de Arundell. 'I have even thought of seeking out the king in Normandy to ask for justice.'

Joan looked frightened at this. 'The risks of trying to escape the country and finding King Richard are too great, Nicholas. You are as much an outlaw in Normandy as you are over here.'

'It may be the only path open to us, Joan,' he muttered.

'But would you ever get audience with him?' she persisted. 'You are just a poor knight, with even the small manor of Hempston snatched from you now. You need a strong champion to plead your case – or even to get it noticed by those in high places.'

Nicholas moodily had to agree with her. 'What champion could I find?' he said bitterly. 'Though I was in Sicily fighting for our king as well as in the Holy Land, I never distinguished myself in any way. I was just another country knight amongst thousands. I never even got within shouting distance of the Lionheart, I've only ever seen him from afar.'

Joan gripped his arm and hugged him to her, desolate at seeing him so despondent. 'There must be some good men somewhere,' she whispered. 'Surely all those in positions of authority are not as corrupt as de Revelle and John Lackland?'

Nicholas shrugged listlessly. 'Maybe there are – but I don't know any, Joan.'

She tried to lift him from his gloom. 'I have heard that Hubert Walter, the Chief Justiciar, is a fair-minded man. He virtually rules England now that the king has gone permanently to France.'

Her husband sighed. 'That may well be, dearest woman. But he might as well be on the moon for all the chance I have of putting my case before him.'

The thought of Hubert Walter, who was also Archbishop of Canterbury as well as being England's chief law officer, triggered a chain of thought in Joan's active mind, which was desperate to help her husband in his dangerous predicament.

'I have heard that the Justiciar was responsible for appointing the coroner in Devon and that they are good friends since their time in Palestine.'

Nicholas looked at her blankly. 'What has that to do with us?'

'Talking with Cousin Gillian these past few weeks, she has told me many things, for she is knowledgeable about all that goes on in Exeter. She says that the coroner, Sir John de Wolfe, is a most upright and honourable man. It so happens that I have become acquainted with his wife Matilda, as she kindly befriended me when I began attending Mass at the cathedral.'

Nicholas was suddenly anxious. 'The coroner's wife! For the Virgin's sake, be careful, Joan! You did not let slip who you really are, I trust?'

His wife shook her head emphatically. 'In Exeter, I

am Lady Whiteford, the widow of a minor knight from the far end of Somerset, staying with my dear cousin Gillian here.'

Her husband still failed to see the point of her sudden diversion. 'He might be as upright as the Archangel Gabriel, but what help is that?'

Joan sat up on the bench, suddenly enthusiastic about her idea. 'Two things, Nicholas. He was a Crusader like you – and a very distinguished one, for he formed part of the king's bodyguard on his journey home. But more important, he hates Richard de Revelle and it was he who had him ejected as sheriff a few months back.'

De Arundell scratched at the itching stubble on his face. He could follow the way his wife's mind was working, but failed to see how it could accomplish anything helpful. 'What can I do about it, Joan? For an outlaw to approach a senior law officer would be as good as laying my neck down on the block. Apart from the sheriff, he is about the most dangerous person in England I could fear to meet!'

Although the celebration of Christ's birth was a week away, the Guild of Mercers decided to include some premature Yuletide festivities in their regular quarterly feast. The Guildhall was decked out with holly and bay branches and the traditional mistletoe. The food provided was even more lavish than usual, as was the music and entertainment. The mercers were one of the leading guilds, for although they dealt in most types of cloth, their speciality was the more luxurious fabrics, such as silk and velvet. Though not the most numerous of the Exeter merchants, they were amongst the most prosperous, and they certainly considered themselves the elite of the trading classes. The warden of the guild in Devon was Benedict de Buttelscumbe who, though only the son of a weaver, thought himself the primate of the Exeter burgesses and was eternally resentful of the fact that his fellow members of the city council had not elected him as one of the two portreeves.

John and Matilda arrived at the Guildhall at dusk, as feasts traditionally began early, though the drinking afterwards might last until midnight. John wore his best tunic of sombre grey, with a heavy surcoat of black serge against the cold night air. In stark contrast, Matilda wore her voluminous new mantle of blue velvet over a kirtle of red satin, the knotted tippets of her bell-shaped sleeves reaching almost to the floor. As became all married women appearing in public, her head was swathed in a linen wimple, secured around the forehead by a narrow band that matched her gown.

She clutched John's arm possessively as they entered the large door from the High Street and was gratified to have the guild treasurer meet them inside and conduct them to their places on the top table, enabling her to gesture condescendingly to several of her friends who were seated lower down the hall.

The large chamber, which had recently been rebuilt in stone, had two chimneyed hearths on each side, but there was still a chill in the air which would persist until the sweat and body heat of over a hundred guests warmed the atmosphere. The table for the important personages was set across the full width of the top of the hall, with two more stretching at right angles down the length of the room, leaving a wide space between for the entertainers. Three musicians were already hard at work, trying to make themselves heard above the buzz of talking, laughing and shouting that was already rising in volume. Merry music on sackbut, fiddle and drum helped create a festive atmosphere, but fell a long way behind the effects of the large quantities of ale, cider and wine that were being liberally dispensed.

Sir John de Wolfe and his lady were led down the side of the hall to their seats near one end of the top table. Matilda had insisted on arriving late so that her entrance could be seen by those already there, and all the other places on the warden's table were filled. Apart from Benedict de Buttelscumbe himself, who occupied a large carved chair in the centre, everyone sat on benches. They obligingly stood and moved a bench back so that Matilda, beaming at the attention she was receiving, could more decorously slide her skirts around the end. When they were settled, John found himself between his friend and partner Hugh de Relaga and a man he recognised as a former warden of the Bakers' Guild.

Matilda was on the other side of de Relaga, with the Mercers' treasurer next to her, so John knew that she would be happy in their company. Hugh was one of his few friends that she tolerated, as he was rich, overdressed, jolly and unfailing flattered her, albeit with tongue in cheek. Matilda also found it most congenial to be seated next to a senior official of the most prominent guild in the city.

Serving men arrived with wine and ale, and soon the feasting began. Thick wheaten bread trenchers were loaded with many kinds of meat, whole fowls arrived on platters, and in front of the warden, a roast swan appeared alongside a suckling pig, which was carved for them by one of the cooks. There was goose and woodcock, as well as venison with frumenty, a type of pudding made from wheat boiled in sugared milk, then flavoured with cloves, cinnamon and nutmeg.

The eating went on for almost two hours, with a wide range of delicacies presented that were rarely seen by the lesser mortals of Devon, many of whom had only umble pie as their Yuletide luxury.

As the wine flowed the noise increased, but John was able to engage both his fellow diners in useful conversation. Hugh de Relaga brought him up to date on the latest activities – and profits – of their wool trading. John tried to limit this particular topic to times when Matilda was engrossed in conversation with the treasurer, as any mention of their new maritime venture was apt to revive her jealous disapproval of Hilda's role in the partnership.

Above the hubbub in the hall, his conversation with the guildsman from the bakers and pastrycooks was of some use. He raised the matter of the death of Matthew Morcok and asked the former warden, a man of some sixty years, if he had any opinions about the murder.

'I knew Matthew quite well,' the man replied, shaking his head sadly. 'He was a queer old fellow, though with an illness like that, who could blame him?'

'Can you think of any reason why he should have met such a violent end?' asked John.

The guildsman shrugged and reached for his wine cup. 'We have all puzzled over this for the last few days,' he said. 'Matthew was such an inoffensive old man there seems no reason at all why he should have been slain.'

'When he was active in his own guild, did anything happen that might have made him enemies?' queried John.

Again the older man shook his head. 'He did nothing out of the ordinary, he went about his business making saddles and kept to himself. He took part in the business of his guild and there was never a breath of scandal, even though he was treasurer, which can sometimes put temptation in men's way.' He took a deep draught of his wine and wiped his mouth with the back of his hand. 'The only other activity he seemed to be involved in was being one of the examiners when journeymen presented their master-pieces. Unless he had some secret that we all knew nothing about, it remains a mystery. I can't see old Matthew being attacked by a jealous husband for making him a cuckold.'

John could get no more from the man that was of any use, and when the eating had finally come to an end he wandered down into the hall with a cup of wine, leaving Matilda deep in conversation with Hugh de

Relaga and the Mercers' guild master. There were a number of men he knew, and with his usual gruff manner softened by the substantial amount he had had to drink, he chatted amiably with acquaintances, who included several more members of various guilds, from butchers to wood-turners and from sawyers to fish-mongers.

With all of them he raised the matter of Morcok's death, but everywhere he was answered with the same incomprehension that such a mild old fellow should meet such a violent end. Several were outright in their disbelief of the manner of his death, until de Wolfe assured them that he had indeed been killed in a particularly bizarre manner. They all gave him a picture of a rather reserved, solitary man, bereft of wife and daughter, who had worked faithfully for his guild for many years until his illness had overtaken him.

Frustrated with facing such a blank wall, John wandered back to his wife and sat for a time talking with his partner in the wool business. As those who had drunk too much became raucous and argumentative, with several scuffles breaking out on the floor below, Matilda decided it was time for decent ladies to absent themselves. Demanding that John drape her best cloak over her shoulders, she bade goodnight to her neighbours on the top table and sailed out, determined to show off her finery one last time before her other lady friends also decided that it was time to leave. Sated with food and wine, John made no protest and escorted her out into the night, past the beggars waiting at the door for the used trenchers and other scraps, then made for Martin's Lane and a welcome bed.

chapter six

In which Crowner John views another bizarre death

The next few days up to the Sabbath passed uneventfully, with no more deaths reported to the coroner. The cold weather intensified and even the foul sludge in the central gutters of the streets froze solid, though the snow held off despite the leaden skies.

De Wolfe had some routine matters to deal with, such as taking a confession from an approver in the foetid cells that served as a prison under the castle keep. The thief had been caught red-handed when a gang robbed a house near the East Gate, mainly because he had broken his ankle when he jumped from a window, his confederates having escaped. Now he was trying to save his neck by incriminating them as well, and the coroner's clerk had to take down his pleas to present to the justices when they eventually arrived. Matilda was still in a moderately amiable mood, anticipating the social and religious celebrations that would accompany the feast of Christ's Mass. This would begin in a few days' time and continue until Twelfth Night at Epiphany.

John woke early on Monday to another bitterly cold morning. After breaking his fast on honeyed gruel, bread and boiled eggs in Mary's cook-shed, he made his way up to Rougemont on foot, treading carefully where runnels of ice coated the steep lane up to the castle gatehouse. His stark room at the top of the spiral stairs was too cold to endure and he found Thomas and Gwyn down in the guardroom, where Sergeant Gabriel and a man-at-arms had a log fire going inside a ring of stones in the centre of the bleak stone chamber.

'Don't get yourself too comfortable, Crowner,' warned Gwyn, brushing the crumbs of a large fish pasty from his moustache. 'We've had warning of a new corpse discovered out on the high road towards Ashburton.'

'Who is it, do we know?' John asked as he accepted a pint pot of ale from Gabriel, who had just warmed it up by mulling it with a hot poker taken from the fire.

Gwyn shook his tousled head. 'Some carter reported it late last night. The local bailiff told him to take the news to the city, as he was going that way from Totnes.'

De Wolfe groaned at the casual way that people ignored the king's regulations. 'God's guts, Gwyn, does no one ever learn? It's been well over a year since the law was laid down about dead men, yet few take the slightest bloody notice!'

An hour later, the three members of the coroner's team were riding out of the West Gate, Thomas bemoaning the fact that he had to get on his pony so early in the day. Though after months of taunting by Gwyn, he had at last abandoned riding sidesaddle like a woman, he was still a reluctant horseman and jogged miserably along in the wake of the two bigger men, who were perched comfortably on their larger mounts.

The carter, who could not be found that morning, had left vague instructions as to the location of the body, which allegedly would be guarded by some local villagers – though de Wolfe doubted that they would have stayed overnight, in the hard frost, just to keep a corpse company. They splashed through the ford across the

Exe, trying to ignore the icy water which was thrown up on to their legs, and took the high road which eventually led to Plymouth. After well over an hour's riding, delayed by the poor performance of their clerk, they reached a point about seven miles from the city, where they were approached by a rider wearing a heavy green cloak. As he cantered towards them on a brown mare, Gwyn automatically felt for the hilt of his sword, though a lone horseman was hardly a threat.

'Are you the crowner, sir?' asked the man diffidently as he came up to them. He was a lean, tanned individual, wearing a woollen hat under the hood of his cloak. John did not need to see the insignia of a hunting horn embroidered on his tunic to guess correctly that he was one of the forest officers, the Royal Forest beginning several miles nearer Exeter.

'I am Robert Lacey, sir,' he announced. 'The body lies about three miles further on from here.' He turned his horse and as he rode alongside them as they continued westward, de Wolfe questioned him about the corpse.

'There is little I can tell you, sir,' said Lacey. 'I knew nothing of it until late last night when a cottar came to my dwelling. I went to view it this morning, but though they had told a carter to notify you, I thought I had better ride towards the city in case he had not found you.'

'What manner of death is this?' demanded De Wolfe.

The forester shook his head as if bemused. 'I've seen nothing like it before, sir,' he said as they jogged along. 'It's strange indeed, as you will see.'

And so it proved, as John was to discover when they arrived at the scene. Rounding a bend in the hard, rutted track, they saw several men huddled under a tree at the side of the road, clutching ragged cloaks and sacks about themselves in an effort to keep warm. That section of the road went through dense forest, with bare trees lining the road for a half-mile in each direction. Dismounting, they approached the group who appeared to be villeins, together with one man obviously of somewhat higher status, who introduced himself as the reeve of Chudleigh, the nearest village half a mile away. They were led through the dead bracken and brown, leafless bushes to the edge of the trees and there saw an extraordinary sight.

'He was just like this when Walter here found him,' muttered the reeve, a cadaveric man who looked almost as bad as the corpse.

Slumped against the bole of a young beech tree was the body of a middle-aged man, his knees resting on the frozen ground. Though his head was drooped so that his chin rested on his chest, his body was prevented from falling forwards by a chain passing around both his neck and the narrow trunk of the tree. He was fully dressed in a tunic of good brown serge, and on the ground nearby was a cloak of similar colour. All John could see of his head was sparse, sandy hair, for his face was buried in the folds of his tunic.

'God's guts, what's been going on here?' boomed Gwyn, standing with his hands on his hips, looking at the bizarre scene. Thomas, peering fearfully around the Cornishman, crossed himself vigorously and began muttering under his breath in Latin. De Wolfe said nothing and, without touching the body, walked around the tree and looked at the chain which was supporting the body. He saw that it was of rusty iron with links each about two inches in length, typical of those used on ploughs or cart harnesses. The two end links had been joined together by a wooden spike jammed through them, and another, thicker piece of branch had been forced between the chain and the tree trunk, tightening it closely against the corpse's neck.

Coming back to the front of the body, de Wolfe bent

and grasped the hair, pulling up the head against the rigor so that he could see the face. Several of the villagers gasped when they saw the features, and Thomas fell to crossing himself again, for the tongue was protruding and the face was mottled with red and purple patches.

'When was he found?' demanded the coroner, glaring at the group of men peering at the corpse.

'Just before dusk last evening, sir,' gabbled one of the men. 'I was searching for a goat that had strayed and came across him as I walked down the track.'

Gwyn bent down and lifted one of the arms, nodding knowingly. 'Stiff as a plank!' he declared.

As it was obvious that death had occurred many hours earlier, de Wolfe did not bother to pursue the matter. What concerned him more was the method of death, and he prised up the eyelids to confirm that the whites were spattered with tiny blood spots.

'Untie that damned chain, Gwyn,' he commanded. His officer pulled out the pieces of wood and the chain fell free, the dead body slumping forwards as its restraint was removed. The Cornishman lifted it with surprising gentleness and laid it flat on the ground, though death stiffness kept the knees bent upwards.

'No doubt he was throttled by that thing,' Gwyn grunted, holding up the chain by one end and displaying its length, which was considerably more than a yard.

De Wolfe was crouching again, examining the neck of the corpse. A pattern of blue bruises lay across the front of the neck, each one corresponding to the links of the chain. Below this the skin was pale, but above it the blueness was marked, and was peppered with small bleeding points in the skin. 'This chain was tightened while he was still alive, the poor bastard!' he snapped.

Standing up again, he glared at the handful of men who were staring bemused at the body. 'Anyone here know who he might be? And how he got to this spot?'

There was a shuffling and a murmuring, then the reeve spoke up. 'Not anyone from Chudleigh, sir, that's for certain. And by his dress, he's a townsman, not grand, but certainly no pauper.' He gestured at the decent clothing and the good pair of riding boots on the corpse. 'The poor fellow must have been on a horse, but God knows where that is by now.'

This was a veiled hint that any good beast left wandering in the wilds of Devon would be spirited away by anyone lucky enough to catch it, for a decent nag was worth a good many shillings.

Thomas ventured his usual good sense in a practical suggestion. 'He has a scrip on his belt, Crowner,' he offered. 'Maybe there is something in that which might tell us who he was.'

A large leather purse was attached next to the buckle on his belt, which was plain, but of good quality. Gwyn crouched and undid the laces which held the flap of the purse closed, then poked his fingers inside.

'He's not been robbed, that's for sure,' he said, displaying a handful of silver pennies and a crude tin medallion of Saint Christopher, the patron saint of travellers. 'That didn't do him much good, did it?'

'Anything else in there?' demanded de Wolfe.

Gwyn fished around again and produced a piece of parchment, folded into four. Knowing that the only one who could read was their clerk, he handed it up to Thomas. 'See if there's anything on that, genius!'

The little priest opened out the yellowed sheet and rapidly scanned it. 'It's a merchant's order, Crowner. For window glass and lead fixings, with a list of shapes and sizes, with some drawings.'

John's black brows came together in surprise. 'He must be a glazier, then. Is there any name we can put to him?'

Thomas shook his head. 'No, but we know where this

came from. It's from Berry Pomeroy Castle. Sealed with de la Pomeroy's crest in wax.'

John's bushy eyebrows went up. 'Odd! One of my damned brother-in-law's partners in crime. He must be wanting to spend some of his ill-gotten gains.' Glazing was extremely uncommon, only the houses of rich merchants, a few barons and some of the wealthier cathedrals and churches having anything but wooden shutters or oiled linen screens across their windows.

'The steward or bailiff there would be able to tell us his name,' grunted Gwyn.

'But the victim must surely be from Exeter,' exclaimed Thomas. 'There can be no more than two glaziers in the city, so it should be easy to identify him.'

De Wolfe pondered the best plan of action. Though he was supposed to hold the inquest where the body was found, it was obvious that these country bumpkins would know nothing of the circumstances of the victim's death. There was no one else in the vicinity to ask, and it seemed pointless to go through the rigmarole of sending for a jury from the four nearest villages and determining presentment of Englishry. However, the law was the law and he made up his mind quickly, deciding at least to make a gesture at the proper formality.

'I will hold a short inquest here and now, using these good folk as the jury. Then we will take him back to Exeter, where he surely must belong. Thomas, quickly record the names and place of dwelling of all these men here – and you, Forester Lacey.'

Within minutes, he had raced through a form of inquiry, getting Thomas to record the few salient facts. He directed the vestigial jury to return a verdict of murder and then turned to Gwyn, waving a hand at the corpse on the ground.

'Wrap him decently in his cloak and lash him across your mare, behind the saddle. And bring that length of chain with you – we'll see what we can discover about him back in the city.'

After such an early start, they were back at Rougemont by noon. The dead merchant was temporarily laid to rest in a cart shed, one of the lean-to shacks that lined the walls of the inner ward. John went back to Martin's Lane to stable Odin with the farrier opposite his house, then went in to dinner.

Matilda was still in what was for her a relatively benign mood, and as they ate their poached salmon, she deigned to listen to his story about the corpse on the Plymouth highway. When he mentioned the likelihood that the victim was an Exeter glazier, her interest was aroused.

'What was his appearance, John?' she snapped, with apparent concern.

'Difficult to say, as his face was discoloured and distorted by the mode of his killing. Why do you ask?'

His wife looked genuinely worried. 'One of my friends at the church is the wife of a glazier, the warden of his guild and a man in a very good way of business, too.' Even in such circumstances, Matilda could not resist emphasising the importance of her acquaintances. 'There are only two master glaziers in the city; may God grant that he is not her husband.'

'The victim was of middling height and had thin, fair hair,' answered John. 'He looked about fifty years of age, though it was hard to tell.'

Matilda heaved a sigh of relief. 'Then it is not him, thank Jesus Christ! I have seen Adele's husband occasionally at St Olave's and he is tall, fat and, like you, has an abundance of black hair.'

At least, thought de Wolfe, this seemed to point to the other glazier, though Matilda could not put a name to him. As soon as the meal was over, he grabbed his cloak and hurried round to Hugh de Relaga's burgage in North Gate Street, a fine town house that befitted a rich merchant. De Wolfe's portly friend was in his hall, digesting his dinner over a glass of wine imported from Gascony. After John exchanged a few pleasantries with his wife, she tactfully withdrew to her solar to leave the men to their talk, and soon John was sitting across the firepit from Hugh, a glass in his own hand. Without preamble, he told his friend that another of his guild masters had met a violent end, and soon the shocked portreeve had named the strangled victim as Hamelin de Beaufort, a glazier with a house and workshop in Rack Lane, which led down towards the quayside. Hugh was horrified to hear of the cruel method of killing and as with Matthew Morcok, was totally mystified as to why such an unremarkable craftsman should have been murdered.

'Surely it must have been highway robbery?' he protested. 'Our roads are becoming unsafe for honest folk to travel upon. I don't know what the world is coming to!'

De Wolfe shook his head firmly. 'His purse still contained a good handful of silver. No footpads would have left that behind. And the garrotting was utterly unlike what some thieving outlaw would inflict.'

The portreeve seized upon John's words. 'Outlaw! What about Richard de Revelle's claim I've heard rumoured, that this Nick o' the Moor was responsible for the killing in Smythen Street? This spot on the Plymouth road is not that far from Dartmoor.'

John shrugged. 'I see not the slightest reason to give that any credence, Hugh. Why should an outlaw want to slay a glazier, for God's sake? And with Morcok, how would a Dartmoor outlaw carry a body to a loft in the middle of the city?'

Hugh threw down his unfinished glass of wine and hauled his rotund body to its feet. 'I must go down to Rack Lane this instant,' he announced. 'Perhaps de

Beaufort will be there, perhaps it's all some horrible mistake. If not, I must convey the sad news to his wife and offer her some comfort on behalf of the guilds.'

The coroner laid a restraining hand on the impetuous merchant's arm. 'If you know this Hamelin by sight, it is best that you come with me to Rougemont and look at the body just to make sure. We don't want to upset his wife needlessly if it's not him.'

The hope was ill-founded, however, and half an hour later, a pale-faced Hugh stood outside the cart shed in the castle, wiping his clammy forehead with a gaudy silk kerchief.

'Poor fellow, it's him right enough. But what a ghastly way to die. There are some evil bastards about, John!'

De Wolfe gently steered his friend across the inner ward towards the keep. 'We had better have a word with Henry de Furnellis first, then go down to the glazier's shop to break the news and ask a few questions.'

The sheriff was equally concerned and mystified at this second death of a senior guildsman and in spite of his usual reluctance to get involved with investigations, he decided to accompany them down to Rack Lane.

'At this rate, we'll be getting short of masters to run the merchant guilds,' he said as they marched down Castle Hill, with Gwyn and Thomas trailing behind the three senior officials. 'Maybe Bridport or Southampton are trying to rid themselves of Exeter as a trading competitor.'

His weak attempt at levity fell on deaf ears and they hurried on through the chill afternoon down to the bottom end of the city where it sloped sharply down towards the river. Near the Water Gate which led directly to the quayside, many workshops and storehouses had congregated. They were thriving on Exeter's economic growth, which was based mainly on the export of tin, wool and cloth, though many other trades flourished in the city.

Almost at the bottom of the slope was a house with a shop at the front, the wide shutter on the large window of the ground floor being let down on hinges and legs to form a display stall for the wares of Hamelin de Beaufort's business. Some fine glass drinking goblets imported from Cologne, a few chalices for religious use and a number of glass ornaments and bowls were carefully placed on view, as were some small panels of leaded light, segments of coloured glass intended for rich men's houses or some church where money had been donated for a window, in return for masses said for a departed soul.

De Wolfe turned in to a door at the side of the stall and entered the front workshop, where several craftsmen and a couple of young apprentices were working away at glass panels set on benches. In a room behind, he could hear the rhythmic squeak of a bellows and see the glare of a small furnace where glass was being reheated by a journeyman and another apprentice. Looking around the faces raised expectantly towards him, he chose the eldest, that of a heavily built fellow of about forty wearing a thick leather apron scarred with burns down the front.

'Your master is not here?' he asked neutrally, in a last faint hope that there had been some error about identity. The man's swarthy features took on a worried expression, as he recognised both the sheriff and the county coroner.

'I wish he was, sir. There's business to attend to and he should have been back from his trip last evening.'

De Wolfe soon confirmed that it was indeed Hamelin de Beaufort who had gone to Berry Pomeroy Castle and failed to return. The workshop was thrown into turmoil when the coroner gravely explained that their master was dead. John assumed that their panic was due to the thought of losing their employment, but it transpired that the glazier's business was a partnership with

Hamelin's brother, who would no doubt carry on trading.

Hugh de Relaga, discovering that Hamelin's wife – now his widow – was in the living quarters upstairs, took himself off to deliver the sad news, much to de Wolfe's relief, as he hated and almost feared that task and the emotions it provoked.

Henry de Furnellis, feeling that perhaps he should make some contribution to the case, asked a number of questions about Hamelin's movements and affairs, but the journeymen and apprentices knew nothing to throw any light on his murder.

'He was a strict master, but a fair one,' said the older craftsman. 'We had no cause for complaint. He was a good guild member and abided by the rules to the letter. It's a real tragedy that he should be struck down so foully.'

Further enquiries amongst all the workers yielded nothing. The coroner's team took a description of de Beaufort's missing horse, which was a tan-coloured gelding, but John suspected it had probably been sold already by whoever had caught it after it ran from the scene of the killing. There were plenty of unscrupulous horse dealers who would not hesitate to spirit away a stolen horse to Totnes or Tavistock and sell it well away from anywhere where it could be recognised.

The sheriff and de Wolfe left the portreeve with the family to console them and to make arrangements for the burial of the dead man, which the guilds would organise. As they were near the Bush tavern, the pair decided to call in for refreshment. Gwyn came with them, though Thomas, never keen on drinking, made his way to his lodgings in nearby Priest Street.

The inn was fairly quiet at that hour of the afternoon and Nesta had time to sit with them near the fire. As always, her soft heart was saddened to hear of the death of Hamelin, though she had never met him.

'I grieve for his poor widow, suddenly being told of his cruel death,' she said sadly. 'I sometimes worry about you, John, also putting yourself at risk with all these unsavoury people you have to deal with.'

She was thinking particularly of last month's escapade down on the south coast, when John had rescued his wife and brother-in-law from a very dangerous situation.

Henry de Furnellis, bluff and to the point as always, leaned forward, his bloodhound face staring into the glowing logs. 'Why two guildsmen, killed in such strange ways? Are we going to see more such deaths?'

De Wolfe shrugged as old Edwin limped across to refill his ale jar. 'We've not the slightest notion as to why these two were slain, so no one can answer that,' he grunted. 'I had better talk to some more guild wardens, to see if they can throw any light on the mystery.'

Gwyn, who had sat himself down at the far end of the table in deference to the presence of the two king's officers, entered the discussion. 'Are you really sure that this outlaw fellow has nothing to do with it, Crowner?' he rumbled. 'Why should de Revelle be so worked up about him?'

'Because one of them was found dead in his precious schoolhouse, that's why. If he had turned up next door, he'd not have shown the slightest interest.'

The sheriff scratched the sparse grey hair behind his ear, where a flea was irritating him. 'And now there is this connection to de Revelle's crony. Would it not be worth trying to find this Nicholas to see if he had any involvement?'

Nesta, who had heard about Nicholas from John, made some tutting noises. 'He sounds a decent enough outlaw, who's been persecuted by that damned de Revelle, so it seems a pity to seek him out to hang him.'

De Furnellis took a pull at the quart pot of cider he had grasped in his brawny hand. 'Maybe we could catch him, then let him gain sanctuary and allow him to abjure the realm after you've questioned him?' he suggested.

The coroner snorted in derision. 'Some hope, Henry! Those moor men can vanish like magic into that huge wilderness. And imagine it in this weather: a posse would die of exposure before they laid eyes on a single hair of those outlaws.' The *posse comitatus* was a band of men raised by the sheriff, charged with hunting down criminals or traitors anywhere in the county. Though John was a seasoned warrior, having fought in Ireland, France and Outremer, he was no moor man, but he knew what a vast area of inhospitable hills, heathland and deep valleys made up the central part of the county. Scores of men had died up there, lost and exhausted in the mists and blizzards that could sweep in at a moment's notice.

Gwyn nodded in agreement. 'There are a dozen gangs of outlaws on the moor, all living in burrows and ruins. We've no idea where this Nick o' the Moors is hiding – probably he has a half-dozen different lairs, miles apart. Looking for a needle in a hayrick would be easy compared with that!'

The sheriff abandoned his idea without rancour. 'I suppose you're right – and I don't want to spend Christ Mass freezing my arse off on Dartmoor, so we'll give up the notion of having a talk with this Nicholas.'

But Nicholas had not given up the notion of having a talk with them – or, more specifically, with Sir John de Wolfe.

Out on the high moor, a freezing fog filled the valley of the West Webburn stream, rolling into the bleak vale between Challacombe Down and Hameldown Beacon. At the bottom, a scraggy collection of bare trees stood alongside the brook like black skeletons in the almost crystalline air. Amongst them, four men worked up a welcome sweat as they swung axes at logs felled some months back, which by now were dried out sufficiently for the fire.

The thud of the blades was muffled by the mist, but a steady morning's work had produced a respectable heap of firewood, and eventually Nicholas de Arundell called a halt. 'That should satisfy Gunilda for a day or two,' he declared, picking a leather jerkin from a bush and shrugging it on before the icy cold could bite into him again. 'I'll miss all this exercise when I recover Hempston.'

Robert Hereward threw down his own axe and wiped his brow with his sleeve. He looked disapprovingly at Nicholas, who had been his master in their previous life.

'It's not seemly for you to have to chop kindling, sir. You are still a manor lord, even if you have been shamefully deprived of your inheritance.'

Nicholas slapped him on the back as they walked up the slope from the stream towards the huts. 'Being outlawed levels all men, Robert. There is no aristocracy on the moor, only leaders of men and those who follow.'

With the ginger Peter Cuffe following behind dragging a sledge full of logs and with Philip Girard clutching an armful of sticks, they made their way up to the largest hut, which had a wreath of blue smoke climbing from a hole in the roof. The village, consisting of a few part-ruined dwellings, had been abandoned long before. A few years of unusually severe weather had forced the last batch of settlers to give up trying to scratch a living from the thin soil and to move back down the valley to the lower and more hospitable land beyond Ponsworthy. No doubt this cycle of pioneering and then disillusion had been repeated many times over the centuries – and would be again in the future. But at the moment, the crudely built shelters of large moorstone blocks were empty and the wall enclosing them had fallen in many places. Most of the thatched or turfed roofs had collapsed as their timbers had rotted, and only those intermittently colonised by tinners had been roughly repaired. The hamlet lay a hundred paces uphill from the Webburn brook, safe from the occasional flooding that occurred after cloudbursts on Hookney Tor and Headland Warren.

With Challacombe Down looming above it, the derelict houses stood in a sloping enclosure, some of them solitary huts, others in short terraces of square rooms. Crude openings for windows and doors were formed by lintels made from long slabs of grey moorstone. As timber was in short supply in that generally treeless heathland, all building was in drystone, apart from the rough branches used to support the roofs.

The late afternoon was drawing on as they unloaded their logs and stacked them against the wall in the communal living house. Gunilda was cooking a large pike that Peter Cuffe had caught yesterday in a pool downstream, but their supper was still an hour away. To calm their hungry stomachs, they each helped themselves to a bowl of thin potage, drawn from an iron cauldron simmering at the side of the fire.

'Cedric should be back from his post soon,' said Gunilda in her harsh voice. 'Not much point in him staying there in this fog.'

The outlaw band always kept a sentinel on watch further down the remote valley, perched up on the southern spur of Hamel Down. From there in clear weather, he could see a long way down the track that came up from Buckland. At any sign of men approaching, he could run back to Challacombe, and within minutes the gang could disperse up the sides of the valley and wait to see who came. If necessary, they could evacuate up to Grimspound, their next hideout a mile further away, which was an even more ancient village, set high in a side valley.

'He'll not be able to see his own toecaps up there,'

agreed Girard. 'The higher you go, the thicker it gets.'

'By the same token, no one is going to come looking for us in this weather,' grunted Nicholas, blowing on the soup in his wooden spoon to cool it. They had rarely suffered any trouble in this respect: the law officers had only once attempted to seek them out, knowing that it was an almost hopeless task even if they had sufficient men and determination. Both the previous sheriff and the new one had lacked both these resources and left them well alone, as they did the other gangs that inhabited Dartmoor.

It was these last who posed the only real threat, as outlaw bands were sometimes jealous of the success of others and especially resented them poaching on what they considered their territory. Twice in the past year, gangs of even worse ruffians had tried to evict Nicholas from his village, but the superior tactics of a former Crusader and his more intelligent members, who had been manorial servants in Hempston, saw off the badly organised thugs who tried to overcome them, especially as a few of Nicholas's men were accomplished archers.

As the damp vapours brought on an early dusk, other members of the gang returned to the village. Cedric appeared from his eyrie, cold and shivering, then the remaining half-dozen men who had been on a foraging expedition down towards Moretonhampstead returned with a side of bacon stolen from a butcher's cart. In addition, they had six fowls taken from the manor farm at North Bovey and a purse containing fifty silver pence from a fat monk unwisely riding alone towards Ashburton. The dead chickens and the bacon were presented to an appreciative Gunilda, and the money was shared out equally amongst all the members of the illegal fraternity.

As darkness fell, they sat on the floor around the firepit and celebrated their successful day with ale and cider, until their leader turned the talk to a more serious vein.

'I told you yesterday, when I returned from Exeter, that I am determined to regain my birthright at Hempston,' he began. There were solemn mutterings of agreement from the men, though Robert Hereward deepened his habitual expression of resigned pessimism.

'My good wife, Lady Joan, planted a suggestion in my mind that has grown into a firm resolution,' he went on, his square chin lifted in stubborn resolve. 'The coroner, Sir John de Wolfe, is reputed to be a fair-minded man who despises injustice. My wife's cousin, who is now sheltering her in the city, has learned much about him since he returned from the Holy Land, where he served our king most faithfully.'

The men muttered 'God save the Lionheart' and 'Bless King Richard', as they felt their present exile was in good part due to the avarice of Prince John and his minions. The revenues of six counties, including Devon and Cornwall, had been granted to him by his carelessly generous elder brother at his coronation – and even though John had been deprived of them after his treacherous rebellion two years before, the king had forgiven him and rashly restored many of his perquisites.

'What has this coroner got to do with our predicament?' asked Cedric, a young man who came from one of the old Celtic families on the Cornish border.

'My wife's cousin says that he has much to do with enforcing the king's peace, as the sheriff is not inclined to stir himself too much. But even more significant, this de Wolfe has the ear of King Richard and his Chief Justiciar, Hubert Walter.'

Nicholas explained that Sir John had fought closely with the Lionheart in Palestine and had been part of his bodyguard on the journey home from the Third Crusade. Robert Hereward, who had already heard the story, added a final recommendation.

'The coroner is well known to detest Sir Richard de Revelle, who is also his brother-in-law. He might welcome yet another chance to discomfort him.'

'The problem is the means of approaching this upright coroner,' said Nicholas, taking up the tale again. 'As a wolf's head, I dare not appear openly before him in Exeter or anywhere in Devon. He is said to be a stickler for the law, whatever his personal inclinations, and would be duty-bound to seize me on the spot, which would be fatal.'

There was a murmuring as the men discussed this dilemma.

'So how can you ever plead your case to him?' demanded Peter Cuffe, the most outspoken of the younger men.

'You need a go-between to arrange a safe-conduct,' called out one of the others. Nicholas nodded at this sensible suggestion.

'That was my exact way of thinking, Rolf. How to accomplish it is the difficult part.'

'Can your good lady's cousin not intercede on your behalf?' asked another, but de Arundell shook his head emphatically.

'I cannot expose her to any risk – and my wife lodges with her, so I wish to keep them well away from any fear of discovery. No, it must be someone else.'

The men were now hanging on every word. This scheme might bring them back within the pale of the law and let them return to their homes – or if it went wrong, it might take them to the gibbet. They waited for their leader to explain his intentions.

'We need him to come out here, where we can fully explain the situation and plead for him to put our case before this royal justiciar.'

Robert Hereward looked even more pessimistic than usual. 'And how in the name of the Holy Mother could you hope to do that?'

The noble outlaw leaned forward as if to impart a secret and his men instinctively did the same.

'At the moment, I have not the faintest idea,' he admitted.

CHAPTER SEVEN

In which Matilda attends midnight Mass

Early on Tuesday morning, the Eve of Christ Mass, it was still bitterly cold. The grey clouds that threatened snow had rolled away during the night, and a pale blue sky had left a heavy frost that glistened on every exposed surface. Over his undershirt, tunic and surcoat, John wore his thickest cloak, long and black, and reaching almost to the ground. It was wrapped tightly around him and secured on his left shoulder by a bulky bronze ring with a pin skewered through the cloth. He wore a grey felt helmet lined with cat fur, yet his ears were tingling before he reached the further end of High Street, on his way to the castle.

Up in Rougemont Castle, he again shunned his freezing chamber and went over to the hall in the keep, where a blazing fire had attracted a throng of people, all standing around warming their hands and, in some cases, their backsides, as they waited to see officials or did business with others clustered around the firepit. He saw Gwyn towering over his neighbours at one side of the throng, with Sergeant Gabriel at his side, both holding earthenware mugs. As a gesture to the bitter weather, Ralph Morin, the castle constable, had ordered the servants to bring in a cask of ale and a supply of iron pokers. Over the growl of conversation, the sizzle of mulling was frequently heard, and John got himself a pot, warming his hands on the sides as he went over to join his officer.

'Where's our miserable little clerk?' he asked, after greetings were made. The description was no longer accurate, as Thomas had cheered up remarkably since being restored to the priesthood the previous month.

'Doing his duty in the cathedral,' growled Gwyn. 'Praying for the souls of some rich buggers, while the rest of us paupers can go to hell.'

As part of his reinstatement, Thomas's uncle, Archdeacon John de Alencon, had arranged for him to be given the clerical appointment of a *preabenda doctoralis,* one of the duties of which was to act as a chantry priest. Thomas had to intercede daily for the spirits of some deceased merchants who had left money in their wills for prayers to release them early from purgatory and wing them quickly on their way to heaven. Every morning, he went on his knees before one of the side altars in the cathedral and prayed before saying Mass on behalf of his dead patrons before the altar of St Paul, then went about his duties as coroner's clerk. Today no new deaths, assaults or rapes had been reported overnight, so the coroner and his officer had no need for their clerk and had a free couple of hours until the hangings just before noon, out on Magdalene Street. The fact that it was the eve of Christ's nativity made no difference to the final act in the administration of justice.

'What about the inquest on our dead glazier?' asked Gwyn. 'Are those few words out on the high road going to be sufficient?'

Though John was a stickler for the application of the law, he was flexible enough to bend some of the administrative rules when it seemed the sensible thing to do. Theoretically, he had held the inquest, albeit with insufficient numbers in the jury, and now could have the body buried.

'There's little else we can do, unless some further facts come to light,' he said harshly. 'We're in the same position as with that cadaver from Smythen Street.'

'Do you think there's any connection between them, Crowner?' asked Gabriel, his rubicund face appearing above the rim of his ale jar.

John pulled the pin from the clasp of his cloak, as he warmed up in the heat of the fire and the hot drink. 'Impossible to say! Two master craftsmen, murdered in different ways in very different places. Apart from being senior guildsmen, they have nothing else in common, apart from a vague connection with those arch bastards farther down the county.'

'So what do we do now?' persisted Gwyn, using his fingers to wipe ale from his drooping moustaches.

'Might as well do what our clerk is probably doing at this moment,' grunted de Wolfe. 'Get down on our knees and pray for enlightenment!'

By the time de Wolfe walked back into the city from the gallows, the weak winter sun had melted much of the frost, but in the many shadowed areas of the narrow streets, there was still white hoar and crackling ice.

At home, Mary had cooked a meal designed to counter the effects of the severe cold: hot rabbit broth with vegetables and a spicy concoction of mutton, onions and rice, the latter imported from France on the same ships that took their wool to Barfleur. Away from the direct heat of the hearth, the gloomy hall was petrifyingly cold, the sombre tapestries that hung from the high walls doing little to insulate the timbers from the outside frost. Even in the house, John wore a heavy serge surcoat over his long linen tunic, and two pairs of hose to keep some warmth in his legs. Matilda was swaddled like a babe in one of her older velvet mantles, brought out of retirement because of its lining of marten fur. They sat huddled near the fire, where a pile of split oak logs had been placed ready by Simon, the old man who chopped their wood and emptied their privy.

As usual, silence was the order of the day, but at least Matilda seemed to have run out of things about which she could nag him. As the hanging of two thieves and a captured outlaw was too mundane for conversation, there was little left to talk about and they both stared sleepily into the flames, cupping their hands around mugs of wine warmed with hot water. John had no duties that afternoon and was waiting for Matilda to go either to snooze in her solar or out to her devotions at St Olave's, when he could slip down to the Bush to see Nesta. Soon Mary came in with another jug of hot wine, but before he could hold out his cup for a refill, there was a loud pounding on their front door and the cook-maid went to answer it.

'It's Gwyn, with an urgent message,' she reported, putting her head around the draught screens that shielded the inner door. Both she and Gwyn knew better than to invite him in when Matilda was at home, as she regarded the Cornishman as a common Celtic savage, almost as objectionable as the deviant pervert Thomas.

John hauled himself out of his chair and stiffly walked to the vestibule, shutting the inner door behind him. 'What is it, Gwyn?' he asked sourly, anticipating that the visit to his Welsh mistress was about to be postponed.

'Another killing, Crowner,' announced his officer with considerable relish. 'A right beauty this time!'

Gwyn's idea of artistry would be thought bizarre by anyone outside the profession of sudden death. De Wolfe stared at him, well aware of his officer's penchant for long-winded and sometimes dramatic explanations. 'What in hell d'you mean . . . a beauty?'

'Another guildsman, but we know who he is this time. A master candlemaker from North Gate Street, by the name of Robert de Hokesham.'

The coroner groaned. Another prominent burgess of

the City of Exeter done to death – what the hell was going on? 'Don't tell, let me guess! Was he strangled with a chain or did he have his neck punctured with a bloody great nail?'

The hairy giant, his bulbous nose almost glowing red with the cold and the ale he had drunk over dinner, grinned mischievously at his master. 'Neither, Crowner. He was pinned to a tree in St Bartholomew's churchyard by a long spike thrust through his left eye!'

St Bartholomew's churchyard was situated in the north-west corner of the city, just inside the encircling ramparts. Surrounded by the mean huts and alleys of Bretayne, the small church had a relatively large plot of land for burials, used for those who had purchased a special dispensation to avoid being interred in the cathedral Close.

John de Wolfe and Gwyn marched through the narrow lanes, with Thomas pattering behind. This part of the city was the most disreputable, Bretayne being named after the original Britons, the Celtic inhabitants who had been pushed into this corner by the invading Saxons centuries before. It had remained poor, and the narrow alleys and passages between the rickety hovels were foetid and rat-infested. They passed St Nicholas's Priory with Osric, one of the town constables, hurrying on ahead. He was the one who had sounded the alarm and had found Gwyn in his usual haunt, the guardroom of Rougemont, gambling with Gabriel and a couple of other soldiers.

'According to Osric, the dead 'un was seen early this morning, but the First Finder ran away,' grunted Gwyn as they turned the last corner.

'So who reported it?' demanded John.

'The sexton of the church,' replied his officer. 'It seems that no one else noticed it because the corpse is on the other side of the tree, facing away from the nearest lane.'

By now they were at the low wall running around the churchyard, which was an untidy plot with a number of large trees growing around it. The small church was towards the town side of the burial ground, which was dotted with irregular grave mounds, some carrying wooden crosses, but most being covered with grass and weeds. A small crowd had already gathered around the wicket gate that led into the churchyard, held at bay by Theobald, the other constable. John pushed his way through the throng of curious sightseers, consisting mostly of old women and noisy urchins.

'Where's the sexton?' snapped the coroner. Theobald, almost as fat as Osric was thin, pointed to the side of the church, an old wooden building with a small bell tower. Against the pine end was a bench and on it sat an aged figure in a shabby brown tunic, with thin bare legs ending incongruously in large leather boots. As John strode across to him, he raised his head, revealing a face badly disfigured by old cowpox scars. He looked shaken and John, in an uncharacteristic mood of gentleness, sat beside him and placed a hand on his shoulder.

'Tell me what you found,' he said quietly to the old man.

The sexton turned to him, his toothless mouth quivering with emotion. 'It was horrible, Crowner,' he quavered. 'I am well used to foul sights after forty years of putting corpses into the ground here, but this was different.' He ran a dirty hand through his sparse hair. 'To see a man standing on his own two feet, stone dead yet held up by a spear through his head, was almost too much to bear.'

'When did you find him?'

'Soon after the second morning service. St Bartholomew is no cathedral and our priest does not keep the canonical hours, but his Mass finished shortly before dinner time. Yet I was not the first one to see him.'

John nodded, yet cursed under his breath that these crimes were dealt with so casually by the populace. 'So who was that?' he asked with forced calmness.

'Willy Madman, a young fellow from Pig Lane. He's not right in the head, but our priest gives him a penny a week to help clear up the churchyard – not that it does much good.' This last was said with a scathing look around the tattered plot, the first sign that he was recovering from his shock.

'Where can I find this lad?' grunted John, eager to get to view the body.

'There he is, behind that tree,' said the sexton, lifting a wavering hand and pointing across the yard. De Wolfe saw a ragged figure cowering at the base of an old elm, one arm raised over his head, as if sheltering from some peril. John rose and began walking over towards him, but as if prodded by a sharp knife, the lad took off and vanished over the boundary wall.

'Bloody hell!' snarled the coroner. 'Osric, get after that fellow and bring him back here.'

With mounting impatience, de Wolfe beckoned to Gwyn and Thomas, who were speaking to Theobald at the gate, and began making his way between the irregular grassy mounds towards the trees on the further side of the churchyard. Osric had been right: the body was not easily visible from the lane nearest the church, and it was not until they had reached the further wall, almost in the shadow of the city battlements, that John could see the corpse.

He stopped to look as his officer and clerk came up to him. Thomas de Peyne gave an audible gulp of horror, and for a moment John was afraid that he would vomit over his boots, but Gwyn surveyed the scene with professional admiration.

'I've seen many a death in my time, but this one is new even for me,' he proclaimed.

Standing with his back flat against a stout oak was a

man dressed in a good tunic of blue serge, with cross-gartered breeches visible beneath. His arms hung by his side, palms facing outward, and his head was held stiffly erect, because it was skewered to the tree by a metal shaft penetrating one eye. The other eye was wide open, and with a slack jaw revealing toothless gums, the face carried an expression of indignant surprise. Some blood was running down the cheek below the left eye, but otherwise there appeared to be no signs of violence. On the ground nearby was a crumpled cloak and a woollen hat, presumably belonging to the dead man.

John went up close and inspected the bizarre tableau, peering behind the victim's head to see how deeply the missile was embedded. Thomas had backed off as far as he dared, but Gwyn was anxious to get on with the examination.

'Can I pull the poor bastard down, Crowner?'

De Wolfe stepped back and nodded, noting that the morbid audience from the gate had moved around the outside of the wall and was gazing slack-jawed at the dramatic sight.

'Yes, get him off there,' he growled. 'This isn't a mummer's play for the benefit of those nosey swine.' He turned and shouted at the score of onlookers, but though they shuffled back a few yards, they refused to disperse.

Gwyn went up to the oak tree and as he supported the corpse under the armpits, John wrenched the weapon out of the wood. It took quite an effort, as it was stuck three fingers' breadth into the trunk. As the body sagged, Gwyn lowered it to the ground, the long spike still stuck through the head.

'The point has come a long way through the skull at the back,' reported the Cornishman. 'Much more blood there, running down the nape of his neck. And he's as stiff as board and freezing cold.'

John bent to look at the instrument of death. It was

a cylindrical metal rod, well over a yard long, blunt at one end, but tapered to a point where it had stuck in the tree.

'What the hell is this thing?' fretted John. 'It's not a spear or a lance.'

Gwyn, coming from a more rural background, suggested that it looked more like a crowbar. 'The sort of thing they use in the villages for levering rocks and tree stumps out of newly won ground.'

The coroner shrugged. 'Could equally well be part of a railing or one of the bars of a gate. Whatever it is, it hasn't been used for a long time. It's covered in rust.' Indeed, the rod was roughened with shards of brown-red flakes that had stained John's hands as he tugged at it.

'Are you going to pull it out here?' asked his officer as they stared down at the body on the grass.

'May as well – he can't be carried through the town with a pole sticking out of his eye.'

With Thomas looking on in horrified fascination, de Wolfe held the head steady while Gwyn pulled and rotated the spike out of the murdered man's eye socket. With a grinding of fragmented bone, it finally jerked free with a soughing sound as the suction of the soft tissues was overcome. The last foot of the iron was plastered in blood and brain and Gwyn casually wiped it in the weeds growing on a nearby grave mound.

'Now what?' he asked gruffly. 'Here's Osric with that simple fellow.'

Across the graveyard came the lanky Saxon constable and the old sexton, each firmly gripping the arm of a reluctant youth. William, as he was known to his mother, was short and squat, with bandy legs and a round, vacant face. He had loose, blubbery lips and pale blue eyes that kept rolling upwards as if he was seeking heaven every five heartbeats.

'You'll not get much sense out of Will,' predicted Osric

gloomily. 'He's harmless, poor fellow, but was missing when the good Lord handed out wits.'

The next few minutes confirmed the constable's predictions, as the youth was hardly able to make himself understood, fearful of these strange men's presence. The sexton was the only one who could get any sense from him, and he translated for the coroner.

'He says that he saw the man when he went around the yard picking up fallen twigs for the parson's fire. He was so frightened that he ran away and hid in his mother's chicken shed. It wasn't until after second Mass that he plucked up enough courage to come and tell me.'

'I doubt you'll bother to call *him* at the inquest!' muttered Gwyn. John ignored this and spoke again to the sexton. 'What did you do then?'

'Came across to look. I thought Will might have been crazier than usual, but this time he was right. I ran and told the priest, who was still in the church taking off his vestments. He came out to look for himself – he hasn't recovered yet.'

Osric chimed in here. 'It was Father Robin who recognised the dead man, Crowner. Seems he buys all his church candles from him.'

John looked down at the corpse and then around the churchyard. The gawping crowd was still there, staring from a distance. 'Have you got a dead-house here?' he asked the sexton.

The old man indicated a dilapidated shed leaning against the back of the church. 'We can put him in there, sir. There's a bier inside the hut, he can be carried on that.'

Leaving Osric and the sexton to see to the moving of the body, John went back to the church, Gwyn carrying the iron rod like a javelin. Inside the small building, they found Father Robin slumped in the only chair, placed in the tiny chancel in case the archdeacon or even the bishop might one day visit. The parish priest was a corpulent, red-faced man, and to John's experienced eye it looked as if he had been treating his shock with communion wine.

'There's little I can tell you, sir,' he said thickly. 'This is a shocking thing to happen in my churchyard. I will never fully get over it. I must consult the archdeacon to see if the grounds need reconsecration.'

De Wolfe was more concerned with the dead man than with the father's religious dilemma. 'This man was your candle supplier?'

The priest nodded, but his eyes roved as if he was seeking a wineskin. 'Robert de Hokesham, of Goldsmiths Street. A master craftsman and a prominent guildsman. He makes candles and other articles of wax and tallow for virtually all the churches, as well as the cathedral.'

'Why should he be in your churchyard today?' asked the coroner.

The parson shuddered. 'Because he must have been there all night. He came yesterday evening to receive his payment for the last batch of altar and chancel candles. He came regularly every two weeks to collect.' Father Robin put his face in his hands. 'I saw and spoke to the poor man only last evening. He must have met his terrible end soon after he left – and has been there all night, poor soul.'

There was nothing else the priest could offer, and when John and Gwyn left the church, the compassionate Thomas stayed behind to try to comfort his fellow cleric. Outside, the constables were carrying the body on a wooden stretcher. When it was on the floor of the shack, the coroner made one last examination, pulling up the clothing to make sure that there were no other wounds. Attached to the man's belt was a bulky purse, which contained a large number of silver pennies, amounting to almost one pound's worth.

'So again, this wasn't a robbery, Gwyn,' he mused.

'Many people would know that he collected his debts on certain days, but this can't be some cut-purse chancing his luck.'

'No thief walks the city streets carrying a four-foot crowbar,' boomed his officer. 'He must have lain in wait for de Hokesham, perhaps with the rod already hidden here beforehand.'

De Wolfe shook his head in perplexity. 'Three guild members found dead inside a week. Admittedly, the first one must have been killed months ago, but it's still beyond my understanding.'

Having seen the body decently covered until the inquest could be held, John and Gwyn left St Bartholomew's, Thomas de Peyne staying behind. He had done his best to console Father Robin – a task that seemed better achieved with a flagon than with soothing words. Then the kindly little clerk took himself to the dead-house, where with much mumbling of Latin and signing of the Cross, he attempted to put the candle-maker's soul on the right path to Purgatory and thence onwards to Heaven.

John had been cheated of his afternoon rendezvous with his Welsh mistress, but fate allowed him to get down to the Bush that evening. Though Matilda had spent an hour that afternoon on her knees in St Olave's – and another hour gossiping with her matronly friends afterwards – she announced that as it was the eve of the celebration of Christ's birth, she was off to the cathedral that evening to attend the traditional special service leading up to Matins.

This was the cue for Brutus to need his daily exercise, and by the eighth hour, John was sitting comfortably at his favourite table near the firepit of the Bush. Gwyn was at a nearby table when he arrived, just finishing a gargantuan meal, and again proclaimed the Bush to be the best cook-shop in Exeter. A boiled pork knuckle and a pile of fried onions, cabbage and carrots were being augmented by half a fresh loaf and some goat's cheese. He had failed to leave the city before the gates slammed shut at curfew and could not get home to his cottage in St Sidwell's, a village just beyond the east walls. There was nothing new in this, and his placid wife was used to his spending many a night in the soldiers' quarters at Rougemont, the eve of Christ Mass not excepted.

'Where's the little fellow?' asked John, as he sat with his arm around the landlady.

'In the cathedral, I'll wager,' declared Nesta. 'He said this is his first Christ Mass since he was restored to the priesthood and he's going to join the rest of them in the celebrations there tonight. I don't know how he manages it, for every day he has to get up before dawn to get to the cathedral and prepare his duties for the dead – yet he's always there at midnight to attend Matins!'

Gwyn came across and lowered himself to the bench opposite with a quart pot of Nesta's famous ale in his fist. Though he wanted to avoid playing gooseberry to his master's dalliance, he needed some guidance as to the morning's duties.

'What are we going to do about this candlemaker, Crowner?' he growled. 'Did you get any more news of him this afternoon?'

'No more than we did with the last one,' admitted John dolefully. 'He has a good house in the centre of the city and a plump wife and three strapping sons to carry on the business. But as to any clue as to why someone should use his head for target practice, there was not a whisper.'

Nesta squeezed his arm compassionately. She knew how de Wolfe hated having to give bad news to families. 'Did the poor woman take it badly, John?' she asked.

'If screaming and fainting is taking it badly, then yes,

she did. Thankfully, I took Thomas with me, he is always good at such tragic moments.' He sounded sombre at the memory of that visit.

Gwyn swallowed the better part of a pint before coming up for air and then wiped his soaking moustache with his fingers. 'What about the other guild people – any opinions from them?'

'I spoke to the men in his workshop – he has a large place behind the house, where they make all types of candle, as well as wax for seals and dubbin and polishes for saddlery and leather goods. He was in a good way of business, with four journeymen and the same number of apprentices.'

One of the maids called across to Nesta about some problem out in the cook-shed and she rose to attend to it, but before leaving said, 'I knew Robert de Hokesham slightly. I bought candles, tallow and oil from him. He used to call regularly to collect the money due. He seemed a pleasant, honest man.'

As she hurried away, Gwyn pursued the matter. 'Did you gain anything about the guild aspect, Crowner? All three of these dead men were prominent masters and had been active in their guilds. Is that just a coincidence?'

De Wolfe sighed as he reached down to fondle Brutus's head under the table. 'Once again I consulted Hugh de Relaga, but he had nothing to offer. Of course, he knew de Hokesham well, he was a member of the city council, but as with the glazier Hamelin de Beaufort, there seems nothing whatsoever in his background to make him a candidate for such a gruesome killing.'

'So what happens next?' demanded Gwyn.

'As this obviously concerns members of guilds, I've arranged with Hugh de Relaga to have a meeting the day after tomorrow with the wardens of most of the major guilds in the city,' answered John. 'Maybe they can throw some light on this matter, as it concerns them so closely.'

Gwyn saw Nesta returning across the crowded taproom and hauled himself to his feet, as he diplomatically prepared to leave.

'What about the inquest on this fellow today?' he enquired as he shrugged his scuffed leather jacket around his massive shoulders.

'We can't hold it tomorrow, so arrange it for Thursday,' commanded the coroner. 'Though if the information is as sparse as with the other deaths, it will be another waste of time.'

Gwyn planted a kiss on Nesta's cheek, getting an affectionate smile in return, then lumbered towards the door. She sat down again alongside de Wolfe and slid her hand under the table to rest on his thigh.

'Forget dead bodies for a while, John,' she pleaded. 'If I get a nice big bone for Brutus, maybe he can wait a while before you go back to Martin's Lane.'

She gave his leg a hard pinch and looked meaningfully at the wide ladder that led to the upper floor.

That evening, in the great cathedral of St Peter and St Mary, one of the most important festivals of the religious year was being celebrated as the last hours of the eve of Christmas moved inexorably towards the day itself.

As the evening wore on, Matilda de Wolfe, attired in her best gown and a heavy hooded mantle of fleece-lined velvet, left her house in Martin's Lane and made her way across the Close to the cathedral doors in the West Front. Her maid Lucille dragged behind her mistress, as a reluctant chaperone. They joined the stream of several hundred other worshippers, many of whom had, like Matilda herself, forsaken their parish churches for the spectacle in the cathedral, which was now virtually complete, more than eighty years since Bishop Warelwast began rebuilding on the site of the old Saxon church, his huge twin towers pushing up into the sky as if they intended to last for a thousand years.

In the great nave, she pushed her way as far as possible to the front of the crowd standing on the bare flagged floor, so that she could get a good view of the great wooden screen that separated the common people from the quire and chancel, where the priests and their acolytes performed their mysteries. The cathedral was not intended to cater for the devotional needs of the general population, being a place where God could be praised endlessly by the clergy in the nine religious offices that punctuated every day and night. The twenty-seven parish churches and their priests were deemed sufficient to cater for the pastoral needs of Exeter folk, but the feast of Christ's birthday was an exception, when a show was put on by the cathedral chapter, partly for the benefit of the public. The usual time for Matins was brought forward from after midnight to the tenth hour, so that devotions could lead up to the vital first minutes of the new day, when Mass was celebrated, the only occasion in the year when it was so timed.

Matilda genuflected and crossed herself, then peered around in the dim light afforded by pitch-brands burning in iron rings on the main pillars, as well as by some soft candlelight percolating from the quire through the fenestrated carvings of the screen. In the distance, she could just glimpse the presbytery and the High Altar, but her gaze was mainly directed to identifying some of her friends from St Olave's, who had promised to be present this evening. As the bells in the great towers began to ring out, she shuffled across to where she saw some familiar figures and soon was with a group of her cronies, enjoying a subdued gossip while they waited for the service to begin. All around her, the crowd murmured, stamped their feet and rubbed their hands against the biting cold. High above, a few birds that had flown in through the unglazed clerestory windows chirruped as they squabbled for places on the roof beams – and occasionally, members of the congregation cursed as the sparrows fouled their best clothes.

Matilda was pleased to find that her new friend Joan de Whiteford had come to partake of the Mass, along with her cousin Mistress le Bret. For some reason, John's wife seemed attracted to the younger woman with an almost maternal urge to take her under her wing. Perhaps it was the misfortune of her early widowhood, as well as the undoubted cachet of her knightly status, that made Matilda warm to her. The coroner's wife preferred the company of women to men, because in general she disliked men. Being married to John was a burden she had suffered for years – she had once even entered a local nunnery, but found the life too spartan for her liking.

She chatted amiably with Joan for a few moments and was glad to find that the pretty woman was also devoutly religious, which made her even more to be cherished. They avidly shared the atmosphere of this special evening and eagerly anticipated the ceremony that was about to begin.

At about the tenth hour, sweet chanting from the choristers began in the distance and a solemn procession entered the quire and chancel. Held high, a gilded cross led in a cortege of splendidly robed priests and their followers, who all peeled off to take their appointed places. Bishop Henry Marshal, for once giving up his political journeying to be present in his diocese, took himself with his mitre and golden crook to his throne near the altar, while his four archdeacons, the other twenty canons and a multitude of vicars-choral, secondaries and choristers distributed themselves around the quire and presbytery.

Chanting, responses, psalms and prayers echoed through the vaulted building and though the proceedings were conducted entirely in Latin, of which no one below the screen could understand a word, the ethereal effect, combined with the cloying thin smoke of incense, created a mystical mind-state so far removed from the rigors of everyday life, that all present felt that they could feel the presence of the Holy Spirit in that great building. Matilda felt her new friend clutch her arm as the melodious chanting of the choir wafted over them and she patted her hand in mutual companionship.

Soon, a canon inside the quire began reading the first lesson, again in Latin, but as the words were being intoned, a young chorister in a white gown appeared on the steps of the distant altar, holding aloft a flaming torch. Then he turned and with the audience breathlessly entranced, he began singing the *Hodie natus celorum rex* in a high, sweet voice, proclaiming that 'the King of Heaven on this day consented to be born for us of a virgin'. Then the boy pointed with his right hand at the statue of the Virgin beside the altar and went down on one knee, at which the assembled clergy responded with *Ut hominen perditem* – 'that he should call home outcast man to the kingdom of heaven'.

Matilda felt Joan quiver with almost ecstatic emotion and her own eyes misted when three choristers from each side of the choir, again dressed all in white albs, came to the altar steps and, with the first lad, turned to sing the *Gloria in excelsis deo* as they walked slowly down through the quire and out through the great carved screen to face the congregation.

When Matins was finished, the midnight Mass was celebrated, and when at last all the clergy and their acolytes had processed out of the cathedral, the spellbound congregation began to make their way home in the biting cold. Matilda stood with her friends just inside the west door, making final conversation and exchanging seasonal goodwill greetings. Rather reluctantly, she said farewell to Joan who, with her cousin for company, left to walk back to Raden Lane. As everyone drifted off, muffling themselves against the keen east wind that had sprung up, Matilda found herself almost alone in the cavernous nave, where most of the torches had now burnt themselves out and the remainder were guttering to a feeble light.

Reluctant to have the almost divine atmosphere come to an end, she told Lucille to wait on the steps and made her way back towards the intricately carved screen which carried the huge central crucifix almost to the apex of the chancel arch high above. The many candles in the choir beyond were still burning, throwing a pale light for a few yards into the nave. Gripped in an aura of religious awe, Matilda went down on her knees on the cold slabs, for once careless of her best raiment, and prayed fervently for herself and almost everyone she knew. She even included her wayward husband and her brother, the idol who had turned out to have feet of clay. Especially she prayed for her new friend Joan, pleading that she should obtain solace and peace of mind after her widowhood. Eventually, as a sexton began snuffing out the candles inside the quire, the ritual-induced state of grace faded and as she could think of no one else for her prayers, she rose and made her way through the empty nave towards the doors.

Out on the steps, she beckoned impatiently to the shivering Lucille, pulled her hood forwards and tugged her cloak more closely to her neck, then set off along the path that led diagonally towards St Martin's Church and the entrance of the lane that led to her house. The icy weather had driven even the beggars out of the Close to seek better shelter, and the tumbled, rubbish-strewn area, with its untidy grave mounds, was completely deserted. The only light came from a waning quarter-moon, often obscured by clouds, together with the distant flickering of a few torches set at the various entrances to the Close, but Matilda had walked this way a thousand times and knew every rut in the path. Halfway to Martin's Lane, she commanded her maid to run ahead and tell Mary to prepare a hot possett of wine for her as a nightcap. Urged on by the snap in her mistress's voice, Lucille hurried away, leaving Matilda to cover the last few hundred paces to her front door.

Still abstracted by the aura of the Mass, Matilda failed to notice soft footsteps coming up behind her. Suddenly a violent push against her shoulders sent her flying to the ground. Her forehead struck a lump of frozen earth thrown from a gravepit and the scream that had formed in her throat turned to a croak, as she almost lost consciousness.

A moment later, she was rolled on to her back and a menacing figure straddled her, his hands groping for her neck. As her wits returned, her first thought was that she was about to be ravished, and she struggled violently. Matilda was a solidly built woman, and desperation gave her the will to buck and twist under her assailant, but he was too strong for her. Again she drew in a deep breath to scream, but now his fingers scrabbled aside her mantle to grab her neck and squeeze, her shriek for help dying in her mouth. The fingers tightened and now she feared for her life, rather than her honour, as the strong hands continued to throttle her. Her head felt about to burst and red flashes appeared inside her eyes as she frantically tried to draw a breath. A feeling of unreality and disbelief coursed through her muddled brain, as she tried to convince herself that this could not really be happening. A buzzing began in her ears, but she was still able to hear a voice hissing sibilantly a few inches from her face.

'You old bitch! Tell that evil bastard you call a brother, that the body in his damned college – and the two that followed – shows what happens to people who cross me.'

Suddenly, the grip on her throat was released and the weight of her assailant's body lifted as he rose to his feet. Then Matilda felt a violent kick in her ribs, thankfully somewhat blunted by her thick mantle, before the harsh voice spoke again.

'And you can tell him that his own time is coming, as it is for his foul accomplice Henry Pomeroy! I want revenge for Hempston, which ruined my life.'

Then she heard footsteps loping away towards Bear Gate and Southgate Street. Gasping, then sobbing with pain and fear, she turned on to her side and lay crumpled into a ball, shivering first with distress and then with cold. Slowly, she dragged herself to her knees and painfully rose to her feet. There was still not a soul in the Close that could come to her aid, and weeping she staggered like a drunken person towards the end of Martin's Lane, only a hundred paces away. As she went, she put her fingers to a newly recognised pain in her forehead and sobbed anew as they came away moist with seeping blood.

The little church on the corner was deserted, as the Mass held by its Saxon priest had finished before the cathedral service, but as she tottered unsteadily into the blackness of the lane, she saw a faint light bobbing towards her. With a moan of mixed hope and fear, she slid back to the ground just as the skinny figure of Osric, one of the city's watchmen, hurried to her solicitously, his horn lantern revealing the coroner's wife, her face bloodied and her garments dishevelled.

Though John had dallied in Nesta's upper chamber until late in the evening, he was home long before the cathedral service had finished, at well after midnight. Promising his conscience that he would attend the traditional High Mass in the middle of Christmas morning, he went straight to bed and was sound asleep when Osric began pounding on the front door with the end of his staff. It failed to wake him, but moments later Mary clattered up the steps to the solar and burst in to shake him by the shoulder.

'Come quickly, the mistress has been attacked!' she yelled, then dived back down to the yard below. Fuddled but soon fully awake, he clambered up from his pallet and threw on breeches and a tunic to cover his nakedness, thrust his feet into shoes and hurried after the maid. In the hall, lit by a bundle of kindling thrown urgently on to the smouldering logs, he found a scene of chaos, with an almost hysterical Lucille cradling Matilda's head as she lay slumped in one of the monk's chairs. The more practical Mary was bathing a wound on his wife's head with a cloth and warm water from her kitchen, whilst Osric was dancing from foot to foot, unable to decide whether to run out and start scouring the darkened streets for the assailant or to wait for de Wolfe's orders.

'The mistress was attacked in the Close, on the way home from midnight Mass,' announced Mary, glaring at John as if it was his fault. She knew where he had been that evening and, as sometimes happened when she had a bout of righteousness, she placed some of the blame upon him, even though the poor man had been asleep in his own bed when it happened.

He pushed Lucille out of the way, telling her to get some brandy wine for her mistress, then knelt on the floor alongside Matilda, his head level with hers.

'Tell me what happened, good wife,' he said with surprising gentleness. 'Who did this to you, eh?'

Snuffles and groans were the only response, then she winced as Mary gave a final wipe to the injury on her temple. It was not a deep cut, rather a deep ragged graze, but it had bled profusely.

'I think she must have fallen to the ground,' murmured Mary. 'But look at her neck and her eyes.' John saw that her eyelids were much more puffy and swollen than usual and in the whites were some bright flecks of blood. When Mary gently eased aside her wimple and collar, several fresh bruises were evident under the angles of her jaw.

'Some bastard has tried to throttle her,' growled John. He slid his arm around her shoulders and pulled her to him. 'You are safe now, wife,' he said gently. 'We'll get to the bottom of this, never fear!'

Chapter Eight

In which Crowner John becomes vindictive

For the first time in his life, John de Wolfe made a grudging apology to his brother-in-law. They were seated on either side of the fire in John's hall, drinking a mid-morning cup of wine, for once united in their concern for Matilda and in cold anger at whoever had committed this outrage upon her.

'It seems that I have to agree with you, Richard,' grunted de Wolfe, reaching across to refill his guest's glass goblet with Loire red. 'I admit I disbelieved your accusation about the corpse in your college being the work of outlaws, but now it seems that you may be right.'

De Revelle was too worried to crow over John's backing-down, as what he had just learned from the coroner indicated a frightening threat to himself.

'I suppose there's no doubt about what this swine said to my sister?' he asked anxiously. 'Could she have been so overwrought as to imagine it?'

De Wolfe shook his head. 'Matilda is a very strong-willed woman, as you very well know. After she had recovered a little last night, she was lucid and definite about what happened.'

When the immediate panic had subsided following her return home, a few glasses of strong brandy wine restored his wife enough for Mary and Lucille to help her up the stairs to the solar, with John and Osric hovering ineffectively behind. The two maids undressed her and got her into bed, heaping blankets and fleeces on her against the cold and plying her with more hot mulled wine. Lucille, the rabbit-toothed French maid from the Vexin, sat with her for the rest of the night, but John crouched for a time at the edge of the pallet and spoke gently to her as she recovered. As he had told her brother, Matilda was a tough, resilient woman not given to fainting or hysterics, and she soon was able to describe what had happened, though this was a pretty sparse tale, as she had seen nothing of her attacker apart from a hooded shape in black clothing. However, she was in no doubt about what he had threatened, though she could not identify his voice.

Osric had rushed away to seek the other constable and to rouse Gwyn from his bag of straw in the soldiers' quarters in Rougemont. They had searched the streets around the cathedral, but it was a futile gesture in the early hours of the morning, when only a few drunks were still abroad. Richard de Revelle had hurried after his breakfast to Martin's Lane as soon as he heard the news, which had travelled rapidly around the city's grapevine, sparked off by the enquiries being made by the two constables.

'I'll strangle the bastard with my own hands when I catch him,' grated John. 'Matilda was quite definite that he said he had killed the poor fellow in Smythen Street and then boasted of the "other two", which must surely mean the bizarre slayings out on the Ashburton Road and in St Bartholomew's churchyard.'

Richard stared at him uneasily. 'But he threatened both Henry de la Pomeroy and myself,' he repeated. 'It must be that bloody outlaw and his gang from Dartmoor.'

John shrugged. 'Unlikely as it seems, I have to agree with you. It was that mention of Hempston that clinches it. Your sins are coming home to roost, Richard, but I wish your sister was not involved in the fruits of whatever crafty schemes you've been up to.'

In his agitation, de Revelle ignored this shaft from John and stayed with the potential dangers to himself. 'I see how they could have slain that glazier out on the high road, but how do they manage to kill and attack within the city itself? This idle sheriff and the portreeves must immediately tighten up the security at the gates.'

De Wolfe gave a scornful laugh. 'How the hell can you stop any man coming into the city, Richard, unless you know his face? Hundreds enter through the five gates every day. Any man pushing a barrowful of hay or a fellow driving a pig could be an outlaw – they don't carry a placard around their neck, you know.'

De Revelle glowered at him, their temporary truce already under strain. 'So what are you going to do about it? I hear de Furnellis has delegated all his work to you,' he added sarcastically.

'I must somehow find this man Nicholas de Arundell – though looking for him in the wastes of Dartmoor will be like looking for a grain of barley in a wheatfield! Have you any idea where he might be, as you and Pomeroy were the cause of him being there in the first place?'

The former sheriff bridled at this. 'And good cause it was. The bloody men started a riot and killed one of my servants. Then they ran away and when they repeatedly failed to answer at court, they were rightly declared outlaw.'

John was too distracted to argue the merits of the case at the moment and wearily turned to more immediate matters. 'The cowardly swine that assaulted Matilda not only half-throttled her, but kicked her when she lay on the ground. Lucille found a great bruise over her ribs.' He swallowed the rest of his wine in an angry gesture. 'What I want to know is why she was attacked and not you? And what have these other killings got to do with it?'

'They are all directed at me or Pomeroy, John,' brayed

Richard fearfully. 'It was *my* college enterprise that he wished to damage. It was *my* sister that he injured. It was Henry de la Pomeroy's glazier, tenuous though that connection might be . . . but he is attacking anything to do with Henry and myself in order to discomfort us.'

Richard was now gabbling his words. 'In fact, I feel he assaulted my poor sister just in order to pass on the message via her lips. That is why, thank Christ, he did not finish the job and strangle her completely!'

John considered this for a moment. 'But he said "two other killings" which can only include the candlemaker in the churchyard. What possible connection can that have with you?'

Richard stroked his neat, pointed beard as he reflected. 'What was he killed with?' he asked.

'An iron rod, rusted and pointed at one end. The thickness of a fat thumb and about a yard and a half long.'

His brother-in-law gestured with his hands. 'Means nothing to me. Maybe this killing was nothing to do with him.'

'Then why claim it as his?' objected John. 'There have been no other slayings this week.'

Neither man had an answer, and soon Richard left for his own house, an armed manservant accompanying him every step of the way.

That Yuletide day was different from all others, in that the de Wolfe household remained very subdued, with Matilda resting in bed. In spite of her refusal to have any medical attention, which John could have obtained from Brother Saulf at St John's, in the afternoon he sent around for Richard Lustcote, who came at once and gave Matilda a pain-relieving herbal infusion for her bruised ribs. The elderly apothecary was well known to her, and after a well-chaperoned examination of her head, neck and side, he declared that nothing was broken or seriously amiss and that she would be restored to health in a few days.

Their dinner was a muted affair compared to what Mary had planned for the festive day, but Matilda forced down a respectable amount of food and several cups of wine as she sat up on her pallet. John ate down in the hall, getting through the poached salmon, roast goose and plum pudding with full appreciation of his cook-maid's skill.

Afterwards, he sat with Matilda for some time, with little to say, but at least he felt that his presence reassured her that some maniac could not climb the solar steps to finish throttling her. His wife's memory of those few terrifying minutes in the cathedral Close was still perfectly lucid and there seemed no doubt that her assailant had clearly linked the three deaths with her brother and his crony Pomeroy, together with Hempston, seemingly unequivocal proof that all were connected.

John stayed with her for well over an hour, but when she fell heavily asleep from the effects of the apothecary's drug, he surrendered his post to Lucille and made a quick trip to the Bush, where Gwyn, Thomas and Nesta were anxiously awaiting his news.

As was to be expected from her nature, Nesta was the most upset and solicitous for Matilda's welfare, even though his wife was the main impediment to their love affair.

'Poor woman, to be so sorely set upon at dead of night – and on her own in a darkened churchyard!' she gasped, rather illogically. 'You should be with her, John, it is your duty.' Both of them were relieved that he had not been down at the Bush when the attack took place, as this would have been an even greater burden on their consciences. After relating all the facts he knew over a jug of mulled wine, the coroner discussed with his three friends the significance of the assault until they ran out of suggestions.

'I'm not convinced that this is the work of that Nicholas de Arundell,' said John finally. 'Whatever that bastard said to Matilda, it seems totally at odds with the nature of a knight and a former Crusader. Unless the fellow's mind has become unhinged, such a nobleman would hardly strangle a defenceless woman coming from Mass!'

'Maybe he has become mad, Crowner,' grunted Gwyn. 'To be so badly treated by de Revelle and Pomeroy and then be banished to Dartmoor is enough to twist any man's wits.'

Thomas repeated the query that John had put to his brother-in-law.

'Why should he claim responsibility for this killing in St Bartholomew's?' he squeaked. 'What can a candle-maker have to do with the old sheriff? And why are all three senior men in the city guilds?'

De Wolfe threw up his hands in despair. 'It's all beyond me, maybe things will sort themselves out eventually. I'll have to see Henry de Furnellis and try to decide what we do about this gang of outlaws. It will be business as usual tomorrow, Yuletide or not.'

He drained his wine cup and reluctantly rose to his feet.

'You're right, Nesta, I'd better get back home. If Matilda wakes and finds me absent, maybe she'll have a relapse – though considering what happened to her, she's remarkably well.'

Nesta walked with him to the door, John acknowledging the murmured sympathy of some of the other patrons, who had all heard, like the rest of Exeter, what had happened the previous night.

She laid a hand on his arm as he bent to give her a kiss before leaving.

'It's spoilt all our Christ Mass festivities, *cariad*,' he said in the Welsh they always used when together. 'I'm sorry for it, but we'll make up for it when all this is settled.'

Sadly, she watched him vanish into the darkness, Gwyn following him ponderously. If there was an assailant lurking in the shadows, the Cornishman was going to watch his master's back like a hawk.

Though the period from Christ Mass until Twelfth Night was looked upon as a season for festivities, normal life went on to a large extent. In the villages, livestock had to be fed and watered, and though it was not a time for ploughing and harrowing, some agricultural tasks had to be carried on – leaky thatch mended and overflowing ditches cleared. In the towns, people had to eat and buy food, especially as those who could afford it ate and drank to excess at Yuletide. Goods had to be brought in and cattle and sheep had to be slaughtered in the streets, so that the markets could be kept stocked.

John's work was no exception and though the courts gave up their sessions for a week, people still died and houses still caught fire, giving him his usual tasks to perform. In fact, this festive season was usually even busier than normal times, as more drinking meant more rowdiness in the taverns and so more likelihood of assaults and killings. Even the risk of fire was greater, with more cooking to be done and larger fires in the icy weather – and again more drunks to stumble and knock over candles and lamps.

On the day following Christmas, John went to his chamber in the castle as usual, after making sure that Matilda was settled as well as she could be. The sedative potion had done its work, and she appeared much recovered, her main complaints being an aching side and a sore throat. This last seemed to make little difference to her voice, which had rapidly regained its stern vibrancy – and certainly was not preventing her from eating. As soon as he could, he took all the facts to Henry de Furnellis and in the sheriff's chamber in the keep, they chewed over what could be done, if anything, to follow up this alleged connection with Nick o' the Moor's outlaws.

'Hempston seems the obvious starting point,' growled the sheriff. 'Never been there myself, but if de Arundell and his gang came from there, someone might know something of their whereabouts.'

De Wolfe agreed and said he would get down there as soon as he was satisfied that his wife was fit to be left alone.

'She's a tough old bird,' he said, with almost a note of pride. 'Many ladies would have died of fright or been in a state of shock for a month after such an experience, but not my Matilda! If he hadn't come up on her unexpectedly from behind, I'd not be surprised if she'd have laid him out with a couple of punches!'

The old sheriff grinned at the exaggeration, then returned to practicalities. 'Do you want a posse or some of Ralph Morin's men-at-arms to go with you?' he asked.

John shook his head. 'I'm not going hunting them across Dartmoor, especially in this weather.' He jerked a thumb at the window slit, through which snowflakes could be seen whirling in the wind. 'As soon as I can travel, I'll go down to see what Henry de la Pomeroy has to say for himself, as he's also been threatened now. I'll go across to this nearby Hempston Arundell, to find out what really happened there. Then we can decide if we are going after these outlaws, but God knows how we'll ever find them in that wilderness.'

De Furnellis was only too ready to let John take the initiative, though he was genuinely worried about the killing of prominent craftsmen in the city. When the Eyre eventually arrived in Exeter, the royal justices would want a full account of everything that had been going on in the county, and to have an unsolved series of murders of guildsmen would reflect badly on the man who was responsible for law and order in Devon.

'Do your best then, John,' he said encouragingly. 'What's the next move?'

'We are meeting the guild masters today to see if they have any bright ideas. I arranged that before we had this news about Hempston, but I still don't see why the bloody man's victims have to be from the guilds.'

At his noon dinner, John was gratified that Matilda felt strong enough to come down to the hall to eat, though her bruised ribs caused her to wince every time she moved. She wore a heavy silk georgette to hide the bruises on her neck, but John could still see the little bleeding points in the whites of her eyes, the result of being throttled.

After they had eaten and he had settled her in her chair by the fire with a pewter cup of wine, he muffled himself in his cloak and with a felt helmet tied securely under his chin and a wide-brimmed pilgrim's hat on top, he set out into the snow, which was about an inch deep in the lane. John turned left into High Street, dropping a penny into the battered hat of a blind beggar who was crouched shivering on the corner. He walked on to the Guildhall, not long rebuilt in stone to serve the increasing needs of the prospering city. Inside the large hall, under its high beamed ceiling, he found a group of men sitting at one of the tables that he usually saw loaded with food and drink at festive dinners. Now the rest of the trestles were stacked against one wall and more than a score of men stood uneasily in the centre, talking amongst themselves and to the seven behind the table.

When he saw the coroner enter, the man in the middle rose to greet him. It was Benedict de Buttelscumbe, the warden of the Mercers, to whom John had spoken before.

'Welcome, Sir John, make yourself comfortable over there,' he said in a lordly manner, indicating a stool at one end of the table. 'The sheriff has kindly agreed to attend as well.' A similar seat at the opposite end of the trestle was obviously reserved for Henry de Furnellis. As de Wolfe eased himself down on to the stool, he saw that Archibald Wasteper, the warden of the Cordwainers was sitting next to him. Beyond him were the two portreeves of Exeter, John's partner Hugh de Relaga and Henry Rifford, a rich leather merchant. They had all heard of Matilda's plight and enquired of her condition, with hopes for a speedy recovery.

John recognised all the other wardens by sight, one being Robert de Helion of the Weavers' Guild and another Ranulph de Cerne of the Fishmongers. Another old acquaintance was Richard Lustcote, who had attended Matilda, being the most senior of the three apothecaries in Exeter.

There were familiar faces too amongst the men standing in the hall, though some were much younger than the wardens, and John assumed that some were masters without their own businesses and the rest were journeymen, skilled men but without the status of a master craftsman.

A moment later, the sheriff ambled into the hall accompanied, as befitted his status, by Sergeant Gabriel and a man-at-arms. Unobtrusively the two soldiers took up their positions just inside the door, and Henry de Furnellis came across to sit at the other end of the table from John. When greetings had been concluded, Benedict rose to his feet and tapped the boards with an intricately carved gavel. The mutter of conversation died away and the self-important warden of the Mercers began a long-winded introduction.

'I have called this emergency meeting of the leaders of the craft and merchant guilds in response to the shocking events that have taken place, the last being only yesterday,' he began. As everyone there knew exactly what had happened and why they were summoned, there was a restless stirring amongst the crowd. After a few more minutes of his platitudes, one man spoke up from the floor.

'Let's get on with it, Warden. We're all losing valuable working time, standing around here with our tongues wagging to little effect.'

The speaker was a burly man of about thirty, wearing a leather jerkin that appeared to have many scorch marks on the front.

John leaned over to murmur to Archibald Wasteper. 'Who's that fellow? He seems very outspoken.'

'A journeyman working for a metal founder on Exe Island. Name of Geoffrey Trove, as I recall.'

If John felt that Trove was outspoken, he discovered in the course of the next hour that a number of other guildsmen were even more frank in expressing their views. In contrast to the more deferential manners of both the knightly class and the clergy, the tradesmen were far more egalitarian and outspoken, the juniors being unafraid to dispute with their more senior colleagues in their craft. As the meeting went on, the speakers at the table were frequently interrupted by voices from the floor, sometimes making scathing or caustic comments about what had been said. One guildsman, a tall blond man who Wasteper said was a fletcher called William Alissandre, even claimed that the killings of the older guild officials might have been plotted by a jealous guild master. There was tutting from the seniors and catcalls from the other journeymen at this preposterous suggestion. The general consensus was that someone or some group was attempting to undermine Exeter's burgeoning trade expansion by a campaign of terror against prominent guild leaders.

'All the men murdered were officials in our organisations,' brayed Buttelscumbe. 'Surely this can only mean that someone intends to intimidate us – perhaps worse is to come.'

There was mixed reaction to this, some jabbering agreement, others ridiculing the idea.

'How can slaying a few men damage our trading prospects, for God's sake?' called a red-haired man with a florid, pugnacious face. 'Our customers here and our agents in France and Flanders are not concerned with a couple of corpses, so long as they get sent the best broadcloth or the finest fleeces.'

Wasteper whispered to de Wolfe that the ginger-headed man was Rupert Penyll, who owned a fulling mill on the river and was well known for expressing outspoken opinions at every guild meeting. Now Benedict de Buttelscumbe invited John de Wolfe to address the gathering, having already determined that Henry de Furnellis declined to speak, typically claiming that he had delegated his authority on this matter to the coroner.

John rose to his feet and hunched over the table, his fists resting on the edge as he glowered around at the assembly. 'I have little to say, as I came here to listen, not to speak,' he proclaimed. 'But you will have heard that my own wife was sorely assaulted the night before last. The swine who attacked her claimed that he had perpetrated these three killings.'

There was an excited buzz of voices around the room as John explained in detail what had happened. He held up his hand for quiet.

'I am not entirely satisfied that this is the whole truth, as I fail to see why guildsmen should have been chosen for this maniac's victims. Anyone would suffice for a corpse, if the only object was to discomfit Sir Richard de Revelle or Sir Henry de la Pomeroy. But I have to make all proper investigations to get to the bottom of the matter.'

The coroner slapped his hand upon the table to emphasise his words. 'You guildsmen are a tight community, you all know your leaders and each other.

The three dead men were prominent amongst you, so does that have any significance? They were not journeymen or apprentices, but masters or officials.' He paused to glare around the men whose faces showed that they were listening attentively to this knight with the strong personality and respected reputation.

'So far, there seems nothing in their business affairs or family matters which marks out any of the victims as being targets for hate or even dislike. Yet there must be something that drove a killer to use such vicious means to bring about their deaths. Surely someone amongst you might hazard a guess as to what that might be?'

He sat down in a silence that was almost palpable, but then murmurs grew into animated voices until they rose to fervent discussion. De Buttelscumbe, intent on showing his own importance, waved his arms and yelled above the tumult. 'Quiet, all of you! Let us have some useful suggestions for the king's coroner, for it is he who has to take the responsibility for accounting to the royal justices for these deaths.' Several voices were conflicting with outspoken advice, but Buttelscumbe managed to get their owners to speak one at a time.

'Surely it must be the work of a madman, Crowner,' called out the red-haired mill owner. 'I knew all three of these dead men and I can vouch for their goodness and honesty. Only a crazed person would want to kill them.'

'That's damned nonsense,' yelled the journeyman Trove. 'From what I hear of these murders, they were well planned – and the proof that whoever did them is sane and clever is that our coroner here has not been able to get so much as a whiff of his identity. Why else would he be here today to ask for our help?'

De Wolfe was not overpleased with this criticism of his effectiveness, but as it was largely true, he held his tongue. The last speaker was one of the wardens, Ranulph de Cerne, who managed to avoid smelling of fish, being now too elevated in his craft actually to handle the produce.

'What I wish to know is whether more of us may be at risk?' he demanded. 'I suggest that we all take more care of ourselves and not wander dark lanes at night, especially the officers of the guilds. We have seen what happened to the unfortunate wife of our coroner here.'

John half rose at this and declined to give any assurances about their safety. 'Certainly the second victim was not in dark lanes, he was attacked in open country, so no one is secure at any time or at any place. I suggest that senior guildsmen try not to be abroad alone, but take a servant with a good sword or a club with them as a bodyguard, until we can lay our hands on this assailant.'

He paused and again scowled around the circle of faces.

'But does anyone know of any common thread that could join these men to Hempston Arundell? Or indeed, to our former sheriff or the lord of Berry Pomeroy?'

No one offered any answer to this last plea, men looking at each other and shrugging. There was a further half-hour of discussion, which was heated at times, but nothing constructive came of it and as de Wolfe had expected, he gained no new information about any of the dead men that was of any use to him.

Eventually, he went back home, anxious to confirm that his wife's improvement was continuing. He was experiencing a nagging mental conflict, for though his conscience was clear in that nothing he had done had brought this calamity upon her – and he was safely asleep in their bed when it happened – his long-lasting infidelity and his endless disgruntlement with their hopeless marriage preyed upon him, as if these sins might have called down misfortune upon Matilda.

He found her still sitting by the hearth, a good fire blazing beneath the stone canopy that took the fumes out through the roof. She was swaddled in a heavy serge mantle, with a bearskin draped across her knees. Lucille squatted on a cushion to one side and a cup of his best Anjou red stood on a stool on the other. The French maid, who seemed perpetually afraid of this tall, dark man, scuttled out of the room as he came in and took the other chair, pushing Brutus gently aside to get his feet on the stone surround of the firepit.

'I have had several callers, John,' announced Matilda with some satisfaction in her voice. 'Four of my friends from St Olave's came to enquire after my condition and pray for my speedy recovery. And Lady Joan de Whiteford also called, she was most anxious about me, bless her.' John made appropriate rumbles in his throat and made his own enquiries about her progress.

'My throat is almost recovered, but this pain in my side troubles me, especially when I breathe,' she complained. 'But I shall be up and about as usual very soon. I do not wish to miss the Feast of Holy Innocents in the cathedral.'

She was referring to the light-hearted – even raucous – celebrations which began on the feast of St John, the third day of Christmas, when the choristers took over the cathedral for a day, one of them being chosen as the 'boy-bishop', complete with mitre and staff. Sometimes the jollity, in which most of the clergy took part, got out of hand: more than once the archdeacons had had to send in the cathedral proctors with their staffs to curb the excesses, which on occasion even spilled over into the city streets.

John listened patiently as at great length she recounted the conversation of her recent visitors, especially those of Joan de Whiteford. Despite the frightening experience Matilda must have suffered, he suspected that she welcomed this episode, and especially the fawning attention of her matronly friends, as a break in the dull routine of her life. When she had exhausted her account, he turned to more serious matters.

'The guild masters and their members could throw no light upon this attack – or upon the deaths of three of their fellows,' he said grimly. 'There seems to be no connection between Hempston and the killing of the guildsmen. I will have to travel to that manor as soon as I am able, to begin my enquiries.'

He hesitated and then continued in a more subdued voice. 'It may be that your brother's conduct in the way that he and Henry de la Pomeroy acquired Hempston Arundell may give rise to some problems, but I will not judge the issue until I have learned a great deal more. It was before my time as coroner when that occurred.'

Not wishing to upset his wife any more, he left it at that. Matilda was silent when he finished speaking. She had come to realise that her brother seemed incapable of keeping out of trouble, most of which he brought upon himself by his greed and his search for advancement.

'You cannot go in this snow, John,' she said eventually.

Chapter Nine

In which Crowner John rides into the country

Matilda was right about the weather and it was another two days before he could set out for Hempston Arundell with Gwyn. The sky cleared, and though the weather remained very cold, a weak sun dispersed most of the snow, leaving only patches here and there in the shadows. Thomas was left behind, much to his relief, as he was a reluctant horseman who would only slow them down as they rode along the frozen ruts of the country tracks. Also, he was anxious to take part in the cathedral's remaining Yuletide festivities.

With unusual solicitude for his wife's welfare while he was away, John made sure that Mary and Lucille would attend to her every need, though he knew there would be a constant stream of well-wishers coming to the house from amongst her friends at St Olave's.

With the Cornishman close alongside, as Gwyn still seemed determined not to let him out of sight for fear of some ambush, de Wolfe rode out of the city early in the morning and crossed the ford beyond the West Gate to reach the southern road to the west of the county. The track was in better condition than John had expected and the weather had improved, so they made good time. They stopped at a tavern in Kingsteignton to feed and water their horses and themselves, then carried on in the direction of Totnes until, about noon, they reached Berry Pomeroy. The castle there was a forbidding pile, built on the edge of a cliff amongst dense woodland, almost within arrow-shot of Hempston Arundell. Rebuilt in stone after the original timber stockade became outdated, the castle had sufficient clearance around it for defence, though this had never been needed. Its main strength was the precipice that fell from its walls down to the gorge beneath,

The twin towers of the gatehouse were guarded by a sentinel who grudgingly allowed them into the bailey, where John growled at a servant to take him to his lord. They were shown into a hall built against the curtain wall of the inner ward. Here Gwyn soon managed to find some more food and drink, while a steward conducted John to a chamber on an upper floor, where Henry de la Pomeroy received him with more than a little suspicion. The thick-set, stocky knight had not yet heard from Richard de Revelle about the attacker in Exeter, and when de Wolfe tersely related that the assailant had threatened the pair of them, Henry thawed somewhat and sent for wine, inviting the coroner to sit with him before the hearth of the draughty room, where wind moaned through two slit windows high up in the bleak walls.

'This man connected his killings with Hempston Arundell,' said John bluntly. 'It sounded like an act of revenge, with more to follow, which is why I have come here today. I intend to go over to Hempston after leaving here.'

'What did de Revelle have to say about this?' asked Henry. Unlike John's brother-in-law, the burly manor lord seemed unperturbed by the possibility of a direct threat to himself.

'He was mainly concerned for his own safety, but had no suggestions as to who might be the perpetrator. Whoever he is, when I get my hands on him, I'll strangle the bastard for what he did to my wife.'

Henry's head nodded on his thick neck. He was still wary of this dark man, who exactly a year earlier had been instrumental in defeating his efforts to revive a rebellion on behalf of Prince John. Both he and de Revelle had wriggled out of serious trouble over that, but he knew they were both marked men in the eyes of the king's loyalists, and that the Chief Justiciar had appointed de Wolfe partly to keep an eye on them.

'If he tries any tricks here, he'll get short shrift,' promised Henry. 'I've had a new gallows erected in the village and I'd be happy to let him try it out.'

'Have you any notion of who this might be?' demanded de Wolfe. 'The obvious choice is one of the outlaw gang that left Hempston when you took it from its lawful owner.' He had no compunction about being direct and possibly offensive towards Henry, as he knew that he, like Richard, still had ambitions to further himself within Prince John's camp.

De la Pomeroy glowered at this, but managed to turn the other cheek. 'It could be Nicholas himself,' he answered, his face reddening. 'He and his gang have stolen from our bartons, poached endlessly from my deer park, and generally made damned nuisances of themselves. This might just be a new departure for him in his attempts to discomfit me.'

The coroner shook his head. 'I can't believe a knight and a Crusader would attack a lone woman in a churchyard, especially one he knew was the wife of a fellow Crusader.'

'But he knew she was a sister to de Revelle, or he wouldn't have left that message with her,' objected Henry stubbornly.

'It's far more likely that it was one of his men, one of those who was ejected by you and Richard from Hempston. Have you no suggestion as to which of them it might be?'

Pomeroy made a rude noise. 'How the hell do I know

who ran off with the bloody man? I don't know the names of villagers in the next manor. I only recall that the old steward was called Hereward or somesuch.'

De Wolfe found the manners and company of the lord not much to his liking and, swallowing the rest of his wine, he stood up and made to leave.

'I really wanted to discover how we could track these outlaws down. Have you any idea where they might be?'

Henry lumbered to his feet and stood with his fists aggressively planted on his hips. 'We chased them off a few times when they came raiding down to Berry or Hempston, but they are like quicksilver on a tray. God knows where on the moor they live, no doubt they have several hideouts.' He marched to the door and opened it, ready to hand John over to the servant waiting outside. 'You'll never find them, especially in this weather. I don't know how they survive out in that wilderness.'

John turned as he went to the head of the stairs. 'I'm off to Hempston now, to see if anyone there has better memories than you. There may be questions at the next Eyre about how the place came into your possession!'

With this veiled threat, he stumped down to collect Gwyn and soon they were back in the saddle. After enquiring of the surly guard at the gate, they went back along the track and turned off on a narrow lane through dense trees until they reached the Gatcombe brook, which they followed down to the little River Hems which flowed through a shallow valley that contained the hamlet. Hempston was built on the opposite bank, a cluster of cottages on a rise of ground with a wooden church right against the small manor house. A bank, ditch and stockade surrounded both buildings, which were obviously old and in need of repair.

'Not much of a place,' grunted Gwyn as they walked their horses up the hill from the small wooden bridge over the Hems, which was little more than a large stream.

'Good fertile soil, by the look of it. Plenty of water

and shelter from the winds in this valley,' countered John, who liked the look of the village.

A few villeins were digging out turnips in the strip fields on each side of the track, looking as if they were muffled up in every garment they possessed against the bitter weather. They cast wary eyes over the two strangers and watched uneasily as they entered the open gates in the fence around the manor house. Here again there were signs of neglect: the compound was unkempt, with weeds growing in the paths, loose shingles on the roof, and tattered thatch on the various outbuildings.

Two men were shoeing a mare at one side, and they also looked suspiciously at the visitors.

'Don't seem a very happy place, this,' grunted Gwyn. 'Reminds me of Sampford Peverel, where we had all that trouble a few months back.'

As they dismounted, one of the men, a short fellow of about twenty with a crop of pustules under his chin, came across. 'And who might you be?' he asked rudely.

John towered over him and glared down into his face. 'I might be the Pope, but in fact I'm the king's coroner for this county. Where's your master, whoever he is?'

Suddenly servile, the septic young man tugged at his dirty forelock. 'Begging your pardon, sir. The bailiff is inside the house there.'

He pointed to the open door, where a couple of chickens were exploring across the threshold. John and his officer thrust the reins of their steeds into his hands and walked across to the front of the manor house, a rectangular block made of heavy timbers and surrounded by another ditch, over which a few planks led to the door.

Inside, there was one large hall and several small rooms partitioned off at the back. A central firepit was ringed with whitewashed stones, inside which a glowing heap of logs cast some warmth on those sitting nearby.

A few trestle tables, some benches and stools completed the furniture. Half a dozen men were sitting there, an old woman and a young girl waiting on them with jugs of ale and bowls of potage brought in through a back entrance from the cook-shed behind.

'Which one of you is in charge?' snapped de Wolfe.

A heavily built man of about forty, with an acne-scarred face, rose from a bench. 'That's me, sir. Ogerus Coffin, the bailiff.' His tone was cautiously respectful, as he recognised John for a Norman knight by his manner and by the quality of the sword hilt that was visible under his open mantle.

Several of the men rose from the table and stood aside as the bailiff waved the visitors to a seat and then sat down himself.

'What can I do for you, sir?' asked Ogerus. 'You'll have some meat and drink, no doubt?'

As another man gestured to the old woman to bring more ale, mugs and food, John brusquely introduced himself and his officer.

'We have several murders and an assault in or near Exeter, which may have been committed by someone connected with this manor. I am seeking out any information, especially about the outlaws who left here with the former manor lord, Sir Nicholas de Arundell.'

Ogerus Coffin gave a guttural laugh, but several of the other men looked uneasy at this news.

'Nick o' the Moor and his gang of ruffians? That's ancient history, that is. Must be better part of three years since he ran off.'

The crone poured ale for John and Gwyn, and a platter of cold pork and thick slabs of coarse bread was bumped on the table before them.

'Have they been around here lately?'

The bailiff's small eyes roved around, surveilling his companions. 'Haven't seen much of them lately, have we, lads? Last time must have been three months back, when they came by night and stole half a dozen chickens and a couple of suckling pigs.'

'How do you know it was them?' asked Gwyn.

'They scratched a sign on the door of the tithe barn, like they did a couple of times before.'

'What sort of sign?' demanded John.

One of the older men pointed up at the wall above the door, where a crude shield had been painted on the timbers. Though faded and deliberately defaced, six white swallows on a black ground were still visible.

'They left that Arundell device on the barn door, cut with the point of a dagger. That one up there has been here since his father, old Roger, built the house.'

'The place is looking pretty shabby now,' observed Gwyn. 'Does no one care for it any longer?'

Ogerus shrugged. 'It's only the land that interests Sir Henry and Sir Richard. They share the income, but don't need the house. I live here most of the time, though I'm really bailiff of Berry Pomeroy. My lord has put me here as caretaker, to supervise the working of the fields.'

John decided they were wandering off the subject. 'Do you know of any among them who might descend to murdering?'

One of the others, the one who had pointed out the shield, broke in ahead of the bailiff, apparently anxious to defend the former lord.

'They get up to some thieving, that's for sure, but they have to live and only steal food or money. They've never killed anyone nor even grievously harmed a soul.'

Ogerus scowled at the man. 'I know where your sympathies lie, Alfred Gooch! You should have gone off and joined them. Didn't they kill that man from Berry when the first squabble started?'

'That was an accident,' mumbled Alfred, sitting down and shutting his mouth.

'And you can think of no one who might have a

particular grudge against Sir Henry or Sir Richard?' persisted de Wolfe.

There were a few muffled sniggers. 'I can't say as to that, Crowner,' grunted the bailiff. 'It's not my place to relate tittle-tattle. But no doubt Arundell and all his tribe up on the moor would gladly see them both dead.'

John seized on part of what the man had said. 'Up on the moor. Where up on the moor might they be?'

Again there were snorts and chuckles of derision from the others.

'Like bloody will-o'-the-wisps, they are,' said another fellow, who had a hunting horn at his belt. 'They got half a dozen places they can hide, and can flit from one to the other at the drop of a hat. Not that they're alone up there, there's plenty of outlaws besides them. Dartmoor is big enough to hide a couple of armies.'

Having no help on that score, de Wolfe turned to another aspect of his investigation. 'What exactly happened when Sir Nicholas was turned out of this place? I've heard different tales from different people.'

Alfred spoke up again, braving the bailiff's obvious displeasure. 'It was a bloody scandal, sir! First they threw out his wife with some yarn about him being dead in foreign parts, then when he shows up at that very door there, hale and hearty, he gets set upon and sent packing.'

Ogerus Coffin glared at him again. 'Watch your mouth, Alfred Gooch. That's not how it was at all.'

'I was there, for Christ's sake,' retorted Alfred, defiantly.

'And so was I – and got two broken ribs for my trouble,' shouted the bailiff. 'De Arundell set upon us, calling on some of the men who were here before we took over to join him. They killed Walter Frome and were only defeated when we sent to the castle for help.'

There were some subdued grumbles of disagreement from a couple of the men, but they seemed afraid to defy their bailiff openly.

John decided he would only get a censored version of the truth from Ogerus Coffin and turned the discussion into questions about the geography of the manor and how men would get there from Dartmoor. It seemed that the obvious way would be to come down the Dart Valley, into which the little Hems stream joined only a mile away. The valley ran inland to reach Buckfast and, beyond it, Ponsworthy and Widecombe which were at the southern edge of the high moor.

'I reckon wherever they are, they keep mostly to the eastern part of the moor,' said another fellow. 'I doubt they dwell over towards Lydford or Tavistock way, for there are other big gangs of outlaws in that direction who wouldn't take kindly to too much competition.'

Even this opinion was of little use in tracking down Nick o' the Moor, as the areas involved were still enormous, a rugged terrain of heathland, bogs, stony ground and tors, all subject to dense cloud, gales, horizontal rain and deep snow, according to the season.

When they had eaten and drunk the plain fare, de Wolfe decided that there was nothing more to be gained by staying. A final demand to the men to search their minds for anyone who might have a particular reason to want Pomeroy and de Revelle dead was met by shrugs and surly looks, without any helpful suggestions. Gwyn would have liked to take Alfred Gooch aside and have some quiet words with him, but the bailiff and the others gave him no chance to steer Alfred away from their company, and a few minutes later they turned their horses' heads towards Exeter, which they hoped to reach before dark.

As her husband was trotting his stallion homewards that afternoon, Matilda had another visitor, after several of her St Olave's friends had come and gone. Joan de Whiteford arrived bearing a gift of 'wardonys in syrup', a sweet concoction of preserved pears flavoured with cinnamon, ginger and saffron, prepared by her cousin's cook-maid.

'It is said to be very nutritious, Lady Matilda. It will help build you up after your awful ordeal,' she said virtuously. Matilda, whose solid body seemed in little need of rebuilding, thanked her effusively and glowed in the warmth of the friendship of this comely, cultured and altogether delightful young woman. John's wife, who seemed already restored to her normal health and spirits after the attack, sent Lucille scurrying out to the cook-shed for some of Mary's sweet pastries and invited Joan to be seated in the other cowled chair before the good fire that was crackling in the wide hearth.

They spent a few minutes in polite conversation about Matilda's rapid recovery, the icy weather and the Holy Innocents' festivities in the cathedral the previous day. The pastries arrived, but Joan declined the offer of wine, as befitted a sober, abstemious widow. Matilda had tried on several occasions to winkle out more detail about Joan's previous life, such as where exactly in Somerset she had lived and how her late husband had died, but she had seemed somewhat evasive, which increased Matilda's curiosity all the more. She tried again now, with little more success, and eventually decided that grief was causing the younger woman to suppress her memories of her former life.

Though the rest of the hall was as cold as a church crypt, the blazing fire overheated their fronts, and the wooden wraparound seats with the arched cowls above kept off much of the pervasive chill. The radiance of the logs, which had driven Brutus back a few feet, encouraged the two ladies to open their pelisses, the lined overgarments they wore on top of their kirtles. Joan had arrived with a heavy hooded mantle as an outer garment, which Mary had draped across the table, and Matilda noticed that it and Joan's pelisse, though of excellent quality, were worn from much laundering and had some patching and darning here and there. It was clear that she was in straightened circumstances compared to her previous life as the lady of a manor, and the older woman's heart went out to her new friend. She even toyed with the idea of subterfuges to improve Joan's wardrobe without appearing to be offering charity.

The warmth of their companionship was evident, the talk moving on to their mutual acquaintances in the congregations of St Olave's and the cathedral: Joan's cousin, Gillian le Bret, seemed to have already introduced her to a considerable number of people in the city.

Their amiable talk went on for almost an hour until disaster struck. On her previous visits, Matilda had not told Joan all the details of her frightening experience, but now that the event was fading a little, she felt able to relate what had actually happened.

'The devil who assaulted me so cruelly said that he had killed three times already and that my brother Richard and another would also pay the price for Hempston!'

Matilda said this in a tone of high drama, not noticing the sudden effect the single word had on her friend. Joan went white and she almost gaped at Matilda.

'Hempston? Did you say Hempston? Surely that cannot be true,' she uttered in an intense whisper.

'It was indeed – some manor down near Totnes, so my husband says,' continued Matilda, blithely unaware of the fuse she was lighting. 'It seems that a rogue knight was expelled from there several years ago and now heads a band of moorland outlaws. Now he is embarking on a murderous crusade against those he claims wronged him. He attacked me so that I might convey his threats to his intended victims!'

Joan stood up so suddenly that the chair grated against the flagstones with a squeal that startled Brutus from his dozing. She stood and stared down at Matilda as if the lady of the house had suddenly grown horns and forked tail.

'That is impossible, mistress! Why are you making such a monstrous accusation?'

Matilda gaped up at her for a moment, then her mouth snapped shut like a steel trap. This was her house, and she was not going to be spoken to in that fashion.

'Watch your tongue, young lady. That is hardly a courteous thing to say!' She was torn between astonishment and annoyance.

'What you allege cannot be true!' blurted out Joan, shaking with emotion. Then she seemed to crumple and flopped back into the chair to bury her face in her hands. 'I have not been entirely frank with you, Lady Matilda,' she sobbed through her fingers. 'I am not who I say I am!'

By now the lady of the house was bewildered. She stared at the woman weeping in her hall, wondering for a moment who was going mad, the visitor or herself. 'Explain yourself, for heaven's sake!' she demanded.

Joan raised her face, tears streaming down her cheeks. 'You have been so kind to me, and I repay you thus, Matilda,' she gulped. 'My name really is Joan and I am the wife of a Crusader and a knight – but his name is not de Whiteford, it is Sir Nicholas de Arundell, of Hempston Arundell.'

Matilda rose slowly from her chair, her face suffused with anger. 'You are the wife of the devil who attacked me? How dare you come to this house, woman?'

'He did not attack you, madam,' screamed Joan. 'He would never do such a thing, he is an honourable man and was many miles away that night.'

'Get out of my house, damn you!' thundered the coroner's wife. 'If it was not your man in person, then it was some villain sent by him to carry out his vile deeds.'

She advanced on the hapless woman, who left her chair and backed away towards the door, her hands held out in supplication.

'I swear Nicholas is innocent, we were deprived of our manor and our life together by unscrupulous men, your brother being one of them.'

This was hardly the right thing to say in the circumstances and caused Matilda, her rage clouding her common sense, to become even more incensed. She bore down on the near-hysterical Joan, who turned tail and scurried to the door, sobbing as she fumbled with the latch. A moment later, there was a thud as the heavy street door swung shut behind her.

Matilda was left standing in the middle of the flagged floor, her anger subsiding as quickly as it had arisen. She looked around and saw that Joan's cloak was still thrown across the table, the younger woman having run out into the icy weather with only her pelisse to shelter her. Matilda picked up the cloak and sadly put her cheek to it, already deeply regretting the irremediable loss of such a special friend. She was still not able to get her mind around the extraordinary claim that Joan had made, but instinctively she knew it to be true. Unusually for her, she vehemently wished that John was here now, so that he could explain what all this meant and reassure her that her friend had merely had a temporary fit of aberration, though she knew that this was wishful thinking.

Her dazed mind was suddenly interrupted by Mary appearing at the inner door.

'Is everything all right, mistress?' she asked concernedly, looking around the empty hall. 'I thought I heard shouting. Has your guest gone?'

Matilda, who was usually brusque with the cook-maid, slowly shook her head and replied quietly, 'There's nothing amiss, girl. And, yes, the lady has gone.'

When Mary had left, Matilda sank back into her chair, still clutching the mantle, and stared into the fire. 'Oh God, what's happening?' she murmured to the Almighty.

* * *

De Wolfe and his officer reached Exeter just as the gates were closing at dusk, and Gwyn went straight up to Rougemont to eat, drink and play dice with the men-at-arms for the rest of the evening. John made his way back to Martin's Lane and, after seeing Odin settled in the stables opposite his house, went home in mellow anticipation of at last getting warm before a good fire, with a jug of mulled wine and the pleasure of Mary's cooking.

What met him in his hall dashed his hopes, as he found his wife slumped in her chair, a linen kerchief pressed to her face. Her wimple was hanging awry and strands of her mousy hair were poking from beneath it.

'Matilda? Are you unwell? Shall I call Richard Lustcote for you?'

When she looked mournfully up at him, he saw that her eyes were reddened and tears welled from the lids. 'I am not ill, John. Just sick at heart.'

He crouched at the side of her chair as she haltingly told him everything that had happened. 'Her name was false, John, she deceived me!'

Privately, he thought it was only natural that the woman would not advertise the fact that she was the wife of a hunted outlaw, but he patted Matilda awkwardly on the shoulder. 'Never mind that, she no doubt wanted to spare you embarrassment,' he said instead. 'But this is a most extraordinary revelation. So she's not a de Whiteford from Somerset, but wife to Nick o' the Moor.'

Matilda sniffed back her tears and wiped her face with the linen cloth. 'She loudly denied that he had anything to do with my ordeal, John. She claimed that they had both been wronged by my brother. How can such a wicked, deceitful woman say such things, when she seemed at first to be such a nice, devout woman?'

De Wolfe groped for a stool and pulled it up to squat near his wife's chair. 'I have spoken to a number of people, including the sheriff – and today I have been down myself to Hempston and Berry Pomeroy. There may well be some truth in what she says, Matilda,' he added gently.

She glared at him with a return of her old antagonism. 'You too, John? You never miss a chance to defame Richard, do you?'

He held his temper in check with an effort. 'Come, Matilda, you cannot deceive yourself that your brother is a pillar of righteousness, after all the dangerous escapades that he has become embroiled in. What I say comes not from my mouth or my imagination – it is a fact that the Arundell manor was, shall we say, *acquired* by Richard and Henry de la Pomeroy in dubious circumstances. I am still not clear about the details; there are conflicting accounts, depending on who one speaks to.'

Matilda was not mollified by this. 'So who half killed me and spat the poison in my ear that it was revenge for Hempston, answer me that? Who could it have been but this Arundell knave or some hired assassin of his?'

Her husband had no answer for this and shook his head in frustration. 'I must get to the bottom of this, and quickly, before anyone else is killed. Where does this lady live? I must speak to her urgently.'

'Speak to her? Surely you mean seize her, arrest her, throw her into the cells at the castle. She is the wife of a condemned outlaw.'

John hauled himself from the stool and backed away to the other monk's seat, where Joan had sat that fateful afternoon.

'I cannot arrest her, Matilda, even if I saw some merit in doing so. It is not against the law to be married to a criminal, unless she gives him aid and succour. And as he is far away on Dartmoor, that hardly seems possible.'

'She lodges in Raden Lane with her cousin, Gillian le Bret – though after her vile deception, even that is open to question!'

John sensed that Matilda was torn between hating Joan

de Arundell and trying to save her affection for her. Her words seemed aimed at bolstering her outrage, but there was an undercurrent pleading for her to be proved wrong. John tried to placate her as much as possible.

'I truly cannot see a knight and a fellow Crusader stooping to attack a defenceless woman in the cathedral precincts at Christ Mass,' he said confidently. 'It would be against all the instincts of honour and chivalry. Though I don't for a moment deny your recollection of that foul assault, it could have been another man, as when he was ejected from his manor, many other men went with him and have suffered ever since.'

The logic of this struck home, and Matilda began to grasp at the faint hope that her rift with Lady Joan was not irrevocable.

'Then you had better set about finding out, husband,' she said with a hint of her habitual grimness. 'Now being unmasked, she may leave the city and hide herself away somewhere.'

The same thought had occurred to John. 'She can go nowhere until the gates open at dawn. I'll confront her tonight – though after a day in the saddle, I'll first need some of Mary's victuals to fill my empty belly, even if it's only umble pie.'

An hour later, the coroner and his wife were standing outside the gate to the burgage plot in Raden Lane. Matilda had insisted on accompanying him, saying that she was the one most concerned in this matter and that she was determined to see it resolved. Though often a surly, selfish person, she was lacking in neither intelligence nor fortitude, and nothing John could say would deter her from coming with him.

It was dark and cold, but the wind had dropped, reducing the chill considerably. Both wrapped in their mantles, they waited for someone to answer the loud rapping that John had made on the gate with the handle of his dagger. Eventually, footsteps were heard on the other side and the quavering voice of the elderly servant, Maurice, called out to ask who was there. No one readily opened their doors to unexpected callers in the dark of a winter's evening, but the authoritarian voice of the king's coroner persuaded Maurice to pull the bolts and lift the bar to allow them inside.

He led them into the main room where, lit by the fire and a number of tallow dips, they found Gillian le Bret standing protectively in front of Joan de Arundell, who like Matilda earlier had obviously been weeping.

'With what intent have you come, Sir John?' demanded Gillian stiffly. 'My cousin has done no wrong. The mild deception about her name was to protect her from the gossips who abound in this city.'

'The lady need have no fear of me, Mistress le Bret. But those same gossips will no doubt have informed you that my wife here was grievously assaulted a few nights ago, and I have certain information that links that with the manor of Hempston. That is why I am here, to urgently seek information.'

Matilda stood stock still behind him, her eyes on Joan at the far side of the room. She said nothing, and John was unsure whether her attitude was hostile or forgiving. For her part, the younger woman displayed only apprehension, as if she expected to be clapped into irons at any moment. Gillian seemed to have taken on the role of interlocutor in this matter.

'My cousin knows nothing of this, but we can swear, by any means you desire, that her husband had no part in any attack upon the good lady.'

'How would you know that, lady, if her husband is many miles away and has no contact with his wife?' asked John in a reasonable tone.

Joan spoke up, more firmly and resolutely than the coroner had expected.

'I know my husband, Sir John. He is a fine man,

honourable and fair. He was a Crusader like yourself, but his absence in the service of our king has brought us nothing but ruin and despair.'

She broke down in tears, and Matilda, undergoing a rapid reversal of mood, lumbered forward to put a consoling arm around Joan's shoulders and to press her head against her own bosom.

Gillian and John looked at the pair and then at each other.

'There seems to have been a miraculous reconciliation,' murmured the elder cousin. 'We had better be seated and talk this through.'

They arranged themselves on a padded settle near the firepit and on a wooden chair and a stool, Joan now linking her arm through Matilda's. Alternately smiling and blinking back tears, Joan told how she had been callously told of the death of her husband and then been evicted from Hempston by de la Pomeroy and de Revelle, on the claim that the manor had escheated to Prince John.

John looked covertly at his wife when her brother's name was given, but apart from a tightening of her lips, she made no comment.

'I know little of what happened when Nicholas came back to Hempston, as I was far away down at the tip of Cornwall. In fact, I knew nothing of his return from the dead for some months, until he got word to my kinsmen down there, through some carters.'

'So have you seen him since then, mistress?' asked John. Joan looked warily at Gillian, who sighed and nodded.

'Yes, she has, just a couple of times. They met briefly at covert assignations, when he came secretly off the moor.' Her voice became more defiant. 'I doubt that is a crime, Crowner, as she gave him no aid whatsoever, for she has none to give.'

The two women said nothing about Nicholas's visit into Exeter, but John spotted an important void in their story.

'So you must be able to contact your husband, lady? Otherwise you would not have been able to set up these meetings?'

Joan flushed, as the conversation was leading into dangerous paths. 'It is difficult and complicated, sir. But he is my husband, we are still young, yet deprived of each other's rightful company, due to the greed of evil men.'

Again Matilda did not react to this innuendo which included her brother. John nodded, accepting the truth of her words.

'I am concerned that as you claim that your husband cannot be personally involved in these murders and in the assault on my wife, then someone in his band of men might be. What have you to say to that?'

On safer ground, Joan considered the proposition. 'Truly, I cannot help you much, as I have no knowledge of how he lives on the moor, except that he says the hardships are barely tolerable. But certainly, men from the manor went into exile with him of their own account, not wishing to suffer serfdom to those who pillage other men's property. Some of those men may well be very aggrieved and desire to strike back at those who ruined their lives. But why would they wait almost three years?'

De Wolfe had no answer to this, but persisted with his questions. 'Is there any one man you might recall who was particularly angry at what happened at Hempston?'

Joan shook her head again. 'I knew Robert Hereward, of course. He was our steward and a kind, steady man. There was also Martin the manor reeve, but I don't recall much about all the others. I had little to do with the running of the manor, Robert Hereward saw to all that, especially after Nicholas was so gallant as to go off and take the Cross.'

She sounded bitter about this, her husband leaving for the Holy Land and leaving her to cope with his alleged death and then the sequestration of her home.

Matilda spoke for the first time since she arrived. 'I

was wrong to speak as I did this afternoon, dear Joan. I was distressed by what had happened to me and to discover that you were no widow, and that your husband was whom I assumed to be my assailant threw me into a unreasonable temper.' She patted the other woman's arm. 'I shall make confession and do penance for my impetuousness, never fear.'

De Wolfe gave one of his loud throat rumblings to halt the possible decline into sentimentality. 'What is to be done, that is the problem? I quite understand why you are firm in your defence of your husband, but you are hardly an unbiased witness.'

Gillian came back into the debate. 'There is nothing further we can tell you, Crowner. All the fault lies in those who took advantage of Nicholas's absence in Palestine to falsely take possession of his manor. That is where the answer lies, surely.'

Matilda turned to look across the room at her husband, having so rapidly moved from accuser to protector of her young friend.

'John, it occurs to me that the swine who accosted me might certainly have been from Hempston, but may have long left that place and be nothing at all to do with the men on Dartmoor.'

Gillian agreed with her. 'In fact, it seems more likely, as how else could these crimes have been committed within the city?'

She forbore to mention that Nicholas de Arundell had entered and left Exeter without any problem, and instead raised the subject of how to lift the fatal stigma of outlaw from him.

'We had already wondered if we could implore you to intercede for Nicholas with the king's council,' she said earnestly. At this, Joan stood up and passionately added her own pleas.

'Sir John, you are a man with a reputation for honesty and a sense of justice, which is more than can be said for so many in positions of authority. Is there nothing that can be done to obtain a pardon for him? Though surely pardon is the wrong word, for he did nothing wrong to deserve being outlawed for trying to defend our home against these pillagers.'

Matilda nodded vigorously, even though her own brother was implicitly being accused by Joan's words. 'John, you are well acquainted with the Chief Justiciar and even King Richard himself. Surely you can make some representations?' Even in this highly charged discussion, she could not resist dropping names to emphasise how well connected her husband was.

He cleared his throat again, cursing Matilda for pressing him too far. 'There is much to be discovered about all aspects of this. The events occurred before I was coroner, and before I can make any move I need to know exactly what went on in Hempston almost three years ago. There is no doubt that your husband and these men on the moor were properly declared exigent, as there are court records to that effect. Thus, legally, no law officer can approach them except to arrest them.'

They spoke together for some time longer, but John gained no more information. The wife was fiercely defensive of her husband, as was to be expected, but claimed that she knew virtually nothing of his present circumstances or whereabouts on the moor. Neither could she suggest anyone from Hempston who might have homicidal tendencies.

Eventually, he prised Matilda away from her *rapprochement* with Joan de Arundell and they left, his wife making ardent invitations to both Joan and Gillian le Bret to visit her to discuss the matter further.

On the walk back through streets dimly lit by a hazy gibbous moon, Matilda repeated her repentance at having dealt so impetuously with Joan that afternoon and pressed John to do all he could to obtain a pardon for Joan's husband.

Almost in retaliation, John raised the matter of her brother. 'You realise that pursuing this will reflect badly upon Richard, to say nothing of that treacherous bastard Henry de la Pomeroy.' He could not see her face in the gloom, but he could imagine her lips tightening.

'Richard is my flesh and blood, John, but if this story is true, then he should be ashamed of himself. No doubt he was led astray by Pomeroy, but he should have restrained himself. My brother has always been greedy for wealth and power, but this time he has gone too far.'

John wondered at her logic, which placed cheating a minor landowner out of his small manor as a worse crime than treachery and sedition in repeatedly supporting the rebellious attempts of Prince John to unseat their rightful king.

'This places me in a difficult position, Matilda,' he said gravely as they reached the corner of Martin's Lane. 'My duty as a law officer obliges me to apprehend all outlaws and either slay them or bring them to the gallows. Now I am being petitioned to seek a royal pardon for these men, yet I cannot approach them other than to arrest them.'

Matilda saw no problem in this. 'As you have no idea where they are, how can you even consider trying to arrest them? That does not affect your ability to seek some resolution of the scandal from Winchester or London.'

As they reached their door, she added grimly, 'When I next see Richard, I will speak my mind to him in no uncertain way. And I'll get the whole truth out of him about how he came to have a share of this Hempston place.'

'And I need to find out much more before I go haring off to the Chief Justiciar,' muttered her husband. 'What in hell this has to do with three murdered guild masters, I just do not know.'

* * *

By next morning it had warmed up considerably, but a depressing winter rain was falling from a grey sky, washing away the remnants of the snow. John went up to his bleak chamber in the castle gatehouse and chewed over the recent events with Gwyn and Thomas, who had just returned from his early duties in the cathedral.

'God's guts, fancy Nick's woman living here in the city as bold as brass,' observed Gwyn. 'Can't you get her hanged for that, Crowner?'

John gave a rare grin as he shook his head. 'It's no crime, she's not the outlaw. And even if it was, Matilda would skin me alive if I as much as harmed a hair of her head, she's almost adopted this Joan as a daughter.'

The thought suddenly came to him that maybe that was not too far from the truth. They had had no children, and given the little time John had spent at home with his wife over the past seventeen years it was not surprising – especially as for many a year now, their marital bed had been used solely for sleeping.

'So what's to be done, master?' asked Thomas, who had listened to the updated tale with interest. 'Are you going to bring this to the notice of Hubert Walter?'

'He should have known all about it, but we've not had a General Eyre visit the county since all this happened three years ago, so the judges would not yet have wind of the fracas in Hempston, even if they were made aware of it, which I doubt they would be. It was before I was made coroner, and with the bloody Count of Mortain nominally the sheriff, followed by Richard de Revelle, I'll wager none of it would have been reported to them anyway.'

That didn't answer Thomas's question about telling the Chief Justiciar, and when he asked again, the coroner sighed.

'I don't know what to do, I'll have to talk it over with the sheriff. My wife will badger me about it from now until kingdom come, but I need to get at the absolute truth first. These outlaws may not be the wronged angels some make them out to be, they could be the usual vicious pack of scum that infest the forests and moors.'

'And what's the connection between them and these murdered burgesses?' grunted Gwyn. 'If this bastard who attacked Lady Matilda hadn't dropped the word Hempston, we'd have no reason to link Nick o' the Moor with the killings.'

His words brought de Wolfe back to what was the more urgent of his investigations. 'Have you any better idea of what that iron spike was and where it came from?' he asked his officer.

Gwyn admitted he had made no progress. 'I feel it must have been part of a railing of some sort. I'll have a wander round the streets later and see if I can spot anything similar.'

John rapped irritably on the table with his fingers. 'I've got the feeling that Joan de Arundell knows more about her husband's whereabouts than she's admitting. She let drop a word or two about him saying how rough the life was up on the moor. I'll wager she has some way of getting in touch with him – and will probably do so now, to tell him that she has been exposed and she is trying to get him a pardon.'

The others considered this possibility. 'How's she going to manage it?' asked Gwyn dubiously.

'There would have to be some arrangement already in place,' observed the astute clerk. 'A rendezvous somewhere on certain days, perhaps?'

'And a go-between – or maybe more than one. There's no way she could go up on the moor herself,' added Gwyn, talking himself into agreeing with them.

John nodded. 'Neither would the cousin risk herself. The only other person is the manservant, an oldish fellow with a deformed face – but he looks fit and active enough.'

'We can hardly watch him day in, day out,' objected Thomas. 'And we might be totally wrong about the whole idea anyway.'

Gwyn stood up and reached for his worn leather jerkin which hung from a peg driven between the stones of the wall. 'I'll have a wander round the town – you never know what gossip I may pick up. I'll keep an eye out for that spike and see if any of the gatekeepers know of this servant.'

John thought it was a long shot and that Gwyn's investigations would undoubtedly be centred on a succession of city taverns, but he had no better suggestions and left the draughty chamber for the more comfortable room of the sheriff, where over a cup of good wine, he could inform de Furnellis of the latest twist in this tortuous tale.

Chapter Ten

In which Crowner John rides to Dartmoor

Part of Gwyn's expedition was to prove successful, but his intention of trying to match the metal rod that had killed the candlemaker was overtaken by events. Towards noon, John de Wolfe was making for his house, his mind on what Mary might have cooked for his dinner. Both he and Matilda were enthusiastic eaters and food played an important part in their lives. He allowed Mary a liberal allowance for her housekeeping and she was a seasoned hand at the market, as well as being a good cook. Soon after dawn each day, she would take her basket around the stalls and booths in Carfoix and Southgate Street and judiciously choose the best meats, fish and vegetables that were on offer. When he had broken his fast with gruel, boiled eggs and bread in her kitchen-shed early that morning, she said she had bought a fine hare for dinner and now he looked forward to having it boiled in its own blood, with red wine, lemon, onions and cloves.

This pleasant reverie was rudely ended when he saw his brother-in-law coming along the High Street towards him, just as they both reached the narrow entrance to Martin's Lane.

'I was just coming to see you, John,' he brayed, and brandished what looked like a short lance in the coroner's face. As they turned towards his house, John saw that Richard was grasping an iron rod seemingly identical to the one that had been stuck through the eye of Robert de Hokesham.

'Where the devil did you get this?' he demanded, taking the rusty metal from him.

'You may well invoke Satan, John,' cried Richard, with a touch of panic. 'It came from the side gate of my house in North Gate Street. And the one alongside it is missing, no doubt pulled out by the murdering swine to use on your candlemaker.'

Somewhat reluctantly, John took him into the house, and they stood in the small vestibule to examine the rod more closely. As Richard had claimed, it was the exact twin of the one used in St Bartholomew's churchyard.

'The gate is made of an oaken frame with holes top and bottom, into which half a dozen of these stout rods are fixed,' gabbled his brother-in-law. 'The gate must be old, and the bars are loose enough to be lifted out.' He grabbed at John's arm. 'I tell you, this proves that the killing was meant to be linked to me! Just as the first corpse was dumped in my college, then the next was Pomeroy's glazier. Matilda's assailant was telling the truth, God blast him – that bastard de Arundell is playing with us, telling us that we might be next. You must do something, John!'

Just then, the inner door to the hall jerked open and Matilda stood there, looking like some Old Testament prophet on Judgment Day.

'Richard. I thought I heard your voice,' she grated. 'Come inside, I have much to say to you.'

Behind his bemused brother-in-law, John grinned to himself as he anticipated the tongue-lashing that Richard was going to get from his sister.

It was almost worth the delay in sitting down to his jugged hare.

Though Gwyn had failed to find the depradations to

the gate of de Revelle's yard, he had made a fortunate discovery about Maurice, Gillian le Bret's servant. The Cornishman had visited a few alehouses and toured some streets looking for suitable iron rods. One fellow – a drinker in the Anchor Inn – was acquainted with the servant at the le Bret house, who also patronised that tavern. Although he knew nothing of Maurice's comings and goings, he described the man graphically.

'Like a beanpole he is, tall and thin. Got this curse all down his face, poor sod. A great thick, purple patch – they say his mother must have been frightened by the devil when she was a-carrying of him.'

Gwyn had intended speaking to the porters at each of the city's five gates and now he had a better description of his quarry. As anyone going to Dartmoor would probably choose either the West or the North Gate, he tried those first and struck gold at the second attempt. At the top of North Gate Street he spoke to one of the gatekeepers, who was one of his hundreds of drinking acquaintances across the city. The fellow's job was to open and close the great doors at dawn and dusk, as well as to collect tolls from those who were bringing goods or beasts into the city. Without hesitation, he said he knew Maurice Axeworthy.

'Who doesn't, poor sod?' he exclaimed. 'Hardly miss him, with a face like that. Often riding through here, he is.'

Gwyn felt a tingle of excitement, as it was unusual for a mere house servant to have the frequent use of a horse to leave the city. Further questioning revealed that Gillian le Bret's man had for some weeks been in the habit of riding out early every Monday morning and returning later the same day.

'Reckon he must be going to visit a sick relative or something, maybe up Crediton way?' hazarded the porter.

Gwyn hurried back to Rougemont with his news and

found his master in the hall of the keep, maliciously regaling the sheriff with an account of the verbal drubbing his wife had given to her brother that dinnertime.

'By Saint Peter's nose, didn't she let him have it,' he said with ill-concealed glee. 'Her tongue is sharp enough when she spears me with it, but for him, she dipped it in acid as well!'

Matilda had released all her pent-up disillusion and indignation at her brother's incessant wrongdoings which for years, she now realised, had blighted her life. This time, her extraordinary affection for her new friend Joan de Arundell had heightened her exasperation and she had torn into Richard.

As de Revelle escaped from her tirade, she had hurled final threats at him and demanded that he undo the damage he and Henry de la Pomeroy had wreaked on the unfortunate de Arundells.

'You had best hurry, for my husband is about to petition Hubert Walter, and perhaps the king himself, for restitution of their manor – and retribution on you grasping pair of villains.' With this final barb, she had slammed the door on him, then promptly gone back into the hall, where she threw herself into a chair and burst into tears.

When de Wolfe had finished telling the sheriff his dramatic story, he turned to his officer. Gwyn told him of his discoveries about Maurice Axeworthy, and together with Henry de Furnellis, they discussed how they might use the information to their advantage.

'I'm sure this fellow meets someone out there in the country, so that news can pass back and forth between them,' claimed John. 'If we can follow this Maurice, we might be led to where Nicholas and his gang hide out.'

'A force of soldiers large enough to capture them would never be able to track men over open country,' objected the sheriff. 'They'd just melt away as soon as they spotted anyone following them.'

De Wolfe agreed. 'I'm not proposing a confrontation in the first instance,' he said. 'But if one or two of us could shadow this messenger, he may lead us to where they have their camp. Then we can return with enough of Ralph Morin's men-at-arms to overpower them and find out the truth about this alleged seizure of their manor – and see if our murderer is amongst them.'

'This servant can hardly be going deep into the moor,' observed Henry. 'Your porter says he goes out in the morning and is back before dusk. That must mean he meets someone on the way.'

'It's always on Monday,' Gwyn reminded them. 'That's the day after tomorrow.'

'Then the sooner the better,' grunted De Wolfe. 'This is a task just for you and me, Gwyn. We'll leave the little clerk to his devotions and his parchments.'

Knowing that Maurice always left by the North Gate – if he indeed was making a trip this week – his two trackers rode out early and concealed themselves in a clump of trees several miles beyond the city but, within sight of the first fork in the road. Straight on was Crediton, an unlikely destination for someone aiming for the high moor. Sure enough, when the tall horseman with the stained face passed by, he turned left, aiming west for Dunsford. His horse was a palfrey, a favourite with ladies, and this one had distinctive dappled grey markings.

They allowed him to get a considerable distance ahead before following. Both John and Gwyn had discarded their usual big steeds as being too conspicuous and had hired a pair of docile rounseys from Andrew's stables. At Dunsford, they asked a shepherd driving a flock towards them whether he had seen 'their friend' on the road, a man with a discoloured face, and were told that he was not more than half a mile ahead of them. Reassured that he had not already vanished into the woods, they carried on at the same pace and eventually came into Moretonhampstead, a village about twelve miles from Exeter. It was almost a small town, a busy place with a stock market and a few taverns that were thronged with freeman smallholders, horse traders and tinners.

'This Maurice knows me, so I'll keep out of the way,' said de Wolfe, as they reined in at the edge of the straggle of cottages and shacks. 'Leave your horse with me and go around the alehouses to see if you can spot that dappled palfrey.'

Ten minutes later, his officer was back, wiping his luxuriant moustaches with the back of his hand. 'Found him easy enough, in the inn with the sign of the plough outside. He's in a corner, eating a pie and talking head to head with a big, rough-looking fellow.' Gwyn pointed back to the village, which was spread around a cross-roads. The tavern was a large thatched hut, almost on the corner of the road that went up towards Chagford.

'Would you know this other man again?' demanded de Wolfe.

Gwyn nodded. 'He's young, not above twenty, I reckon. And a thatch of ginger hair, brighter than mine, a real red-knob he is!'

John chewed his lip in indecision. 'Do we follow this one? Did he seem just a casual drinking mate, or are they meeting on purpose?'

'I've a gut feeling it's the real thing, Crowner. They were muttering close together, as if they wanted to keep their talk to themselves.'

'Right, get back in the saddle and hang around there until this ginger fellow leaves. We'll have to track him as best we can, though God knows it will be difficult once he leaves the road.'

And difficult it proved to be, following a horseman in open country without giving themselves away. They had had to wait for half an hour, until the carrot-haired man emerged and trotted off on a sturdy moorland pony. John and Gwyn split up, keeping just out of sight of each other, then alternating their positions in respect of the presumed outlaw so that he would not glimpse the same man every time if they inadvertently came within his view. For a couple of miles they were on a proper road, the one that ran southwards to Ashburton, but then the distant man turned right on to a track that went to the hamlet of North Bovey.

When they reached the village, there was no sign of him, and a boy herding goats at the side of the road said that no one had passed by in the last hour. Cursing, they wheeled around and, almost in desperation, took the only side track a quarter of a mile back. This led through trees to a bare heathland and Gwyn was able to find some hoofprints in a boggy area where water was still oozing back into the cavities.

'Trodden very recently, I reckon,' he grunted. 'He must have come this way.'

Cautiously, they followed the track which began to climb on to the moor, a land of bare ridges with valleys which were filled with a patchwork of woods, waste and strip fields. As they went a mile or so beyond the village, now seen down below, the track became little more than a beaten path, with scrub and bushes on each side. Though it was not raining, a thin mist hung over the countryside and the higher parts of the moor were lost in grey cloud. Gwyn and the coroner rode cautiously, their eyes straining for a glimpse of the man ahead, and their hands never far from the hilts of their swords.

After another two miles or so, the landscape grew bleaker as they rose towards the upper plateau of Dartmoor. The mist thickened into wreathing shapes as the breeze whispered through dead grass. Eventually, the path dipped steeply down into a combe along the bottom of which ran a clear stream; bushes, dead brambles and some stunted trees filled the glen. As they splashed through the brook, Gwyn, who was in the lead on this narrow path, suddenly stopped and whipped out his sword with a hiss of steel. A man on a short-legged moorland pony had moved out from behind the bushes and now confronted them. It was not the ginger youth they had been following, but suddenly he also appeared behind the first fellow, an older man with unkempt dark hair. The redhead jabbed a finger at them and spoke excitedly.

'That's them, Philip. Been following Maurice and then me all the way from Exeter.'

So much for our clever plan, thought John as he hauled out his own sword. The two men who confronted them kept at a distance and made no move to threaten them. They had daggers in their belts, and the dark one had a short spear across his saddle, but he let it lie there undisturbed.

'Sir John de Wolfe, the crowner?' he asked in a broad, rural accent.

De Wolfe stared at him in surprise. 'How the hell do you know who I am?' he demanded, holding his sword at the ready. 'And what do you want? Who are you anyway?'

The man smiled thinly. 'A lot of questions, Crowner! Old Maurice told Peter here who you were, though God knows how you got on to him. And I am Philip Girard, once a huntmaster in happier times.'

He was a thin, haggard man of about John's age, the skin of his face looking as if it had been dried over an open fire. He wore a tattered leather jerkin over worsted breeches and an open cloak of frayed moleskin with a round hood. John noticed that he had a hunting horn on his belt, as well as the dagger and a short sword.

The coroner gruffly acknowledged his identity. 'And this is my officer, Gwyn of Polruan. Now, are you proposing to prevent us from continuing our journey?' he added with a hint of sarcasm.

Girard grinned. 'And just where were you proposing

to journey to, sir? With no one to follow?' He pulled the horn from his belt and gave a long double blast that echoed around the banks of the little glen.

'What's that for?' demanded Gwyn aggressively, waving his sword at the huntsman.

'You'll see in a moment, sirs. Until then, can I invite you to follow us for a few miles? The choice is yours, you can turn back now, if you wish.'

Gwyn flushed and moved his horse forwards a few feet towards the speaker. 'Don't tell us what we can or can't do. I'll cut your bloody head off if you don't get out of the way!'

'Hold fast a moment, Gwyn,' called de Wolfe, then directed his piercing gaze at Girard. 'Am I right in thinking that you are one of de Arundell's outlaws?'

'I am one of Sir Nicholas's men, yes,' admitted the man, emphasising the noble title of his leader. 'He has been hoping to have the chance to talk to you, as long as it was on equal terms . . . Though I never thought we would come across you in this fashion. Maybe it is the will of God.'

'Equal terms?' snapped John. 'I am a law officer and you and your master have been legally declared outwith that law. The only true terms would be for me to lead you back to the gallows in Exeter on the end of a rope.'

Philip Girard smiled wanly. 'That won't be happening today, Crowner.' He gave another single mournful blast on his horn, and almost immediately three men on horseback burst through the bushes. Muffled in ragged clothes, they were a menacing trio, bearded and long-haired.

'You are still welcome to come or go, Sir John, but I doubt even fighters with such a doughty reputation as you and your squire would prevail against we five, if you contemplated arresting us.'

John was intrigued by the situation, sharing little of Gwyn's truculent indignation at being ambushed.

'So what are you proposing, eh?'

Girard, who was obviously the senior member of this bunch, answered for all of them. 'We know from Maurice, when he comes each week to Moreton, that Lady Joan wants her husband to take our predicament to the highest authorities. Sir Nicholas ardently wishes to explain everything to you in person, but could not devise a way of bringing this about. Now you seem to have taken the matter into your own hands.'

Gwyn was still smarting from being outmanoeuvred by the outlaws. 'We followed your carrot-knob to discover your hideout, so that we could return with a troop of men-at-arms to flush you out,' he growled.

All the men grinned at this. 'It's been tried more than once,' retorted the ginger youth. 'But have you ever tried catching a ferret in a cornfield?'

De Wolfe kept to the main issue. 'So you want us to come and talk to Nicholas de Arundell, is that it?'

The former huntsman inclined his head. 'As a matter of honour – and we still have that left, in spite of every misfortune that has been heaped upon us – we swear that we will conduct you to him and see that you return safely.'

John looked acoss at Gwyn, 'It's up to you, you can turn back if you wish. But we came to find Nick o' the Moor and now we are being offered guides to that very end.'

Gwyn seemed to accept his master's confidence and he settled back into his usual amiable humour. He slid his sword back into its scabbard. 'Very well, as long as they've got something to eat and drink in their den, wherever it is.'

The atmosphere suddenly lightened, and John also sheathed his weapon. 'We'll come with you, then, on those terms. How long a journey will it be, for it looks as if we'll not get back to Exeter this day?'

'More than an hour from here, sir. We can feed and

bed you for the night, primitive as it might be. Though I'm sure that will be no novelty to the pair of you.' He pulled his pony around and led the way along the path, the other four outlaws falling in behind Gwyn and de Wolfe.

'We must soon leave this track and cut across country,' said Girard. 'My friends and I are not popular with villagers and smallholders in these parts.' He smiled rather sadly. 'Neither would I be pleased if my hens and goats vanished and the cabbages disappeared from my croft.'

They struck off up the valley and followed the stream, then went through woodland until they came out on the lower slopes of a bare hill with strangely rounded rocks on the top.

'That must be Easdon Down, where we fought last year,' muttered Gwyn, as he recognised the scene of a fight against a different band of outlaws. The man in front continued around the base of the down, and once again they plunged into the forest, avoiding a small village on their left.

Philip Girard rode his pony without saddle or stirrups, with just a folded blanket over the beast's back and a bridle to control it. Even so, he kept up a fair pace given the difficult terrain, especially when they were in dense woodland.

'Is it much further?' demanded Gwyn, seeing another and much higher barren hill appear in front of them. Their guide turned and pointed ahead.

'We're passing Heathercombe Down, then we'll go between King Tor and Hamel Down. A mile beyond that and we're there.'

They left the trees and climbed up across desolate moorland, the east wind now catching them again, blowing wreaths of thin cloud across the upper slopes. Reaching a saddle between two high bluffs, they began descending towards a distant valley, but before they reached it, they crossed an odd structure.

'What the hell's this place?' asked Gwyn, his Celtic sensitivity tuned to some ancient vibrations. In the bowl of moorland between the two bluffs, a waist-high wall of blackened moorstones made an almost perfect circle, a bow-shot across. The stones were in a double line and the remains of a ditch lay outside the circle. Dotted around inside were the remains of small round huts, most with stone doorposts and some with angled entrance passages. Three or four had rough roofs of branches and turf, though these seemed to have been added recently. Girard stopped his horse at the far side, where there was a flagstoned entrance to the compound.

'This is Grimspound, an ancient village,' he said. 'Far older than Christ's birth, so the wise men say, though how they can tell, I don't know. The folk that used to live in the place we use now, claimed it's haunted and certainly most people down the valley wouldn't come near here at night, for fear of seeing the little folk.'

They jogged on, riding down steeply from the mysterious stone camp into the main valley, but John was still intrigued.

'Who put roofs on some of those huts?' he questioned.

'A couple were made by passing tinners, as a shelter when caught by bad weather, but we repaired some others as a refuge should some large force come against us in Challacombe,' he replied.

John had heard of Challacombe but never been near it, as it was in a remote part of the moor. At the bottom of the slopes they reached a track that ran southwards down a valley through which a stream babbled. On each side were high bare hills and at the bottom, alongside the brook, a few sparse trees grew. The old huntsman took them about half a mile farther, as the wind dropped and the mist crept down from the moor.

'That's where we live, if you can call it living,' said Philip Girard bitterly. He pointed across the stream where, beyond a thin copse of stunted, black trees, the irregular outlines of some low, crude buildings could be seen behind an old wall. In single file, they rode towards them and crossed the stream over a rough bridge of fallen logs. As they approached the enclosure, men came out through a gap in the surrounding walls and waited for them to dismount.

'That's Sir Nicholas, our lord,' murmured Girard to the coroner, indicating the figure standing in the middle of the small group, staring at the newcomers. John saw a stocky man in his mid thirties, dressed in much the same type of clothing as his men. A leather jerkin and worsted breeches seemed the most practical garb for living in these wild conditions. Girard dismounted and hurried ahead to explain to his master what had happened.

De Wolfe stepped forward, as did Nicholas de Arundell, so that they met on the patch of rough ground that separated the two groups.

'You are welcome, Sir John,' said Nicholas in his deep voice. 'I only wish it was in more civilised surroundings.'

The two men weighed each other up, making no move to grasp each other's arm in greeting. John took in de Arundell's strong, rather stubborn features, but Nicholas held his gaze unwaveringly. The younger man recognised an even tougher character, de Wolfe's dark face carrying the stamp of grim resolve and determination.

'We are both old Crusaders, I understand?' grunted de Wolfe. 'We never met in Outremer, which is hardly surprising given the chaos and turmoil we all suffered.'

'I was delayed for almost a year in Sicily, fighting another war,' explained Nicholas. 'But we have other matters to discuss first, so please come into our shelter, which at least will be warm and where we can feed you.'

As they walked into the compound where the stone shacks were built, the former steward, Robert Hereward, made himself known. Then Philip Girard introduced Gwyn to the other men. Inside the largest of the huts, the fire had been built up to defeat the cold outside; though the fumes seeking to escape through the gaps under the thatch prickled the men's eyeballs. Daylight from the open door and the flames gave enough illumination for the visitors to see the sparse furnishings and the piles of bracken where some of the men slept. At Nicholas's invitation, they sat at the trestle table and from the other end, the old woman shuffled forward, carrying some wooden bowls and a loaf of bread.

'This is Gunilda, the most important member of our tribe,' said Nicholas. 'She keeps us fed and moderately clean, God bless her.'

The woman put her load on the table and nodded at the visitors, before going to the firepit to take a blackened cauldron off the stones near the edge. After she had ladled out a thick vegetable potage into their bowls, the other men crowded round with their own pots and dishes, then went to sit or crouch around the fire to eat.

'There'll be venison later on,' promised Hereward. 'Peter Cuffe, our best archer, got a hind yesterday down towards Widecombe. That's a hanging offence, I know, but you can't be hanged more than once!'

There was a guffaw of laughter from the outlaws; Gunilda distributed more hunks of bread to them and went back for the ale pitcher.

De Wolfe, who had been silently taking in the situation, began asking questions of de Arundell.

'Are these all your company?'

'They are, apart from a lookout down the valley. We are now only twelve men – and a woman.'

'And this is your permanent home?' asked John.

'At present, though we have several smaller hideouts scattered over the moor. We need to be able to vanish within minutes if anyone comes against us.'

Gwyn raised his head from his soup bowl. 'Does that ever happen?' he asked.

Robert Hereward, also sitting at the table, answered with a nod. 'Yes, but not often, thank God. A year ago, a large gang of desperate men from over the Tavistock end of the moor took it into their heads to finish us off, but we melted away and they achieved nothing but wrecking this place. It is poor, but soon mended.'

De Wolfe picked up the ale pot which Gunilda placed before him.

'So no law officers have come against you?'

Nicholas shook his head. 'Not for a long time, thank God. In the earlier days, Richard de Revelle tried to pursue us here with the excuse that he was sheriff, but he sent only a few men and we soon lost them in the wildness of the moor.'

'This place is very remote, being near the centre of Dartmoor,' added Philip Girard. 'There is often bad weather and it is easy to evade those clodhoppers who march up the valley. Our sentinel spots them in plenty of time and we just vanish.'

There was a pause, then the coroner spoke again. The tone of the meeting changed perceptibly and the other men around the hut listened attentively, for possibly their lives depended upon what was to be said.

'You must understand that as a senior law officer, I should not be here, except to arrest you all or strike off your heads. But I have heard certain things about you, which I need to investigate further.' He paused and looked sternly around the ring of faces seen dimly in the poor light. 'Officially, I am not here – understand?'

There was a muttered chorus of agreement.

'Now, I need to know exactly what happened at your former manor – and what has transpired since then.' He took a gulp of ale and looked expectantly at Nicholas de Arundell.

The blue eyes in a handsome, rather flushed face looked

back at him steadily. 'I will start at the beginning, Crowner. Probably like your own family, we Arundells came over at the time of William's conquest, and settled mainly in Sussex and the West Country. The Bastard gave much land to Roger, the first of the Arundells down here in the west, most of it in Somerset and Devon, though lately many of the family have settled in Cornwall.'

'Sensible people,' grunted Gwyn.

'His son Robert was my grandfather,' continued Nicholas. 'He gave Roger's name to my father, who acquired the manor of Hempston, near Totnes, from the descendants of Judhael who was granted all the land thereabouts by the Conqueror.'

'How did your father come by it?' asked de Wolfe, who wanted to exclude any false title to the land before they went any further.

'It was all quite legitimate,' answered Nicholas, anticipating the coroner's caution. 'He was left land in Somerset by my grandfather and he exchanged it for Hempston, which was part of the adjacent Pomeroy estate. The bargain was sealed with a witnessed deed in the proper way.'

'Where is that deed now?'

The noble outlaw's face darkened. 'If I know de Revelle and Henry de la Pomeroy, the parchment is ash scattered to the winds by now. It was in my chest at Hempston, but when I had to run for my life, I had no chance to recover such things.'

John looked over the horn spoon that he was dipping into his stew. 'Such a deed of transfer for such a significant item as a manor would have a copy lodged in the Chancery in Winchester or London. But carry on with your tale, sir.'

'When my father died some eight years ago, I inherited the manor as his only son. I married Joan and all was well for a few years until I decided to take the Cross and go off to Palestine.'

He paused and rubbed his forehead in some anguish. 'If I had stayed at home, none of this would have happened. I sometimes wonder why God called me to the Holy Land, then stabbed me in the back after I went.'

De Wolfe gave one of his throat clearings, this time intended to convey sympathy. 'Why indeed? Why did any of us go, for there was little booty to be gained, unless it was for our souls?'

'My father was always keen on my supporting the Pope when he declared a Crusade. He had been on the ill-fated one in the forties. Anyway, go I did and was away almost three years. When I got back, that bastard de Revelle and his crony at Berry Pomeroy had annexed Hempston, claiming that I had been assumed dead and that the land had reverted to the original freeholders.'

'Why should they consider you dead?' demanded the coroner.

'Because it suited their purpose,' snapped Nicholas, banging the table and making the ale pots rattle. 'I had twice sent messages home to my wife, written by our chaplain, as I have no skill with letters. But I later learnt that one certainly never arrived, as the friend to whom I had entrusted it was shipwrecked off Italy. God knows what happened to the other; I have never heard since of the knight who promised to deliver it.'

'Then what?' prompted John, as his host seemed to go into a gloomy reverie at these evil memories.

'Almost three years ago, having arrived by ship at Dartmouth, I arrived unannounced at my manor. I found the house occupied by strangers, my wife gone, and my steward and reeve replaced by men from Berry.' He looked across at the dour Robert Hereward. 'He can tell you better what had happened, Crowner.'

The older man nodded and leaned forwards across the table. 'Three months before my lord came home, a group of horsemen rode up to the manor house one day and confronted Lady Joan and myself. They were led by Henry de la Pomeroy, Lord of Berry, and Richard de Revelle, who at that time was not yet the sheriff.'

He stopped and shook his head as if trying to rid himself of the memory. 'They said that Sir Nicholas was dead, so that the manor now escheated to the tenant-in-chief – John, Count of Mortain – who had decreed that Hempston would in future be held by the former freeholders, the Pomeroys.'

There was a murmur of anger from the men around; though they knew the sad tale backwards, it never failed to stir their emotions.

'So how did de Revelle come into this?' asked Gwyn.

'No one mentioned it at the time, but later it seems that Henry de la Pomeroy and Richard de Revelle made some deal with each other, to divide up the revenues of Hempston between them. Anyway, I was thrown out and a bailiff from Revelstoke, Richard's main manor near Plympton, was installed for a time – then Pomeroy's man Ogerus Coffin arrived, and he remains there to this day, God curse his guts!'

'And my wife was also turned out,' snarled Nicholas, returning to the story. 'Those two swine declared her a widow, though she had no proof of it except my absence in Outremer and my silence. They even had the bloody gall to offer her some damned Pomeroy cousin as a husband, the bait being that she could then stay on in Hempston as the new lady of the manor.'

'So what did she do?' asked de Wolfe, impressed by the sincerity of the outlaw's complaints.

'Joan is a spirited woman, right enough. It seems she told them to go to hell and take their miserable cousin with them.'

'The lady actually spat in Pomeroy's face,' said Hereward with some relish. 'She screamed and raved at them and tried to get us servants to attack them, but it was hopeless. They had men-at-arms and a whole crowd of retainers to manhandle us out of the hall. I ended up living with Martin there, in the reeve's cottage – though he wasn't the reeve any longer. They imported their own from de Revelle's place near Tiverton and built him a new house.'

Gunilda came around with her jug to refill their pots. 'I lived in Totnes at the time,' she said indignantly. 'Not a word of the real truth reached there, all that was said was that Sir Nicholas had died on Crusade and that Lady Joan had sold up the manor and gone back to Cornwall.'

De Arundell took a deep drink and moodily continued his saga. 'They were right in that she went back to Cornwall, for she had nowhere else to go. She threw herself on the mercy of her second cousin, Humphrey de Arundell of Trefry, who has been good enough to support her.'

John de Wolfe scratched at his bristly face and scowled at his host. 'But we have not come to an explanation of why you are now outlawed,' he said bluntly.

'I arrived at Hempston with only a few attendants, my squire Philip Girard there and a couple of men.' He waved at the lean, wiry fellow with the horn at his belt. 'Philip had been the chief huntsman at the manor and came with me to Palestine. Like your man Gwyn here, he has been a constant and faithful companion to me.'

'That was a terrible day, it still haunts me in my dreams,' contributed Girard. 'We expected a rapturous welcome – and all we got was black disaster.'

Nicholas nodded in agreement. 'In my hall, I looked for my wife and her tire-women – and was met by a total stranger, this bailiff, who claimed we were impostors and threatened to have us whipped out of the village. Some of the old servants were hanging back behind him, too afraid to come forward and greet us.'

'We tried to throw him out,' said Philip Girard. 'But he hollered for help and half a dozen strangers ran in and forcibly pushed us out of the house and into the road outside the stockade, threatening to cut our throats if we tried to come in again.'

'I saw a horseman ride out as if the devil was after him,' added Nicholas. 'I later learned that he had been sent to Berry Castle, to warn the Pomeroys of our return. By now, some of our villagers had come around the gate, attracted by the noise. Robert Hereward was one and he told us what had happened, so we went back to the reeve's house to recover our wits.'

The rest of the story came out, a catalogue of deceit and violence. While the shaken Crusaders sat taking some food and ale in Martin's cottage, a force arrived from Berry. Henry de la Pomeroy was the leader, and brought with him not only his steward, castellan and a score of men, but also Richard de Revelle, who had been staying with him at Berry.

De Wolfe, working out the time-scale, strongly suspected that this must have happened during the very period when the two malcontents were plotting to join the rebellion of Prince John against the captured king languishing in Germany. But Nicholas and his men were still describing what had happened at Hempston.

'We confronted them in the compound surrounding my manor house,' he went on. 'I admit I was in a towering rage – and who could blame me? We shouted and abused each other roundly, each becoming more angry with every passing moment. My own men, good Hereward here and Martin and Philip, joined in the shouting, for they had suffered almost as much as me, with the loss of their positions in the manor.'

The haggard steward fervently agreed with his lord. 'This was the first time we had the opportunity to vent our feelings, Crowner,' he said. 'It seemed that at last Sir Nicholas had returned to rid us of these interlopers, so we stood together and trusted that our righteous cause would prevail.'

Nicholas shook his head sadly. 'When the words

became inflamed, then Pomeroy and de Revelle turned nasty and ordered their men to eject us from the village. A riot began, with my men and some more of the villagers turning on the guards from Berry, though they outnumbered us and were better armed. In fact, I and Philip Girard were the only ones wearing swords, as we had just arrived.'

'In a trice, it became violent,' said Robert Hereward. 'We were set upon by these oafs belonging to de la Pomeroy and had to fight back as best we could, with staves and cudgels.' His voice dropped as he recollected that day. 'A fellow came at me with a dagger and I hit him with my staff. He fell, as did others, but this one never got up. He died later of some unlucky damage to his brain.'

'We were being steadily pressed back by the armed men,' declared de Arundell. 'We had no chance of winning and I realised that those devils would either kill us or fabricate some charge against us to get us hanged. They could not afford to do otherwise: if they let us live they would lose their claim to the manor and probably be hauled before the king's justices themselves.'

'So what did you do?' asked John, gripped by the drama of the story.

'When I saw we had no hope of prevailing, I yelled to my men to run for the church. It is built close against the manor house, within the palisade hardly a score of paces away. Some of the other villagers, God bless them, threw themselves in the way of the usurpers for long enough for a few of us to stagger into the porch and slam the door shut. Henry Pomeroy was yelling for us to be dragged out, but our parish priest, old Father Herbert, screamed defiance at them and waved his crucifix in their faces, threatening them with eternal damnation and excommunication if they dared to break sanctuary.'

'Eight of us were in there, all of them here now,' said

Philip Girard, waving his hand around the hut to encompass the faces gazing intently at the storytellers. 'De Revelle and Henry posted their men all around the church and shouted that they would starve us out well before the forty days that we were entitled to hide there.'

'That's against the law,' boomed Gwyn indignantly. 'Sanctuary seekers are entitled to be fed by the village for those forty days.'

'The law was whatever those bastards wanted it to be,' said Martin Wimund. 'We starved and thirsted for three days, as they stopped our people from coming near us . . . even the priest was kept from his own church until he promised not to bring us any aid.'

'Then Pomeroy's bailiff, that arrogant swine Coffin, shouted to us that one of their men was dead and that we were all murderers, with nothing to expect but a hanging when we were dragged out,' continued Hereward. 'I offered to surrender myself, as I was the one who had cracked his head – but my master and the others said that we would all shoulder the blame together.'

There was a growl of agreement from the men as the manor lord took up the story again. 'On the fourth night, we were sorely affected by hunger and thirst – all we had had between us was a pitcher of holy water for filling the stoup. There was nothing to lose, and for once the good Lord was with us, for around midnight we heard the few guards singing drunkenly, as they had been at the ale. By then, the rest had gone back to Berry, thinking that as we were within the stockade around the church and manor house, a few sentries would be sufficient when the gate was closed.'

'So I gather you made your escape that night?' suggested the coroner.

'It was the only choice other than starvation or hanging, especially when later the priest crept up to the door and told us that half the guards were fast asleep.

Then the good old man set fire to the thatch of one of the privies on the other side of the house, and in the confusion we just ran for the gate, beat up the one sentry left there and ran like hell out of the village into the night.'

'Thus putting yourself outside the law,' observed de Wolfe, not without sympathy.

Nicholas smiled wryly. 'There was no way we were going back to the Hundred Court in Totnes to answer charges. That would only have ended in a hanging, with de la Pomeroy and de Revelle the most powerful lords in the district.'

'So in due course, I presume that when you failed to answer four times to your attachments to the county court, you were all declared exigent?' concluded John. 'And here you are now, outlawed and at the mercy of any man who wishes to claim five shillings for your wolf's head.'

Robert Hereward nodded ruefully. 'They've got to catch us first. But I'm getting too old to live like a badger on the moor, skulking from one hole to another. This place is not too bad, but before we came here six months ago, we lived like rats.'

Gwyn looked around the hut. 'You said eight of you left Hempston – so where did the others come from?'

Nicholas looked around the hut at his faithful band. 'Two more from the village eventually ran away to join us; they were unmarried and weary of the oppressive ways of this bailiff. The others, including Mother Gunilda, drifted here for refuge – and very welcome they have been. Others have come and gone over the years, a few found living on the moor too arduous for them and slunk away, God knows where.'

The tale was now told, and de Wolfe sat back thoughtfully to digest what he had heard. 'One reason that I needed to seek you out,' he said grimly, 'was the matter of some bizarre killings in Exeter recently. Have you heard anything of those?'

Nicholas looked mystified and shook his head. John realised that he had not yet had a chance to hear any news from his wife from Peter Cuffe, who would have collected any messages from the servant Maurice. De Wolfe briefly described the slaying of the three guildsmen and then rounded off his narrative with an account of the attack on Matilda and the accusations made by her assailant.

De Arundell seemed genuinely shocked. 'I can scarcely credit this, Sir John. My wife last week sent me news that your wife had kindly befriended her – and now to hear that some swine has so badly used her! That's terrible.'

'It was indeed,' growled de Wolfe. 'But what of this claim the bastard made that he was avenging Hempston? The only thing to be read into that is that he was one of your band here.'

Nicholas was clearly aghast at this suggestion, and the growls from the men around showed that they were equally horrified.

'Impossible! No one here would do that – and anyway, what chance would they get of wandering around Exeter intent on mayhem and murder?' Nicholas avoided mentioning that he had entered the city with little trouble.

'So why should he say such a thing?' persisted John. 'Why would he want to link his attacks with de Revelle and Pomeroy, then claim it was for Hempston, unless he was connected with you?'

Nicholas, his face flushed with anger, stood up and faced his own followers. Gunilda stopped in the middle of bringing more bread and watched the tense scene with her hand to her mouth.

'Have any of you anything to tell me about this?' Nicholas demanded, glaring around the ring of faces. 'The coroner would not tell us anything other than the truth, so how can this be explained?'

There was silence, each man looking at his fellows with a mixture of apprehension and suspicion. 'I can't believe any of us are involved,' replied Robert Hereward. 'Could it be one of those men who used to be here, but have now gone?'

'What men have left, over the years you have been outlawed?' asked the coroner, as this seemed a reasonable possibility. There was an immediate buzz of voices, as this avenue of escape was seized upon.

'Probably six or eight have joined us and then drifted away,' said Martin Wimund. 'Mostly those who came from elsewhere, though several were originally Hempston villagers.'

There were murmurs of agreement around the room and one older man spoke up. 'That blacksmith, James de Pessy, he was a bad lot. Then there was William de Leghe, who thieved from us – but he had the phthisis badly and his chest could not stand the damp, so he's probably long dead by now.'

Several other men were mentioned, including a thatcher, Walter Lovetrot, who had stabbed another man and then run off into the hills.

'What happened to these other men?' asked Gwyn.

Robert Hereward shrugged. 'God knows, but several who went said that they were going to walk to distant towns like Bristol and Southampton and try their luck at staying undetected. As long as they were not identified as outlaws, they could claim their freedom after a year and a day.'

'Why d'you say this blacksmith was a bad lot?' queried the coroner.

'He was a freeman who had come from somewhere a few years earlier and set up a forge in the village. Always protesting and complaining about something, he was a pain in the arse. Though he joined us in our fight and was outlawed with the rest of us, he never stopped whining about the loss of his forge. One day, he said he'd had enough and just walked away. He was one of those who said he was going to try to settle elsewhere, maybe in Brittany.'

John tried to get a description of him, but the result was so vague as to be useless. 'Just a man in his thirties with dark hair,' was the best he could extract from the gang. The same applied to Walter Lovetrot, the murderous thatcher, so de Wolfe turned to another matter.

'This man who died, you swear it was not a deliberate killing?' he demanded sternly.

Robert Hereward leaned forward again. 'It was a free-for-all fight, sir. They were hitting the hell out of us and we were flailing around in response. This fellow pulled a knife on me and I swung at him with a stave. I've done it before and caused nothing but a sore head. It was just unfortunate that he must have had a thin skull or some such.'

'And as this was more than two years ago, before the coroners were introduced, there would have been no inquest,' mused de Wolfe. 'Was the sheriff involved in this at all?'

Nicholas de Arundell shrugged his broad shoulders. 'Hard for us to know, Crowner, being tucked away up here in Dartmoor. But we never heard any more of it, so I think Pomeroy and de Revelle kept their heads well down over the whole affair, so as not to draw attention to their misdeeds.'

'The sheriff then would have been the one before Richard de Revelle – and guess who that was?' cut in Gwyn cynically. 'The Count of bloody Mortain himself.'

De Wolfe nodded. 'Quite so. Though Prince John never showed his face in the county all the years he was supposed to be sheriff, after William Brewer gave up in '79. He left all the work to his serjeants and bailiffs.'

Robert Hereward voiced his continued indignation. 'No wonder the outrage was never challenged. As sheriff, he was hardly likely to condemn what his treacherous supporters had done. De Revelle undoubtedly got the shrievalty handed on to him because of Prince John's patronage.'

'So the whole bloody affair was nicely sewn up between them,' sneered Gwyn. 'I doubt it ever came to the ears of the judges or the Justiciar, let alone the king himself.'

Nicholas sighed and motioned Gunilda to go around again with her jug. 'That's the whole story, Sir John,' he said. 'That's what I get for going off to the Crusades, losing my manor and my wife – and if I'm caught, my very life. To say nothing of my honour and reputation sacrificed in this injustice.'

'What's to be done about it, that's the thing?' said Martin Wimund. 'You are our last and only hope, Crowner.'

There was a tense silence, as all the hardened men looked at de Wolfe, who was turning the situation over in his mind.

'You have lived as fugitives up here on Dartmoor for almost three years, robbing travellers, poaching and stealing from honest men?' he asked harshly.

Nicholas glared at him, sudden suspicion showing on his face. 'What else should we do, starve or freeze to death? If it were not for those bastard swine de Revelle and de la Pomeroy, we would be hard-working, peaceful men, tending our acres down in Hempston.'

Robert Hereward's voice was vibrant with emotion: 'I killed a man without intent when he drew a blade on me during a mêlée, Crowner. I am more than willing to pay the price: I would give myself up to be hanged tomorrow if it would help these others – but it would be futile.' He thumped the table. 'But I swear by Mary, Mother of God and all the saints you wish to name, that we have never killed a single person these past two years. Yes, we have cut purses from fat priests and wealthy merchants – and we have stolen geese, sheep and the occasional deer for Gunilda to cook for our bellies. But that was for survival, nothing else.'

His voice shook with sincerity and John believed him.

Next morning the coroner and his companion were riding back through Dunsford as the bell in the village church tolled for the noon hour. They had spent the night in Challacombe with their outlaw hosts, lying wrapped in their own cloaks on a pile of dried bracken around the firepit. At dawn, after a meagre breakfast provided by Gunilda, Robert Hereward and Martin Wimund had escorted them back over the moor and left them within sight of Bovey.

'So what did you think of all that?' grunted the coroner after they had ridden in silence for a mile.

'Their tale rang very true, Crowner,' answered Gwyn. 'The whole sad story is typical of that bastard Richard de Revelle and that swine Henry de la Pomeroy. He's every bit as bad as his treacherous father, who may be dead, but I don't mind speaking ill of him!'

John's face remained dour, and he remained silent for another few minutes as he assembled his thoughts. 'I too believe what those men told me, and I intend to seek justice for them,' he said finally. 'The stumbling block is that they are undoubtedly outlaws and criminals, having preyed on the population for a couple of years. Every one of their legion of thefts is a capital offence, and even if it were not so, just being outlaws earns them a hanging.'

'But none of that would have happened if it were not for the vile crime that those lords committed,' protested the Cornishman. 'They are victims of circumstance and deserve better than to be stranded on Dartmoor with every man's hand against them.'

'I agree with you,' replied the coroner. 'But though they slipped into becoming a gang of desperate men with little difficulty, finding a solution will be a great deal harder.'

'So what are you going to do about it?' boomed the ever-practical Gwyn.

John leaned back against the cantle of his saddle, easing his back which had stiffened during the ride. He was getting old and soft, he thought, not like the days when he could spend a week on a horse and think nothing of it. He dragged his mind back to the immediate problem.

'Henry de la Pomeroy seems to be the prime instigator of this plot, but my dearly beloved brother-in-law is also very much involved. He is the first person I must confront about this, though my wife has already given him a drubbing over it.'

'But remember, he's the one who is accusing Sir Nicholas of planting that murdered body in his school,' said Gwyn. 'Perhaps he's saying that just as a means of further blackening Arundell's name, as an extra safeguard for keeping him beyond the law.'

John nodded. 'De Revelle will no doubt remember the body, too, when I tackle him about Hempston.'

'You'll get short shrift from that slippery eel,' prophesied Gwyn. 'Whatever you say, he'll twist your words and try to put you in the wrong. But it's bloody daft to think that Nicholas and his men had anything to do with these guild killings.'

'Though the second murder was on the high road near Ashburton – a place that outlaws and footpads habitually haunt in order to attack travellers,' said de Wolfe, playing at devil's advocate himself to tease Gwyn.

'But if you get nowhere with de Revelle, what else can be done?'

They were trudging uphill now, their horses labouring against the gradient of the rutted track.

'I'll go to see Lady Joan again,' answered de Wolfe. 'She has no reason to hide now, for being the wife of an outlaw is no crime. She may be able to tell me something that's of use. But in the circumstances, the only real solution is a royal pardon. Even in the highly unlikely event of de Revelle agreeing to hand back the manor, that still leaves those men outlaws, unless the royal justices feel able to revoke the writ of exigent – or the king grants a pardon.'

Gwyn pulled up the hood of his leather jerkin as they crested the hill and met the full force of an icy wind. 'And how the hell do you get a royal pardon?' he shouted. 'Sail the winter sea to France to seek King Richard?'

'Not in this weather! Nicholas can wait on the moor a few more months. But perhaps I'll take a ride to Winchester to seek Hubert Walter and talk it over with him. Maybe he can offer a pardon on the king's behalf, if he thinks the case is strong enough.' The Chief Justiciar had been in charge of the army in Palestine after the king left for home, and he knew John de Wolfe well – in fact, it was he who had suggested to the Lionheart that John be appointed coroner in Devon. Since the king had left for France again the previous year, Hubert had become the virtual ruler of England, as well as being Archbishop of Canterbury.

They rode on, conversation stalling as they sank their chins into their hoods against the numbing wind. A few more miles and the great twin towers of Exeter's cathedral were in sight, outlined against grey clouds that threatened more snow.

They had missed their dinner, so Gwyn made for the nearest inn as soon as they entered the city and John went home to Martin's Lane, where he could always depend on Mary to find him something substantial to eat in her cook-shed.

chapter eleven

In which Crowner John goes to visit a lady

On Wednesday morning, the coroner rose later than usual; after the long ride across the moors, his back and buttocks ached as if they had been beaten with a pike handle. After eating his morning gruel, bread and salt bacon in Mary's warm hut, he found his cloak and boots and ventured out into the streets. A light covering of snow had fallen during the night. It was barely an inch deep, but the icy breeze kept it from thawing, and his boots made a crisp crunching noise as he walked up to the castle. The passage of men, beasts and wheels would soon churn the snow into a dirty grey paste, but while it was still pristine it was attractive even to the unimaginative de Wolfe, especially as it covered up the filth that lay in the gutters in the middle of the streets.

Up in his chamber, high in the gatehouse, it was freezing as there was no means of having a fire. The floor was wooden and there was no modern hearth or chimney. The tower had been the first place built on the orders of William the Bastard when he demolished forty-eight houses to make room for the castle, immediately after quelling the Saxon rebellion of 1068. Sometimes, one of the guards brought up a charcoal brazier and lit it on a large slab of slate in a corner of the room, but today there was nothing.

Gwyn had abandoned his usual seat on one of the windowsills, as the icy wind was moaning through the narrow gap, having already blown a powdering of snow across the floor. He sat on Thomas's stool at the table, hugging his thick leather jerkin to his chest, his pointed hood sticking up over his untidy red locks.

'Colder than a nun's backside,' he complained. 'I would have gone back to the soldiers' barracks, only I waited to see if you had any orders for me.'

De Wolfe stood a moment, rubbing his hands together and looking at the pile of parchments on the table – unreadable until Thomas came from saying his Masses. John sat for a few minutes attempting to concentrate on the reading lessons the vicar in the cathedral had given him in his lack-lustre attempt to teach John to read. Boredom soon made him seek some excuse to abandon the attempt, and he got up from his bench.

'Too bloody cold to stay here, Gwyn! Makes the heat in the Holy Land seem almost welcome – though when we were there, we yearned for cold weather.' He turned to the staircase. 'Until the little fellow arrives, there's nothing to be done, so let's get to the fire in the hall. I presume there are no new deaths reported overnight?'

The Cornishman shook his head and lumbered over to join him.

'What's to be done today, Crowner?' he enquired as he followed John down the winding steps.

'No court or hangings today, so I thought I would have a word with our good sheriff about Nicholas de Arundell, then go and talk to his wife.'

'What about tackling de Revelle again? You'll have to do that sooner or later.'

With the memory of Matilda's verbal assault still fresh in his mind, John was reluctant to think about that problem, though he knew he would have to challenge his brother-in-law before long. For now, John was content to make Joan de Arundell his next target.

They walked across the inner ward, where the usual crusted mud was temporarily hidden under the thin blanket of snow, and climbed the high wooden steps to the entrance of the keep, whose two storeys squatted on the undercroft which housed the castle gaol and torture chamber.

Inside the hall, crowded even at this early hour, Gwyn made for the firepit, where he could scrounge some food and ale and talk to his many acquaintances, while John headed for the door on the left wall which led into the sheriff's chamber.

Henry de Furnellis was hunched over his fireplace, which did have a chimney running up through the outer wall. 'I'm damned cold, John! My blood must be running thin in my old age,' he complained as de Wolfe joined him. He was still a fit man, if rather lazy – he had once confided to John that after more than forty years fighting for several kings, he felt he now deserved an easier time in his dotage.

Ignoring his chief clerk's pained expression as he surveyed the heap of neglected documents on the sheriff's table, Henry retrieved a wineskin from a shelf, and poured two cups for John and himself.

After they had settled down, hunched on two stools close to the fire, de Wolfe told him of the journey out to Dartmoor and his partial abduction. The sheriff's lugubrious features showed mild surprise.

'The county coroner consorting with outlaws! What's the world coming to?' Then he grinned and topped up John's cup. 'What's to stop me raising a posse and going out there and hanging the lot of them?'

De Wolfe could have retorted that Henry's usual regime of masterly inactivity made that highly unlikely, but he knew that the sheriff was not serious. 'I haven't told you where they are, for one thing. And I promised, as one old Crusader to another, not to reveal it,' he said.

'Though I'll admit, it would take very little enquiry amongst the folk around the edge of the moor to discover their hideout.'

He drank some of the wine and stared into the leaping flames of the burning logs. 'What's to be done about it, that's the thing? That bastard de Revelle has stolen a nice little manor and is getting away with it, thanks to the fact that de Arundell got himself outlawed, through no real fault of his own.'

'You say his steward actually felled this man who died?' asked de Furnellis.

'He swears it was not deliberate, just an unlucky blow during a free-for-all in which they were outnumbered. And I believe him, but of course there was no inquest or any sort of court hearing.'

De Furnellis grunted in disgust. 'And if there had been, who would be the judges down around Totnes? Pomeroy and de Revelle! But what trapped Nicholas was running for sanctuary and then escaping.'

John nodded gloomily. 'That's the problem, Henry. Not answering to their attachments in the county court has put them outside the law and bans him from any attempt at getting legal redress.'

They sat in silence for a moment.

'The king seems the only hope in this matter,' said the sheriff finally. 'I can do nothing, as it was my own county court that made them outlaws – though before I was in office – so I can't turn round now and say it never happened. The writs of exigent will still be lying in the court records.'

John finished his drink and stood up. 'It's not really any of my business, either. All this happened before the office of coroner was set up, so I've no power to look into the death of that man almost three years ago.'

Henry looked up at his friend with a knowing expression. 'But you're going to make it your business, I can tell. How will you set about it?'

De Wolfe hauled his cloak higher and wrapped it around himself before leaving the relative warmth of the chamber. 'It's no good waiting for the next visit of the Commissioners of Gaol Delivery, or even the judges at the next Eyre, whenever that might be. They're not likely to be sympathetic to an outlaw's plight. I'll need to talk to Hubert Walter and see what he can do. I might even have to cross the Channel to seek King Richard, come the spring sailing season.'

Henry rose and walked to the door with him. 'Let me know if there is anything I can do, as I would hate to see that crafty swine de Revelle getting away with this. He's kept it pretty well hidden, for very few people know what happened in Hempston. It was put about that de la Pomeroy bought it back from the so-called widow.'

The coroner left, content at least that de Furnellis was not going to send a contingent of soldiers on to Dartmoor to hunt down Nick o' the Moor and either slay him or drag him back for hanging. John went across the hall, which had become even more crowded as the morning went on, and found Gwyn sitting at a trestle table with a quart of ale which had been sizzled with a red-hot poker. Before him lay a bowl of potage, ladled from a blackened cauldron sitting on an iron tripod at the side of the firepit. The Cornishman was noisily sucking from a wooden spoon with every sign of relish.

'D'you never stop eating, man?' demanded the coroner.

His officer grinned up at him, his red hair sticking out from his head like a hedgehog's spines. 'I've got a bigger body than most folk, so it needs more sustenance,' he claimed. 'Is there something you want me to do now?' He began to rise, but John pressed a hand on his shoulder.

'No, you sit there and make a pig of yourself, good man. I'm off to see a lady.'

His officer grunted. 'It's a bit early for Idle Lane, isn't it?'

His master shook his head. 'I'm off to see de Arundell's wife. I'll be back before dinnertime.'

He loped away, his tall, black-clad figure parting the crowd like a ship cleaving through the waves. Going along towards the East Gate, he turned off into Raden Lane and soon was admitted into the le Bret household by the servant with the prominent birthmark.

'You led us a fine dance across the moor,' said John good-humouredly. Maurice grinned.

'I spotted you right from where the road turned off to Crediton, Crowner!' he chortled. 'But I didn't let on, for having you follow me to the tavern was just what Lady Joan would have wanted. I told Peter Cuffe what was going on and he played along with it.'

He escorted de Wolfe inside, where a warm welcome awaited him from Gillian and her cousin Joan. Matilda had already been there to pass on the welcome news and all John could do was to confirm it more formally.

'But don't expect too much of this yet, my ladies,' he warned before he left. 'Finding Hubert Walter is a task in itself, and I have no means of knowing whether he will have any sympathy with the appeal. Officially, your husband is still an outlaw and must keep clear of any risk of being seized.'

In spite of the caution, Joan was effusive in her thanks. 'Both you and your good wife have been kindness itself to me. I feel sure that God will see fit to right this wrong done to us, and you are his instrument.'

John had never been given such an accolade before and hawked and cleared his throat in his usual way when he wished to disguise his embarrassment. 'One thing I can say is that you have no need to hide yourself away now,' he advised. 'You have committed no crime and can appear as Lady Joan de Arundell with no fear or shame.'

De Wolfe stood in the doorway, adjusting his cloak ready for the cold outside. 'As soon as circumstances and the weather permit, I will ride to Winchester and if necessary to London, to seek out the Chief Justiciar and put the case before him. That is as far as my powers will extend and it will be up to him to decide what, if anything, shall be done.'

Heavy snow brought many activities to a stop, including crime. The streets were layered by half a foot of snow and outside the walls, travel was brought almost to a standstill. Traders in the city had a hard time in getting supplies of meat, fish and vegetables from the surrounding countryside and though they shovelled the dirty white slush from around their stalls, the range of goods on display was much reduced. Many households were becoming anxious about obtaining their staple provisions, and in the mean lanes of Bretayne the rapidly rising prices made the poverty-stricken existence of the poor even more miserable. The slowdown in the pace of life also meant that John de Wolfe had little to do, as the January Fair had to be cancelled, which meant a hiatus in the usual crimes always associated with such events. The cut-purses, armed robbers and thieves who normally infested the fair-ground never arrived, and even the usual violent rowdiness in the ale-houses abated.

Every morning, the coroner trudged up through the snow to Rougemont, where he discussed with Gwyn his proposed visit to Winchester. As they sat in the keep, warming before a huge log fire and supping the castle ale, he broached the subject of Thomas.

'Should we take him? He'll slow us down, the way he rides that damned rounsey,' observed John.

His officer shrugged, squeezing the ale from his whiskers with his fingers. 'Thank God, he's at last throwing a leg over its saddle now, instead of sitting on his arse sideways like a bloody woman. But he's still so damned nervous on the back of a horse, you'd think he was riding a tiger.'

'He'd be much happier playing bishop in his little side chapel every morning,' conceded de Wolfe. 'So I think we'll give the poor little fellow a holiday and leave him here to commune with his Maker, rather than drag him half across England.'

This agreed, they talked about the journey itself. The distance a horse and rider could travel in a day was very variable. In the depths of winter, there were only about nine hours of daylight, as opposed to more than double that in high summer. Without changes of horses, as were provided for the royal messengers and heralds, a beast could not be expected to toil along all day without rest and fodder. Then the state of the tracks was paramount – heavy rain which turned the surface into glutinous mud made it almost impossible to get very far. Hard frost, in which the ruts were frozen into stone, could cripple a horse's legs. Floods and the crossing of swollen rivers were additional hazards, so it was never really predictable how long a journey would take. In good conditions in winter, the most a rider could hope for was thirty miles a day, not the fifty that the official messengers might achieve with relays of mounts.

'We'll have to reckon on five days to Winchester, if the weather improves,' grunted de Wolfe. 'And another three if we have to go on to London.'

Two days after Twelfth Night, the weather warmed up a little and most of the snow melted, with the sages and wiseacres in the taverns forecasting that January would be relatively mild.

But it was not only the coroner and his officer who had an interest in the weather – twenty miles to the west, two men in Berry Pomeroy castle were considering the same problem.

The lord of Berry, Henry de la Pomeroy, was entertaining some of his friends, one of these being Sir Richard de Revelle.

The main bond between Henry and Richard – apart from a venal love of money and power – was their continued, though covert, attachment to the cause of Prince John, Count of Mortain. When King Richard, the Lionheart, was imprisoned on the way home from the Holy Land, Prince John had made an abortive attempt to seize the English throne. He had been supported by many barons and high clergy, including Bishop Henry Marshal of Exeter – and amongst the hangers-on, who hoped for advancement under a new monarch, were Henry de la Pomeroy's father and Richard de Revelle.

The two manor lords were sitting in a chamber in one of the twin towers that flanked the main gate. The ladies were in another room with their companions and tirewomen, having left the men alone to drink wine before one of the several large braziers set around the chamber.

They sat in heavy folding chairs with thick hide seats and backs, keeping them close to the fire. The wooden shutters on the window-slits kept out most of the wind, though even the easterly breeze had died down considerably.

'There should be no problem getting up to the moor in this,' observed Henry. 'There will still be snow on the slopes, but the valley bottoms should be clear by then, unless it turns bad again.'

De Revelle nodded, holding out his heavy glass goblet for a refill of the excellent red wine that Henry imported from Bordeaux. 'How many men will you muster?' he asked. 'I have arranged for a dozen of my retainers to come up on Monday.'

De la Pomeroy fingered his heavy jowls thoughtfully. 'I thought to take about the same number. That will be double the strength of Arundell's gang.'

'Are you sure that he can be found up in that great

wilderness?' asked de Revelle, concened both for his comfort and his safety.

'I sent one of my bailiffs up to Widecombe, to scout around and listen to the local gossip. Though there are a number of these cursed outlaw bands up on Dartmoor, it seems no secret that this Nick o' the Moor, as they call him, is the best known.'

'But is it clear exactly where he hides out?' persisted de Revelle.

'There is little doubt that he camps somewhere up in the vale of the Webburn. When we get near there, I have no doubt that my men will soon flush them out.'

Richard still looked anxious. 'Are you sure that we will have enough men for this? We want no survivors to go carrying tales to my damned brother-in-law or the Justiciar.'

His host rang a hand bell to summon a servant to bring more charcoal for the braziers. When he had gone, Henry answered his guest.

'These men of Arundell's are village clods, who ran away with him when he fled. They have no talent for fighting, whereas most of the men I will take are men-at-arms from the garrison here. Together with your fellows, they will be able to wipe out this bunch with one arm tied behind their backs.'

'When will we ride out then?' asked de Revelle.

'As soon as possible, Richard. You said that your sister forcefully informed you that her husband is setting off to seek the Justiciar immediately the roads are clear of this snow. God knows how long he'll be gone if he has to chase Hubert Walter over half the country. So we should have a clear field to complete our business before he returns, if we set out at the same time.'

Richard still looked uneasy, drumming his fingers nervously on the arm of his chair. 'There'll be hell to pay when he finds out, especially if he managed to obtain the support of the Justiciar over this.'

'Kill these bloody outlaws now and then all we can be accused of is doing our duty!' reasoned Pomeroy. 'If your bloody brother-in-law has no one left to champion, the whole affair will fade away.'

Henry de la Pomeroy shrugged his burly shoulders. He was a tougher character than the former sheriff. 'We are respected landowners who have been pestered by the depredations of outlaws, who steal and rob on our lands, Richard! We have every right, indeed a duty, to flush them out by raising a posse to exterminate them.'

He grinned wolfishly, showing his stained and chipped teeth. 'I might even claim the five-shilling bounty on each wolf's head that we collect up on the moor!'

The following night, John de Wolfe strode away towards the Bush Inn, heedless of the steady rain that had moved in overnight, washing away the remnants of the snow and making the air feel almost mild after a month of continuous frost.

'This will hamper your journey tomorrow, John,' said Nesta solicitously. 'The highway will be a morass of mud if it keeps on raining.'

She put a quart of best ale in front of him, but was unable to sit with him for the moment, as the inn was busy. He looked up at her trim figure, her delicious bosom sheathed in a green linen kirtle, over which was a long apron. He hoped that he could have at least a few hours with her later that day, up in her little room in the loft, for it might be weeks before he could touch her soft flesh again. Nesta seemed to read his thoughts, for her green eyes twinkled and she bent to give him a quick kiss before gliding off to chivvy her kitchen maids in the cook-hut in the back yard.

He sat alone at his table by the firepit, but his isolation was short-lived. The huge figure of Gwyn rolled in through the door from Idle Lane and, a moment later, Thomas de Peyne appeared, both of them sitting down opposite him.

'Bloody rain!' began the Cornishman, echoing Nesta's complaint as he signalled to old Edwin to bring him a drink. 'This will add at least a day to our journey.'

The little clerk looked smug, having been excused the torture of a long horseride. 'I'll pray for you every day, Gwyn, in the hope that that great fat backside of yours doesn't develop saddle sores.'

John gave instructions to Thomas about the conduct of the coroner's business in his absence. The clerk was to record all details of every case reported and seek the aid and advice of the sheriff if any death, rape or assault occurred. There was now a second coroner in the north of the county, who in desperate circumstances could be summoned.

After they had thrashed out the routine for putting the coroner system on hold for at least a couple of weeks, de Wolfe turned to Gwyn.

'Are you all set for an early start tomorrow? Has your family given you grief over your absences?'

The ginger scarecrow grinned. 'My wife is usually glad to see the back of me every now and then. We love each other dearly, but absence makes the heart grow fonder. And I've promised my two lads that I'll buy them new knives at Candlemas if we're back by then.'

'Candlemas? You'll not be away that long, surely?' Nesta had come back and was shocked that she might not see her lover again until the second day of February. 'I'll be looking for a new suitor by then, John de Wolfe.'

John hastened to reassure his mistress that if the Chief Justiciar could be found at Winchester, they should be back within little more than ten days. He omitted to mention that if they had to go on to London, that time could be at least doubled.

'You are going to great deal of trouble and discomfort for this Lady Joan,' observed Nesta, with a tightening of her lips which suggested the dawning of disapproval. 'I presume she is pretty? You could never resist a damsel in distress, could you?'

John grabbed her wrist and pulled her down on to the bench alongside him, throwing his arm around her shoulders and hugging her to his chest. 'Jealous, are we?' he growled, planting a smacking kiss on her cheek. 'Yes, she is fair, though not at all my type. You are my type, you Welsh hussy.'

Mollified, Nesta cuddled closer to him, oblivious of the grinning Cornishman opposite and the slightly askance glances of the celibate Thomas.

'Very well, Sir Crowner, as long as you deliver her husband to her and don't get up to any of your tricks with the fair lady.' Like Matilda, Nesta was well aware that John had a roving eye, and though she felt that during the past months he had remained faithful to her, she accepted that like most active men he would have difficulty in resisting temptation if it was placed squarely in his path.

'I'll keep an eye on him, *cariad*,' said Gwyn in the Welsh-Cornish patois they used between them. When Thomas was there, they usually reverted to English, but just to tease him Gwyn sometimes lapsed into the Celtic that was the first tongue of Nesta and himself, and which John had picked up from his mother when a child. Thomas scowled and in reprisal said something in Latin, which none of them understood, but which sounded sarcastic.

John placated his clerk by telling him how much he depended upon him to look after the coroner's business while they were away. 'You know as much about the system as I do, Thomas. I have no doubt that all will be recorded on your immaculate rolls when we get back.'

'What happens if another guildsman gets murdered, Crowner?' asked the priest rather tremulously.

'Tell the sheriff and Ralph Morin, that's all that can

be done. After all, it's their business to chase criminals, not mine. But don't meet trouble halfway, my lad. We've had no problems of that sort for a while, so offer up some spare prayers in that chapel of yours so that it continues that way.'

chapter twelve

In which Richard de Revelle goes hunting on Dartmoor

The coroner and his officer made better progress eastwards than they had expected, as the rain had melted away the snow but had stopped before the roads became totally mired. A moderate east wind helped to dry up the tracks and by the early morning of the day after they left Exeter, they were leaving an inn at Bridport and making their way at a brisk trot towards Dorchester.

At dawn that day, men were also on the move many miles to the west, riding out from Berry Pomeroy Castle. Henry's bailiff Ogerus Coffin and the reeve from Hempston Arundell were at the head of the column, with the two lords behind them. Then came the rest of the men, a collection of castle guards, yeomen and freemen from Berry, seated on a motley collection of horses, ranging from an old destrier to several rounseys, and from a lady's palfrey to a few packhorses taken from a baggage train.

Their armament was equally diverse, the guards having pikes and maces, the lords their swords, and the rest of the men a variety of weapons, including axes, staves and a couple of chipped, dented swords. One of the posse was the chief huntsman from Berry Pomeroy and he had brought four of his hounds with him, who loped at his horse's heels, when they were not darting off into the bushes to investigate the scent of foxes and badgers.

Altogether, the posse consisted of twenty-two men, some ill at ease with this task, which was far removed from their usual occupation of ditching, thatching and ploughing – and several of them were secretly unhappy at having to harass the rightful inhabitants of Hempston, who they felt had already suffered enough.

One of their leaders was also not all that enamoured of the affair. Sir Richard de Revelle felt that the day would be far better spent in his comfortable manor at Revelstoke, sitting before a large fire with a glass of brandy-wine in his hand, and with another large meal when dinnertime came along. Instead, he was jogging along a winding track alongside the River Dart, shivering inside his riding cloak in spite of the padded gambeson under his chainmail hauberk. He was the only one wearing any form of armour, apart from a few men with iron helmets. Henry de la Pomeroy had a thick tunic of boiled leather under his colourful tabard emblazoned with his family crest, though little of this could be seen for the heavy, fleece-lined serge cape that he wore over the top.

The rest of the men were dressed in an irregular collection of outfits, including leather jerkins and several layers of woollen tunics; almost all wore breeches with cross-gartering on the legs.

'At least that damned frost has gone,' bawled Henry, riding alongside de Revelle. He seemed eager for a fight, having been in several campaigns in France and Ireland in former years. Richard was a reluctant soldier, he had wanted to become a lawyer as a stepping stone to politics, but his Crusader father had insisted that after attending the cathedral school at Wells, he became a squire to a local knight. Richard had managed to avoid any serious fighting, though he had become a hanger-on to several campaigns in northern France, which was where he had come to the attention of John, Count of Mortain.

Now he was trying to look as if he was enjoying this military escapade, having been persuaded by Henry that unless Nicholas was dealt with before the damned coroner persuaded Hubert Walter of the righteousness of de Arundell's claim, they would be in deep trouble.

As the column trotted through Buckfastleigh an hour later, curious stares followed them, as the sight of a troop of armed men riding purposefully along was a disturbing sight. A number of villagers ran inside, bolted their doors and crossed themselves fervently.

On they went, past the great Abbey of Buckfast, and then they began weaving through the valleys and over the downs of the rising ground that led on to the moor. By noon they had covered another seven miles to Widecombe, where they halted to rest their horses and eat the provisions they had brought in their saddlebags – hard bread, cheese or scraps of meat in the case of the villagers, though the bailiff had carried better fare and a flask of wine for himself and the two manor lords.

'We'll not get back home by tonight, sirs,' he announced, stating the obvious. 'But I've told the innkeeper here that you two gentlemen will need a place to sleep, even if it's only by the firepit. The men can find themselves a barn or a cowshed.'

After an hour's rest, they mounted up again and Henry de la Pomeroy conferred again with bailiff Coffin. 'Where do we go from here?' he demanded, being unfamiliar with this remote area of the county.

'Those miscreants are said to be somewhere on the West Webburn, the next valley to the west, Sir Henry. The alehouse keeper here is vague about it, I think he's afraid of vengeance from the outlaws if things go wrong.'

'How good is that information, bailiff?' snapped de Revelle, still unhappy with this whole expedition, especially if there was likely to be any danger to himself.

'Another of my spies from Ashburton says he has heard of Nick o' the Moor being camped somewhere up the vale of the West Webburn stream – though these villains are usually always on the move.'

'Where the devil is that?' brayed de Revelle.

'Widecombe is on the East Webburn brook, so it must be over there somewhere.' Ogerus Coffin waved vaguely to his left, where a misty grey hill obscured the view. 'The innkeeper says we must go back a little way, then cross over the foot of that hill towards Ponsworthy, then follow the next stream northwards.'

With these somewhat imprecise directions, the posse struggled back into the saddle and plodded off in the wake of the bailiff. An hour later, they were moving up a shallow valley, with grey-green slopes on either side and a small stream babbling down between straggling bushes and a few trees. There was no sign of habitation and the path was now reduced almost to a sheep track, forcing them to ride in single file.

Heavy low cloud darkened the day, but there was only a slight mist and no sign of the dense fog that could roll down within minutes and make the moor a dangerous place for travellers. In spite of the reasonably good visibility, none of them noticed a figure high up to their left, peering over a large slab of moorstone. Having noted their appearance and numbers, the ginger-headed lookout slipped back over the skyline of the ridge and ran like a hare ahead of them, easily outpacing the horses who were stepping delicately along the stony path, anxious to avoid twisting a hoof.

'Right, everyone take what they can carry and let's clear out.' Nicholas de Arundell spoke urgently, his commanding manner, honed on the battlefields of Palestine, spurring his men to frenzied activity. Peter Cuffe had just sprinted into the compound, bringing news of the approach of many armed men.

'I reckon we've got about half an hour before they're within sight,' he panted, as he seized a bow and bag of arrows that had been propped against the wall near the pile of ferns that was his mattress. The other men ran to the other two huts and collected their arms, as well as a few treasured possessions. Robert Hereward took the time to dump a bucket of earth on the fire, in the faint hope that the smoke would not give away the position of the ruined village. Others grabbed the best parts of their food supplies, a haunch of venison, some bread and two dead coneys.

Within minutes, they had assembled within the stone walls that marked the yard, ready to flee from the place that had been their home for many months.

'Who d'you reckon it is, Peter?' snapped Nicholas as he stared down the valley.

'Too far away to see, but I'm sure there were two destriers carrying men in long riding cloaks. The rest were a mixed bunch, at least twenty armed men.'

'Those bastards Henry Pomeroy and Richard Revelle, I'll wager,' snarled Hereward. 'Thinking they'll catch us unawares.'

'They want to finish us off,' growled Philip Girard. 'Maybe they've had wind of the coroner's promise to plead our case with the king?'

Nicholas tore his eyes away from the distant opening into the valley and turned to face the bleaker hills to the north.

'Let's go, we can talk about it later. Did you see any bowmen amongst them, Peter?'

The red-headed youth shrugged. 'Hard to tell, but I don't think so. They seemed a ragged lot, except for a few who may have been from a castle guard.'

As they spoke, Nicholas led the dozen men towards the gap in the wall that led up on to the moor on the western side of the valley.

'We'll get up high and walk along the crest of the

down, then cross the valley at Headland Warren, up on to Hookney Tor.'

As he left the compound, he cast a regretful glance at the tumbledown huts that had been their home. He wondered how many times it had been abandoned like this since men first came to Dartmoor. As they were filing through in orderly haste, the last man, Robert Hereward, suddenly stopped. 'Gunilda. What about Gunilda?' he exclaimed.

The others halted in their tracks and stared at each other. 'She went to the other side of the valley to set rabbit snares,' said one of the men. 'That was a couple of hours ago.'

'We can't leave her,' said Peter Cuffe, to whom the old woman had become a second mother.

'She'll hear these swine coming,' said Girard. 'Gunilda's a tough old bird, she'll go to ground until they're past.'

Nicholas swore all the oaths he had picked up in years of soldiering.

'We can't go looking for her now, we'd walk right into the path of these bastards.'

There was a hurried debate and though opinions were divided, de Arundell was forced to make a quick decision. 'We have to leave her or we'll all be caught down here in the open. I'm sure she'll hide out somewhere. God knows there are enough holes in the ground around here.'

Reluctantly, they began hurrying up the hillside, half a dozen of them carrying long yew bows over their shoulders. Within ten minutes, Challacombe Down looked as deserted as on the Day of Creation, the outlaws having vanished into the grey-green void that was the moor in winter.

The solitude did not last long, however: before long a faint jingle of harness and soft thud of hoofs could be heard as the intruders came tentatively into the valley of the West Webburn stream. Richard de Revelle did not like the feel of this country, he was tense and his eyes roved ceaselessly from side to side, in spite of Henry's brash assurances that they would wipe out these outlaws like a pack of rats. Once again, Richard earnestly wished that he was back in his hall at Revelstoke instead of sitting on a horse in the cold damp of Dartmoor, where violence and mayhem might break out at any moment.

'God's teeth, where are those swine hiding themselves?' growled Henry, his square head swivelling back and forth as he surveyed the bare hills and the scrubby trees along the stream. 'Ogerus, come here,' he yelled and the bailiff wheeled his horse around and walked back to his master.

'Do none of your men know this damned place?' he demanded. 'Where are we supposed to be looking for the bastards?'

Ogerus Coffin shook his head. 'We are all from down south, sire, this is a foreign land to us. But according to that man who gave the information, there is a ruined village here where the outlaws set up one of their camps.'

Half a mile further on, he was proved to be right, for one of the men-at-arms from Berry Castle gave a shout and pointed over to the left. 'There are some buildings of sorts, across the stream, my lord.'

They looked past some shabby trees bare as firewood, and saw the dark shapes of a few huts, built of almost black moorstone. There was no movement anywhere and no smoke wreathed up into the leaden sky.

'We'll go across and look, but it seems our birds have flown,' snarled Henry, angry and disappointed. The posse turned off the track and began treading carefully through the boggy ground to the bank of the stream. Before the leading man reached it, there was a sudden commotion behind them, on the far side of the track. The four hounds belonging to the huntsman began barking furiously and streaked away up the lower slopes of the hill.

'They've scented something, bailiff,' yelled the huntsman, slipping from his saddle and running after his dogs. A moment later, as the halted cavalcade turned to watch, the man vanished from view, apparently into a hollow in the ground. His shouts of command silenced the dogs, then he reappeared, dragging what seemed to be a large bundle of damp rags. Ogerus Coffin turned his horse and walked it up towards the huntsman, then turned in his saddle and shouted back.

'It's a woman, sir. By Jesus, the ugliest old hag you ever saw.'

A mile away, Nicholas led his men down into a bowl of marshland, where the stream spread out before the valley narrowed and bent to the left. Ahead was the high swell of Hookney Tor with a clump of misshapen stones on top. Between that and Hameldown Tor was the small pass through which the coroner had been taken on his journey from Moretonhampstead.

'Any signs of them?' Nicholas asked Peter Cuffe, who had been in the rear, but who now came running up as the column merged into a ragged circle.

'Nothing yet, though I fancied I heard hounds barking just now.'

De Arundell stared back down the silent valley. 'I hope to God that Gunilda has hidden herself somewhere. It never occurred to me that they would have dogs with them.'

Hereward was philosophical about it. 'God wills whatever is to happen, Nicholas. We have to look after ourselves now, until we can get back down there when they have gone.' He looked up at the slopes of rough grass, clumps of it in yellowed tussocks where it had died back for the winter. 'We must get up there and lie low.'

They moved on, climbing up steeply alongside a stream that had cut deep, irregular channels in the black peat. In a few minutes they were on the sloping saucer between the two high tors, where the ancient circle of Grimspound sheltered a dozen crumbling huts, tiny structures like stone rings, some with a tattered roof of branches and turf.

From there, they could look down on the upper end of the valley, but could not see back to Challacombe because of the bulk of Hameldown Tor on their left.

'You are our best pair of eyes – and have the fastest legs, Peter,' said the leader to the ginger lad. 'Get up along the ridge again and keep a sharp lookout down towards the village.'

When he had loped off, Nicholas went wearily through the gap in the double palisade of stones that reached to waist height in a huge circle around the ancient encampment.

'We may as well rest, until either something – or nothing – happens,' he suggested. The men broke up into three groups and each found a place in one of the primitive huts to sit and worry about their situation – and especially about Gunilda. The little food they had managed to carry away was shared out, and one of the men went to fill an empty wineskin with the clear water from a small stream that trickled past the circle.

They sat and waited, the silence broken only by a thin moan of wind across the uplands and the occasional squawk of a crow scavenging amongst the heather.

The raiding party from Berry Castle had rampaged through the primitive dwellings at Challacombe, angry and disappointed that there was virtually nothing worth looting. They kicked apart the piles of ferns that the outlaws had used for beds and overturned the crude table and stools that were the only furnishings. A couple of men grabbed the paltry remnants of food that lay on a shelf and swallowed the dregs of home-brewed ale that remained in a small barrel in a corner.

The bailiff kicked at the debris in the firepit. 'The ashes are still hot under that soil,' he reported to his master. 'They must have smothered it within the past hour.'

Henry stood with Richard de Revelle in the middle of the main hut, glowering around at the deserted room. 'So where the hell are they? They must have had good warning of our approach.'

'The bastards have had a couple of years to get used to these God-forsaken moors,' replied Ogerus. 'They've slipped away up one of these bloody hills.'

De Revelle was secretly relieved, hoping this meant that there was to be no pitched battle. 'So what do we do now? Burn this place down and go home?'

Henry looked at him with more than a hint of contempt, for he had long become aware of de Revelle's physical cowardice. 'I suppose so, though little good it will do. These damned stones won't burn – and they can rebuild the roofs in half a day!'

'What about this old hag, my lord?' asked the bailiff. 'She must be something to do with these men, there's no hamlet within four miles of here.'

The two leaders walked out into the yard outside, where Gunilda was slumped on a log, two men from Hempston standing guard over her.

'Sweet Jesus, what a disgusting old sow,' barked Henry, using the Norman French that he and Richard spoke together. He marched up to the old woman and snarled at her in the same language. 'Who the hell are you, woman?'

She looked at him blankly and made no response, so he repeated himself in English. Gunilda rolled her bloodshot eyes up at him and gabbled something he failed to understand, so thick was her local accent.

'Bailiff, speak to this animal, I can't understand her monkey language.'

Ogerus translated, with rather too much relish to suit his master. 'She says, may your member turn green and rot off, to be devoured by wolves, sir.'

With a snarl of rage, Henry stepped forward and gave the old woman a blow across the side of her head with his fist that knocked her off the log to sprawl on the floor. The two men standing behind her looked askance at de la Pomeroy, but wisely held their tongues.

'Pick the old cow up, damn you,' he yelled at them. 'Perhaps she knows where these other villains have gone to.'

They dragged her from the floor and held her between them, other men now drifting towards the group, curious to see what was happening.

Gunilda sagged between her guards, her head drooped on to her chest, blood welling from a wound on her temple where one of Pomeroy's rings had gashed her.

'Do you think she is part of this gang?' brayed de Revelle. He seemed unconcerned by this savage attack on an old woman, though the looks on some of the faces of the men from Berry and Hempston showed that they were not happy with the situation.

'Ask her again, bailiff,' snapped Henry. He drew his sword and prodded the front of her ragged kirtle with the tip, as if to indicate what would happen if she spat out further abuse.

Ogerus Coffin jerked Gunilda's head up by grabbing her hairy chin and glared into her face. There was a short exchange in the thick Devon patois, the woman mumbling her words, obviously still dazed from the blow to her head.

'She says she was collecting herbs and knows nothing of any men, sir.'

'A liar, if there ever was one,' snapped de Revelle, determined not to be subservient to Henry Pomeroy's leadership. 'What herbs are about in the depths of winter? She's miles from any village and only yards from a hut with a fire barely dampened down. Of course she belongs to them!'

'Probably a waif, there's a few of them in the county, consorting with outlaws,' suggested the bailiff.

Henry raised his sword high in the air. 'Hear that, wretch,' he yelled. 'Anyone is entitled to remove your head. I could even claim five shillings for it if I took it to the sheriff.'

Gunilda looked at him dully from the eyes that stared from above loose pouches of skin on her dirty, lined face. 'Do it then, damn you,' she muttered apathetically.

'Perhaps she knows where her fellow criminals have gone,' suggested de Revelle. 'Ask her, bailiff, you seem to possess the same strange speech that she employs.'

Ogerus grabbed her by the shoulder and shook it as he gabbled something at her. The old woman shook her bleeding head wearily and he repeated the question, shouting at her with his mouth inches from her face. Again she shook her head, but momentarily her eyes flickered to her right as she looked anxiously up the valley. Ogerus, by no means a stupid man, caught the glance and began ranting at her again, shaking her by the shoulder, but she stubbornly refused to answer.

'She won't say a thing, my lord,' said the bailiff, looking over his shoulder at the two knights. 'But I've got a notion that they went up the valley, that way.' He gestured in the direction that Gunilda's eyes had turned, towards the distant hump of Hameldown Tor.

Henry Pomeroy, still red with anger, lifted his sword again and threatened the Saxon woman. 'Where are they, damn you? Did they go that way? Answer me, you ugly old hag.'

For answer, Gunilda spat in his face. Enraged, Henry punched her in the chest with his powerful fist. Caught by surprise, the two guards lost their grip on her arms and she tumbled backwards, falling full length and hitting her head on a large moorstone which had tumbled from the old wall behind her. There was an ominous crack and she lay inert – never to move again.

Several of the men muttered their concern, but were soon stilled as Henry glared around. 'What are you staring at, damn you?' he yelled. 'Get to your horses, we are going farther up the valley to find these swine. Go on, move!'

Without a second glance at the still body on the grass, Henry de la Pomeroy beckoned to de Revelle and the two men strode away towards their steeds, Richard by no means enthusiastic about the imminent prospect of a fight.

Within half an hour, Peter Cuffe came pounding down the slope from the brow of the hill where he had been keeping watch.

'They're coming, Sir Nicholas,' he shouted breathlessly as he dashed in through the gap in the boundary wall. 'And they must have fired the huts, for I see a column of smoke down the valley.'

The men stumbled from the shelters where they had been resting and congregated around their leader and the ginger youth who had brought the unwelcome news.

'We are going to have to fight, after all,' exclaimed de Arundell. 'I had hoped that when they found the place empty they would give up and go home.'

'What about Gunilda? Has she been taken, I wonder?' asked Philip Girard. 'If so, perhaps they forced her tell them where we were.'

Robert Hereward shook his head vehemently. 'Never. She would have her tongue cut out before she would give us away,' he snapped.

'If they failed to find us down in Challacombe, then they must realise that we are up this way, for they came on the only track southwards,' observed Nicholas.

'And they have dogs, which will pick up our trail,' added Peter.

Their leader stared down the slope to the track, thinking hard. 'What remains now is to defeat the bastards – or at least harry them until it becomes too dark, then we can slip away.' For five minutes, de Arundell described their plan of campaign, giving instructions to each man as to how they were going to carry out the ambush. The men made hasty preparations to their weapons, the half-dozen with bows now stringing them with the animal-gut filaments that they kept under their caps to protect them from rain. The others had swords, axes, iron-tipped staves, a couple of long pikes and a few wicked-looking ball maces swinging on chains from a short handle.

'Did you check again on their numbers, Peter?' demanded their leader.

'As I first thought, about twenty, all on horses of varying sorts. The two riding destriers must be that swine Henry Pomeroy and Richard de Revelle.'

'But no bowmen?' rasped Nicholas. 'Are you sure about that?'

The redhead nodded. 'I saw none, and the way most of them are sitting on their saddles suggests that they would be more at home with a cabbage hoe or a thatcher's rake!'

Nick o' the Moor gave rapid orders to his band of outlaws. He sent most of them up the two hillsides that sloped away from the great circle of Grimspound, ordering them to find somewhere to conceal themselves, either in hollows in the ground or behind large rocks. He placed an archer on each side of the shallow gully down which the stream tumbled to the valley below, the only practical approach to Grimspound. The other four bowmen he sent to hide in strategic positions on the slopes around the camp. Once again, he dispatched Peter up to the corner of the ridge, to signal when the intruders had reached the nearest point on the main track below. With luck, they might pass by and continue up the narrowing valley towards the Chagford road.

Together with Robert Hereward, he climbed up the flank of Hookney Tor to the north and they hunkered down in a slight hollow behind large tussocks of coarse grass.

'They are all mounted, so do you think they'll climb up here still on horseback?' queried Robert.

Nicholas shook his head, his face grim but lit with the expectation of battle, such as he had not experienced since the Holy Land. 'It's too steep and slippery with yesterday's rain. They'll have to leave their mounts down on the track, probably leaving a couple of men to look after them.'

Hereward crossed himself and muttered some prayer under his breath, then took a firmer hold on the long-shafted battleaxe that he held with a knuckle-whitening grip. They waited and shivered in the cold air, every man now silent in order not to betray their presence, as in that wilderness sounds carried a long way.

They watched intently, looking up at the ridge where Peter crouched on the edge of Hameldown Tor. A layer of grey cloud hovered like a moist blanket, blotting out the extreme tops of the hills, but leaving the lower slopes and the valley clear apart from a few wraiths of detached mist that drifted on the breeze. Nicholas de Arundell remembered similar ambushes in other campaigns and had the same thoughts: whether or not he would be dead within the next few minutes – and whether it would hurt so very much with a spear or sword through his belly.

His eyes strayed down to the steep slope where the stream cut its way through the peat to the track below, but suddenly he felt a nudge from Robert's elbow.

'Peter must have spotted them,' he hissed. They swivelled their eyes up and saw Cuffe running down the hillside, bent low and keeping out of sight of the road below. He stopped for a second and made urgent pointing gestures, then ran a few hundred paces more and dropped out of sight behind a slab of moorstone.

Silence fell again, but soon they could all hear the intermittent neigh of a horse and the faint jingle of harness, as well as the bark of a hound. A human shout next broke the stillness, and a muffled curse as a fretful stallion kicked out at another beast.

A few moments later, they saw the first heads appear, bobbing over the curve of rank grass as they climbed up the sheep track alongside the stream. The horses and hounds had obviously been left down below. Nicholas had hoped to evade detection altogether, but he realised that it was a forlorn hope. Amongst these men were huntsmen and even poachers, who could easily recognise a recent footmark in the wet soil and realise than men had trodden the same path not long before.

Soon about a score of figures had risen out of the valley and were cautiously approaching the two stone pillars that marked the entrance to the ancient settlement. They were led by a pair who wore thick leather curiasses and round iron helmets, suggesting that they were part of the Berry Castle guard. Behind them strutted the sturdy figure of Henry de la Pomeroy, followed more hesitantly by the slimmer Richard de Revelle.

Nicholas stared across the few hundred paces of ground with loathing in his eyes. These were the men who had dispossessed him, driven his wife from her home and made him an outcast. He almost wished he had given his archers orders to strike them down where they stood, but even after the tribulations that had forced him to live like a hunted fox, remnants of his chivalrous upbringing prevented him from killing without warning.

He watched as all the invading force gathered inside

the wide circle of Grimspound. There was much waving of arms on the part of de la Pomeroy, then some of the men went around the low circular huts, peering inside those that had not collapsed or lost their roofs. Soon there was a shout, clearly heard in the still air, and one of the searchers came out with what could have been a crust of bread – then another found a recently chewed piece of bacon. After a hurried conference, the faces of all the posse turned to scan the surrounding hills, their hands clutching their weapons in readiness for an attack.

De Arundell cursed under his breath. Though his men had been careless in leaving signs of such recent occupation, he was realistic enough to accept that he could not prevent the searchers from discovering their presence in the area. All he could do now was wait and see what happened.

After a hurried discussion between the two manor lords, their bailiff and the leading man-at-arms, and half a dozen of the more soldierly men came out of the enclosure and began walking cautiously up the slopes on each side. They had their swords or pikes at the ready and began searching behind each large rock and in every hollow. It was only a matter of time before they came upon one or other of the outlaws, and Nicholas felt it was beholden upon him to take the initiative. As he saw a big fellow wearing an iron helmet with a wide nosepiece clambering up towards his hideout, he suddenly stood up and brandished his sword, the light of battle glowing in his eyes.

'Stop there, or I'll slit your gizzard, damn you,' he yelled, his volatile temper flaring up. The man almost dropped his sword in surprise as the apparition seemed to appear from the very earth in front of him.

There was a roar from the rest of the posse down below as they caught their first sight of their quarry, but almost simultaneously, almost all the outlaws, except the archers, popped up from their hiding places and gave answering yells of defiance as they waved their weapons at the foe.

The big man in front of Nicholas soon got over his shock and with a roar of triumph launched himself towards the outlaw leader. However, he was lumbering uphill and suddenly found himself facing two adversaries, as Robert Hereward hoisted himself from his crouch and stood alongside his master, brandishing a long staff with a wicked spike on the end. With a great shout, Nicholas went to meet the man, parried a swing from the big sword and kicked him hard on his shin. As the man grunted with pain, de Arundell swung the flat of his yard-long sword against the side of the fellow's head and he fell to his knees, blood streaming from his lacerated ear.

'Clear off, you bastard,' screamed Hereward, his own battle lust awakened. He prodded the man in his sword arm with his spiked staff and though the tough leather jerkin prevented any deep injury, the man screamed with pain.

By now, other single combats had begun, as the few invaders outside the enclosure were being attacked by Nicholas's men. They had the advantage of the higher ground and within a few moments, two of the Berry men were lying wounded and the others had taken flight back down the slope. Most of those in the compound were racing to the opening to join the affray, though a few were scrambling over the wall, a difficult task as it was not only chest-high, but was double, with a space between the two layers of moorstone.

As a dozen men began jostling through the entrance, the outlaw archers made themselves known, standing up to loose off a rapid succession of arrows into the press of figures pushing through the narrow gap. There were screams of pain and the rest of the men dived back to take cover behind the grey stones of the palisade. Amongst them were the two knights, with Richard de

Revelle lying almost flat on the ground, shaking with fear as he watched two wounded men dragging themselves into cover.

'Bloody archers,' yelled Henry de la Pomeroy, livid with anger rather than fear. 'Where in hell did they get archers?'

Had he but known it, the six men in the outlaw band had made themselves expert bowmen by sheer dint of practice. Often with little to do between forays, they had spent their time in learning the skill from Morgan, a man from Gwent in South Wales, the home of the longbow. Outlawed for an alehouse brawl in Plymouth, which had left a man dead, he had joined the band almost at the beginning and taught those interested how to make bows and how to use them. Hundreds of hours of practice had strengthened their arms and sharpened their eyes so that, though not up to the standard of professionals in an army, they were more than proficient in a close-quarter situation like this.

As most of the Berry posse cowered behind the protective wall, the few that had clambered over it were in various stages of fight with Nicholas's men. One was set upon by Martin Wimund and another outlaw, receiving a hearty kicking that left him senseless on the ground, while another had managed to fell Peter Cuffe with a blow from a heavy staff. His assailant was about to finish off the ginger-headed youngster, with his dagger, when the nearest archer saved Peter's life with an arrow through the assailant's throat.

'What in Christ's name do we do now?' hissed Richard de Revelle to Henry, as he cowered against the boundary wall.

'Break out and attack the swine,' snarled Pomeroy, his temper getting the better of his good sense. 'They had luck and surprise on their side just then, but it can't hold.'

He was wrong. As Henry waved to the men sheltering

around him and got them to dash with him to the gap in the palisade, they ran into another shower of arrows that killed another man-at-arms and slightly wounded Henry in the leg.

Cursing, he dragged himself back into the shelter of the wall, where de Revelle, who had not stirred an inch, looked at the injury and declared it not to be serious, just a glancing cut above Pomeroy's ankle.

As the blaspheming lord bound a kerchief around his leg to staunch the bleeding, there was a loud shout from the nearby slopes.

'Pomeroy! De Revelle! Are you listening? This is Sir Nicholas de Arundell. Can you hear me?'

Henry struggled to stand up, putting his weight on his good ankle and using the lumpy stones of the wall to pull himself erect.

'Be careful, man,' hissed de Revelle desperately. 'He may put an arrow through your head.'

De la Pomeroy might be a bully and a boor, but he was no coward, and ignoring Richard's warning he hoisted himself high enough to peer over the palisade. He saw Arundell, looking much rougher than he remembered him, standing on higher ground a hundred paces distant. Two other men, one an archer with an arrow ready on the string, stood alongside him. Looking round, Henry saw a dozen men encircling the camp, several more of them archers.

'What do you want, you murdering thief!' he yelled at Nicholas.

'I've murdered no one,' de Arundell called back. 'And neither am I a thief, like you and that snivelling coward de Revelle. Where is he, anyway, has he died of fright?'

Pomeroy looked down and hissed at his co-conspirator. 'Stand up, for God's sake! Show yourself, will you?'

Reluctantly, Richard slowly rose and peered over the wall. When he saw the archers, he dropped again, but

Henry grabbed his cloak and hauled him up to stand alongside him.

'Give yourself up, de Arundell,' blustered Pomeroy. 'You are outnumbered.'

This was met by a chorus of laughter from the men surrounding Grimspound and for devilment, one of the archers loosed off an arrow which smacked against a stone within a foot of de la Pomeroy's head. He jumped and de Revelle ducked below the parapet once more.

'And for what shall we give ourselves up to you, Pomeroy?' shouted Nicholas. 'To be hanged or beheaded?'

'You are outlaws, damn you,' raved Henry. 'We are a lawful posse, come to cleanse the moor of your evil presence.'

'Lawful posse, my arse,' retorted de Arundell. 'Only the sheriff can raise a posse – and he knows the righteousness of my case, as does the coroner, who is riding to petition the king about your wrongdoing.'

Henry ground his teeth in frustrated anger. There was nothing he could do to confound this bold outlaw. He and his men were trapped inside the ring-wall, with half a dozen archers able to massacre anyone who tried to make a dash for it through the narrow portal.

'Can't we hide inside these little huts?' quavered de Revelle.

Henry looked down at him with contempt. 'What good would that do, you fool? They could come to the doorways and pick us off like rats in a barrel.'

The knight they had ousted from Hempston was calling to them again. 'You started this fight, damn you. I wanted no part of it, and if you had not followed us up here and tried to kill us, we would have left for another part of the moor.'

Pomeroy, thankful that Nicholas did not yet know that his old woman retainer had been killed, now realised that there was nothing to do except save his skin and whatever dignity he could salvage.

'So what do you propose, outlaw?'

'I want no more killing or wounding. I never wanted any in the first place. If you throw down your arms, you can walk out of this place and take your dead and wounded with you.'

There was a mutter of agreement from the men cowering inside the pound, echoed fervently by Richard de Revelle. 'Agree to it, accept his offer at once!' he hissed.

Henry gave him a scathing glance, but realised that he was right – they were trapped and had nothing left to bargain with. He shouted across to Nicholas, still standing on a tussock with a sword in his hand.

'Very well, but remember, there will be another day, and next time you will be overwhelmed.'

De Arundell gave a cynical laugh. 'Tell that to King Richard or his Chief Justiciar when they haul you before them. For now, just drop your weapons and clear out of here! You'll not find us in this area again, if you are foolish enough to come seeking us before royal retribution is visited upon you.'

The light was failing by the time the men from Berry had tramped despondently down to the road to regain their horses. They carried two dead men and two who had suffered arrow wounds. Two more who had lesser injuries were helped along by their compatriots, including Henry de la Pomeroy himself, who leaned heavily on the arm of his bailiff as he limped along to his stallion on a damaged leg.

A pile of swords, pikes, maces and staffs lay inside Grimspound, though Nicholas chivalrously agreed that the two knights could keep their swords, so long as they promised not to unsheath them again that day. As the winter dusk approached, the outlaws watched the defeated posse ride away down the valley, the archers keeping a watchful eye for any last-minute treachery until the cavalcade had vanished out of sight. Two of their men had slight injuries, though Peter Cuffe had soon recovered from his blow on the head.

'Where do we go from here?' asked Robert Hereward as the gloom thickened.

'We can stay up here tonight, sheltering in the huts. But some of us must go back down to Challacombe to make sure that the place is unusable after that fire. And of course, to seek for Gunilda. I have a bad feeling about her,' he added grimly.

After their ignominious defeat at Grimspound, Henry de la Pomeroy and Richard de Revelle headed back to Berry Pomeroy Castle to lick their wounds and to hold an inquest on their failure and the possible consequences. The darkness obliged them to spend the night at Widecombe and it was noon the next day before they limped home. That afternoon, the east wind moaned around the towers of the gatehouse as the two men sat in Henry's chamber easing their aching limbs after their long ride back from the moor. The gash in Pomeroy's leg had been cleaned and bound by one of the servants, but it still smarted enough to be a reminder of the fiasco at Grimspound.

They had eaten and now settled in chairs set on each side of a large brazier, a jug of Loire wine on a nearby table providing frequent refills for the silver goblets they held.

'It was those bastard archers who undid us,' snarled Henry for the fifth time. 'I'm going to hire a couple of Welshmen to train those clods of mine to shoot!'

Richard was more of a realist. 'Don't waste your money, Henry. It takes years to make a man competent with a longbow – and I'll warrant we'll get no second chance against Arundell and his gang.'

'So what do we do about it now?' rasped de la Pomeroy, splashing more wine into his goblet. 'Run and shelter under Prince John's skirts, I suppose?' His tone was bitterly sarcastic.

'What else do you suggest?' retorted Richard huffily. 'Without his support, we could be in serious trouble. Do you want to go the same way as your father?' he added maliciously, referring to the elder Pomeroy's suicide at St Michael's Mount. When accused of treachery to King Richard, he had ordered his physician to open the blood-vessels in his wrists, so that he bled to death, rather than face the Lionheart.

Henry was too worried to take offence. 'So how do we go about it? You are close to the Count of Mortain.'

A shutter rattled in the wind as de Revelle considered his answer.

'We must get ourselves to Gloucester as soon as we can and hope that the Prince is there. His support is vital to us. After all, he was nominally the sheriff of Devon when we seized de Arundell's manor – and he had had Devon and Cornwall in his fief at the time, so he could be considered to be Nicholas's ultimate landlord.'

Henry saw little that was helpful in this tortuous argument, but grudgingly agreed that a clever lawyer might be able to draw some legal justification from it. 'Sounds a thin excuse for us kicking out de Arundell's family and sequestering his lands,' he said. 'Still, if you think we are in personal danger over this, then by all means let us ride to Gloucester.'

Richard de Revelle, who had a much more perceptive and cunning brain than the boorish de la Pomeroy, was adamant. 'It's our only defence, Henry! I know this damned man de Wolfe. He's like a bull-baiting dog, he never lets go once he's got his teeth into something. Comes of being a bloody Crusader, I suppose. We need to speak to Prince John before de Wolfe gets back from kissing Hubert Walter's arse!'

At the same time that afternoon, in a workroom behind a large forge on Exe Island, just outside the western wall of the city, a man was bent over a complicated device lying on a bench.

He murmured under his breath as he worked, filing a slot in a piece of iron that was part of a mechanism that consisted mainly of a powerful leaf-spring held back by a trigger device. The contraption seemed to owe much of its design to a cross bow, except that it was very much smaller and the bow part was replaced by a single arm.

The man, a fellow with a heavy, sullen face, was fashioning every piece with loving care, working from a diagram scratched on a square of slate with a sharp nail. A lock of hair fell incessantly across his forehead and he brushed it aside with almost obsessional regularity. Alongside the device he was fashioning, were several other metal articles, including large door locks, parts for ox-cart axles, iron swivels, and rings for horse harness.

From the yard outside came the rhythmic clang of hammer on anvil and, from an adjacent workshop, the tapping of a punch clinching over rivets, as other journeymen and apprentices went about their business. Although he was absorbed in his task, the man kept one ear tuned for approaching footsteps. Whenever it sounded as if someone might come into his back room, he rapidly covered up the device with a piece of sacking and seized some other article to work upon. Usually, it was a false alarm and as soon as the footsteps receded, he went back to his careful filing again.

Chapter Thirteen

In which Crowner John travels across England

The journey to Winchester was tedious but unremarkable. Both John de Wolfe and his officer had made it a number of times over the years and the road was familiar. The weather remained cold, but free from snow or significant rain, so their progress was good. The coroner was not riding his old destrier Odin, who was too heavy for a long haul like this. He had once again hired a younger gelding from Andrew the farrier who kept the stable in Martin's Lane, and the good beast kept up a brisk trot hour after hour, covering a good twenty-five miles each day.

Being in the saddle from dawn to dusk was enough for any man, even though the winter days were short. A good supper, some ale and a gossip with whoever was in their lodging was a prelude to sound sleep, whether it was on the rushes alongside an alehouse firepit or in a castle hall. Two nights were spent at inns and another at Dorchester Castle, as the coroner considered that he was on the king's business and therefore entitled to accommodation there.

When, on the fourth day, they entered the walls of Winchester a few hours after noon, enquiry at the castle at the top of the sloping High Street soon brought about disappointment. Hubert Walter, the Chief Justiciar and virtual regent of England, was not there, but had left for London the previous week. One of the senior Chancery clerks, with whom de Wolfe was acquainted from previous visits, told him that as far he knew, Hubert was not planning to cross the Channel to see the Lionheart in the near future and could probably be found in Westminster or the Tower if John could get there within the next few days.

'We'll rest up today and tomorrow, to give both the horses and ourselves some respite,' he announced to Gwyn. 'Then hack on to London, as I half expected we would need to.'

The clerk readily found accommodation for the Devon coroner in one of the tower chambers in the castle, while Gwyn found a mattress in the soldiers' quarters, where he could drink and play dice to his heart's content. John spent the next day renewing old friendships with a number of knights and clerks he knew from either Outremer or Ireland, as the faithful service of many old campaigners was rewarded with official posts – as indeed John himself had been. Winchester, the old capital of Anglo-Saxon England, was still an important seat of government, though gradually London was becoming predominant.

When their rest was over, they set off again eastwards, this time through less familiar countryside, passing through Hampshire and Surrey. The distance of this leg of the journey was much less and they needed only two nights' accommodation, the first at an inn in Farnham, the second by claiming hospitality at Chertsey Abbey.

On the third day, now over a week away from Exeter, they rode wearily along the bank of the Thames into Southwark and across the bridge into the swarming streets of London. Both men had been there a number of times before and were not overawed by its size or its frenetic activity, but as they passed over the old wooden bridge, they stared curiously at the new one which was slowly being built nearby. Started a long time before, it was evidently still many years away from completion: only the bases of the nineteen piers showed above the turbulent water.

'Where do we look first, Crowner?' grunted Gwyn as they halted their steeds at the corner of Eastcheap in the city itself. De Wolfe looked downriver to where the grim pile of the Conqueror's White Tower stood high above the city wall. He pondered whether to try there first or make the longer journey in the opposite direction to Westminster.

'Hubert is almost king these days, so let's try the palace,' he said rather cynically. They plodded westwards, passing through the walls near the huge headquarters of the Knights Templar and onwards through the fields along the Strand, around the curve of the Thames until they came to the village of Westminster where the great Saxon abbey stood. Opposite, nearer the river bank, was the palace built a century before, its huge hall a legacy of William Rufus. As well as being the residence of an absent king, it was now surrounded by a cluster of buildings to house the ever-increasing bureaucracy of government, making it a bewildering maze for anyone unfamiliar with its layout.

They stopped outside the main gatehouse and stared at the imposing buildings. 'Can we cadge lodgings here, Crowner?' asked Gwyn, looking doubtfully at the crowded courtyards and the hurrying clerks and monks who were crossing back and forth to the Abbey opposite.

'We can but try, but first I need to see if Hubert is actually in residence,' grunted de Wolfe, kicking his mare into motion again. The gates were open, but guarded by two soldiers wearing tabards displaying the three couchant lions of King Richard's royal arms. John displayed a small parchment roll from which dangled the impressive wax seal of the Chief Justiciar, which Hubert had given him on a previous occasion. Though the sentinels could not read, they recognised the seal and directed the two visitors to a guardroom inside the gates, where in addition to a sergeant-at-arms they found a tonsured clerk sitting behind a table covered in documents.

John explained who he was and proffered the warrant again, which this time the black-garbed official was able to read. It was an authority which Hubert Walter had given de Wolfe when Richard de Revelle needed disciplining the previous year. It ordered every one of the King's subjects to provide John with any aid he required and made it clear that the bearer was well known to both Justiciar and King Richard himself. After scanning it, the clerk rose to his feet and spoke respectfully to the coroner.

'I have heard of you, sir, you have a certain reputation at the court.' He said this without any trace of sarcasm and went on to offer both good news and bad news.

'I regret that the Archbishop has gone to attend to his episcopal duties at Canterbury and will not return until tonight. But I am sure he can give you audience in the morning – and in the meantime, I would be happy to arrange accommodation for you – and your officer.' He looked rather doubtfully at the dishevelled Cornish giant who stood behind the coroner, but wisely refrained from any comment.

An hour later, after seeing that their horses were fed and watered, John and Gwyn were taken into the Great Hall by a servant, who placed them at a table near one of the several firepits and arranged for food and drink to be brought. The place was huge, a double row of columns supporting a vast roof, under which hundreds of people were milling about. Sections of the hall had been partitioned off, and it seemed to be part courthouse, part official chambers. The rest was a turbulent meeting place for those who either governed England or sought audience with those who governed England.

'What the hell do we do now?' queried Gwyn as he started to demolish a platter of fried pork and onions which a serving lad had placed in front of him, along with a jug of ale. John, similarly engaged in tearing the meat from a boiled fowl, peered at his henchman from under his black brows.

'You may do as you wish, Gwyn, but after a week in the saddle, I'm going to my bed and staying there until the morning.'

Though Hubert Walter was the most powerful man in the country, he eschewed ostentation and dressed soberly, unlike many of the popinjays that strutted about the court. With Richard Coeur de Lion absent in France, the Chief Justiciar carried much of the burden of government on his shoulders, especially the task of endlessly finding money.

'Little more than half the 150,000 marks ransom has so far been paid to Henry of Germany,' he confided to John de Wolfe the next morning. 'I have stripped most of the churches of their silver plate, taxed the wool producers until they groan and installed you and your fellow coroners, as well as the new Keepers of the Peace to squeeze all I can from the legal system.'

They were sitting in a barely furnished room that Hubert used as his working office when in the palace of Westminster. A good fire burned in the hearth, which was modern enough to have a chimney, and the two chairs on either side of the large table were comfortable enough, but otherwise it hardly looked like the chamber of an archbishop and the virtual ruler of a country.

Hubert was a lean, tanned man with a face like leather, his cropped brown hair greying at the temples. He wore a plain red tunic, the only gesture to his ecclesiastical rank being a small gold cross hanging on a slender chain around his neck. They sat each with a silver cup of wine before them, like old comrades. Hubert had been in Palestine ostensibly as chaplain to the English Crusaders, but his role became more and more military as time went on. He acted as chief negotiator between King Richard and Saladin, and when the Lionheart had left for home on his ill-fated voyage, Hubert was left to command the army and arrange for its withdrawal. When Richard was captured in Vienna and imprisoned first in Durnstein Castle on the Danube and then in Germany, it was Hubert who visited him and arranged the lengthy process of negotiating the huge ransom to get him released. It was during this time that he had come to know and respect Sir John de Wolfe.

Now they sat opposite each other in the chilly morning, at first reminiscing about their dusty, dirty and dangerous days in Palestine, then getting down to the business that had brought de Wolfe to London.

'I guessed it would be de Revelle again,' sighed the Justiciar. 'I suppose it would have saved a lot of trouble if we had hanged the bastard a couple of years ago.'

'He never seems to learn, damn him,' replied John in exasperation. 'But he is my wife's brother and it would be difficult for me to see him swinging on the gallows-tree.'

He explained in detail what had happened over the seizure of the manor of Hempston and the banishment of Nicholas de Arundell.

'So you see the difficulty, that Nicholas was forced into outlawry and is unable to sue for restitution,' he concluded.

Hubert Walter stared at the base of his goblet as he twisted it on the table. 'He was with us in Outremer, you say?'

John nodded. 'I never met him there, but he was at the battle of Arsulf. Who wasn't?' he added rather bitterly, for that was a day of great slaughter on both sides.

'De Arundell? Yes, I remember the name, amongst so many others. That family came over with William the Bastard at the time of Hastings. This is a poor reward for a staunch Crusader, John.'

As Hubert refilled their cups, John added some more explanation. 'From what I've heard, Henry de la Pomeroy was the prime schemer in this. Hempston lies against his lands and though de Revelle has been a beneficiary of the theft, Henry has annexed the manor into his own estate and the two of them are splitting the revenues between them.'

The archbishop shook his head sadly. 'There's been too much of this petty anarchy going on, John. Even though we crushed Prince John's major treachery, thanks to Queen Eleanor's vigilance, since then many lords have been whittling away at their neighbours' property. Too many of the damned sheriffs are either absentees or corrupt; they rarely take any action – and some are party to it themselves.'

John thought of saying that it was a pity that the king did not spend more time in England to take a firm grip on his wayward nobles, but decided to hold his tongue. Instead, he pointed out one fact.

'Both the miscreants in this are covert supporters of the Count of Mortain, sire. I don't claim this particular act is anything to do with that, it's just plain greed and opportunism on their part. But it goes a long way to explaining why they could get away with it, as John was the original tenant-in-chief.'

The Justiciar looked enquiringly at the coroner. 'In what way?' he asked.

'Well, this happened before you established the coroners, so I was not around to be involved. And you well know who the sheriff of Devon was at that time.'

Hubert nodded. 'Prince John Lackland, of course. As Sheriff of Devon he was remarkable for his complete absence from the county. God knows who did his work, some serjeant or bailiff, no doubt. They wouldn't have lifted a finger against de Revelle or Pomeroy, of course.'

He absently fingered the cross on his breast as he stared into the fire. 'What's to be done about it, that's the thing? You didn't ride all the way from Devon just for my sympathy, you want some action, eh?'

De Wolfe nodded. 'It's a gross injustice, sire. They mustn't be allowed to get away with it.'

'Indeed not. If it was up to me, I would ride back with you and either clap the bastards into irons or hang them from the nearest tree, for the trouble they have wrought these past few years. But they have powerful allies amongst both the barons and the churchmen. Even I have to work with circumspection, as there are those who would delight in seeing me humbled.'

John, who took no great interest in the politics of the court, gave a noncommittal rumble in his throat and waited.

'The prince still has a substantial following, all waiting like a pack of dogs to fall upon a lame deer,' continued Hubert Walter. 'Many lesser nobles, like de la Pomeroy and de Revelle, have ingratiated themselves with these and expect protection when they get into trouble.' He drank some of his wine and looked directly into John's eyes. 'I know from the complaints and veiled threats I've had before, that Bishop Henry of Exeter is one of these. And he is brother to William the Marshal of England, also effectively the Earl of Pembroke. There are others too, who would delight in seeing me fall, especially as I am so obviously the King's man.'

This was all getting too rarefied for de Wolfe, who always considered himself a simple fighting man.

'So what's to be done?' He returned to the same basic question, afraid that the Justiciar was working around to a refusal to take any action, but Hubert reassured him.

'This must be properly brought before the royal

judges, to ensure that justice is seen to be done. I know that the Eyres are grossly lagging behind in their visitations to the counties, but I will appoint a special commission to hear this matter.' He gave a wry smile and winked at de Wolfe. 'I think that Walter de Ralegh might be an appropriate person, being from Devon himself.'

Walter, one of the senior royal justices, was well aware of the situation in the west of the country, being a local man. He had had brushes with de Revelle before and in fact had been responsible for dismissing him from office as sheriff, and had also sworn in his successor, Henry de Furnellis.

'I'll appoint Walter and one other reliable judge to come down as soon as possible,' continued the Justiciar. 'They can resolve this matter speedily and firmly at a special sitting in Exeter.'

'But what about Nicholas de Arundell?' asked John. 'He is still marooned on Dartmoor as an outlaw. I'd not put it past Pomeroy and Richard to murder him under the excuse that he is still "as the wolf's head".'

Hubert rubbed his clean-shaven chin thoughtfully. 'I'll take a chance on that. I'll grant him and his men the king's pardon and get the Lionheart to ratify it when I see him, probably in a month's time. It will certainly serve to allow de Arundell to attend the court and put his side of the dispute.'

De Wolfe was gratified and relieved to hear this, but was still cautious. 'Is that really possible, sire?'

Hubert looked sternly at de Wolfe. 'Anything is possible when you possess the king's writ to manage his kingdom in his absence. And here I have a twofold power, for as Head of the Church as well as Justiciar, I could enforce my decision on the grounds that it is an offence punishable by excommunication for anyone to take advantage of a man who is on Crusade. Even the other crowned heads of Europe, evil swine though most of them are, respect that rule. It was what prevented Prince

John from getting aid from abroad when he rose up in revolt against his brother, when Richard was returning from Palestine.'

They spent a few more minutes discussing the details of the procedure before John took his leave. The two men had a deep mutual respect, and de Wolfe knew that he could depend upon Hubert Walter to keep his word. For his part, the Justiciar promised as John left the chamber that the clerks in Chancery would deliver a writ of command to him later that day, which would order the Sheriff of Devon to deliver Nicholas from his predicament as an outcast.

'We will have to wait for Ralegh to make his deliberations before this Arundell can enter into his manor again, but that should not be long. At least, the fellow and his men can be reunited with their wives in the meantime.'

With a great sense of relief, the coroner strode after an attending clerk through the tortuous passages of the palace, eager to find Gwyn and tell him the good news over a celebratory quart of ale.

Chapter Fourteen

In which Crowner John comes home

When the coroner and Gwyn were again at Dorchester, with still two days to go on their journey home, a curious injury occurred in Exeter.

That evening, a master weaver, Gilbert le Batur, left the back door of his house in Rock Lane, at the lower end of town near the Water Gate, to visit his privy. This was against the fence at the end of his yard, past the kitchen hut and pigsty. Inside the house, he had left his buxom wife Martha and his two adult sons, who were shocked to see their father stagger back into the hall a few minutes later, bleeding profusely from a wound in his shoulder.

Half an hour later, apothecary Richard Lustcote arrived, having been urgently summoned by one of the sons. It was not usual for him to attend upon customers, as they normally came to his shop, but he was well acquainted with Gilbert from their activities in the guilds – and the son's concern at his father's injury was too intense to be ignored.

Lustcote found his friend lying on a pallet in the solar that was built on to the side of the hall, anxiously attended by his wife and younger son. The weaver was pale and shocked, lying shivering under a thick blanket of his own manufacture, and responded to questions only with a mumbled grunt. The son had only been able to tell Lustcote that some kind of missile was lodged in his father's shoulder, and with some calming words, the apothecary turned down the blanket and saw a mess of blood across Gilbert's tunic, spreading down from the shoulder to his waist. At the upper part of the garment, a short stub of what appeared to be rusty metal was protruding. Feeling gently around the back of the shoulder, Richard Lustcote touched more metal, this time a sharp spike protruding through the fold of skin at the bottom of the left armpit.

'What's this, for pity's sake?' he exclaimed. Gilbert screeched when he touched it and the apothecary fumbled in his bag for a vial of strong poppy syrup, a large dose of which he administered to the weaver. 'That will deaden the pain very soon,' he said reassuringly, covering up the shoulder again, after checking that the bleeding was now almost stopped.

He turned to the despairing wife and the two sons, then motioned them to move a little further away. 'While that drug works its effect, tell me what you know of this,' he said in a low voice.

'My father went out to the privy and came back like this,' growled the elder lad, a stocky youth of about eighteen. 'It looks as if someone has shot him with a crossbow, yet the missile looks too small.'

'Have you been out to see if some miscreant is in the yard?' asked Lustcote.

'I saw no one, but it is so dark and all I had was a flickering candle.'

Richard shook his head wonderingly at the strange things that happened at night, then waited for the poppy extract to take effect. He considered having the injured man taken up to St John's Hospital, but the journey up to the East Gate would be very painful for Gilbert and would increase his shocked condition. Lustcote used half an hour to try to reassure the wife that the wound was not mortal, as the arrow or whatever it was had gone through the flaps of skin and muscle under the armpit and had thankfully missed any vital structures. What he did not tell them was that the main risk was from suppuration and gangrene, if the object had carried any dirt into the wound. By now, Gilbert le Batur had subsided into a drugged stupor, his breath puffing between slack lips, and the apothecary, with the help of the sons, turned him on to his side. With relative ease, Lustcote slid the projectile out of the wound at the back of the armpit. After seeing the wife clean up the dried blood and place new linen over the two wounds, he walked over to the firepit, where the flames from a pile of logs augmented the rush lights and candles.

'What do you make of this?' he asked the sons, holding out the object he had taken from the wound. It was a short iron rod, somewhat longer than a hand, with a very sharp arrowhead on one end, being plain on the other. 'Just as well it had no fletching or I would never have removed it as easily as I did,' he said thankfully. 'Any idea what it is?'

The sons inspected the missile, then denied all knowledge of it. 'It's not a crossbow bolt,' said the elder. 'Too short and it has no leather flights.'

'Your father is a very lucky man,' exclaimed Richard. 'This thing had the power to completely transfix his armpit. If it had hit him a few inches to the right, it would have gone into his heart. This was an attempt at murder.'

The wife left her ministrations and came across, holding a bowl of water stained pink with blood. She and her boys were well aware of the fate of the three other guildmasters in recent weeks.

'My husband was a master weaver, as you well know, Richard,' she said quaveringly. 'Is this yet another such attempt, d'you think?'

The avuncular Lustcote put a hand gently on her shoulder. 'I do not know, Martha; that will be for the sheriff and maybe coroner to investigate. But at least this time it was an attempt, not a success. For that we must be thankful.'

Cold and weary, muddy and hungry, the coroner and his officer reached Exeter just before dusk two days later. Gwyn went off to his dwelling in St Sidwell's to let his family know that he was still alive, whilst John took the valiant gelding back to Andrew's livery stables, then crossed the lane to his own house. After a warm welcome and a surreptitious kiss from Mary in the vestibule as he shed his cloak and boots, he went into the hall, wondering what sort of reception he would get from his wife after two weeks' absence.

Matilda proved to be remarkably benign, as she had been just before he left. She even enquired if he was tired, which for her showed unusual solicitude. He sank into his chair by the fire and fondled the soft ears of old Brutus, who crawled up to greet him. Mary bustled in with mulled ale and hurried off again to bring him food from the kitchen shed.

'Did you have a favourable response from the Archbishop?' demanded Matilda, preferring Hubert's episcopal title to his more worldly rank. John, encouraged by her interest, launched into an account of his doings.

'So I have brought a personal commission from Hubert Walter to bring the matter before the royal justices as soon as it can be arranged,' he concluded, passing the document across to her. Though like him she could not read it, the impressive seal gratified her, and John decided to play along with his new-found importance in her eyes to keep her in a sweeter mood for as long as possible.

Mary came in with a wooden bowl of hot mutton stew and a small barley loaf. When John moved to the table to attack it enthusiastically, Matilda came to sit opposite, and she continued to surprise him.

'While you were away, I kept closely in touch with that poor lady, Joan de Arundell,' she announced. 'I have tried to keep her spirits up by telling her that you will undoubtedly use your influence in Winchester and London to right this wrong, so I am glad that I have been proved right.' She said this as if she had personally arranged with the Almighty for the Archbishop of Canterbury to be sympathetic to her husband's petition.

'And I have seen my brother again,' she added with a marked tightening of her thin lips. 'He called here a few days ago and seemed rather chastened. He was much more chastened when he left, after once more getting the length of my tongue about his deplorable conspiracy with that evil Henry de la Pomeroy.'

There was a pause while Mary placed a trencher in front of him carrying a spit-roasted capon, accompanied by a platter of cabbage, beans and onions. At this time of year, the choice of food was becoming limited, but a fresh white loaf and hunk of cheese was to follow.

When the maid had left, his wife resumed her monologue. 'Richard still maintains that the Hempston manor was escheated when it was thought that the lord had died, but that good lady assures me there was no evidence at all that her husband had perished.'

John cut a thick slice of bread with his dagger and covered it with butter-fried onions. He paused with it halfway to his mouth. 'What did your brother say to that?'

Matilda scowled at the memory. 'He told me to mind my own business and tell you to mind yours. He says he is aware you consorted with outlaws and intends reporting it to a higher authority.'

De Wolfe gave a humourless laugh. 'Higher authority? I suppose he means that traitor Prince John. I doubt he'll do that, or the Chief Justiciar and his justices will come down harder on him than ever.'

Matilda was in a difficult position: although her former

loyalty to her brother had been whittled down to almost nothing, she was afraid that any worsening of his position might cost him his life.

'I pray daily to God in Heaven that he would just retire to his manors and lead a quiet life.' Her voice quavered a little. John felt sorry for her, a strange feeling that beset him every so often.

'If he just returns this manor to the rightful owner and cuts himself adrift from Pomeroy, then he might survive yet another fiasco,' he said gently, though he was not at all sure that the king's judges would agree with him.

When he had finished his meal, he went back to the hearth with his wife and they sat silently for a while. Then he told her again about Hubert Walter's provisional royal pardon for the outlaws and Matilda brightened up.

'Will you let me tell Lady Joan the good news?' she asked. 'I have befriended her well since you left and would like to be the bearer of such welcome tidings.'

John nodded, pleased to have something to lift her from her despondency. 'It means that Nicholas de Arundell can now leave the moor and come to live with his wife,' he said. 'He cannot yet return to his manor until the justices have deliberated, but no doubt her cousin will find room for him in that large house.'

Matilda preened herself at the prospect of meeting another Crusading knight, who would no doubt be grateful for her support to his wife. Soon, a dog-tired John announced that he would seek his bed when he had finished the jug of wine. Even the prospect of walking Brutus down to Idle Lane failed to seduce him from the blessed prospect of sleep. As he wearily took his saddle-bruised body up to the solar, the ever-cautious de Wolfe thought that things seemed to be going so well that maybe they might be going a little too well – perhaps

Fate still had something unexpected in store for them all.

As the coroner half expected, the next morning brought a multitude of problems that had accumulated during his absence. The faithful Thomas was genuinely delighted to see him when he climbed to the lofty garret in the gatehouse, then reported on a string of cases that had been either dealt with or shelved during the past two weeks. Most were routine, and a number had already been dealt with by the sheriff, rather to John's surprise, as Henry de Furnellis rarely exerted himself. Several men were rotting in the cells below the keep until the coroner could get around to taking their confessions, and several accidental deaths needed inquests, based on the depositions that Thomas had recorded earlier. However, the day soon brought some more pressing matters. The first was the arrival of Richard Lustcote, who appeared out of breath at the top of the winding stairs. The coroner sat him on a stool and listened with increasing concern to the apothecary's story.

'This victim is another guild master?' he asked with a feeling of foreboding.

'One of the best-known weavers in the city,' replied the apothecary. 'That is why I feared that this might be another one of those murderous attacks, though thankfully one that failed.'

'How badly is he injured?'

Richard pursed his lips in doubt. 'He lost some blood, but the damage is not mortal, unless it turns purulent. It depends on where that damned iron rod had been before it was used.' Feeling in his apothecary's bag, he produced the iron rod and handed it to the coroner. 'This is the object that caused his wound – you had better keep it as evidence.'

John and Gwyn examined the rusty metal with interest, but came to no conclusion about what it was, other than some crude form of crossbow bolt. De Wolfe scratched his stubble, in dire need of scraping with a sharp knife since he had last shaved in London. 'Did you seek the cause of this injury at the house?' he asked. 'I mean, the device that fired this thing at the weaver?'

'I went out to the yard and the privy with his sons, but it was dark and all we had was a candle. I am an apothecary, not a constable.'

The coroner accepted this and decided to go and look for himself. The apothecary took himself off to his shop and John went down to Rock Lane with his two acolytes behind him. They found Martha le Batur ministering to her husband with the assistance of another motherly woman who was her maid. Gilbert was on a low truckle bed in the solar, muffled up against the cold air under a pile of blankets. He was pale, which at least seemed to indicate that so far he had no fever from an infection of his wound.

When they entered, he struggled to sit up, but he groaned at the pain in his heavily bandaged shoulder and fell back on to his pallet.

'What do you recall about this affair?' demanded de Wolfe, sitting on a stool alongside the victim's bed, the wife and elder son hovering anxiously behind him.

Gilbert was lucid, though his face was puckered with pain. 'Very little, Crowner, it was all over so quickly. I had the urge to visit the privy, as I often do after my supper. I put my hand on the latch and pulled the door open and immediately was struck in the shoulder.'

'You were lucky it was only your shoulder, father,' said the son. 'A few inches to one side and it would have been your heart.'

'I have the old elder tree to thank for that,' replied the weaver. 'It grew so much last summer that a branch now hangs across the privy door and makes you lean to the side to avoid scratching your head. I was going to cut it down, but now I'll spare it out of gratitude.'

Further questions drew out nothing useful, as none of the family members saw or heard anyone lurking about the yard that night. John decided to examine the scene of the crime for himself, and Edwin, the elder son, took them across their yard at the back of the house to the privy, a simple structure of rough-hewn planks with a tattered roof of mouldy thatch. It backed on to a lane at the rear of the burgage plot, where the night-soil man came with his cart once a week to shovel out the ordure that had accumulated. A trap at the back of the tiny hut gave him access to the foul space under the seating-board, which had a circular hole cut in the top. John examined the door, which was a crude panel of planks with thick leather hinges. It was held shut by a wooden latch that dropped into a slot on the doorpost, being opened from inside by lifting with a finger pushed through a hole. He looked at the inside and outside of the door and at first sight found nothing remarkable. Similarly, the walls of the privy appeared normal, being covered in peeling whitewash. It smelled less offensive than most buildings of this type.

'Can you get into the lane from the yard?' asked Gwyn. Edwin nodded and led them around behind the adjacent pigsty, which smelled far worse than the privy, and opened a small gate in the wooden fence. They went out and studied the back wall of the latrine. Partly covered in shrivelled ivy, the boards were warped and shrunken in places, but Gwyn's sharp eye soon spotted something amiss.

'The edge of that plank has been gouged away – and recently, by the looks of it.' He pointed to a place in the middle of the wall, yellowish heartwood being exposed where a small semicircle had been hacked out of the board. Above it, there was a gap between the planks, so given the depth of the gouge, the total defect in the back wall was at least an inch.

'About chest height, too,' piped up Thomas. 'That iron rod would easily pass through that gap.'

De Wolfe was running his fingertip over the planks within a hand's span of the hole. 'What about these, Gwyn?' he asked gruffly. He often sought his officer's opinion on practical matters.

Gwyn peered closely at what John had indicated, his big red nose almost touching the planks. Then he felt them delicately, as the coroner had done. 'Screw holes, four of them,' he declared. 'Spaced evenly around that central gouge, and just as fresh, by the colour of the exposed wood.'

They all stepped back into the lane, the son Edwin looking with admiration at these sleuths who could discover such obscure signs.

'What does it mean, sir?' he asked.

'Some device had been screwed to the outside of the back wall, then removed after the deed was done,' said de Wolfe.

'What sort of device?' asked Thomas, always the most curious member.

De Wolfe shrugged. 'How the hell would I know? Some sort of bow or spring, I suppose.'

'But how would it be discharged?' persisted Thomas. 'Did the assailant wait there all night in the hope that the man would go to the privy?'

'My father is very regular in his habits, sirs,' offered Edwin. 'He goes to relieve himself about the same time every evening. If someone watched for a few nights, they could easily discover his routine.'

John nodded his agreement, then walked back around into the yard and pulled open the latrine door once again. 'Use those keen eyes of your again, Gwyn,' he commanded, pointing at the inside of the door.

His officer soon found what they were looking for, another fresh screwhole in the centre of one of the upper planks.

'A booby trap, must have been,' said Gwyn. 'A cord tied around a hook or screwhead in the door, passed across to the back wall, then through the planks to whatever trigger was on this device.'

The clerk, the least mechanically minded of them all, nodded in understanding. 'When the door was opened, the string tightened and fired the arrow. But there were no flights on it.'

Gwyn grunted. 'At that short range, it would hardly matter. The distance from the door to the back of the privy is less that two paces. It could hardly miss!'

'And if my father had not twisted to avoid that elder branch, it would have killed him,' added the son tremulously.

Back in their bleak chamber in the gatehouse, the coroner and his team revived themselves with bread, cheese and cider, their usual routine for a late extra breakfast. John sat at his trestle table and turned the metal bolt over in his fingers, staring at it intently, as if he could make it tell him who had planted it in the master weaver's latrine.

'He must have set up his device just before Gilbert was due to attend to his bowels,' said Gwyn. 'Otherwise, he might have shot the wrong person.'

'And removed it soon after, so as to get rid of the evidence,' said Thomas.

There was silence, broken only by the sound of Gwyn champing his crusts and slurping his drink. 'What can be done to investigate this, Crowner?' asked Thomas eventually.

'Damn all, once again,' replied John angrily. 'This is the fourth attack on guild masters and we've not the slightest idea of who or what's behind them.'

There was another silence, then Thomas de Peyne spoke up rather diffidently. 'I've been thinking, sir,' he said. 'An odd notion has come to my mind.'

Gwyn groaned in mock exasperation. 'Has God been talking to you again, little man?'

The clerk ignored him and began to expound his theory to the coroner.

'There is something common to all these four attacks, apart from the victims being prominent guild members.'

John stared at his clerk from under his black brows. He had learned to respect Thomas's ideas, as the small priest was well-read and highly intelligent. 'And what might that be, Thomas?'

'Think of the means of death in each case, master,' replied the clerk. 'Matthew Morcok, the man found in Smythen Street, was killed by an iron spike driven into his spine. Then Hamelin de Beaufort, the glazier, was found along the Buckfastleigh road, strangled with an iron chain. The next was Robert de Hokesham, the candlemaker, speared to a tree in St Bartholomew's by an iron spike. And last of all, we have Gilbert le Batur shot by an iron bolt.'

Gwyn, not as quick on the uptake as the other two, demanded to know what was so significant about all that.

Thomas made a rude face at him. 'You big oaf, don't you see that every death was caused by iron! And probably the device that shot that bolt will be constructed from iron. I feel it in my bones that iron plays some part in this unhappy series of tragedies.'

While Gwyn digested this theory, the coroner began to evaluate it.

'So iron and senior guildsmen are the common factors, Thomas? How can we link them together? None of the victims were ironmasters.'

Looking a little crestfallen, the clerk had only one suggestion. 'Perhaps it would be worth talking to the warden of the Guild of Ironworkers. I don't recall his name, but I seem to have heard that he is only recently elevated to that position.'

For lack of any other ideas, John vowed to seek the man out later that day. The rest of the morning was partly spent with the sheriff, as he needed to be told of John's visit to London – then John and Thomas took confessions from several prisoners in the cells below the keep. Gwyn had been sent off to arrange two inquests for the afternoon, and it was noon before John got back to Martin's Lane for his dinner.

Matilda was still in an amenable state of mind and announced her intention of going to Raden Lane after the meal, to take the good news to Joan de Arundell. John promised to call there later, to explain more officially what the Chief Justiciar had said about righting the wrong done to Nicholas.

Over mutton stew and a tough boiled pheasant, John took advantage of his wife's good mood and her compendious knowledge of the upper strata of Exeter society, to enquire about the current warden of the Ironworkers' Guild.

'That will be Stephen de Radone, a new man in the post,' she said straightaway. 'I know his wife well through our attendance at the cathedral, though she attends St Petroc's Church rather than St Olave's.' Matilda said this as though the other church was affiliated to Sodom and Gomorrah.

'Is he a new man in Exeter?' asked John, pulling a piece of gristle from his teeth.

'Not at all, he was born and bred in the city. But he was elected Warden a few weeks ago, as the previous man, John Barlet, recently died from falling from his horse.'

Matilda informed John that like many ironmasters, de Radone had his home and business in Smythen Street. John resolved to call upon him later, when he might also slip into the nearby Bush to see Nesta for the first time in almost a fortnight. In the past, he had had some problems with his mistress when he had neglected her for too long, even though his absences were inevitable because his duties took him out of the city, and he didn't want her wrath again.

The two inquests were held in the Shire Hall in the inner ward of Rougemont, the gaunt building being used for a variety of legal purposes, including the county court, the coroner's enquiries, the regular Commission of Gaol Delivery and, with much more pomp and formality, the infrequent Eyres, when the royal justices came to Devon to try serious cases and enquire into the administration of the county.

Today's inquests were routine, low-key proceedings, one into the death of a miller who had fallen into his own mill-stream when drunk and had been dragged under the wheel and drowned. The other would have been a criminal case, had not both parties been killed. It concerned a fight in the Saracen Inn, Exeter's meanest tavern, where a rowdy sailor from a ship at the quayside had stabbed an argumentative porter from Bretayne. Before the latter had expired from loss of blood, he had punched the sailor so hard that the man had cracked his head on one of the stones that ringed the firepit and died within the hour.

The coroner dealt with the witnesses in record time and directed the jury so forcibly that they returned an acquiescent verdict within half a minute.

Leaving Thomas de Peyne to finish writing his account of the proceedings, John marched with Gwyn down through the town and into the top end of Smythen Street. They passed the school where all this had begun, and John idly wondered if Magister James Anglicus had finished converting the old forge into a new lecture room.

There were half a dozen metal-working establishments in the street, and the thump and clanging of hammer on anvil echoed from some as they passed. Further downhill, John could see the crude sign of the Saracen tavern hanging over the door and, beneath it, the gross figure of the innkeeper, Willem the Fleming, as he threw stinking rushes from the floor into the street.

'Which one of these places do we seek?' asked Gwyn. As John had no idea, he accosted a man pushing a barrow full of charcoal, who indicated a house a few yards away. The lower front chamber was wide open to the street, and several apprentices and a journeyman were busy at benches, hammering, drilling and filing. As with almost all the blacksmiths' premises, a side lane led into a back yard, where the heavier work of forging was carried on.

They found the owner, Stephen de Radone, in a back room where he was busy with his clerk, checking tally sticks against a parchment which the literate clerk held in his bony hands. His master was a tough-looking fellow in his mid-forties, with hair as black as John's and muscles almost as powerful as Gwyn's. De Wolfe decided that here was a man who could do every metalworking task as well as any of his employees – and probably better than most. It seemed no wonder that his fellow guildsmen had elected him as Warden of their trade organisation.

Stephen received them courteously and led them upstairs to the living quarters above his business. Here his comely wife greeted them, then diplomatically vanished, leaving them to talk privately to her husband. Refusing refreshment, much to Gwyn's disappointment, the coroner reminded de Radone about the three previous deaths and explained the recent development concerning Gilbert le Batur.

'It occurred to my clerk that all these incidents employed iron implements and we wondered if this has any significance.'

The smith pondered for a moment. 'Of course, Crowner, most weapons are of necessity made of iron – swords, daggers, maces and the like.'

De Wolfe nodded his agreement. 'It may be sheer coincidence, but we are grasping at straws. However, no death was due to wooden arrows or a club – nor to drowning, nor throttling by hand.'

They discussed the matter for a time, but try as he would, Stephen could think of no logical connection between his trade and the series of deaths. De Wolfe made one last attempt at rationalising the problem.

'Look, all the victims were prominent in the activities of their trade guild. All these trades were different, no two men practised the same profession. Is there anything at all that might bring them together?'

The ironmaster thought about this for a moment. 'We attend each other's feasts and dinners from time to time, though probably all four would not have been at any one event at the same time.'

He chewed his lip contemplatively, then held up a forefinger. 'I wonder if they might have come together at the judging of a masterpiece,' he said. John gave a frown to show that he failed to understand.

'In every trade, a young lad is apprenticed for, say, seven years,' explained Stephen. 'Then he may become a journeyman, proficient to carry on his work without supervision and to train apprentices in his turn. But he cannot set up in business for himself until he proves his competence to his guild and becomes a master in his own right.'

Gwyn was floundering, though he knew the rudiments of the system. 'So what's that got to do with our problem?'

'A journeyman has to make a "master-piece", at his own expense in time and materials, to present to his guild for examination and approval, before he can go out into the world and set up as an independent trader.'

John began to see where this was leading. 'And who judges his master-piece?' he asked.

'In the first instance, it is the warden and officers of

his own guild, for they are obviously most competent to assess the object – whether it be a glass goblet, a pair of shoes, a turned wooden bowl or a sword.'

De Radone became more animated as the strength of his own argument increasingly appealed to him. 'But he may be refused, as sometimes there is animosity and jealousy between a master and his journeyman, especially if the master does not want to lose the man or have him set up in opposition. Then the candidate may appeal against the decision and the guild will summon senior members of other guilds to act as independent assessors.'

The coroner fixed Stephen with a steely eye. 'How can we tell if that happened recently – possibly to a member of your own guild?

De Radone turned up his hands in supplication. 'I have no idea, Sir John. I can affirm that it has never happened in my own forge here, but I cannot speak for the other metalworkers in the city – nor in the towns further afield, for there are guild members in Totnes, Dartmouth, Crediton and other places.'

'How can we find out?' demanded de Wolfe.

'There will be records in the Guildhall, Crowner. I have only been warden a short time, so I cannot speak from memory, but the clerks to the guilds will have scrolls recording all these matters for years past.'

After thanking Stephen for his help, the coroner and his officer marched out into Smythen Street again and turned towards Idle Lane.

'This may be a wild goose chase, Gwyn, but it sounds like a job for our worthy clerk. He thought up this daft idea, so he can go and wade through the dusty rolls in the Guildhall.'

Neither mentioned that, in any case, Thomas was the only one who could read them.

CHAPTER FIFTEEN

In which Crowner John rides again to Dartmoor

In the late afternoon, John walked alone through the best part of the city to Raden Lane. When he reached the house of Gillian le Bret, he was relieved to find that Matilda was no longer there, having gone to her devotions in church. He was received in the hall by Joan and her cousin and pressed to wine and pastry wafers, though the fair young woman was too excited herself to eat or drink. John had the impression that only modesty and good manners prevented her from flinging her arms around his neck in exuberant thanks for the good news that Matilda had brought earlier – he was rather disappointed that she did not.

He repeated all that had passed between Hubert Walter and himself, the two women hanging on his every word. 'So there is now no hindrance to your husband reappearing in Exeter or anywhere else,' he concluded.

He was surprised to see a shadow pass over Joan's pretty face.

'There is only one problem, Sir John,' she said. 'I have not heard from Nicholas since you left for London. Normally, we get a message every week or so, but this week and the previous one, there has been no messenger waiting at the usual rendezvous in Moretonhampstead. I am so worried. What can have happened?'

De Wolfe had no answer to this or any reassuring words, other than vague platitudes that all would be well. It would certainly make his plans more difficult to carry out, if the object of his rescue operation was nowhere to be found.

'When is the next meeting due to take place in Moreton?' he asked.

Joan twisted a kerchief nervously between her fingers. 'Not until next Monday, sir. We sent our servant there only yesterday, but there was no sign of anyone from Challacombe.'

John thought rapidly of his commitments. 'I cannot ride tomorrow, but on Thursday my officer and I will go up on to the moor and seek him out. It may be that he has had to move camp for some reason.'

With further profuse thanks, in which Matilda was also lauded as an angel of mercy, the two ladies saw John off at their door. As he walked back to Martin's Lane in the gathering dusk, he was more concerned than he had admitted about Nicholas's apparent disappearance. Had de Revelle and de la Pomeroy decided to act to wipe Nicholas from the map before any action could be taken by London? No news of such an escapade had reached Exeter, but the two villains would be hardly likely to proclaim it abroad.

De Wolfe decided to have more words with the sheriff over this and made his way to the keep of Rougemont. He found Henry de Furnellis sitting near the firepit in the hall, a quart of ale in his fist, spinning yarns with Ralph Morin, Sergeant Gabriel and a few of the older men-at-arms. John shouted to a servant for a jug and settled down with the group, all of whom he knew and trusted as loyal king's men. He told them of his new concerns for Nicholas de Arundell.

'We have heard nothing of any foray on Dartmoor,' said Ralph. 'Though news travels very slowly in those remote places, especially if people desire to conceal their actions.'

When John told them of his intention to search for de Arundell, the sheriff offered to send armed men with him. De Wolfe accepted a small escort, as the search would perhaps need to be wide.

'Sergeant Gabriel and a couple of mounted men would suffice,' he said. 'We're not looking to fight anyone, just to discover where the hell he has got to.'

'What's to happen about the Justiciar's decision to right this wrong?' asked the castle constable, twisting his forked beard pugnaciously. 'Are we going to hang those two bastards at long last?'

Henry de Furnellis held up a placatory hand. 'Easy, Ralph! Hubert says that he's sending Walter de Ralegh down to hold a special court to settle the issue. Then you can talk about hanging them.'

The burly constable buried his face in his ale jar. 'Those crafty swine will find some way to wriggle out of it, I'll wager. They've got Prince John and half the bloody clergy on their side.'

After supper that evening, Matilda went off to visit her 'poor relation', a cousin in Fore Street. Although the woman was the contented wife of a thriving merchant, she had been adopted as a charity case by John's overbearing wife, who called upon her at intervals to make sure she was not starving on account of marrying a mere tradesman.

John took the opportunity to 'take the dog for a walk', and although he had already called in at the Bush Inn earlier in the day to make his peace with Nesta, he went down again to Idle Lane as soon as his wife's back was turned.

Sitting at ease at his table near the hearth, he had time to recount all the details of his trip to Winchester and London, places that Nesta had only heard of, as her travels had taken her only between her home in Gwent and the city of Exeter. She was the widow of a

Welsh archer, who had fought alongside John de Wolfe in several French campaigns. When Meredydd finally hung up his longbow, John suggested that he move to Devon, and with his accumulated loot from fifteen years of fighting he had bought the Bush, then a rundown alehouse. The archer brought his wife from Gwent, and they worked hard to make it successful, but then Meredydd was stricken with a sudden fever and died. John had helped Nesta financially to keep the tavern going until it finally paid its way again – and in the process, they had become lovers in every sense of the word.

'You are a good man, John,' she said softly, putting a hand affectionately on his arm. 'Going all that way to fight an injustice. And I'm not even jealous, though I'll wager that this Lady Joan is pretty.'

He gave her a crooked grin and squeezed her thigh under the table.

'When was my head ever turned by a pretty face – apart from yours, *cariad*?' he replied in Welsh. 'My main reason was to do down that damned brother-in-law of mine.'

The inn was fairly quiet that evening, though Nesta was called away several times by either old Edwin or one of the serving maids to attend to some cooking problem or see to a new arrival who wanted a penny mattress in the loft for the night. When she came back to John after dealing with one such customer, he solemnly placed a penny before her on the table.

'Any chance of me also getting a bed tonight, mistress?' he asked with a straight face. The pert answer she had ready was interrupted by the appearance in front of them of Thomas de Peyne, who had just slunk in through the back door. His natural reluctance to frequent taverns had increased since he had been recently restored to the priesthood, so John knew that he must have something important to tell him. However, this had to wait until Nesta had finished fussing over the clerk, as she was always convinced that he never get enough to eat in his mean lodgings in Priest Street. She went off to order a maid to find him a bowl of stew and a couple of chicken legs, and while she was in the kitchen, Thomas blurted out his news.

'I have been in the Guildhall, as you instructed, Crowner. Their records are in some disorder, but they are all there. I went through the rolls pertaining to the guild of Ironworkers and found that last summer, one of the journeymen was refused advancement because his master-work was deemed insufficient.'

The little clerk's pinched face was pink with cold as he wiped a dewdrop from the end of his long nose with the sleeve of his black cassock.

'What was the name of the master who failed him?' asked John tensely, expecting that it might be one of the four dead guildsmen, until he remembered that they were not in the same trade.

'It was John Barlet, the previous warden of the iron-masters,' said Thomas. Deflated, the coroner then recalled that Stephen de Radone had said that his predecessor had died after a fall from a horse – an accident . . . or was it? It had not been one of John's inquests, but the man might have died outside south Devon, under the jurisdiction of a different coroner.

But Thomas had by no means finished his tale and as Nesta returned with a cup of wine and slipped back alongside John, he continued.

'The most interesting part, Crowner, is that the journeyman appealed against the decision and it was heard by four senior members of the city guilds – and again rejected.'

John was almost afraid to ask his clerk the names of the adjudicators, but when Thomas delivered them in a dramatic whisper, the coroner slammed his fist on the table and let out a shout that turned every head in the taproom.

'Thomas, you're a bloody genius! We've got him, thanks to you.' Then he glowered at his clerk from under his beetling black brows. 'But you've not yet told me the name of this damned journeyman!'

Thomas looked furtively over his shoulder, as if he was about to impart some state secret. 'It was Geoffrey Trove, who works on Exe Island.'

De Wolfe stared at his clerk. The name rang some faint bell in the back of his mind and he struggled to retrieve it. 'Trove? Trove? That name is somehow familiar.'

Then the memory of the meeting in the Guildhall with the members of various guilds came back to him. He recalled the pompous Benedict de Buttelscumbe who was the convenor and then the general discussion afterwards. Yes, that was it, there was a fellow, a journeyman smith, who had some sarcastic remarks to offer about the failure of the law officers to solve the killings.

The coroner half rose from his bench, as if to dash out and arrest the man at that moment, but Nesta pulled at his sleeve.

'John, it is pitch dark outside,' she scolded. 'These murders have been spread over weeks, so I doubt that waiting until morning will make any difference to your investigation.'

De Wolfe saw the sense in what she said and subsided on to his seat.

'You are right, as usual, woman. But at dawn, I shall visit the warden of the ironworkers and discover what I can about this Geoffrey Trove. And especially where he lives and works.'

And that was the first problem, for Geoffrey Trove was nowhere to be found.

Soon after first light, while Thomas was busy at his devotions in the cathedral, John and his officer were at Stephen de Radone's forge in Smythen Street. When they told him of Thomas's discovery, the warden was aghast.

'Could this really be a motive for murder?' he protested. 'I know this man Trove slightly, he has always been difficult and outspoken in matters concerning our trade – but murder?'

'Is obtaining the rank of a master important?' asked de Wolfe.

'Very much so, especially if a man is ambitious and wishes to set up on his own,' replied Stephen. 'And to have your master-piece rejected once, let alone twice, is indeed a slur on a craftsman's proficiency. It means that he would be condemned to working as a journeyman for ever, certainly in Exeter. His only hope would be to move somewhere far away, where his history is unknown, and to try again.'

The warden told them that Trove worked for an iron founder down on the river, just outside the city on the marshes beyond the West Gate. Plentiful supplies of water flowing along the leets that meandered through the flood plain allowed a number of mills to operate there. Most were fulling mills for the wool industry, but there were also a few iron smelters and founders, who used the power of millwheels to drive bellows and hammers for their metalworking.

The coroner and Gwyn hurried through the early-morning crowds thronging the shops and stalls until they emerged through the West Gate. They took Frog Lane across Exe Island, the swampy ground between the city wall and the river, which curved around to the north where many of the mills were situated. Shacks and shanties were dotted around the edges of the leets and streams, always in danger of being flooded or washed away when the Exe flooded after rainstorms up on Exmoor. But today was dry and cold, and they soon reached the mill which Stephen de Radone had described to them.

The place was a hive of activity. Looking into one of the high, open-fronted sheds, John could imagine that he was on the threshold of Hell. Amidst mounds of ore and charcoal, a bulbous furnace was issuing forth a stream of white-hot iron, around which several foundrymen were capering, holding long rods, guiding the liquid metal into stone and clay moulds. Though fascinated by the sight, John tore himself away and found the ironmaster cloistered with a miserable-looking clerk in a hut that served as their office and counting-house.

John tersely explained their mission to the master, a prosperous-looking man with a large paunch, and a rim of grey beard around his plump face.

'He's gone,' declared the ironmaster. 'Said he was sick, then just walked out two days ago without a word. He always was an awkward fellow, though he worked hard enough.'

'Did you know about his trouble with the guilds?'

'Of course. Mind you, he brought it on himself, he was a cussed individual, wouldn't take advice.' He explained that Geoffrey Trove refused to offer a conventional object as his master-piece, even though he was a competent craftsman.

'Instead of casting an elegant door knocker or forging a handsome dagger, the damned fool insisted on making some strange device. He claimed it was a miniature crossbow that a man could hang from his belt and use to deter robbers.'

John and Gwyn looked at each other on hearing this apparent confirmation that Trove must have been the culprit.

'Was he much incensed at his rejection by the guild masters?' asked John.

'Hard to tell, he was such a surly, close-lipped devil. I wouldn't have thought he would commit murder over it, but you never can tell with these silent ones.'

Further questioning brought out the fact that Geoffrey Trove was unmarried, so far as anyone knew, though he had come several years ago from Bristol as a journey man and no one knew anything of his past history.

'He lived alone in one of those huts on the island,' said the master, waving a podgy, be-ringed hand down towards the distant Exe bridge, still unfinished after several years' construction. 'Don't ask me which one, someone on Frog Lane will tell you. I have to admit that he looked very poorly when he left here.'

'What was wrong with him?' asked de Wolfe.

'God knows, he would rarely give you the time of day. But he held one arm stiffly and his face was flushed as if he had a fever. I told him to seek an apothecary.'

Leaving the master to count his profits with his clerk, the two law officers retraced their steps back across the marshes, shivering as a fresh north wind moaned about them, reminding them that once again, snow might not be all that far away. 'Let's hope it keeps off a bit longer,' grumbled Gwyn, thinking of their proposed search of Dartmoor the next day.

Enquiry led them to a cottage that was larger and more substantial than some of the shacks. It was built on the edge of a muddy channel that had been strengthened by stonework, making the cottage safer than some of the mean huts that were literally sliding into the leets. It was a square box built of cob on a wooden frame and had a thatched roof in fair condition. There were no windows, but a front and back door of oaken planks. The back door was barred from inside and the front door had a complicated metal lock.

'Probably made it himself,' observed John, rattling the massive padlock in a futile attempt to shake it open.

They hammered on the doors, getting no response. Gwyn stood back and studied the door with a critical eye. 'That will take some breaking down. Do you really need to get inside, Crowner?'

John nodded, scowling at the barrier of oak that was frustrating them. 'If that device for shooting iron rods is inside, that would clinch his guilt,' he growled.

'Do you want me to try and smash it open?'

John reluctantly shook his head. 'You'd do yourself an injury. There's no great urgency, I'll get Gabriel to bring a couple of men down here later with a length of tree trunk. If there's no answer then, they can batter it open and see if there's anything incriminating in there.'

As they walked back towards the city de Wolfe wondered where Geoffrey Trove might have got to, if he was not in his place of work or at home.

'Let's try St John's Priory, maybe he's sought the ministrations of Brother Saulf in the infirmary, if he really is ill.'

St John's was the only place in Exeter where sick persons could find a bed and have some sympathetic care offered to them. However, this time Brother Saulf could not help, as no such person as Trove had been to the infirmary and he had never heard of him.

Baffled, de Wolfe and Gwyn returned to Rougemont, where they found Thomas hard at work copying rolls for the next visitation of the Commissioners of Gaol Delivery. But he also had news of a different visitation, one that Hubert Walter had promised.

'The sheriff's clerk asked me to tell you that Sir Walter de Ralegh, together with another justice, will arrive in Exeter one week from now, to hear the case of Nicholas de Arundell,' announced Thomas, with a satisfied smile on his peaky face.

'That makes it all the more urgent to find our Nick o' the Moors,' said the coroner to his officer. As they settled down to their mid-morning ale and bread, John complimented his clerk on his genius in thinking of the iron connection in the murders, which now seemed to have been confirmed beyond any doubt.

'We even know the name of the bastard who's

responsible,' he concluded, as Thomas wriggled in self-conscious delight at this rare praise from his master.

'But like de Arundell, we can't find the bugger!' boomed Gwyn. 'They've both vanished into thin air, so if you really are a genius, tell us where we can find them.'

The little priest took him seriously and began to tick off the possibilities on his thin fingers. 'He's not at his work, or his dwelling. Neither is he sick in the infirmary. He's not likely to be in St Nicholas priory, as they don't encourage outsiders to share their sickbeds.' Thomas stopped with three fingers displayed. 'You say he was a stranger in Exeter, having come from Bristol, so he'll have no relatives to stay with, so either he's left the city or he's holed up in some lodging.'

The big Cornishman grunted derisively. 'Doesn't need a genius to come to that conclusion. Which lodging, that's the point?'

At the lodging in question, a young woman stood uncertainly in the centre of the room and looked down at the bed, a hessian bag stuffed with a random mixture of feathers from fowl, geese and ducks.

It was not this primitive mattress that caused the worried look on her face, but the man who lay on it, groaning as he nursed his left arm. Denise had done her best with a pot of salve from an apothecary and a wide strip of linen torn from her only bedsheet. She had anointed the angry slash on Trove's forearm with the green paste and wrapped it with several turns of the cloth, tying it in place with a length of blue ribbon. But the wound had become redder and more swollen, and pink tracks had begun to climb up the skin of his arm towards the shoulder.

'You need better attention than I can give you, Geoffrey,' she exclaimed for the tenth time. 'I'm no leech or Sister of Mercy, what do I know of tending wounds?'

The journeyman gritted his teeth against the throbbing in his arm as he struggled to a sitting position. 'It will pass, woman. Give it time, it was not much more than a scratch.'

He cursed the carelessness with which he had detached his shooting device from the back of the privy. In the dark and in haste to remove it before anyone came to investigate, he had slashed his bare forearm against the end of the laminated leaf-spring that shot the missile. The injury itself was not serious, but by the next day, the deep scratch had become angry, and by the day after it was oozing pus. He suspected that some evil miasma had splashed upon his device from the ordure pit below, where there was a wide opening for the night-soil man to shovel out the contents.

Denise, a handsome girl of about twenty years, seemed close to tears. 'You'll die, Geoffrey, I know you will, unless you have it seen to properly. I had an uncle who stabbed his foot with a fork when he was hoeing turnips . . . he died in the most awful convulsions a week later.'

The iron-worker glowered at her. 'Thanks, that really cheers me up! Look, if it's worse by tomorrow, you can call an apothecary.' He subsided on to the palliasse again, waves of heat passing over him in spite of the coldness of the room, which was heated only by a charcoal brazier set on a stone slab in the centre of the rush-covered floor. The dwelling was a single room at the back of a silversmith's shop in Waterbeer Lane, behind the High Street. It had been Denise's place of business when she was a working whore, but now Geoffrey's generosity allowed her to keep all her favours for him. He had patronised her for a long period as a regular client, but a brusque affection and sense of possession had gradually developed, so that he had even thought of marrying the wench once he had set up in his own business as a master craftsman, but those bastards rejecting his application had scuppered all his plans.

Still, he had almost got even with them all now; only the last venture against Gilbert le Bator had gone wrong – and left him with a poisoned arm into the bargain.

He had had to leave his employment when the arm became useless and, though his master knew he was sick, he doubted whether he would ever go back. Something told him that the failed attempt on the weaver's life the other night would lead to his exposure if he stayed in the city, so he had abandoned his mean hut on the marshes and moved in with his mistress. As soon as his arm had healed, he would leave Exeter and take Denise away to yet another fresh start, perhaps this time in Gloucester. But first of all, he had one last score to settle.

Matilda's new hobby of being solicitous to Lady Joan de Arundell caused her to be very concerned at the news that Sir Nicholas had disappeared. She made none of her usual complaints when her husband announced that he had to ride off at dawn the next day to look for Nicholas, and she even added her own exhortations to John to spare no effort in finding the former outlaw.

'He must be told of his release from this iniquitous stigma,' she exclaimed. 'That poor woman, at first full of joy at his salvation, is now plunged into misery because he has vanished.'

It was unlike Matilda to be so melodramatic, and John wondered at her state of mind. For a fleeting moment, he wondered if her going mad could be grounds for annulment of their marriage, then forgot the notion.

In the cold light of the following dawn, Gwyn waited patiently outside on his mare while de Wolfe had the farrier saddle up his favourite gelding for the ride to Dartmoor. They met Sergeant Gabriel and two men-at-arms at the end of North Street and sallied out of the nearby gate towards the village of Ide and then onward to Moretonhampstead.

The sky was by now a sullen slate grey, with a suggestion of pinkness nearer the horizon, and the leather-faced sergeant mournfully prophesied snow before evening. The air was cold and still, but the going was good and they made rapid progress at a steady trot up and down the fertile undulations that led to the high moor.

'Where are we aiming for?' asked Gwyn when the little town locally known as Moreton came into sight. 'We haven't the slightest idea where Nicholas may be holed up.'

'Let's talk to the folk in the tavern, maybe someone will have an idea,' growled John. 'It was there that Lady Joan's messenger used to meet one of the men from Challacombe.'

When they reined in at the alehouse and entered for a welcome jug of ale and some hot potage, they learned nothing of Nicholas de Arundell's whereabouts, but picked up many rumours of an attack upon him.

Like all tales in the countryside, they improved with the telling, and the exaggerations of the attack on Challacombe had expanded until it seemed impossible that any of the outlaws could have survived. The patrons that morning were eager to offer their versions of the drama to de Wolfe, until his habitually thin store of patience ran out and he grabbed the taverner by the arm.

'For Christ's sake, man, let's have some sense here,' he snapped. 'Have you any real idea what happened over in Challacombe?'

The chastened landlord held up his hands in supplication. 'It's all gossip, Crowner,' he pleaded. 'But certainly some armed band came up from Widecombe way and there was a fight with Nick o' the Moor's men. One of the locals here, who's not above taking a rabbit or even an injured deer over that way, said he was in the Challacombe valley a week past and saw the old huts burnt out and no sign of any life there.'

'Is there no rumour of where they might have gone?' demanded Gwyn belligerently, for he did not like the look of this crafty fellow.

'Like will-o'-the-wisp is that Nicholas. They do say he has several hideouts across the moor, one of them being up towards Sittaford Tor.' This was one of the most remote parts of the high moor, with vast areas of deserted land around it.

'Might just as well tell us he's somewhere on the bloody moon!' grumbled Gwyn.

They could get nothing more of any use from the men in the tavern and after finishing their food and ale, John decided to strike out for Challacombe, across the indistinct track along which he had been taken when he first visited Nicholas de Arundell. The snow was holding off, and again they made good time over the firm, dry ground so that by noon, they were coming down below Hameldown Tor across the grassy bowl that held the strange ancient stones of Grimspound. There was nothing to tell them that a major ambush had been set here not long before, and they continued down on to the track that led southwards down the valley. The bleak countryside seemed deserted, and apart from birds the only life they saw was a dog fox lurking alongside the Webburn stream. Within a mile, they came to the stunted trees that surrounded the old village where John and his officer had spent a night.

'All burnt out, Crowner,' called Gabriel, who was riding a few yards ahead of them; the two soldiers were at the rear. As they crossed the stream and came up the slope to the old walls, they could see that the rough thatch that had been on several of the huts had collapsed into a blackened mess. When they dismounted and walked inside the wall around the settlement, the acrid smell of scorched branches and bracken assailed their nostrils. Though the large moorstones that made up the walls were still in place, the interiors of the primitive dwellings were reduced to heaps of sodden, blackened debris from the roofs. An ominous silence hung over the old village, broken only by the eerie hoot of a disturbed owl from the nearby trees.

There was nothing to be gained by staying, and the coroner motioned the others back to their horses. Just as they were filing through the gap in the wall, Gabriel stopped and pointed across the yard that lay in front of the nearest huts. 'What's that there? It looks very recent.'

John's gaze followed his finger and saw a heap of earth in a corner, on top of which was fixed a crude wooden cross made from two branches lashed together with cord. When they all went over to look, they saw that the earth was freshly dug; no weeds were on the surface, and the broken ends of the cross were pale where living sticks had been snapped through.

'What poor soul is under there, I wonder?' murmured John. The two soldiers crossed themselves and even the agnostic Gwyn bowed his head in respect. De Wolfe only hoped that the occupant was not Nicholas de Arundell, but there was no way of telling what had happened. It was now obvious from the destruction of the camp and the recent grave that the outlaws had been attacked and that someone had paid with ther life.

'Where do we go from here?' asked Gwyn, as they swung back into the saddle and began walking their horses back through the trees to the place where they had crossed over the little river.

'Deeper into the moor, north from here,' answered the coroner, with a confidence that he did not feel. Dartmoor covered about four hundred square miles and the outlaw band could be almost anywhere within it, assuming that they had not been wiped out in the attack.

As they turned left on the main track, retracing their path towards Grimspound, those behind suddenly saw the sergeant tense in his saddle and grab for the ball mace that hung from his saddlebow.

A voice called out from behind the last tree in the copse that lined the stream, and a figure stepped cautiously out from behind it.

'Crowner! Crowner John!'

A ginger-haired youth, muffled in a cloak made of poorly cured deerskins, advanced on them, his hands held high to show that he was no threat. Gwyn was the first to recognise him as one of the outlaws.

'Peter Cuffe, it is you, Peter?' he roared.

The redhead came up to them, smiling now that he was in no danger of being brained by Gabriel's fearsome mace. Explanations soon followed, and it became clear that the youngest of the gang had been sent as a lookout. He had been three days on his own, sleeping in a shallow cave up on the ridge above and watching for anyone approaching the ruined village.

'Nick hoped that we would be contacted by someone. We were unable to send anyone to Moreton last week to keep the usual rendezvous, though next Monday we were going to be there, as we knew Lady Joan would be worried.'

He described the attack on Challacombe and the tactical withdrawal of the outlaws to Grimspound, where they had outwitted the invaders and made them flee.

'I knew it, roared Gwyn. "Those bastards de Revelle and Pomeroy! Surely they must hang for this.'

De Wolfe shook his head sadly. 'For what? Attempting to clear out a nest of outlaws, as is their right and indeed duty? They could even have claimed the wolf's head bounty had they succeeded.'

'They did succeed in one instance,' said Peter Cuffe sadly. 'Poor old Gunilda died, that's her grave in the yard. We found her body when we crept back after those swine had left.'

There were growls of anger from Gwyn and the men-at-arms, but John kept his mind on the present situation. 'We are hoping for a pardon for you all from the king,' he explained. 'So I need to talk to Sir Nicholas as soon as possible. Where is he now?'

Peter Cuffe explained that after the ruination of Challacombe, they had withdrawn to a temporary camp, in cave shelters that were just about habitable. A few days later, they had moved again to slightly less miserable quarters in old huts belonging to an abandoned tin-streaming works above Chagford.

As the winter's day was rapidly advancing, they set off at once, Cuffe sitting up behind Gwyn. He had no horse, and the back of the Cornishman's big mare was the broadest of the group's steeds. The ginger lad guided their path, which meandered between the bare downs and valleys, going ever northward without ever meeting any habitation. Even though de Wolfe reassured Cuffe that he was no longer in any danger of being beheaded, two years as a fugitive were too deeply ingrained in the lad's soul for him to take any chances.

The early dusk was falling as they reached a small valley, little more than a deep gouge cut into the moor by a fast-running stream. They were near the eastern edge of the high moor, and in the far distance a few glimmers of light showed where a hamlet or farm nestled in the greener, more fertile land down below.

Directed by Cuffe, the riders went carefully down into the small gorge, their horses slithering on the mud and stones of the bank until they reached the stream, which babbled and gurgled between boulders on its rapid journey to join the Teign a few miles away. The ginger youth gave a piercing whistle, and an answering whistle came from a few hundred yards further down. In the gathering gloom, John saw the rotting remnants of wooden sluices and troughs where tin-washing had once been carried on. Underfoot, serried piles of gravel lay in a herringbone fashion, where the river bank had been dug out in the search for ore and the useless tailings had been discarded.

The whistling had come from a pair of low huts, built as usual of dark moorstones piled on top of each other, roofed with branches and turf. Originally shelters for the miners and places to store their tools, the huts were now the refuge of the outlaw band, an even more primitive lodging than the old village at Challacombe.

As de Wolfe's party approached, men hurried out of the holes that formed the doorways and stood awaiting them in anxious anticipation. Foremost was Nicholas de Arundell, unshaven and dishevelled, as were all of his men.

'Thank God it's you, Sir John,' he said fervently, clasping the coroner's hands. 'What news have you for us?'

'Good, certainly hopeful, Nicholas,' replied the coroner, shivering as he slid from his horse's back. 'Your accommodation here looks less luxurious than that when we last met, but I would be glad of some shelter while we talk.'

The outlaw chief hustled them to the doorway of the nearest hut, but Gabriel said he would go with his two men to the other shanty, a few yards away. The dozen or so residents clustered around, and some took the visitors, horses to join their own, which were tethered further down the stream. With much shouting about hot potage and ale, the two groups parted, and de Wolfe and Gwyn squeezed into the main hut, which was barely high enough to allow them to stand upright.

Nicholas waved a hand expressively at the heaps of bracken that lined the walls, inviting them to sit down in a circle around a small ring of stones in the centre, which confined a smoky fire of logs hacked from the stunted trees in the valley.

'Thank God we are old Crusaders, Sir John. These are poor quarters even for us, but I know you will understand that we have little option, as those bastards once again deprived me of my home, simple though the last one was.'

As they squatted on the beds, Philip Girard, Martin Wimund, Robert Hereward and a couple of other men pushed into the hut and shuffled into places opposite, eager to hear any news. Peter Cuffe found a pitcher of cider in a corner and passed around some pottery mugs. 'The stew is being heated in the other place, there's a better fire there than this one,' he explained sheepishly.

'You'll not need to suffer this much longer,' began John, reassuringly. 'From this moment, the Chief Justiciar says that you are no longer outlawed and may return to your homes without fear.'

There was a babble of joyful astonishment and the coroner heard a similar uproar from the other hut, where on John's instructions, Gabriel had passed on the same message. For a few moments, he could hardly speak for a barrage of questions from the men, until Nicholas yelled for quiet.

'We beseech you, Crowner, tell us everything. We have waited so long for this.'

There was silence as John carefully related his visit to Hubert Walter and the promises that the Justiciar had made to them.

'This is virtually as good as the word of King Richard himself,' he concluded. 'But until the royal justices, in the shape of Walter de Ralegh, make a full investigation and pronounce on the matter, we must all tread carefully.'

This sobered the excited men a little, and Nicholas asked what exactly de Wolfe meant by this.

'There is no doubt that the stigma of outlawry has been lifted from you all, as there will be no going back on the word of the king's chief minister. But as to Hempston Arundell, we have to wait for Walter's verdict, though knowing him as I do, I doubt there will be any lack of sympathy for you.'

'So what does that mean as far as we are concerned?' asked Robert Hereward.

'I need Sir Nicholas back in Exeter straightaway, as he must appear before the sheriff, who may wish formally to remove this curse of being an outlaw – and as soon as de Ralegh arrives next week, he will want to see Sir Nicholas.'

'And the rest of us?' demanded Martin Wimund.

'As I said, you are entitled to leave this place as free men. The problem is that Henry de la Pomeroy and Richard de Revelle still occupy the manor they stole from you and will not take kindly to your turning up there before official decisions have been made.'

'So where can we go?' pleaded Philip Girard. 'Most of our band came from Hempston. Our homes are there, and our families.'

John looked across at Gwyn, now dimly visible in the twilight of the unlit hovel. 'No doubt you will all be required as witnesses when Walter de Ralegh begins his enquiry next week, so I do not see any objection to you being housed in Rougemont for that short period. Do you think that is possible, Gwyn?'

His officer bobbed his head over a pot of cider. 'The garrison is small these days, so there's plenty of room. I'll ask Gabriel, and if he thinks it's practicable, we must get permission from Ralph Morin, the castle constable.'

De Wolfe turned back to Nicholas, who looked haunted, as if he feared this was a dream or a cruel joke, and that he would soon wake to find that he was still an outlaw.

'I suggest that you return with us to Exeter in the morning', John said. 'No doubt that kind cousin of your wife will accommodate you in her house. The men must, I'm afraid, stay here for a day or so until we send for them to come down to Rougemont. It would be too risky for them to return to Hempston until the threat of Westminster is held over those bastards down there.'

He suggested that Nicholas go over to the other hut and explain the position to the other half of the band, while he was away, Martin Wimund, the former reeve of Hempston, told John of the attack on Challacombe and the routing of Pomeroy's force up at Grimspound.

'They killed poor Gunilda, a defenceless woman,' growled Girard. 'We found her body, and buried it, when we went back to look at the wreckage of our homes after they fired them.'

'She may have fallen and cracked her skull,' said Hereward. 'But there were bruises on her, and however she came to die, those swine were responsible.'

Nicholas came stooping back into the shed and posed another question: 'We defeated twice our number up at Grimspound,' he said. 'Our archers saved us, but killed two of their men in the battle. Will we be indicted for murder over that?'

John de Wolfe, sticking scrupulously to the law as he saw it, scratched his stubble as he deliberated on this. 'An inquest must be held eventually and I am the coroner for the south of the county. I will hear the evidence, but this was virtually an act of war. You were attacked without provocation by a much larger force, whose members undoubtedly wished to kill you all, so you had no option but to act in self-defence by whatever means you could. That sounds like a good reason to call the deaths justifiable homicide. But we must put her matter to an inquest jury when the time comes.'

The more formal part of the discussion over, the men fell to animated talk about the future and the prospect of seeing their families once again. They trooped out into the open and mixed with their fellows from the other hut. A few who were not from Hempston, but who had drifted into the outlaw band later, wondered what was to become of them, but Nicholas promised that they would be welcome in his manor when it was restored to him. 'We have stuck together in good times and mostly bad, so I'll not see you thrown out to fend for yourselves, good men that you are.'

It was almost dark, but the excited men felt in no mood to sleep, so another hour or more passed before they divided themselves between the two huts and curled up on their crude beds, wrapped in every garment they possessed, but still half-freezing in spite of the glowing wood on the central firepits.

Chapter Sixteen

In which the royal justices arrive

Nicholas returned to the bosom of his family in Raden Lane with great rejoicing, his wife being overjoyed to have him free of the furtive constraints that had required him to skulk into the city in disguise. One of her first tasks was to take him to buy some decent clothes and boots, in place of the worn and dirty raiment he had had on the moor. Her cousin generously gave them both money and two good-quality cloaks that had belonged to her late husband. De Arundell walked with his wife through the crowded streets in a state of nervous awe, hardly able to believe that at any moment he would not feel the heavy hand of arrest on his shoulder.

'We owe everything to Sir John de Wolfe,' said Joan as they walked back towards her cousin's house, the old servant Maurice walking behind them, carrying their purchases from the Serge Market and several shops in High Street.

'Indeed we do, but be cautious, sweet wife,' answered Nicholas. 'Our troubles are not yet over, for we have to see what comes from the deliberations of Walter de Ralegh next week – and to be sure that King Richard has confirmed the Justiciar's promises. I doubt those swine down in the west will give in without a fight.'

'You fought them once and won, husband,' protested Joan loyally.

'I will meet any man in a contest of arms – but those bastards Pomeroy and de Revelle have influential friends and are expert in manipulating the law to their advantage.'

Joan refused to allow her husband's caution to dampen her joy at having him back, and when they returned again to Raden Lane she was able to share her delight with her friend Matilda de Wolfe. The coroner's wife had heard from her husband that Nicholas had returned with him from the moor, and she had hastened to Gillian le Bret's dwelling to offer her felicitations. She was eager to cast her eyes on de Arundell's romantic figure, as he had been by turns a knight, a manor lord, a Crusader, and then a hunted outlaw.

Nicholas welcomed her graciously as the woman who was the wife of his saviour John de Wolfe, as well as someone who had befriended Joan in spite of being the sister of one of the villains. Matilda was instantly charmed by this handsome man, and her resolve to side with John against her brother's cupidity was strengthened on the spot.

'Lady Matilda has been very kind to me, Nicholas,' declared Joan, as they settled around the hearth in Gillian's hall. Over pastries and wine, they discussed the future, and Matilda, a different woman when away from her husband, was encouraging about the outcome.

'My husband, the king's coroner, is very influential,' she affirmed grandly. 'He is acquainted with many powerful people – and indeed the king himself is by no means unaware of his worth, for John was a member of his personal guard when Richard returned from the Holy Land.'

She avoided mentioning that her husband had been unable to prevent the monarch from being captured in Vienna on that ill-fated journey.

'It's not the worth of your John that worries me, good

lady,' responded Nicholas. 'But that other John, Count of Mortain, who may well use his considerable influence to confound the good that your husband has already achieved.'

Gillian le Bret broke in reassuringly. 'Sir Walter de Ralegh is originally a local man, albeit one who has risen high in the chambers of power,' she said. 'He knows the politics of the West Country very well and is a strong character, faithful to King Richard. He is unlikely to be intimidated by the barons and bishops who are beholden to Prince John's ambitions.'

Matilda held her tongue about the fact that it was Walter who had officially ejected her brother from the office of sheriff and had sworn in his successor, Henry de Furnellis. Although she was now firmly against Richard over his part in the seizure of de Arundell's manor, there was a limit to how much she was willing to acknowledge publicly concerning his treachery.

'We can only wait and pray until next week, when the king's judges will hear the matter,' said Joan practically. 'I am sure they will uphold justice and undo the wrong that has been visited upon us. My only wish is to get back to our home in Hempston and live quietly, to pick up the broken threads of my life!'

Matilda laid a comforting hand on the younger woman's shoulder.

'Amen to that,' she said piously. 'I'll add my prayers to yours, twice each day until Walter de Ralegh arrives.'

'We know now that it was definitely this Geoffrey Trove who is the culprit, but where the hell is he?' De Wolfe sounded more aggrieved than angry as he took the stripped bone of a sheep's shank from his platter and dropped it on to the rushes for the expectant Brutus.

'Perhaps he's already in hell, if he was as sick as that ironmaster suggested,' grunted Gwyn from the other side of the table.

'He might have left the city altogether,' said Nesta. 'The fact that he's vanished surely means that he knows he's been marked down as the killer. Wouldn't he want to get as far as possible away from Exeter?'

It was evening, and John was supplementing his supper at home with some extra sustenance at the Bush, with Gwyn enthusiastically following his example. That afternoon, the big Cornishman had returned to Exe Island with Osric, and between them they had kicked down the door of Geoffrey's hut. Amongst the sparse furnishings was a workbench, on which was an iron frame about the size of a quart pot, containing a powerful spring device. It was obviously the machine that had discharged the bolt that had injured the guild master in Rock Lane. Gwyn had brought the strange weapon down to the tavern, where they studied it with interest.

'Evil as he must be, he is a clever fellow and a very good craftsman,' said John, peering appreciatively at the fine workmanship of the mechanism.

'Is that blood on one corner?' observed Nesta, whose younger eyes were the keenest. She pointed to a sharp edge where the end of the strong laminated spring projected beyond the square casing. Gwyn spat on his forefinger and rubbed it on the brown stain. It came away reddened and he nodded in satisfaction.

'Can't be the victim's blood, he was yards away when this thing was fired. So it must have come from the bastard who made it.'

'But where is he?' repeated de Wolfe once more. Having tracked down the identity of the killer, he was now mortified not to be able to lay hands on him. If he had seized him, he could have dragged him before Walter de Ralegh when he held his special court in a few days' time. Geoffrey Trove could have been tried and sentenced without further delay, so that the evil fellow could have been hanged straightaway, relieving the minds of all the other guild officers who had been in fear of their own lives these past few weeks.

Nesta signalled to old Edwin to refill their ale pots, then slipped her arm through John's, as they sat side by side on the bench near the hearth.

'What's the connection between this Trove bastard and Hempston Arundell?' asked Gwyn. 'It must have been him who so foully attacked your wife, Crowner. But what did he mean about it being justice for Hempston or whatever he said?'

De Wolfe frowned as he did when in deep thought. 'He must have been one of those men that left the manor when de Arundell was evicted, then left the outlaw band some time ago. They said one was a freeman blacksmith, which is a bit unusual, but I can't recall what they said his name was. He must have combined getting even with the men who ejected his master-piece with wanting to scare de Revelle and Pomeroy.'

Nesta clutched at his arm. 'Do you think he's still plotting to do some harm to your brother-in-law and that pig of a man down in Berry?'

'He's hardly in a position to do much, is he? He's on the run, he must guess by now that we know who he is. I reckon he'll make tracks for some distant part of England, or even try to take ship across the channel.'

Gwyn shook his head, his wild locks bouncing. 'He could still slip a blade between Richard's ribs one dark night – with a bit of luck,' he added impishly.

Usually, when the royal justices or the Commissioners of Gaol Delivery arrived in the city, there was a considerable amount of pomp and ceremony. They were invariably met on the high road outside Exeter by the sheriff, coroner and portreeves, who escorted them into the city with a score of mounted men-at-arms led by the castle constable.

However, about noon on the following Monday, a small

group of horsemen trotted in without the usual pageant. These were two noblemen with a couple of clerks and a few armed servants, who made their way to the New Inn, the city's largest hostelry, which lay in High Street towards the East Gate. This was the usual lodging for judges, and as soon as the sheriff and coroner heard that Sir Walter de Ralegh had arrived, they hurried down to greet them.

Walter was a tall, grizzled man in his sixties, still with a strong Devon accent that betrayed his origins, having been born near East Budleigh, a village near the coast less than a dozen miles from Exeter. De Ralegh had risen high in the service of the king, both the old Henry and now the Lionheart. He was a senior justice and a man respected both for his forthright views and for his honesty, a rare quality in the corridors of power. Being a local man, he was often chosen by the Chief Justiciar to deal with problems in the West Country, and he had several times been involved with John de Wolfe in such matters.

The sheriff, coroner and judges now sat in a private parlour of the New Inn, Walter with his riding boots off to ease his feet after the ride from Honiton, where they had stayed the previous night on their journey down from Winchester. He introduced his companion judge, who was a former Commissioner who had recently been elevated to the Eyre circuit. This was Reginald de Bohun, a baron from the Welsh Marches who owned manors between Hereford and Shrewsbury, as well as estates in the north. He was a great-nephew of the great Humphrey de Bohun, Steward of England. Younger than Walter, de Bohun was about de Wolfe's age, of average height, with dark brown hair cut in the typical Norman manner, a dense cap left above a closely shaven neck. He spoke only when he had something useful to say, but John felt he was a man who decided matters on the facts, rather than on emotions or the convenience of the situation.

Walter de Ralegh, a blunter and more outspoken character than de Bohun stretched out his legs with a groan as he reached for a jug of cider on the table. 'I'm getting too old for all this hacking around the countryside,' he complained. 'This is the second time this year Hubert has sent me down here to deal with Richard bloody Revelle. Unless we can hang him out of the way, I might as well come back to Devon to live. It would save my arse from wearing out in the saddle.'

Hubert Walter, who had sent the pair of justices down to Exeter, had outlined the problem to them, but now John and the sheriff repeated it and filled in the details of the seizure of Hempston Arundell by the two miscreants.

'And this occurred while Nicholas de Arundell was away at the Crusades?' asked de Bohun.

'It did indeed, which makes it such a despicable trick,' growled de Wolfe. 'De la Pomeroy convinced his poor wife that some mythical man returning from the Holy Land had reported that her husband had perished.'

'And then he and de Revelle claimed that on the death of the freeholder, the manor reverted to the Crown,' added de Furnellis. 'But as Prince John had been granted all of Devon and Cornwall by the king, it actually escheated to him.'

'Who then conveniently passed it over to his favourites,' completed John. 'Pomeroy claimed that he was to get the actual land in fee simple and that de Revelle would share the rents and income with him equally.'

'All based on the basic lie that the manor lord was dead,' grunted de Ralegh.

'Did the wife accept this tale?' asked Reginald de Bohun.

John shrugged. 'It seems so, though her steward told me that she was so distraught by the reports of his death that she was in no fit state to fight back, other than to deny the claim and look to her servants to help her.'

De Bohun looked across at his judicial colleague. 'I think for the sake of fairness, we should not try this case behind closed doors like this,' he said firmly. 'Let us wait and hear what the various parties have to say about it on Wednesday.'

The enquiry into the annexation of Hempston Arundell was not a trial in the same sense as the Eyre of Assize or the Commissioner's hearings, for there was no jury, as the two royal justices would be the sole arbiters of the matter. The proceedings were heard in public in the same Shire Hall that saw so many other legal events, such as the county courts, the burgess courts, inquests and the Eyres and Gaol Delivery themselves. Even though the matter was serious and, given the rank of the disputants, might even have political significance, it attracted little public interest. However, a few spectators assembled on the hard-packed earth of the floor to listen to what was being said on the low platform at the end of the hall.

The sheriff's messengers had previously warned Richard de Revelle and Henry de la Pomeroy of the date of the judge's arrival, and had commanded them in the king's name to present themselves on pain of heavy amercements if they failed to show up. The two defiant defendants duly appeared with a retinue of supporters, including their bailiffs, stewards and reeves.

In deference to their rank, these main players were not obliged to stand in the body of the court with the common witnesses, but were provided with a couple of tables and some benches, set on one side of the dais. On the other side, a similar trestle was placed for Nicholas de Arundell and his wife Joan, with her cousin Gillian le Bret as a chaperone. There were further tables at the back for the clerks, who were drawn from the sheriff's staff and the pair who had accompanied the judges. For once, there was no need for Thomas de

Peyne to be sitting up there with quill and ink, but he stood with Gwyn and the coroner behind the clerks, listening to the proceedings.

In the centre, seats had been brought for the two judges. These were high-backed chairs, borrowed from the sheriff's quarters in the keep, and they were flanked by a more modest pair for the sheriff and a priest, who sat one on each side of the justices. As always, the Church insisted on being present, especially as this case might concern a wrong done to a man on Crusade. Partly at de Wolfe's instigation, the priest was John de Alencon, Archdeacon of Exeter. Though he would play no role in the judgement, he was a firm supporter of the king and a covert antagonist of the Count of Mortain.

At the eighth hour of the morning, the cast of this impending drama assembled, with all of Nicholas's former outlaws standing uneasily below the dais, a row of men-at-arms behind them to separate them from the onlookers. Sergeant Gabriel patrolled the hall, loping around to make sure there was no disturbance, and he in turn was watched from the wide doorway by the massive figure of the castle constable, Ralph Morin, his forked beard jutting out like the prow of a ship.

On the platform, Richard de Revelle, dandified in a bright blue tunic covered with a fur-lined pelisse of red wool, nervously settled himself behind the table, with a more soberly dressed Henry de la Pomeroy scowling on his right hand. Between them was a stranger, a man of about thirty with a smooth, olive face. He was dressed in a plain black tunic and had a clerk's tonsure and a small silver cross hanging from a chain around his neck, suggesting that he was a priest of some kind. Lying before him was a roll of parchment and a large book.

Behind them stood bailiff Coffin of Berry Pomeroy and the steward from de Revelle's manor, together with two of their reeves. Nicholas was similarly supported by his steward Robert Hereward, and the reeve Martin Wimund.

At a signal from the constable, there was a discordant blast on a trumpet wielded by one of Rougemont's soldiers. Gabriel marched towards the platform ahead of the Archdeacon, who had entered the hall followed by the two royal judges, with the sheriff bringing up the rear. As everyone stood in deference, they royal judge climbed the step to the dais and stood before their chairs while John de Alencon delivered a short prayer, calling down the wisdom of God to help them arrive at a just verdict that day.

As soon as everyone had sat down and shuffled themselves into place, Sir Walter de Ralegh lost no time in getting down to business.

'Let this issue be put before us without delay!' He leaned forward and spoke in a loud, authoritative voice in a tone that indicated that he was in time no mood for prevarication. 'The king's officer in this county of Devon, Sir Henry de Furnellis, will state the nature of the dispute and call witnesses as to the facts.'

The grey-haired sheriff climbed to his feet, but before he could open his mouth, the sleek cleric who sat next to Richard de Revelle also rose.

'My lords, I wish to submit that these proceedings cannot proceed, as it would be unlawful so to do.'

Walter de Ralegh turned to glare at the interruption. His eyesight not being what it was, he peered aggressively at the defendants' table.

'Who the hell are you, sir?' he demanded.

'I am Joscelin de Sucote, my lord. A clerk and lawyer, presently chaplain to Prince John, Count of Mortain, at his court in Gloucester.'

Walter squinted again to get the man into sharper focus. 'Oh, it's you again, is it? What the devil do you want here?' He turned to his fellow judge and muttered audibly, 'It's that damned lawyer of John's, who tried to interfere when I kicked de Revelle out of office.'

Joscelin was unperturbed by the jibe. 'I have been assigned by the Count to assist his tenants-in-chief, as the prince himself has a considerable interest in the ownership of the disputed lands.'

Walter scowled at the self-assured man whose manner verged on the patronising. 'I'm not sure that I need to hear anything from you. You have no official standing in this court.'

De Sucote waved a hand airily. 'On the contrary, my lord, at their specific request, I am the legal representative of both Sir Richard de Revelle and Sir Henry de la Pomeroy and thus am fully entitled to speak on their behalf.'

De Ralegh glowered at Joscelin, whose Levantine appearance suggested that in spite of his French name, he came from the southern part of France and possibly had Moorish ancestry. 'Have they suddenly lost the power of speech, that they need you to try to explain their actions?' he bellowed.

Reginald de Bohun discreetly touched his arm. 'It would be best to let him have his say. He is entitled, if he really is acting for these men.'

The senior justice muttered under his breath, but waved a hand reluctantly at Joscelin. 'Say your piece then and get it over with.'

The lawyer leaned on his table with one hand and waved the other towards the group of men standing below him in the hall.

'These are outlaws, as is their leader over there!' He pointed a finger at Nicholas de Arundell sitting opposite. 'They were properly declared exigent by a previous sheriff, and as such have no rights whatsoever to bring a legal suit. In the eyes of the law, they do not even exist and by rights should be executed forthwith, as my clients here recently attempted to do on behalf of the people of this county.'

A buzz of concern went around the court and the former fugitives from Dartmoor looked about them in alarm, afraid that they had been betrayed by the promise of amnesty.

'Sit down, de Sucote or whatever your name is,' bellowed Walter de Ralegh. 'You are totally misinformed and are wasting the time of this court. Sir Nicholas and his men have been granted a free pardon by the king – not that they should have been branded as outlaws in the first place.'

Unabashed, Joscelin remained standing and again addressed the justices in a tone of polite insolence.

'I beg leave to dispute that fact, my lord. As I understand it, the so-called pardon was given by Hubert Walter, not Richard Plantagenet.'

Walter rose to his feet and angrily pointed a quivering finger at the lawyer-priest. 'You are becoming insufferable, sir! Firstly, the Chief Justiciar has been given authority by our blessed monarch to act in his name in all judicial functions and therefore *his* actions in this matter are the *king's* actions. Secondly, despatches that arrived at Southampton three days ago from the court at Rouen contained specific confirmation by King Richard of the Justiciar's action. So sit down and shut up, unless you have anything useful to say.'

Even the arrogant clerk hesitated to continue his defiance of the fiery old warrior, though he would have liked proof of the king's confirmation of Arundell's pardon. A quick calculation in his mind told him that it was just possible for a reply to have arrived from Normandy in the time since the Justiciar had lifted the sentence of outlawry. Though it was not the sailing season in the Channel, vital despatches continued to pass in each direction throughout the year, and with favourable winds the crossing could be made in one day. Reluctantly, he subsided to his bench, his first attempt at defence having failed.

The sheriff then outlined the circumstances of the dispute, from the alleged reports of the death of Nicholas to the riot at Hempston Arundell and the banishment of Nicholas and his men.

Reginald de Bohun began with a very pertinent question to Henry de la Pomeroy.

'Tell me how you heard that de Arundell had been killed in Palestine. Can you prove that you had such a message?'

Henry flushed and looked to de Revelle and his steward for help. 'It was common knowledge, I can't recall where and when I heard it. No doubt my manor officials will confirm that.'

'No doubt they would, but common knowledge is hardly proof,' said de Bohun sarcastically. 'You seem to have no name or details of the mysterious monk who brought news of this supposed death. Have you any evidence to persuade me that this was anything other than a convenient rumour?'

Pomeroy evidently did not, and after getting no help from de Revelle he sat down in confusion, still muttering about 'common knowledge'.

Nicholas then stood to state emphatically that he had not suffered so much as a slight wound during his two years' campaigning in Sicily, Cyprus and the Holy Land, let alone been in danger of being reported dead. The questioning went on for another hour, the two judges relentlessly picking at every item, in spite of Joscelin de Sucote's efforts to bolster the meagre facts and to challenge the judges' right to ask certain questions.

Joan then stepped foward to relate how the two manor lords had arrived on her doorstep with a troop of retainers and armed men, to inform her that her husband was dead and that the manor now escheated to Prince John, as he had previously been granted the whole of the two western counties by his royal brother. In the court she stood alongside her husband, neat and demure in a blue gown under a heavy woollen cloak, and spoke in a clear voice that rang out over the hushed court.

'These men said that the prince had given Hempston into their care and that I was to move out within three days. I protested loud and long, but with no husband to turn to, nor any relatives closer than Trefry in Cornwall, I was helpless. My steward, faithful Robert Hereward who sits here, did all he could, but they beat him and turned him out of his dwelling.'

There were vociferous denials from the defendants' bench, but Hereward, the reeve Martin Wimund and Philip Girard all vehemently confirmed their mistress's account.

The story moved on to the return of Nicholas from Outremer, to find his wife gone and a strange steward installed in the hall of his manor house. The altercation that ensued then was the most controversial part of the evidence, as the riot that broke out when Nicholas's old servants joined him in attempting to evict the intruders had led to the death of one of Pomeroy's men.

'I submit that these soon-to-be outlaws set upon the legitimate servants of the manor and sorely assaulted them,' brayed the lawyer Joscelin. 'They murdered one man and seriously injured others. They fled, realising the enormity of their crime, and when they failed to appear to answer for it at four sessions of the county court, they were quite properly outlawed.'

A red-faced and choleric Henry de la Pomeroy jumped up to confirm this, though de Revelle sat strangely quiet, nods of assent seeming to be the most that he would contribute to his defence.

'But I understand that within an hour of the return of Sir Nicholas, a force of armed men arrived from nearby Berry Pomeroy, bent on ejecting them from the manor,' cut in de Bohun, seizing the weak point of the denials. 'Surely they must have been the greater force, and the returning Crusader with only the support of a few old manor servants would have little chance against them?'

For another hour and more, accusations and counter-claims were bandied back and forth, with Walter de Ralegh forcefully keeping the parties to the relevant issues and Reginald de Bohun more quietly interjecting questions and comments which went to the heart of the matter.

Finally they came to the day of the attack on Challacombe and the fiasco at Grimspound. Here the suave voice of de Sucote laid great emphasis on the killing of the two men from Berry Pomeroy by Nicholas's archers, calling it 'yet more murders which should be punished by hanging'.

Walter de Ralegh dryly observed that when a much greater force turns up fully armed, those attacked must surely be entitled to defend themselves to the best of their ability. Pomeroy and de Revelle, together with their advocate, made great play of the claim that they were doing a public service by marching against outlaws in order to slay them and legitimately rid the Devon countryside of evil thieves and robbers.

'Again, very convenient timing,' observed de Bohun with scarcely veiled sarcasm. 'Having just heard that Sir John de Wolfe, the king's coroner, was riding to London to seek the intervention of the Justiciar, you suddenly decided to rid the high moor of men who had already been there for well over two years.'

The deaths of the soldiers at Grimspound was balanced by statements not only from Nicholas and his men, but also from de Wolfe, to the effect that an old woman, Gunilda Hemforde, had died in the attack and was found hastily buried in the yard at Challacombe. Strident denials of her murder were made by the defendants, but eventually some admissions were made by Pomeroy's men of some rough handling of the lady in an effort to get her to reveal the whereabouts of the outlaws.

Noon was approaching by the time all the evidence and disputation was completed. More citizens had drifted in by now, as news had percolated through the streets that a right royal row was brewing in the castle – a couple of score spectators were now packing in behind the half-circle of soldiers.

Finally, the two justices turned to each other and spent ten minutes in a head-to-head discussion, speaking in low voices that even the sheriff and the archdeacon could not discern. The murmur of conversation in the Shire Hall was muted as the two judges eventually broke apart and Walter de Ralegh stood up in front of his chair, a tall and forbidding figure. His head moved slowly from side to side as he spoke first towards the defendants' table, then at Nicholas de Arundell, the plaintiff.

'This issue perplexes my brother lord and myself, but it must be resolved,' he began in his deep, uncompromising voice. 'The fault is undoubtedly mainly on the side of those two manor lords Henry de la Pomeroy and Richard de Revelle, who have acted shamefully in this matter.'

There was a gush of protest from Joscelin de Sucote at this defamation of his clients, but Walter waved him back into his seat with a peremptory wave of his hand.

'To take advantage of a lady whose courageous husband was absent both on the king's business in Sicily and Cyprus and especially on the Holy Crusade, was despicable. We consider that using the patently fictitious excuse that her husband had died was a cruel falsehood based on an alleged rumour, probably circulated by the defendants themselves.'

He turned to John de Alencon, who sat next to him. 'Archdeacon, I understand that the Church has particular strictures against those who take advantage of absent Crusaders?'

De Ralegh knew this perfectly well, but wanted it voiced from an ecclesiastical throat. De Alencon was happy to oblige.

'Indeed it does. Rome is firm upon the issue, even up to withdrawal of communion from those who offend.'

'Then that may be a matter for your own consistory courts to pursue – but as far as we are concerned today, we have to make judgement on earthly grounds. There is another who bears responsibility for some of the wrongdoing, and that is John, Count of Mortain. The fact that his chaplain is here today shows that he is well aware of what has transpired. Whether he knew of it at the time, I cannot tell, but this allegation that the manor of Hempston was forfeit to him on the alleged death of its lord is a total fabrication. If it escheated to anyone, it would have been to the king.' He ignored another babble of protest from the table on his right.

'However, on the other side of the coin, there is no doubt that an affray took place when Sir Nicholas discovered that he and his family had been evicted. Whatever the truth of the matter, a man died from a blow on the head during the mêlée – though one might say that such a violent reaction was justified in the circumstances.' He paused and looked grimly around the court, reminding Gwyn of his own master at inquests.

'There is also the matter of the deaths at Grimspound. Again, de Arundell and his men were chased from their refuge, which was then burned to the ground – and a defenceless old woman ended up dead, in somewhat doubtful circumstances. They were then pursued by a much larger force under Pomeroy and de Revelle – and who can blame them for resisting to the best of their ability in order to save their lives, though this also ended in further killing?'

John de Wolfe, who had been inwardly rejoicing at the judges' partiality for de Arundell up to this point, suddenly had an inkling that it was not going to be a resounding verdict in his favour. What was the crafty old devil working up to, he wondered? The coroner stared at the judge's back, waiting anxiously for his next words.

'Our first Norman monarch, William of Falaise, encouraged the employment of various ordeals as a means of settling legal disputes. These ancient rites are meant to call upon the aid of the Almighty in determining who is right and who is wrong.' Walter laid a hand on the shoulder of the archdeacon and looked down at him. 'I am well aware that recently, Rome has become less than enthusiastic about the employment of such tests, and indeed I hear that there are calls for the Holy Father to ban them.'

He stared around again. 'But I believe that there is still merit in the ordeal – and what is more important, so do the people of England, who are firmly attached to them as a means of seeking justice.'

'Is the old bugger going to get Richard and Pomeroy to dip their arms into molten lead?' asked Gwyn in a hoarse whisper. 'Or run barefoot across nine red-hot ploughshares?'

De Wolfe shook his head, still intent on listening to Walter de Ralegh, for he now thought he could see where the man's mind was leading him.

'My brother justice and I have decided that this dispute must be settled once and for all, so that no one can then complain that favouritism or political interference tilted the verdict – for the aid of God himself is to be sought, which no man can question.'

The silence in the hall was almost palpable, as every ear strained to know what was going to happen.

'We decree that this dispute is narrowed down to the ownership of the manor of Hempston Arundell, the other issues of improper outlawry and the deaths of persons during armed combat being dismissed inasmuch as they are not contentious between the parties.'

The heavy features of de Ralegh were turned first

towards the table where de Arundell sat, hardly daring to draw breath – then across to de Revelle and Henry Pomeroy, who sat uneasily awaiting whatever was in store for them.

'We further declare that this single issue be resolved by the Ordeal of Battle, where Nicholas de Arundell will engage in combat with Henry de la Pomeroy and Richard de Revelle in succession. If he is vanquished by either, then the manor of Hempston is lost to him.'

There was a shocked silence, then a hubbub broke out, both on the dais and down in the body of the court. Joan de Arundell screamed and threw her arms around her husband, howling that this was just a stratagem to have him killed. Nicholas, however, gently disengaged himself, as Gillian hastened to comfort her cousin.

He stood up, and in a loud voice accepted the challenge with all his heart, confident that right would be on his side.

On the defendants' table, Joscelin de Sucote rose to his feet and began making protests, but de Wolfe suspected that his heart was not in it – the judgement did not affect him personally, and if these Devon barbarians wanted to hack each other to pieces, then let them get on with it, he had done his best for them.

Alongside him, the barbarians in question showed very different reactions to Walter's decision. The burly, pugnacious Henry de la Pomeroy, who had fought in several campaigns and was fond of jousting and hunting, was confident that he could more than hold his own against the slighter Nicholas de Arundell, as long as there were no bowmen in the offing. Richard de Revelle, on the other hand, looked pale and shocked, his hand nervously caressing his pointed beard. De Wolfe saw him tugging at Joscelin's sleeve and gabbling urgently at him, which merely provoked the lawyer into repeated shakings of the head, as he presumably told Richard that there was nothing he could do at that point to reverse the decision of the judges.

As the chatter and catcalls from the floor grew louder, Ralph Morin signalled to Sergeant Gabriel to restore order. With stentorian shouts, buffets across the head and a few blows from their cudgels, the garrison soldiers soon calmed the audience down, allowing Walter de Ralegh to finish announcing the details of the trial by battle.

'As the disputants are all of noble birth, they shall fight with the short sword, rather than with the half-staff of the commoner,' he declared. 'Sir Nicholas, as one man against two, will have the choice as to who shall face him first. If he triumphs at the first bout, there will be an hour's respite for recovery before the second contest.'

John, though worried at the outcome of this affair, grinned to himself as he saw his brother-in-law's face blanch at the prospect of facing de Arundell, whether it be at the first or second bout. But Henry de la Pomeroy was a different matter, thought de Wolfe uneasily.

'I must go up to Raden Lane and offer some comfort to Lady Joan,' fretted Matilda over the dinner table a short while later. John felt like telling her to stop fussing and to mind her own business, but he wisely held his tongue. He knew that she was well-meaning and also that she was worried herself, as her own brother, who until recently she had idolised, was going to be on the receiving end of a sword wielded by a hardened campaigner who had had his physical skills honed by a couple of years' hard living on Dartmoor.

He did his best to reassure her about the outcome. 'This need not be a fight to the death, Matilda. This has been boiled down to a dispute over land and they are not going to hang the losing survivor. A disabling strike with the sword – or a submission if one man is being soundly defeated, will suffice to satisfy honour.'

He did not add that there was nothing to stop one combatant killing the other if he could – and by the angry look in de la Pomeroy's eye, it seemed he would be happy to spill Nicholas's life blood all over the ground.

'When is this barbaric ritual to take place?' demanded his wife.

'The first contest will be at the eighth hour tomorrow morning, in the inner ward of Rougemont,' explained John. 'The second will be an hour later, the actual time depending on how long the first one lasts. Usually, few continue for more than a couple of hours, unless the pair are evenly matched in skill.'

His wife clucked her tongue and bemoaned the blood-thirsty tastes of bestial men, compared to the gentler sensibilities of her own sex. 'If Sir Nicholas perishes, that poor wife of his will be devastated,' she said with genuine concern.

'If he is defeated, he loses his home and his land and everything that goes with it,' pointed out de Wolfe. 'He would be destitute, yet another landless, penurious knight let loose upon the country. He might as well go back to being an outlaw on the moor, thanks to your brother and his grasping friend from Berry Castle.'

For once, his wife had no caustic answer to throw back in his face.

That afternoon, John and his officer and clerk went back to the coroner's chamber in the gatehouse to refresh themselves with bread, cheese and ale – though Thomas drank cider, for which he now grudgingly admitted he was getting a taste. The little priest pulled his quills and parchment towards him, ready to start writing duplicate copies of inquests, but the other two seemed in a talkative mood, wanting to pick over the significance of the proceedings that morning.

'I had hoped old Walter and this new judge would have just hanged those two sods – or at least banished them from the realm or imposed a massive fine that would cripple them,' growled Gwyn, from his usual seat on the window ledge.

De Wolfe, sitting behind his trestle table, shook his head. 'They have too many powerful friends for that, Gwyn. John de Alencon told me afterwards that, on reflection, he felt it was unwise of him to suggest that the bastards could be excommunicated for cheating a man on Crusade, as the bishop is well known as a strong supporter of Prince John and will probably have strong words to say to the archdeacon when he hears about it. And you saw how the prince sent his clever lawyer down to aid them.'

'But what does this strange verdict of Ordeal by Battle mean, Crowner?' asked Thomas, his sharp nose almost twitching with interest. 'What on earth can that achieve?'

The coroner rasped a hand across his stubble thoughtfully. 'It was a clever move, assuming Nicholas wins. It would show that God as well as the king's justices agree that de Arundell was the wronged party, though that seems bloody obvious to everyone. But at least, by invoking the Almighty, it would prevent those who support the prince from claiming that the result was rigged by the Justiciar and his justices.'

'And if he loses?' grunted the Cornishman.

De Wolfe shrugged. 'Political expediency, it's called. Hubert Walter certainly wants Nicholas to triumph and to see de Revelle's nose rubbed in the dirt once again – but if it fails, then he can say that it shows that he was impartial.'

'Will he win, master?' asked Thomas. 'It doesn't seem fair, asking one man to fight two opponents.'

'Some of these ruffians who turn approver have to fight up to five of their accomplices to save their necks,' replied Gwyn. 'As long as there's a decent interval between bouts to allow them to recover, I don't see it makes much difference.'

De Wolfe went back to answer Thomas's first question. 'Who will win? I hope to God that Nicholas can vanquish Henry de la Pomeroy, who is a hard bastard and well used to fighting. De Revelle is a chicken-hearted coward and should be no problem, though I hope Nicholas doesn't kill him, as Matilda will blame me for the rest of my life.'

Gwyn swallowed the rest of his quart with a gurgling noise like a barrel being emptied. Wiping his moustache with an upward sweep of his hand, he became inquisitive.

'I've seen many of these trials by combat, but I still don't understand why bashing your opponent's head with a staff or skewering him on a sword should be a means of solving a legal dispute.'

Their clerk, a fount of knowledge on so many matters, was eager to show off his erudition. 'As the judge said, it's an ancient ritual, though new minds at the Vatican are becoming impatient with what they see as pagan magic, even though Almighty God is invoked.'

'How ancient?' asked de Wolfe, also curious about this odd practice, even though everyone was familiar with it as a part of English legal procedure.

'Ordeals of fire and water go back to ancient times, even in far-off places in the East, but as for the Ordeal of Battle, as the justice said, William of Normandy brought it to England at the time of the Conquest,' explained Thomas. 'But it was originally a German invention or even possibly developed by the pagans in the Northlands.'

Gwyn scratched his crotch vigorously. 'Wherever it came from, let's hope our man Nicholas has the stronger arm tomorrow, after all the effort we've made to help him.'

'Amen to that,' said Thomas, crossing himself devoutly.

Chapter Seventeen

In which Crowner John sees justice done

Though the crowd in the Shire Hall might have been small the previous day, Exeter's gossip grapevine ensured that far more people climbed Castle Hill the next morning to see three knights and manor lords fight it out, possibly to the death.

The constable of Rougemont had been up at dawn to organise the arrangements. The weather was cold, with a leaden sky, but there had been no new snow, and only dirty remnants of the last fall lurked at the foot of the high curtain walls. Sergeant Gabriel and his soldiers from the garrison had cleared the centre of the inner ward of the usual obstructions, such as empty ox-carts, archery targets and heaps of refuse. The pigs and goats that normally snuffled about the bailey were chased down to the outer ward, and a man was stationed at the gate to make sure that they did not return.

Gabriel paced out the requisite square of sixty feet on each side and his men hammered in stakes at intervals, ropes being strung between them to keep the combat area clear of spectators. A dozen men-at-arms spaced out outside this barrier made doubly sure that there would be no interference to the ritual.

By the time the cathedral bell tolled to announce the office of Prime, just before the eighth hour, about a hundred people were gathered in the inner ward. At the end farthest from the gatehouse, towards the squat keep, the supporters of de la Pomeroy and de Revelle gathered along the rope, mainly the bailiffs, reeves and other manor officials. The opposite side of the marked-off square was reserved for de Arundell's men from the moor, together with his wife Joan. Nicholas and her cousin had tried to persuade her to stay away, but the resolute lady adamantly refused, saying that if her husband was to be wounded or killed, it was only right that she should be with him.

Resigned to the stubborn woman's resolve, Gillian le Bret stayed closely by her, and to de Wolfe's surprise, his own wife Matilda insisted on accompanying them. He tried to dissuade her also, saying that it was not proper for a woman to witness bloodshed, injury and possibly death, but taking her cue from Joan de Arundell, Matilda shrugged off his protests. John wondered to what extent she was there in case her brother Richard suffered the same misfortune, so with a sigh he abandoned his attempts to keep her away. He could not stay at her side, as he had his own duties as coroner whenever an ordeal was in progress, and Thomas had to keep a record for eventual presentation to the royal justices of the General Eyre when it arrived, sometime in the future.

At the eighth hour, the major figures in the drama began appearing.

As the Church, however reluctantly, had to participate in this appeal to the Almighty to see justice done, Archdeacon John de Alencon arrived, though the garrison chaplain, Brother Rufus, a jovial Benedictine, actually officiated. The fat monk came out of the tiny chapel of St Mary, which was adjacent to the gatehouse, and waddled across the hard mud of the bailey to greet de Wolfe, with whom he was firm friends. Together they ducked under the rope and stood waiting with the archdeacon for the combatants to arrive.

Henry de Furnellis came across from the keep with

Ralph Morin, just as Nicholas de Arundell appeared from the guardroom in the gatehouse, where he and his 'squire' had been waiting. The squire acted as the fighting man's second and in this case was not unnaturally his steward Robert Hereward, the gaunt Saxon who had so faithfully stood by his master.

The pair joined his other retainers along the rope and Nicholas slid a reassuring arm around his wife and kissed her tear-stained face as they waited, until the sheriff strode up to John and his companions.

'Where are these damned men . . . do you think they've run away?' he demanded.

As if in answer, they heard the sound of hoofs on the drawbridge across the dry moat and five horses trotted into the inner ward. The riders went across to the stables against the further wall to dismount, then walked back to the central arena. John saw that Pomeroy and de Revelle were accompanied by their suave lawyer, and followed by Ogerus Coffin. The other arrival was an elderly man with a very wrinkled face, who he recognised as Richard's steward from his manor of Revelstoke, in the far west of the county. He was Geoffrey de Cottemore de Totensis, and he had a haughty manner in keeping with his ponderous name.

The new arrivals ducked under the barrier and, studiously avoiding the de Arundell camp, strode stony-faced to stand at the opposite end of the arena, next to their few supporters. De Wolfe saw that Henry de la Pomeroy walked with aggressive enthusiasm, his big body exuding confidence and indeed arrogance. His fleshy face seemed redder than usual, in spite of the cold breeze that blew between the castellated walls. In contrast, Richard de Revelle trailed behind him, his usual mincing gait reduced to a reluctant trudge. If he noticed his sister standing with his opponents rather than supporting her own flesh and blood, he made no sign of even acknowledging her presence.

Now a blast by the inexpert trumpeter heralded the arrival of the two royal judges, who came down the steps from the keep with their clerks and a couple of court servants. The constable held up the rope for them to pass under, and they walked to the centre of the square, the rest of the participants gravitating towards them like iron filings to a piece of lodestone. As the king's representative in the county, Henry de Furnellis again had the responsibility of managing the ritual, and he marshalled the various players into their proper places.

Nicholas was stood facing his two opponents, who were a good dozen feet apart, their respective squires standing behind them. The archdeacon, the garrison chaplain and the two justices grouped themselves between the disputing parties, and the sheriff beckoned to John to join them. As he walked across, he saw that Joscelin de Sucote also attempted to enter, but was brusquely warned off by Walter de Ralegh, who told him he had no part to play in this particular drama.

The first act was, not surprisingly, religious. Firstly, John de Alencon offered up a general prayer to seek God's mercy on all present and to plead that His wisdom would ensure that justice would be done that day. Then Brother Rufus stepped forward with a psalter in his hands and set about safeguarding the proceedings from any unfair advantage derived from witchcraft or the machinations of Satan! He advanced on each of the three duellists in turn and made them repeat a solemn oath after him, with both of their hands resting on the holy book, which he held out to them. Nicholas was first, squaring his broad shoulders as he made the sign of the cross and then followed Rufus's words in a strong, confident voice.

'Hear this, ye justices, that I have this day neither eat, drink nor have upon me neither bone, stone nor grass nor any enchantment, sorcery or witchcraft whereby the law of God may be abased or the law of the devil exalted. So help me God and his saints.'

The monk then went across to Pomeroy and repeated the ritual, Henry bawling out the words at the top of his voice in a pugnacious manner. Indeed, de Wolfe wondered if he had been drinking, in spite of the assertion in his oath, for he seemed to be in an abnormally excited mood.

Once again, there was a marked contrast when Rufus took his psalter to Richard de Revelle. Though the weather was cold, de Revelle's fur-lined cloak of green wool should have kept him from shivering, yet John saw his jaw quivering as he hesitantly repeated his oath.

When the chaplain stepped back after completing his task, the sheriff gestured at de Arundell. 'Sir Nicholas, it is your prerogative to choose your first opponent in this wager of battle. Tell us, who do you name?' Without hesitation, Nicholas pulled off his right glove and threw it on to the ground before Henry de la Pomeroy.

'I will fight that man first and may God give the strength of righteousness to my arm.' His voice was strong and clear, provoking a ragged cheer from the throats of the men who had shared his exile on Dartmoor. His wife, supported on each side by her cousin and Matilda, turned even paler and held a kerchief to her mouth to conceal her anguish.

Henry de Furnellis now waved at Ralph Morin, who stood near the rope, and he and Sergeant Gabriel marched across, each carrying an armful of equipment.

'To ensure that you are evenly matched, you will be given identical arms. You will have a short sword, a shield, a helmet and a jerkin of leather.'

The sheriff watched as the two squires examined the articles to make sure that no unfair advantage could be introduced. Then they went to their masters and helped them to remove their cloaks and strap on the short armless tunics of stiff leather, which were almost an inch thick and had been boiled until they had almost the texture of wood. The swords had blades about two feet long, unlike the great weapons that were used on horseback or in battle. Similarly, the shields were much smaller than the oval ones used against lances; these were round bucklers of hardwood covered with thick leather. The helmets were the standard issue, a round iron basin with a nose-guard, tied under the chin with thongs.

When the two men had been equipped, the others left the centre of the arena, apart from the sheriff and chaplain, who stood between the combatants. As de Wolfe loped back to the perimeter, he noticed his brother-in-law wiping his brow with the back of his hand, as if to remove a sudden sweat that, in spite of the frost, had overtaken him when he realised he had at least a short respite – and possibly a reprieve from fighting if Henry de la Pomeroy's boasts about his inevitable victory came true.

The sheriff gave the last formal instructions to the fighters.

'You will fight with might and main until one of you is vanquished, either by death or by being forced to the ground by the point of a sword at your throat or vitals, when the victor can have you hanged. To submit, then the loser must cry "craven" in a loud voice!'

De Furnellis stepped back, his duty done, and the monk had the last word. Raising his hand in the air he made the sign of the cross and cried out, 'May the blessing of God the Father and the Son and the Holy Spirit descend on these weapons, to discern the true judgement of God.'

Brother Rufus then backed slowly towards the rope barrier and the contest began.

Standing with Gwyn behind the coroner, Thomas de Peyne watched the drama with tremulous fascination. His classical education allowed him to compare the scene with some Roman gladiatorial contest, as the two men, out there alone in an empty arena, circled each other while they each took the measure of their opponent. Shields across the chest and swords half lowered, they glared at each other across ten paces of hardened mud. Both were about the same height, but Henry was the heavier, from both muscle and some fat, and there was little doubt that he was a strong and dangerous adversary, for all that he was six years older than Nicholas.

He made a sudden feint, jumping forward with a yell and making de Arundell step back. No blow was exchanged, but Pomeroy shouted at Nicholas to unnerve him.

'You've no bloody archers behind you now! I'm going to cut you to pieces, as I would have done at Grimspound if you'd fought fair!'

Nicholas made no reply, but a moment later, as Henry charged at him, he sidestepped and brought his sword down, making a chip of wood and leather fly from the edge of Pomeroy's shield.

From then on, the fight was fast and furious, a sequence of advances and retreats, shield bosses clashing and then breaking apart. Both men seemed evenly matched as far as skill and courage were concerned, and a rising tide of yells came from the onlookers, urging them on to even greater efforts. Though the sympathy of most people was with de Arundell, as the circumstances of this dispute were widely known, there was no doubt that Henry was putting up an excellent performance and he had a number of spectators shouting for him, in addition to his own men.

As the two combatants hammered away at each other, without so far inflicting any damage except to their shields, Gwyn muttered into the coroner's ear, 'If I was a gambling man – which I am – I'd put my money on Pomeroy at the moment, more's the pity.'

De Wolfe, his eyes glued to the action, replied without

turning his head. 'There's nothing in it so far, Gwyn. Nicholas is the younger man, so maybe he can keep this up for longer. I don't see how they can carry on for very long like this.'

As if they had heard him, the fighters abruptly pushed each other away and circled at a distance, both with heaving chests and gasping for breath. John now saw a long rent down Nicholas's tunic below the jerkin, but there appeared to be no blood, so it looked as if Henry's sword had only slashed the garment, not the flesh underneath.

After a few moments' respite, the younger man returned to the attack, and this time de la Pomeroy backed away, his face almost purple with effort, his lips curled back in a rictus of angry excitement. Then he rallied and, with a burst of energy, forced de Arundell back to the centre of the square. They hammered away for several more minutes, and in spite of the cold, both men were seen to be sweating, perspiration visible on their brows below their helmets. De la Pomeroy, whose activity seemed almost demonical, looked as if he was about to explode, his face engorged and his eyeballs prominent.

As more shouts of encouragement erupted from the sidelines, mostly shouts of 'Nicholas, Nicholas!', the lord of Hempston again began driving Henry back, with a ferocious charge that took them halfway to the ropes. Then catastrophe occurred, as Nicholas stumbled over a hardened clod of earth kicked up by some beast and fell forwards on to his shield and sword hand.

In a flash, Henry Pomeroy leapt towards him with sword raised, and as Nicholas rolled sideways and began pushing himself up, he suffered a glancing blow from the blade on his right arm.

John saw the sleeve rip and blood well out, as the agile de Arundell sprang up and instantly slashed back at his adversary. But it was his sword arm that had been injured, how badly de Wolfe had no means of telling. An experienced campaigner, de Arundell deliberately ran backwards to give himself a few seconds in which to slide his good arm from his shield hoop and change hands, so that his weapon was now in his left hand. Though not so powerful as his right, years of practice had strengthened it to a reasonable degree – but he was now at a considerable disadvantage. Henry came charging at him, yelling at the top of his voice, drowning the cries from the spectators. Nicholas held his ground and managed to strike at Pomeroy's shield so hard that a split appeared in the wood, which was now only held together by the leather covering. Once again a furious hand-to-hand combat ensued, which at least reassured de Wolfe that Nicholas's injury could not be life-threatening or he would have failed already from loss of blood.

'They can't keep this up for much longer,' snapped de Furnellis, standing alongside the coroner. 'Henry de la Pomeroy is like a man possessed. He'll make a mistake in a moment and Arundell will have him.'

But he was wrong, though for a good reason.

After a brief circling, the lord of Berry again came at Nicholas like a madman, roaring and slashing as if he intended to conquer his enemy by sheer weight and speed. The quick-footed Nicholas sidestepped again and, left-handed, jabbed behind Henry's damaged shield. The thick leather cuirass absorbed most of the blow, but the point of his sword pricked Henry's belly and he gave a yell of pain, even though the injury was not serious. The wound put him in a towering rage, and he swung back determined to cut this tormentor in half.

As he bore down on de Arundell, a hush descended on the crowd, who half expected to see this bull-like leviathan trample the slimmer man into the mud. Nicholas expected the same, as he saw Henry's eyes bulging in his puce-tinted face, rage vying with triumph as he saw victory within his grasp.

Suddenly, the charging man stopped. He seemed to crumple at the waist, and his sword fell from his fingers as he grasped the neck of his jerkin and sank to the ground, a gurgling, gasping sound bursting from his purpled lips.

De Arundell gaped in amazement, his own sword still raised, but as de la Pomeroy did nothing but writhe on the frozen mud, still scrabbling at his throat, he cautiously went nearer. Half suspecting some trick, he kicked away the other man's sword so that it was out of reach, then dropped to his knees alongside him. By now, people were racing across the arena towards them, and seconds later the sheriff and coroner were by his side.

'What's happened to him?' demanded de Furnellis.

'God knows. Some kind of seizure, I think.'

'He's bleeding from his belly,' said Brother Rufus.

De Wolfe ripped at the thongs that secured the leather jerkin down the front of Henry's body. 'Give him some air, he's choking,' he commanded, for the stricken man was still gasping and tearing at his neckband. John explored the wound under the tunic and found it to be little more than a surface puncture.

'Nothing to do with that,' he said, looking up at Ralph Morin, who had joined the group clustered around the fallen man. For a fleeting moment, de Wolfe felt it ironic that so many were now solicitous about Henry's welfare, whereas five minutes earlier they were quite prepared to see him mortally wounded on the end of de Arundell's weapon.

By now, Joan de Arundell had broken away from her cousin and John's own wife and had raced across to her husband; hugging him, she demanded to see his wounded arm. The blood was running down his sleeve and dripping off his fingers, but he seemed oblivious of it, being more concerned with the extraordinary turn of events.

'It is the will of God, praise be,' exclaimed Brother Rufus. 'He has decided the outcome in the plainest manner.'

John de Alencon, also kneeling by the stricken lord, looked rather less convinced that this was a show of divine intervention, but he held his tongue.

'We must get him moved,' said the practical sheriff, and yelled at Sergeant Gabriel to find a litter to carry the victim to the keep, where he would at least be out of the biting breeze. At that moment, someone with a better understanding of seizures arrived, in the shape of Richard Lustcote, the apothecary, who had been amongst the spectators.

Dropping to a crouch, he said some soothing words to de la Pomeroy and undid the laces that closed the neck of his tunic beneath the leather jacket. Then with fingers on the pulse at the man's wrist, he cocked his head to try to understand the garbled words that were now punctuating the gasps for breath.

'You have pain, sir? Where is it, d'you say? In your chest and arm?' Gently, the experienced druggist coaxed some sense from Henry, at the same time calming him down, so that the purpling of his face and lips began to recede. Lustcote climbed to his feet and looked around the circle of faces. 'He has had a seizure of the heart and lungs, not a stroke of the brain,' he diagnosed. 'Too much exertion and frantic excitement in a man who should have eaten and drunk less these past few years.'

'What's to be done?' asked the sheriff anxiously. 'Will he live?'

Richard Lustcote pulled him further away, so as not to be discussing prognosis over the patient himself.

'He could die in the next five minutes – or live another twenty years,' he replied. 'Get him to a bed and leave him be in peace for a few hours. I will give him some tincture of poppy to quieten him down.' He groped in the capacious scrip on his belt, as he always carried a few basic medicaments for use in emergencies such as this.

As Henry was hurried away on a wooden stretcher by a couple of soldiers, the apothecary's pouch was put to good use again, as Joan de Arundell, concerned for her husband's injury, petitioned Lustcote to attend to the wounded arm. While this was being done, Henry de Furnellis tried to get some order back into the disrupted proceedings. He conferred with the two justices who had come forward into the centre of the combat zone, then threw up his arms and yelled for attention, the tuneless trumpeter trying to help him with a ragged series of blasts.

When the hubbub had subsided sufficiently, the sheriff bawled out his announcement. 'By whatever means, an Act of God or the frailty of man, there is no doubt that Sir Nicholas de Arundell was the victor of that bout of arms. He has thus satisfied the first part of this wager of battle and in one hour will meet Sir Richard de Revelle to determine the final outcome.'

There was a murmuring from the crowd, some more catcalls and a few yells that it was unfair to match an injured man against a fresh opponent. Richard de Revelle, who with his cadaverous steward, had come up to the group in the centre, pushed his way through to the sheriff. 'I agree with those men,' he said earnestly. 'Surely we can delay this pointless business until he has recovered from his injury?'

De Furnellis glared at the dandified Richard. There was no love lost between the two men who had both been sheriff twice over.

'I would have thought you would have welcomed the chance to fight a wounded man, de Revelle. It's the only way you have a chance of winning.'

The fact that de Revelle had already considered this and weighed it against the chances of having the whole affair postponed or even abandoned, blunted the curtness of the answer that came to his lips – but Nicholas de Arundell broke in with a loud cry.

'No, sheriff, there's no need for an hour's delay! I have suffered nothing but a mere scratch and the disturbance has allowed me to get my breath back. Let us get on with the battle and settle it once and for all!'

Again, de Furnellis went into a huddle with the king's justices, and John saw de Bohun shrug indifferently, while Walter seemed quite happy with de Arundell's proposal.

This time without the aid of the trumpeter, the sheriff's strident voice announced that the bout would continue at once, and all but the leading figures began to drift back to the ropes. Looking as if he was walking directly to the gallows, Richard de Revelle plodded back to his end, where his steward-squire, Geoffrey de Cottemore, and another servant took away his fine cloak and strapped him into his boiled leather jerkin and helmet. The small shield and the sword were handed to him and he stood immobile for a moment, ashen-faced and numb of mind.

An educated man who loved learning and politics, he had never espoused the normal pursuits of most lords, fighting, gaming and hunting – though he was fond of womanising and embezzlement. Now to be thrust into an arena with a hardened Crusader who had spent years surviving on Dartmoor was the most frightening experience of his life, for he knew he had wronged the man and fully expected Nicholas to kill him. He felt frozen to the spot and it took a push in the back from his squire to get him advancing like an automaton towards the middle of the square.

'You have already taken your oath against sorcery,' said the sheriff. 'So after the priest has invoked the wisdom of God, you will begin to fight – if needs be, to the death.'

Brother Rufus came to repeat his call for the Almighty to see justice done, then he and the sheriff retreated, leaving the two men alone in the centre of the lonely field. De Arundell's arm was not nearly as good as he alleged, the lacerated tissues throbbing painfully under the tight bandage that the apothecary had applied. At least he had not lost much blood, so he was not weakened or shocked, and for now he was able to hold his sword in his right hand, though he was prepared to change and fight with the other if needs be.

As the two men circled each other, Gwyn and John de Wolfe watched anxiously from the side. 'Without that wound, there'd be no doubt, Crowner,' growled the Cornishman. 'I'd wager my last ha'penny on Nicholas. But he's tired after that run-around that Pomeroy gave him, apart from that strike on his sword arm.'

John had his eyes fixed on his brother-in-law. 'He's terrified, but all he's going to do is defend himself and hope that our man flags from exhaustion. I wonder if Nicholas intends to kill him?'

As he spoke, de Arundell – tired of slowly wheeling round his adversary – made a sudden lunge towards de Revelle, who jerked up his shield to take a swinging blow that almost knocked it from his arm. John saw a spasm of pain cross Nicholas's face as the impact radiated up his damaged arm and he was not surprised to see him back off and change his sword and shield to the opposite sides.

Richard de Revelle saw it also and attempting to seize his chance, ran in and struck several blows, all parried by Nicholas's shield. De Revelle tried again, then gave a squeal as the tip of de Arundell's sword slid beneath his guard and jabbed him on the wrist that held the buckler. Nicholas followed up without hesitation and kicked out at Richard's leg as he slammed his own shield against that of the other man. De Revelle staggered backwards and only just regained his balance, before his opponent was on him again, hacking left-handed against the shield, shredding the leather and splintering the underlying wood.

Abruptly, it was all over.

De Revelle suddenly dropped to his knees and sent his sword spinning across the dried mud of the bailey. Throwing up his arms, one still inside the thong of his shield, he shrieked out the fateful word '*Craven*!'

Hovering over him, blood now oozing afresh from under his bandage, Nicholas stood with sword upraised. For a long second, de Wolfe wondered if he was going to bring it down to cleave Richard's skull in half. Then he slowly lowered it and, with a contemptuous shove, put his foot against de Revelle's shoulder and rolled him over on to the cold earth.

In the Bush that night, the trial by battle was the talk at every table, not only at the landlady's place near the hearth. To have one defendant felled by a seizure and the other to make the most abject surrender at the hands of a wounded adversary was unique in everyone's memory.

'What I can't get over is Matilda's behaviour,' confessed de Wolfe, about to attack a trencher carrying a slab of fatty fried pork, with onions and beans around the sides. 'She marched on to the field amid the confusion and went up to her brother and slapped his face! Called him a spineless coward and said she never wanted to see him again.'

The tender-hearted Nesta sighed. 'Oh mercy, that's sad! She was always so proud of her brother when he was sheriff, though he was an evil fellow, as we all know to our cost. But I'm sorry she has been so disillusioned.'

'It will do me no good, though,' said John bitterly. 'The fact that she's fallen out with Richard will inevitably be laid at my door, as it always was in the past. Eventually she'll take delight in accusing me of being the one who got a pardon for Nicholas from the Justiciar and so led her brother into this situation with the royal judges.'

'I thought she was big friends with his wife and had broken with Richard for stealing his manor?' objected Gwyn, sitting opposite with a pig's knuckle and his third quart of ale.

'That won't stop her blaming me for his downfall. Women's minds aren't like ours, Gwyn, they can twist logic any way that suits them!' For that he suffered a sharp kick under the table from Nesta.

'If the world was run by women, it would be a much better and more peaceful place,' she announced tartly. 'All you beasts think of is war and killing and making life intolerable for ordinary folk.'

'That's not always so, though I admit there's some truth in it,' conceded John. 'Take today, Nicholas was magnanimous over his success. He could have spitted Richard on his sword or, being the victor, demanded that he be hanged – but he let him off.'

Thomas, who was hunched at the end of the table, eager to hear all the gossip, shook his head. 'That's not strictly true, Crowner, according to the traditions of "wager of battle".'

'Go on then, tell me, fount of all legal knowledge,' challenged John, the events of the day making him good-natured this evening.

'Yes, he could legitimately have slain him any time during the battle, but once he shouted "craven", his life should be spared, but he would be declared outlaw.'

'Ha! There's natural justice for you,' jeered Gwyn. 'Let the punishment fit the crime. I wonder how he would fare, alone on Dartmoor?'

'But it didn't, did it?' pointed out Nesta. 'He walked away free, without hardly a scratch upon him.'

'The bastard's got a charmed life,' complained Gwyn. 'How many times is it now that he's been caught out in treason, embezzlement and theft, yet manages to slither back to his comfortable manor and a life of ease?'

John had to agree that his officer's analysis was very near the mark. 'But it will cost him dear this time, and I feel he'll keep his head well down for a very long while to come.'

'How will it cost him?' demanded Nesta, and waited for John to explain what had happened that morning.

'When de Revelle submitted, the sheriff and the two justices hurried over to see what should be done. Nicholas at once announced that he wanted no retribution against either of his adversaries, other than full restitution of himself, his family and his men in Hempston Arundell and a sworn promise that they would never again interfere in his manor. But as part of this settlement, he wanted full compensation for all that had been taken from there during the time that de la Pomeroy and de Revelle had annexed it – all the freeholders' rents, the sales of crops, animals and wool that would have been earned by him had he been in occupancy during that period.'

Thomas's little eyes opened wide. 'That would come to a hefty sum. Can they calculate what is owed to him?'

'All the manor accounts and tallies are there, it seems. The justices, when they agreed to de Arundell's suggestion, gave the sheriff orders to have all the records seized and pored over by clerks familiar with such things – at the expense of Pomeroy and de Revelle. They have two months in which to pay up or they will be hauled back before the court, assuming Henry lives through this.'

'The shock of paying all that money may well give him another seizure,' said Gwyn with some glee.

They continued the gossiping until there was nothing left to be said about the day's excitement. Thomas slid out of the tavern, bent on visiting the cathedral for some silent prayer, and Gwyn rolled off to the castle to play dice with Sergeant Gabriel and his soldiery, diplomatically leaving his master alone with his mistress. They soon found themselves up in her little chamber in the loft and John discovered that the tensions and stresses of the day had done nothing to dampen his ardour when they made love on the wide feather mattress on the floor.

Afterwards, in the dreamy relaxation that followed, the coroner lay on his back staring up at the dark recesses of the spider-haunted roof trusses, just visible in the light from a single candle. With his arm around Nesta's shoulders, he became contemplative about the events of past weeks.

'Most of my problems have gone, thank God,' he reflected with satisfaction. 'I had begun to despair of even finding a common thread between those guildsmen killings, let alone finding the identity of the actual killer. And now my campaign to get justice for the Arundells has at last succeeded, though it was a finely run thing at the end.'

The auburn-haired landlady nestled closer to his body as they lay under the heavy sheepskins. She could see their breath steaming in the cold air, but even naked as they were, it was warm beneath the covers.

'So what remains to disturb your peace of mind, Sir Crowner?' she asked teasingly.

'Very little – there are hardly any inquests outstanding and Thomas's rolls are up to date for presentation to the next Eyre.' He suddenly scowled up into the gloom. 'Except of course, we have not yet found Geoffrey Trove, and that bastard who assaulted my wife may already have left Devon or even England itself.'

Some time later, afraid that her lover was falling asleep, Nesta prodded him with her elbow.

'Up you get, my man. You can't stay here all night, your dear wife will need your company after such a distressing day.'

He was not sure whether Nesta was being sarcastic, but knowing of her sympathetic nature, he decided she probably meant what she said. In any event, he grumbled his way out of bed and pulled on his clothes, before collecting Brutus from his knuckle bone downstairs and setting off in the freezing evening for home.

Next day, Matilda dragged her husband off to Raden Lane to say farewell to the de Arundells, who were on the eve of leaving for Hempston. They were to meet up next day with all the men who had lived with Nicholas on the moor and were to ride *en masse* along the River Hems to their manor, which would be their home once again.

Nicholas, his arm in a linen sling, was effusive in his thanks to John de Wolfe and pledged his help in anything that the coroner might need in the future. Lady Joan was tearful in her thanks and, with Matilda watching benignly, even ventured to give him a parting kiss on his bristly black cheek. John wryly wondered what his wife would have said and done if any other woman had done the same in public, especially Nesta – or Hilda of Dawlish. A little cynically, he decided that it took other people's misfortunes to temper their own conflicts, then chided himself for such unkind thoughts when his wife was silently suffering from yet another humiliation caused by her brother.

They left the loving couple and returned to Martin's Lane, where after their noontide dinner Matilda pleaded exhaustion. Indeed, she looked pale and wan, so her usual climb up to her solar was earlier than usual, not even delayed by a cup of wine. John had no duties that afternoon and wandered out into the back yard to seek Mary's company in her kitchen-hut. Flurries of snow were twisting about in the east wind, but there were not enough for snow to settle on the ground. He sat on a stool next to Mary's cooking fire with Brutus at his feet and contentedly sipped from a jar of mulled ale which she had made for him. After talking for a while about the remarkable events in Rougemont the previous day, Mary asked him what would happen to Richard de Revelle now.

'A cat has nothing on my brother-in-law when it comes to nine lives,' he replied cynically. 'He seems to weather every storm, even when they are all of his own making. But after this humiliation, I hope to God he just goes back to his manor and keeps very quiet for a very long time.'

'But he's not long bought a dwelling up on North Gate Street,' objected the raven-haired maid. 'I wonder if he and Lady Eleanor intend to live there some of the time?'

'I doubt he'll want to walk the streets of Exeter for a while, after his shameful exhibition up in Rougemont,' said John with ill-concealed satisfaction. 'If he's any sense of honour, which I doubt, he'll go back to Revelstoke, which is his manor furthest away from this city. If I never see him again, it will be too soon.'

But this uncharitable sentiment was shortly to be confounded.

Chapter Eighteen

In which a hound proves his worth

It might have been Denise's ointment or simply the healing power of nature, but Geoffrey Trove's arm had improved over the past two days. Although it was still throbbing and painful, his fever had subsided – and, best of all, his mistress's constant nagging for him to attend an apothecary had faded with the infection.

The journeyman was still afraid to go out in the daytime, for fear of being recognised, but in the old black cloak with a deep hood – the one he had worn to attack the sister of that swine de Revelle – he had ventured out to a low alehouse the previous evening to eavesdrop on the city gossip.

He heard about the battle up at the castle and gloated that the two objects of his hate had both come to grief in different ways. He sincerely hoped that Pomeroy's seizure would prove fatal, but the news that Nicholas de Arundell had contemptuously spared the life of Richard de Revelle annoyed him greatly. If he had killed him and Pomeroy had also died, then Geoffrey, who was basically very religious in spite of his disregard for some of the Commandments, would have considered that God had smitten the evil-doers on his behalf.

Now that de Revelle was not only unharmed but a free man, Geoffrey decided that it was up to him to complete the task that the Almighty seemed to have overlooked. Denise was out, buying some food at the stalls in High Street. Now that she had given up whoring and he had left his job, he had to support them both from the meagre savings he had accumulated from his pay as a journeyman – another reason for seeking violent revenge against those who had prevented him becoming a rich man with his own business.

He went to his small chest in the corner, one of the few things he had brought from his shack on Exe Island, and took out a duplicate of his master-work. It was the prototype of the one he had left behind in his hut, as he was afraid that some poison on the springs of that one might again contaminate him. This other device was slightly smaller, but equally efficient in firing a bolt. He had made the second one with greater care and better metal, finishing it off meticulously to display his skill – yet still those hidebound bastards of guild masters had rejected it. He placed it on the table, checked the mechanism, then fired a bolt against the opposite wall, where it stuck quivering in the whitewashed cob, two inches deep into the plaster. Satisfied, he pulled it out and cleaned it, then wrapped the miniature crossbow in a cloth and put it back into the chest before the nosy Denise returned.

Lady Eleanor de Revelle had been quite satisfied with her new town house in Exeter. When her husband was sheriff, she had firmly refused to spend any time in his official residence in the keep of Rougemont, which she considered a bleak, draughty place unfitting for a woman of her station in life. Eleanor was an even greater snob than Matilda – who she despised – and when Richard was living in Exeter castle, she had insisted on living either at their manor in Tiverton or at Revelstoke. She endured his frequent falls from grace with apparent indifference, keeping his professional life at arm's length. However, his dismissal as sheriff and now his ignominious defeat at the hands of Nicholas de Arundell were hard to bear, but she dealt with this latest embarrassment by keeping herself aloof from any of her husband's activities, and often his very company.

A tall, angular woman with an icy personality, she had long regretted her marriage to Richard de Revelle, as she considered that she had married well beneath her. She was the third daughter of an earl with estates in Somerset and Gloucestershire and, like Matilda, had been married off as one of the least saleable assets of the family to a moderately acceptable young knight. After twenty years of marriage, she had accepted her fate stoically, settling for extravagant creature comforts bought both by Richard's money and a generous allowance from her own family.

It was Eleanor who had prodded her husband into purchasing the house in North Gate Street, partly with the excuse that if he was entering into this respectable venture to establish a college in Smythen Street, then he needed to be much nearer to it than either of their manors at opposite ends of the large county. The house gave her an opportunity to spend as much time as she wished in a city where there were greater market facilities and frequent fairs and festivals, a welcome change from the boring isolation of their manors.

Though she had little affection for her husband, she had become used to him and had no desire to lose him either to another woman or to death – though his neck had come perilously close to the hangman's noose on several occasions. Eleanor was well aware of his predilection for harlots, though she never admitted to herself that it was her own frigidity that was the main reason for this behaviour. As long as he did not shame her over his amorous activities, she was prepared to pretend this situation did not exist.

Thus that evening, when he gruffly told her that he was going out to meet a friend in the New Inn, Eleanor was indifferent to the news, suspecting that he would probably end up in one of the brothels that abounded in the back streets. She retired early, going to the upstairs solar with her tire-maid to prepare for bed. Waking some time during the night, she found that her husband was absent from his side of the large feather palliasse they shared. Again, this was no novelty and she turned over under her blankets and bearskin and went back to sleep.

However, in the morning, there was still no sign of Richard de Revelle and he failed to arrive when their servants brought bread, sweet gruel and coddled eggs to break their fast. This was unusual, as he was fond of his early-morning victuals, but questioning of the three servants they employed threw no light on de Revelle's absence.

Irritated rather than worried, she had herself dressed and went with her maid to morning Mass at the nearby church of St Keryans, for rather like Matilda, attending frequent services was one way of filling the empty life of a gentlewoman. On her return, she was approached deferentially by Matthew, the bottler who took on the role of their steward in that small household.

'My lady, I am becoming concerned about Sir Richard,' he said hesitantly, as his mistress had a sharp tongue when dealing with her servants. 'He has still not returned and the old man who comes to chop kindling and draw water from the well found these in the yard behind the house.' He held out a floppy velvet hat with a crumpled feather and a rusty iron rod longer than his arm.

'That is my husband's hat,' snapped Eleanor, snatching it from him and turning it around in her hands.

'And this is another bar pulled from our back gate, a twin to the one the master told us about – the one that was used to slay some guildsman in a churchyard.'

As Eleanor stared at him with mounting concern, Matthew added, 'And both are stained with blood.'

* * *

'This small amount of blood is not from a stabbing, Eleanor. The smears both on the rod and the hat suggest that he has been struck a blow on the head and this is bleeding from his scalp.'

John de Wolfe tried to make this sound like good news, not mentioning the possibility that Richard's skull might have been cracked like an egg.

He was standing in the yard behind the house in North Gate Street, with Gwyn busy examining the back gate, which now had two of its half-dozen bars missing. The lady of the house was listening to him tight-lipped, with Matilda hovering anxiously behind her, common adversity driving these two women into an attempt to be friendly and supportive to each other. In fact Matilda, for all her recent antagonism to her brother, seemed the more upset, though Eleanor's usual glacial manner might have concealed more concern than was apparent.

'Did he not return home last night?' Matilda asked anxiously. 'Where can he have been?'

Her sister-in-law was not anxious to answer that last question, as she suspected that she knew what had taken her husband out into the dark streets. 'He was not in his bed at all. This accident must have occurred late last evening, after I had retired.'

She had responded to de Wolfe's routine questions with some reluctance, as she thought him little better than an ill-mannered soldier, but the evidence that Matthew had found had left her with little option but to send a message to Richard's sister, since her husband was a senior law officer – albeit one she blamed for Richard's repeated falls from grace.

'I fear this can be no accident, lady,' said John, as gently as he could. 'No one strikes themselves on the head hard enough to draw blood. And the use of this iron rod makes it impossible to believe that the perpetrator is anyone other than the assassin who killed those other men.'

Eleanor de Revelle drew her thin body stiffly upright and fixed him with her pale blue eyes. 'So you think Richard is dead, John?' she asked tonelessly. Already she was readjusting herself to the role of widow and wondering if it might not be preferable to being married to an inveterate scoundrel.

But de Wolfe was not yet ready to go along with her speculations. Strangely, he admitted to himself, though he had often wished his brother-in-law in hell, under these circumstances he ardently hoped that the man was still alive and not another victim of this murdering bastard. If Richard was to forfeit his life, it should be legally at the end of a rope, not by being slain by some crazed journeyman.

'He may well be alive, Eleanor,' he reassured her. 'This spike, whose partner was used to kill another man, has not been used other than as a club.'

He hefted the rod in his hand to assess its weight. 'I think Richard was struck to deprive him of his wits and has been carried off somewhere. Maybe he is being held as a hostage, as we have been seeking this Geoffrey Trove all over the city. At least we know who the villain is that attacked your husband.'

The wife scowled at the coroner. 'And what good is knowing his name, if you cannot find him – or where he has taken my husband?'

Matilda, who cared for her sister-in-law about as much as the Lionheart cared for Philip of France, came to her husband's defence.

'John is doing all he can, Eleanor! This killer has led everyone a merry dance for weeks – as I know to my cost, as he half-killed me in the cathedral Close.'

De Wolfe decided to leave his wife to bandy words with Richard's haughty wife and walked across the muddy yard to where Gwyn was peering at the ground near the gate, which led into a short side lane leading out to North Gate Street. 'There's a real mess of footprints around here, Crowner, but nothing of any use, with so many people in and out of here every day.'

John looked down and agreed with his officer. 'If de Revelle was struck on the head, as he surely must have been, where is he now?' he rasped. 'Dead or alive, I doubt he walked out of here.'

Just then Thomas arrived, out of breath after hurrying from his chantry duties at the cathedral, and the coroner briefly explained what had happened.

'He must have been carried away, or possibly dragged,' suggested the clerk. 'Was this Geoffrey a big man, strong enough to do that?'

'I only saw him once, in that guild meeting,' grunted the coroner. 'But he seemed tough enough, which is what you would expect of a blacksmith and ironworker.'

'No drag marks in the mud,' growled Gwyn, looking again at the ground. 'If he was hauled away, you'd expect his heels to leave a couple of grooves in this soft muck.'

De Wolfe opened the gate, which was now minus two of its rails, and went out into the lane. He looked first up to North Gate Street, only a few yards away.

'I can't see Trove struggling through the main streets with a body in his arms, even late at night. Surely he would have gone the other way?'

They turned and looked down the narrow lane, which was no more than a path between the yards of the burgages on either side. Matthew, the steward of the house, was hovering around, looking lost and anxious, and John beckoned him nearer.

'Where does this lane go?' he demanded.

The servant, a middle-aged fellow with a bad turn in his eye, seemed to stare directly at both Gwyn and the coroner simultaneously.

'It goes past burgage plots and vegetable gardens through to St Mary Arches Lane, sir. Beyond that is St Nicholas Priory and the warren of Bretayne.'

De Wolfe cursed under his breath. From there, the

whole of the bottom quarter of the city was accessible. In the squalor of Bretayne, no one would look twice at a man stumbling along at night with a drunken friend – or even a corpse.

'What about a hound, master?' asked Thomas, as usual having the quickest mind amongst them. 'Could not a lymer sniff out a human quarry, if he is given something with his scent upon it?'

A lymer was one of the several types of hunting dog, the breed with the keenest nose, as opposed to the greyhound, which hunted by sight. John looked at Gwyn questioningly, as neither of them had thought of this novel idea.

'We've got the hat he wore last night, with his blood upon it,' said the coroner. 'Do you think it would work?'

'What dog could we use?' asked Gwyn, then his broad face lit up. 'Your Brutus, why not? He was a grand old lymer when he was younger, and there's nothing wrong with his snout even now.'

The Cornishman was a great dog-lover, and they seemed to respond to him in a similar fashion. A few moments later, he was hurrying back down North Street and soon he had returned with the long-legged brown hound, taken from the coroner's house under Mary's astonished gaze.

John had explained to the two ladies what they were going to try and when Brutus arrived, he stuffed the foppish hat under the dog's nose, hoping that his old hound would grasp what was required.

The animal seemed delighted at this novel outing, which was a change from his usual walk down to the Bush tavern. When Gwyn called him into the lane and set off through the garden plots, he loped ahead in a determined way, stopping every few yards to sniff the weeds and fence posts on either side.

'He's going somewhere, bless him,' yelled Gwyn, as he hurried to keep up with the dog, with the coroner, his clerk and the steward trotting along behind.

At the end of the path, they came out on to a wider lane which came from Fore Street past St Mary Arches church and wound around the compound of St Nicholas Priory, where the few Benedictine monks kept a large vegetable garden in addition to their devotional tasks. Brutus sniffed deeply at a bush on the corner, then cocked his leg against it, before ambling off with the diagonal gait that so many long-legged dogs possessed.

Beyond the priory wall there were no more dwellings, as the city wall loomed ahead, and the land up to the wall for a considerable distance in each direction was taken up by garden plots, some overgrown and neglected. The hound suddenly stopped and raised his muzzle as if sniffing for inspiration. Gwyn caught up with him and held the cap to Brutus's nose to reinforce the reason for their game. The hound lifted one of his forepaws as he took a final sniff, then shook himself and set off more slowly into the rough ground, where old onion beds, coarse grass and nettles had died back for the winter.

'Where's he off to now, Gwyn?' called de Wolfe.

'Maybe he's just got the whiff of a rat, but he seems to know where he's going,' replied the officer, proud of the performance so far of his canine friend. Brutus pushed his way through the frost-shrivelled weeds of a neglected plot and then slowed down and stopped. With his neck outstretched and a forepaw again delicately raised, he gave a throaty growl, then looked up enquiringly at Gwyn.

'I reckon he's telling us something, Crowner,' said Gwyn. 'What's that ahead of us, at the foot of the wall?'

The others came up to stand behind the now wary hound and looked at where Gwyn was pointing. The town wall, built of Saxon and Norman stones on top of the original Roman base, was only about a dozen feet high here, as beyond it the ground dropped off suddenly into Northernhay. Away to the right were the towers of the North Gate and on the left, the wall sloped down past St Bartholomew's churchyard towards the river.

Along the inside of the wall were a few ramshackle huts, little more than shelters for those who worked the many plots that filled the areas where there were no houses. Some were derelict and unused, though a few beggars and homeless poor sometimes camped out in them for want of better lodging. The nearest was no more than six feet square, built of panels of mouldering woven hazel withies, covered by a lean-to roof of tattered reed thatch, the upper end of which rested against the town wall.

'Let's have a look in there, anyway,' growled de Wolfe. 'It may only be a badger or a fox that's upset old Brutus.'

They walked cautiously across the waste ground, the dog now keeping to Gwyn's heels. As they got nearer, John could see that the closed end of the hut faced them, so presumably the entrance was on the opposite side. Both the coroner and his officer drew their swords as a precaution, and Thomas and the steward dropped back, being unwilling to become involved in any possible violence.

'Anyone in there?' yelled Gwyn in a voice that could be heard over half the city. He did not really expect a response and was startled to hear a harsh voice reply from inside the shack.

'Keep away, damn you – or I'll kill him now!'

Eyebrows raised in surprise, de Wolfe motioned to Gwyn to stay where he was, whilst he himself moved quietly around the hut until he could see into the open end, keeping a dozen paces away from it.

'I said stay away, or he'll get it now,' came the same voice, tense and high-pitched with fear and defiance. It was indeed Geoffrey Trove, for now John recognised him as the man from the guild meeting. He was leaning against the stones of the wall, the only place where the sloping roof was high enough for him to stand upright. At his feet was the body of a man, stretched out on the ground, with a sack over his head. From the ornate embroidery around the bottom of the green tunic, John had no doubt that the figure was that of his brother-in-law, though whether dead or alive, he could not tell.

'You are the ironworker called Geoffrey Trove?' snapped the coroner. 'Come out of there and give yourself into custody at once!'

There was a laugh, harsh and hysterical from the swarthy journeyman. 'Not a chance, coroner! I've outwitted you four times already and I'll do it again. Another step nearer and this thieving bastard gets his throat cut.'

Geoffrey bent and pulled off the sack, revealing Richard's face, dried blood crusted on his forehead and cheek. He was conscious, but a length of cloth was tied over his mouth as an effective gag, and cords secured his ankles and wrists. His captor brandished a long dagger and John, knowing Trove's lack of compunction in killing and attacking defenceless people, was prepared to believe his present threat.

'You can never get away with this,' he barked, but stopped moving towards the open end of the shelter. Gwyn had moved to stand alongside him and both held their swords at the slope, ready to dash forwards if the crazy metalworker made any move to strike de Revelle.

'What is it you are hoping to gain by this foolishness?' yelled the coroner. 'You cannot escape, there's nowhere for you to hide now.'

'I have a hostage, unless I decide to kill him,' called Trove, dimly seen in the dark hut. 'I want safe conduct to a church, God knows there are plenty of those near here.'

'The swine wants to seek sanctuary and then abjure the realm,' exclaimed Gwyn. 'Some hope, after all the crimes he's committed.'

John was not so sure that the size of the crime affected the right to sanctuary, unless it was sacrilege. If any fugitive gained a church, or even its churchyard, he could claim forty days' immunity from arrest and then, if he confessed, the right to go to a port and take ship out of England. The irony would be that Trove's confession would have to be taken by a coroner, in this case, the husband of the woman he had attacked!

First, Trove had to reach a church, and John was damned if he was going to get the opportunity.

'Not a chance, Trove!' he shouted back. 'You'll never get ten paces away from that hut with your prisoner, let alone to the nearest church. Is he still alive after that wicked blow you gave him with your precious rod of iron?'

For answer, Trove gave the inert figure a kick and then hauled Richard's head from the ground by the hair. There was a groan and as de Wolfe inched nearer, he saw that de Revelle's eyes were rolling wildly, though the gag prevented him from calling out.

'He's alive all right, though only you coming along stopped me using this on him!' Trove reached down and picked up something from the floor, which he brandished at those outside. John saw it was another of the infernal machines for firing small iron arrows.

'Now he's my bargaining counter for my freedom, Crowner! Make up your mind quickly, who is it you want dead – me or your brother-in-law?'

'Shoot the bastard, for all we care,' muttered Gwyn, but he was careful not to utter the words loudly enough for the man to hear.

'This is madness, Trove!' said de Wolfe in exasperation, beginning to edge forwards towards the hut, lifting his sword a little as he went. 'My officer and I will cut you down the moment you set foot out of that hovel. Throw down those weapons now and let's have an end to this.'

This made no impression on the beleaguered man. Knowing that unless he could gain sanctuary, his life was forfeit whether he surrendered or fought it out, he had nothing to lose.

'If you come a step nearer, I'll shoot you with my master-work,' he threatened, hefting the miniature crossbow in one hand. 'It's drawn back and the bolt's in place, all I need do is pull the trigger. I'll not miss this time – that damned weaver was lucky in that he stumbled at the privy door.'

The prospect of eight inches of iron rod being projected into his chest caused John to stop moving and he stood in the wilted nettles, frustrated by the deadlocked situation. He looked across at Gwyn for inspiration.

'I'll go and get more men, Crowner,' said the Cornishman in a loud voice and gave a knowing wink. He moved away, back past the hut, scuffing his feet noisily until he was a score of yards away. Then he stopped and waited, well out of sight of Geoffrey Trove.

De Wolfe forced himself not to look in Gwyn's direction and called again to the man in the shack to divert his attention.

'Why did you kill all those innocent guildsmen, Trove?'

'You know damn well, Crowner! They conspired against me to deprive me of a decent living. I am a skilled worker and fully deserving of becoming my own master. They were jealous of me and wanted to keep me out of their cosy little society. After all I've suffered, that was the final insult.'

'You killed them by such cruel means, damn you. They didn't deserve that,' snarled the coroner, anxious to keep the man's attention distracted.

'For ruining my life? Of course they did! I stalked them one by one, they were as unsuspecting as sheep coming to slaughter.'

Out of the corner of his eye, De Wolfe sensed Gwyn

slowly creeping towards the back of the hut, putting each foot down carefully to avoid any noise. John carried on with his diversionary tactics.

'Why so angry with de Revelle and Pomeroy, then?'

The figure inside the shack gave Richard another kick. 'The bastards! For the second time, my attempts at settling down to a decent trade were ruined by them. I had to leave Plymouth on some trumped-up accusation of stealing another man's tools, so I took another name and set up as a blacksmith and farrier in Hempston. A lowly job for a craftsman like me, but I could have made a success of it as the first step. Then those sods stole the manor and in my temper, I joined with de Arundell against them – and got outlawed for my pains.'

Gwyn had moved nearer to the back of the hut now. John was half afraid that Brutus, who had been lying down watching the proceedings with interest, might get up and run barking to his big ginger friend, but thankfully he seemed to sense that he should stay where he was.

'So why leave Sir Nicholas, after having been loyal to him against the men from Berry Pomeroy?' he called, still intent on keeping Trove's attention.

'Ha! A fine reward I had for my loyalty. Life on the moor was bad enough, but then one of those louts picked a fight with me and I had to defend myself with a knife. He hardly had a scratch, but I got the blame, so I told them all to go to hell and left them to rot.'

'You came into Exeter, an outlaw?' queried John, still intently watching Trove's grip on both his dagger and his crossbow.

'Nothing to it, if you're careful. I paid some clerk to write me a testimonial from an imaginary ironmaster in Bristol and got a journeyman's post on Exe Island, nearly three years ago now. If it hadn't been for those God-rotten guildsmen, I could have become a master and gone to another city to set up my own business.'

De Wolfe had now lost sight of Gwyn, who had vanished behind the back end of the hut. Then covertly looking under his lowered bushy eyebrows, he saw a hand come up above the further end of the roof and give a wave. Resolutely, he raised his sword and began walking towards the open end of the crude shack. He saw Richard wriggling on the ground, his eyes bulging with terror, faint noises coming from under the gag as he tried to shout or scream.

'Keep back, I say, damn you!' roared Geoffrey, as he ducked his head and moved to the middle of the hut to face the advancing coroner. 'I've three more of these bolts for those others, after I've dispatched you.' He raised the hand that held the device, a dagger still clutched in the other. John gritted his teeth and prepared to duck one way or the other as the bolt flew free. It had almost missed the weaver and it was a matter of chance which way he should swerve, depending on how inaccurate the flight of the missile would be.

'Not another step or I'll let fly!' screamed Trove, instinctively backing to the rear of the shed as the fearsome knight with the long sword continued to advance.

There was a *twang* and John threw himself down and to his right, hoping to God that the crossbow device was not biased to that side as well. Simultaneously he heard an agonised scream, and as he picked himself up from the weeds he feared that Geoffrey had also carried out his promise to cut Richard's throat. But his brother-in-law was gagged, so how could he have screamed?

Staggering to his feet, hoping that Trove could not reload the bow that quickly, he launched himself at the doorway and in the confusion of the moment, was bemused to find himself crashing into Geoffrey, who seemed to crumple out of the opening against his own body.

John had no opportunity to raise his yard of steel as the man was right on top of him: he half expected to feel Trove's dagger drive between his ribs. But the man just slid down his front to the floor and lay twitching on the ground, a wide red stain spreading across the back of his cloak.

Seconds later, Gwyn thundered around the hut and gazed in satisfaction at the body at their feet.

'Got the bastard! Are you all right, Crowner, I left it a bit late?'

An hour later, a cluster of men were gathered on the waste ground where the drama had taken place. As soon as it had ended, John had sent Thomas off at a limping trot to reassure Matilda and Eleanor that Richard was alive, if somewhat battered. Then he carried on to Rougemont to notify the sheriff, before going to Raden Lane to request the presence of Nicholas de Arundell, who would not yet have left for his repossessed manor. At the same time, Matthew the steward hurried to fetch the apothecary Richard Lustcote to attend to Richard de Revelle.

'Saving your worthless life is getting to be a habit,' grumbled John as he used his dagger to cut through the tightened knot that held the gag in place, then the bonds on his limbs. They had dragged his brother-in-law out of the shack into the daylight, leaving the corpse of Geoffrey Trove spreadeagled across the threshold.

As soon as de Revelle's mouth was free, he gave a wail, which seemed to be a combination of relief, self-pity and pain. 'My head. Oh Christ, my head,' he moaned, and indeed, the state of his scalp was not a pleasant sight, as his hair was plastered with dried blood on one side, crusty streaks of it running down his face. They propped him sitting up against the city wall and when he calmed down sufficiently to speak sensibly, there was little useful he could tell them.

'I recall nothing after walking along North Street on my way home from . . . well, from the New Inn.' He seemed evasive about where he had been, but de Wolfe had not the slightest interest in that.

'After a good knock on the head, the wits before the blow often seem to vanish as well,' observed Gwyn cheerfully.

'When did you recover them?' demanded de Wolfe. Now that it seemed unlikely that Richard was going to die or even suffer any lasting effects, he felt little sympathy for his brother-in-law, especially after the cowardly performance he had put up in his trial by combat.

'I don't know. Sometime during the night, it was dark.' He groaned again and put up a hand and tentatively felt around the gash in his scalp. 'I was already bound and gagged. I had no notion of where I was until dawn came and I saw that foul hut and that swine standing over me, calling me obscene names and telling me with relish what he was going to do to me.'

The apothecary came at that point and after feeling Richard's pulse, looking into his eyes and gently palpating his head, declared him fit to be taken home, where he would bathe and dress his scalp wound. Soon Matthew returned with a couple of men lugging a detached door to use as a stretcher, and the former sheriff was carried away, still moaning piteously.

'Let's have a good look at this murdering devil,' decided de Wolfe, and with Gwyn he dragged Trove out of the hut by his arms. One of them had strips of soiled linen wrapped around it, under which was a festering but healing cut. That was of little consequence compared to the wound in the middle of his back, just to one side of his spine.

'I don't like striking a man in the back, it's not fair play,' boomed the Cornishman. 'But I heard him threatening to skewer you with that infernal machine of his, so I reckoned that I'd better act fast!' He ripped Geoffrey's bloodstained tunic from his shoulders and exposed a two-inch wide slit over his ribs, from which oozed dark red blood. 'I felt him move against the wattle wall, so I jammed my sword blade between the withies and pushed like hell. He must have moved away, for I was almost up to the hilt before I hit him.'

'That's another one I owe you for, Gwyn,' said John, slapping his friend on the shoulder in a rare gesture of affection. 'I thought that bloody arrow might have hit me somewhere, but probably you stuck him just as he was letting fly.'

They were examining the 'infernal machine' when voices and the tramp of feet along the path heralded the sheriff, Sergeant Gabriel, two men-at-arms and Sir Nicholas de Arundell. They came and stood in a ring around the body, while John regaled them with what had happened.

'Is this the man that was once with you in Hempston?' he asked, as Gwyn rolled the body over to lie face up.

Nicholas bent to look, then nodded. 'That's James de Pessy, as we knew him. Our blacksmith, though he was adept at making all kinds of objects. A useful man, if he hadn't had that vicious streak in him.'

Henry de Furnellis prodded the corpse with the toe of his boot. 'I wonder why he didn't just kill de Revelle in his yard, instead of clouting him?'

'And how did he get him here from his house?' added Nicholas.

John looked at the powerful frame of the ironworker as it lay outstretched like some hateful crucifixion. 'He must have carried him in his arms; he's a strong man and Richard is only a dapper little fellow.'

'But why keep him alive in this damned hut?' asked the sheriff. 'That could only increase the risks.'

De Wolfe rubbed at the dark stubble on his cheeks. 'I think he intended to kill him at the end, but was hedging his bets. He took him as a hostage, as he plainly boasted to me. Mad as he was, he didn't wish to be caught for a certain hanging.'

'Would you really have let him get to sanctuary, as he wished?' asked Nicholas.

De Wolfe shrugged. 'He had a knife ready to slit de Revelle's throat. My wife would never forgive me if I let that happen! It was only because I knew Gwyn was in position on the other side of that wattle panel that I took the risk of rushing him.'

After the fraught events of the past few days, a sense of anti-climax suddenly seemed to descend on them all. Then John looked down at Brutus, who was lying quietly, watching them with his big head resting on his outstretched paws.

'There's the hero of the hour,' he said fondly. 'Without his nose, we'd never have found them and that bastard might well have got away with it.'

The old hound rose and ambled across, putting his slobbering muzzle into John's outstretched hand. He looked up as if to say, 'It was nothing really, master!'